The Magic of
Painted Creek

Robyn Kilgore

Website: http://www.robynkilgorebooks.com

Instagram: @robynkilgorebooks

Facebook: Robyn Kilgore - Author

To Bruce, Amelia, and Adalynn; the painters of my life.

ONE

THE ALARM CLOCK crashed to the floor as I smacked at it for the last time. "I'm leaving that damn thing here," I grumbled to myself. I felt crazy for having such strong feelings about an inanimate object, but I hated that alarm clock. Sitting upright and running my hands down my face, I felt more like a zombie than a human girl. Woman.

Whatever.

Unfortunately, I'd missed the off button for the alarm and the clock's fall from the table hadn't broken it or ripped the plug from the wall, so it was still happily wailing away from under the bed. And it didn't sound muted. Oh no, now it somehow seemed to reverberate through the entire room as if the under bed acoustics were the perfect amplifier for my morning agony. Flipping myself over the edge of the bed and hanging upside down, I yanked the cord from the wall and huffed in relief at the sudden silence. Calling on core strength I absolutely did not have, I wriggled upright and collapsed back into the pillows.

In the sudden stillness, I took a moment to really look around my bedroom in the apartment I'd had for the last five years, the first place I could call my own when I moved out of my mother's house. Looking at it now though, I wondered if I really could call it *mine*. I paid the rent and other bills, sure, and maintained my responsibilities, and theoretically made all the decisions. But I felt no sense of "me" in this space. The walls were a dull builder grade beige, as was the carpet. Hell, even my comforter was a slightly darker shade of beige. The only pop of personality in the room was my dark purple sheets, and even they were hidden away when the bed was made.

My mother had helped me choose the apartment, and all the things in it, when she finally conceded to my desire to move out at twenty years old. I had been financially self sufficient for a couple years, I was lucky in that way. My painting business had really taken off right after high school, and in a mere year I had acquired a nice little nest egg that continued to grow while I still lived at home.

I shook my head, not wanting to mentally relive the fights we'd had when I told her I wanted a place of my own. But I couldn't help but wonder as I looked around my bedroom if this is what I would have chosen for myself. Even the artwork, now carefully wrapped up and ready to move, was bland and muted in color. Neutral. Safe.

I glanced back over at the offending alarm clock. My mother had even gifted me that alarm clock, saying that productive people got their day started early. "You started this." I narrowed my eyes, pointed at it, and huffed. I realized the clock probably sounded louder because the room was now almost completely empty, and therefore echoey, not because the electronic device was actually yelling at me.

After one more second of reflection, and one more glare at the clock, I squared my shoulders and got out of bed. "No time like a new beginning to change your interior design choices. And I'm

2

more productive at night anyway." With that, I headed to the shower, vowing to leave the alarm clock and all things beige behind in the move.

WALKING INTO THE kitchen for what would be one of the last times after a long hot shower, I couldn't help but continue my train of thought from earlier. Looking around with a cold kind of detachment, I thought *there really is no personality in this space. Oh my God, am I really this boring?*

Maybe I was being too critical. After all, everything was packed in brown moving boxes and taped up tight, holding all my possessions and the feelings I hadn't let myself feel yet. Hopefully I'd only be unboxing the former once I made it to North Carolina. Maybe when I unpacked everything wouldn't feel quite so... bland.

I sat at the tiny little breakfast bar and got out the travel watercolor set that I always kept in my daily tote bag. I wanted to do one last painting in the apartment before I left. Looking around, I cursed under my breath when I realized I'd already packed the coffee maker. "Stupid, stupid girl." There was no way I was going to make it through this whole day without copious amounts of coffee. But I could make it through one painting at least.

Staring at the blank page and still feeling frustrated by my thoughts this morning, I drew a line straight down the center. I sketched out a quick outline of the apartment building on both sides, keeping them the same. On the left, I painted everything in the vivid realistic detail that I was known for in the art world, even if it was fast and a little sloppy. On the right, I focused on extra color, trying to play with color pop and emotions more than capturing every realistic detail.

When they were finished, both sides were good, but I sat frowning down at the paper anyway. The left was almost sterile in its realism, and the right, while vibrant and colorful, still fell flat, lacking any sort of emotion tied to the color.

"Well, I guess I am that boring." Scrunching my nose, I packed up my travel paints and washed everything up. It was time to go.

The movers were scheduled to come with the landlord later

that day. All the big things that wouldn't go in my car, and that I wouldn't need anyway, were going to a storage unit temporarily until I knew where I was going to land permanently. All that was left was my overnight bag, the linens I'd used last night and this morning, and the little bit of food that was left in the kitchen. After three trips to the car and one last once over the whole place, I stood at the front door and glanced over my shoulder. "Bye. Thanks for keeping me safe." I locked the dead bolt and walked away.

4

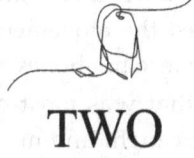

TWO

THE DRIVE WAS long. I didn't mind for the first 100 miles but then I started to get restless. The second performance of the *Wicked* soundtrack had ended... I didn't just sing in the car, I committed... and all my other road trip hacks had failed me. The roads from Columbus, Ohio to Painted Creek, North Carolina were blissfully uneventful and quiet, but that gave my mind time to wander.

They are such cliché sayings really... 'one phone call changed my life', or 'nothing was ever the same again'. I always knew what it meant of course in an abstract kind of way, but I never truly grasped as an adult how completely, permanently life altering one moment in time could be. Not until I got my own life changing call. I couldn't help but replay that phone call in my mind as I flew down the highway.

* * *

I HAD JUST talked to Gram the weekend before so I was surprised to see her name pop up on my phone. We'd always been close in spirit, even if we couldn't be close in proximity, so it wasn't unusual for us to chat on the phone often. But she was the busiest retired lady I knew, always having tea with someone or out gallivanting about. A Wednesday afternoon phone call would never have fit in her normal schedule. Ice began creeping across my stomach as I stared at the phone before finally swiping to answer.

"Hey, Gram!" I said, and my voice sounded brittle even to my own ears. I pressed the phone between my ear and my shoulder so I could keep wiping off the counter after lunch. Multitasking was my default setting, but I needed the movement then to keep the ice in my stomach from creeping into my bones, too.

"Oh, honey," a voice that was most definitely not Gram's on the other end of the phone caught and my stomach dropped to the floor, leaving a hollow ache in it's place. "Mabel, it's not your gram, it's Dottie. Sugar, there's been an incident."

Dottie had been one of Gram's best friends for my entire life, and I loved her like another grandmother. Her voice had slowly trailed off. The silence was suffocating, but I'd have held my breath forever to prevent what I knew was coming. "Your gram passed on this morning. I'm sorry to call you from her phone like this. My what a nasty shock for you dear. Well I am just so sorry." Somewhere in the back of my mind I had registered that Dottie had managed to squeeze in a honey, sugar, and dear in less than a minute. *Impressive.*

"You know how dear your gram was to me, well to everyone in town really, and I'd promised her time and time again if anything were to happen to her I'd call you from her phone as soon as I could. She was always worrying you wouldn't recognize my number and wouldn't pick up and then you'd have to hear the news from some stranger on a voice mail." I made some noncommittal noise in the back of my throat as she sniffed again. It was a fair concern for Gram to have... she was right, I never answered the phone if I didn't have to. But in this case it would've been better to have no news at all.

"Everything seems to be moving along right quick now. I'll tell Mr. Findley, you remember him don't you? Gram's lawyer? I'll make sure he knows I've already talked to you, honey, and that he can call you with all the necessary details."

"What happened, Dottie? I just talked to Gram a few days ago and she was fine."

"Now Mabel, don't you go worrying about the specifics. She went quick like she would've wanted and she loved you more than anything. That's all that really matters. Now sugar, I have to go but I'm sure I'll be seeing you real soon. I love you, Mabel."

True to her word, Dottie talked to Mr. Findley and he called me before the sun had fully set and my apartment was blanketed in darkness. All the arrangements had been made years earlier by Gram. "Just in case," she would say. Turns out just in case was in fact a brain aneurysm no one could have known about or prevented. It was just her time.

The next couple of weeks were a whirlwind of grief and traveling. I'd gone down for the funeral alone and had one brief meeting with Mr. Findley. He'd told me that Gram had left her cottage to me. I stayed in a hotel that trip though, not able to face Gram's beloved cottage without her in it.

"You should come stay awhile, Mabel. The house is yours, so you have a place to stay, and I know you work for yourself so I imagine if you ask real nice your boss will give you the time off to sort things out. And there are things to sort out, other than just the cottage. Maybe if you come back in a few weeks, with a clearer head..."

And then I'd done something so completely out of character I'm still not sure how it happened. I'd agreed. Not only had I agreed, I'd *committed*. I went back home that day to end my lease, make arrangements, and tell my mother.

AS IF THINKING about her had alerted her somehow, my phone's screen lit up in the dash cradle with my mother's name, her ring tone assaulting my ears and breaking me out of my unpleasant train of thought.

"Good morning, Mother," I said with a smile plastered onto my face. That was a thing wasn't it? People could hear it in your voice if you smiled?

"Don't good morning me, Mabel. Why does it sound like you're already driving?" So much for my subliminal smile.

"I am, Mom. I'm actually halfway there and making good time. Thanks again for the send off dinner last night. It was nice not to have take out again since all the food was packed."

"Well you wouldn't have had to pack all your food if you had just said no to this ridiculous plan."

Aaaannnndddd here we go again. My mother was nothing if not persistent, and if there was a millisecond left that she could still try and win this argument she'd take it. "You could have sold off your gram's things without ever going back to that town, much less moving there for a couple of weeks. I just don't know what's gotten into you, honey. You've never been so far from home for so long before. And why in the world would you give up your perfect apartment when you aren't staying in that dreadful little town permanently anyway?"

"Mother, you know I've always wanted a studio space in my house and I just didn't have one at that apartment. It was cute and charming in its own way," I cringed, "but it certainly wasn't perfect." She huffed but didn't interrupt me. "This was the push I needed to find a space that actually works for *me*. And at least Painted Creek is a place I used to know well. And Dottie is there so it isn't like I'll be truly alone. I needed a change, Mother, and this was a great opportunity to come honor Gram. Who knows, maybe I'll keep the house as a summer home. Or rent it out as a vacation rental. Or find a permanent renter. Or..."

"Mabel Morrison, you spend your two weeks there and then come back to Ohio. You'll have a list of commissions by then that you can't neglect if you want to maintain the name you've made for yourself in the art industry. I'll keep an eye on available properties with a space for a studio that are close to me so you can get back on track when you're done with all this foolishness."

After a beat of silence I said, "Mother, the traffic is getting bad and I need to focus. I'll let you know when I arrive safely. Love you, bye!" I hung up without waiting for her to respond. I'd learned a long time ago the best way to deal with my mother when we didn't agree, which was often, was avoidance. "Alright Michael Crawford, sing me home," I said as I clicked on the next soundtrack in my music app.

Snickering to myself, I remembered thinking I was boring this morning in my beige apartment with my safe decor. As the pipe organ blared through the speakers of my car, I realized I may appear boring, but I was definitely different when I was alone at least. I started singing along to the original *The Phantom of the Opera* soundtrack and settled in for the last leg of the trip.

EVERYTHING WAS EXACTLY the same and completely different. The juxtaposition of what my eyes were taking in versus the pictures in my mind was enough to make anxiety tighten my stomach. It'd been fifteen years since I'd stayed in Painted Creek for more than a night during the Christmas holiday, and I usually tried not to pay too much attention as I drove through town to the cottage anyway. The trip back for the funeral had been so brief and so filled with grief, I barely remembered doing it at all, much less mentally cataloging the changes I noticed to the town.

The two weeks out of the summer that I got to spend with Gram in Painted Creek used to be the highlight of my entire year. Mom and Dad would pack me up and bring me to town, stay one night, then leave the next morning. And then it was just me and Gram. And Dottie. And all the other people in town that seemed drawn to Gram and her little house every day. Some with a smile on their faces and some with a problem in their hearts that they needed to share the burden of with another. We would play in the creek behind Gram's house, dance with the fireflies and stay up late every night while she told me stories. Gram would take me to the restaurants in town for 'Ladies' Lunch Out' with all of her girlfriends, and we'd walk up and down Main Street to pop in and out of every one of the little shops.

When Mom and Dad would come back for me two weeks later, I'd have a veritable treasure trove of trinkets; things Gram had spoiled me with from the shops, crafts we'd made together, rocks and feathers I couldn't bear to part with from the park, and even some of Gram's tea to take home.

That was probably my favorite treasure, Gram's tea, and I'd make it last as long as I could for the next six months or so until our Christmas visit. Gram would never mail me any... she'd say it just wasn't the same as being able to put the bag in my hands and whisper her love and best wishes in my ear. And of course nothing from any store had ever come close to the flavor and fragrance of Gram's tea. Dad had died after my eighth summer with Gram, and Mom would never let me come back to stay on my own again. Then, I only got a special bag of tea at Christmas. It was a lot harder to make it last a whole year...

It hit me hard and fast just then, 3 miles outside of town, that the last bag of tea she gave me at Christmas was my *last* bag of tea from Gram. Regret washed over me in a tidal wave. *I should have insisted on coming back here more as an adult,* I thought. Gram made a few trips to Ohio to see me when I was still a child, but things between her and my mother were so strained that eventually no one could take the stress her visits caused and she'd stopped visiting. As soon as I'd gotten my first cell phone though, we were thick as thieves again. Nothing cracked me up quite like an inappropriate meme from Gram.

How much time I had missed with her! I could have gotten to know her as an adult, really listened with my heart instead of the impatient ears of a child when she told me stories about her life. What all had I forgotten or dismissed as irrelevant? And now there was no one left to tell the stories of Dad and Gram's family, of my family.

Thinking of the loss of Gram's tea was just the beginning. I still hadn't scratched the surface of all the little changes that now were a permanent part of my life, whether I wanted them to be or not.

Blinking away the sudden rush of tears, I slid my sunglasses to the top of my head as I crept up on Main Street. I think every small town USA has a Main Street, but none of them held a candle to the one in Painted Creek. The name of the street actually wasn't even Main Street, it was Stone's Throw Road, but I guess that was too much of a mouthful for folks that lived here so everyone just called it Main Street. After all, Main Street was just a stone's throw away from everything in town. Get it?

Most tourists didn't. And that meant the poor, confused tourists were an endless source of humor for the residents. Once, the Mayor had even put up a bulletin in the town hall telling people they had to explain that Main Street was really Stone's Throw Road and give people proper directions and a fighting chance at getting where they were going. It didn't matter though...folks in Painted Creek loved nothing more than to annoy the Mayor, whom they loved dearly, by ignoring him. It was their favorite pastime when I was younger, second only to giving tourists the wrong directions with a polite smile on their faces. I grinned to myself, hoping the town hadn't lost its quirky personality all these years later.

Our Main Street by any other name still functioned as your typical Main Street did though. It was one of the four streets that made up the outside border of the town square. I guess this side of the square was granted the title of Main because it was the side that ran along the front of the fountain. That was really the only difference in the four streets as far as I had ever worked out.

As I drove slowly through, I felt tension I didn't even know I was still holding in my shoulders melt away. There were minor differences, yes, a new paint color here and a different store there, but the majority of my little town looked to be as I'd remembered it.

"And praise the gods there's a new coffee house! I will survive!" I sang the last bit in my best Gloria Gaynor impression and giggled. The gratitude I felt at finding that little bit of sameness and one *good* change was swift and fierce. Gram's passing was an undeniable, permanent alteration I'd have to try and make fit for the rest of my life. But if this town could move forward without losing all of its past, I could learn how to move forward too.

Probably.

Maybe.

THREE

AFTER DRIVING THE length of Main Street and around the square, I circled back around to the new to me coffee shop. This was a change I could voraciously celebrate. I still had some time before my meeting with Mr. Findley and now I could meet him caffeinated!

I parked my car along a side street that was two stores past the coffee shop and took a deep breath. I meant it to be a deep cleansing breath, but it stuck somewhere between a shallow inhale and a cough. I'd been away from Painted Creek too long to know much of anyone anymore, and new places always had me feeling like a fish out of water or a flightless bird, never quite fitting in with the surroundings. But the allure of fresh brewed deliciousness was stronger than my anxiety, so I dropped my shoulders back and got out of the car.

I had always loved walking the streets of downtown Painted Creek with Gram when I came for visits. Everyone was always so friendly, each person as different as the shops that lined the street. Even though all the shops had their own personalities, they all came together in the way a kaleidoscope does, celebrating the differences of all the colors by making one beautiful picture together. The buildings along the street had two or three shops each. Some buildings were still the original brick, some mixed stone and wood siding, and some were even vinyl now.

The building I had parked beside was a triple unit. I loved how the outside was built in such a way that it looked like three individual buildings stuck together with super glue. Each shop had its own color scheme and molding detail, giving each space its own energy. The first shop had beautiful vintage typography style lettering painted on the window, proudly proclaiming a pet shop awaited inside. With a quick glance inside, I kept on moving toward the coffee shop. Somehow, I didn't fully register the handsome man behind the counter, peering back at me through the window.

The next shop in the trio looked worn, like the years had just kept chipping away at its soul along with the paint. In its prime, it must've been a deep forest green and beautiful. It almost felt like it was patiently waiting for someone to notice it again, and it would just enjoy its slumber until then. *Shame*, I thought, but I didn't linger. I could smell the coffee now and it was acting like an olfactory beacon calling me on to the coffee shop.

At first glance, Artful Brew was a normal coffee shop. When you opened the door the aroma of fresh ground coffee beans wrapped around you like a warm hug while the whirl of the steam wand drowned out even your own thoughts. If only for a moment, everything feels right in the world. Or maybe that's just my experience in a coffee shop. My mother always reminds me too much caffeine is bad for you and that I should find healthier coping mechanisms. I'd like to remind her that even artisan coffee is cheaper than bail money, but I've learned to hold my tongue.

After taking a brief moment to appreciate the heavenly sounds and smells of my happy place, I started to scan around the shop. It was perfectly busy for a Friday evening; not so crowded I'd be overwhelmed by the press of bodies and noise, but not so empty I'd feel exposed to curious eyes. A huge bar height counter stood to the left, separating the cozy seating area from the fancy coffee machines taking up the entire left hand wall. Two baristas flitted around behind the bar working together with such synchronization it was like they shared the same brain. There were no seats stationed at the bar, but the floor was worn butter soft in some spots as if people would stand there and shuffle their feet while chatting animatedly with whoever was working. I liked that.

Unlike the outside of the shop, which was a subdued if alluring café au lait color, the inside was an embrace of warm, rich tones. The counter was a deep espresso color and was definitely the focal feature of the whole shop; it was stunning. The walls were a rich brown-grey that managed to reflect the light in a way that kept the vibe airy instead of oppressive. The small smattering of tables and chairs were all intricate scroll iron in tones of light cream, almost like clouds across the stormy sky created by the walls.

My favorite thing though was probably the Bali style carved wood accents that were everywhere. The utensil holders on the counter had carved compartments, a huge cabinet along the back wall by the hallway had the most intricate carved and cut out doors I'd ever seen, and the word 'COFFEE' cut, carved and distress painted a light cream was displayed proudly above all the equipment.

I'd finally made it to the other end of the room where the 'Order Here' sign hung from the ceiling, its vintage typography style hand pointing down ever so helpfully. I was still so distracted trying to take it all in, it took longer than it should have for me to realize the girl behind the register was just looking at me, waiting for me to come back to reality and order my coffee. I startled a little, but she just smiled at me slightly. Not unkind, but like she had met her quota for peopling today. She made it longer than I did, my peopling quota is usually met by around 11 AM.

"Sorry, I was in my own little world for a minute there," I laughed weakly as I finally met her eyes. I realized she really wasn't a girl at all, not that much younger than me, but her tiny stature and cute features made her appear like she was still in her teens. Her eyes, however, held a skepticism that seemed older than both of us.

"Happens all the time. What can I get for you?" she asked.

It was on the tip of my tongue to tell her 'large black coffee', my go to coffee order, but I paused. I may not have had a say in all the changes that had crashed into my life, but I could take some control back and make some changes of my own, couldn't I? Even if it was just changing up my unassuming coffee order.

"Umm…" I glanced up at the biggest chalk board menu I'd ever seen. It stood floor to ceiling behind the end of the counter up against the back wall. I caught myself gawking at the menu with my mouth open as I tried to speed read everything they could make here.

After a moment of unchecked panic at all the options, I finally blurted, "I'd like whatever your favorite is please. In a large." The words tumbled out too fast and probably too loud. I stared down at the counter and had a little inner turmoil freak out, fidgeting with my necklace. After the silence became uncomfortable, I glanced up and met her eyes again. One eyebrow was raised and the opposite hand was on her hip, like she had to balance out the sarcasm in her body. It was obvious she had some thoughts swirling in her mind, so I decided I'd just be patient until they made their way out of her mouth.

"Why would you want my favorite? What if my favorite is a black decaf?" she said, dropping her arm in exasperation. Her collarbone length hair, honey brown and shining with golden highlights, was slipping from her hair clip, adding to her look of irritation.

"Well, that'd be blasphemous, but I'd say thank you and enjoy it, all while making a mental note that you're probably just as boring and lost as I am. Then I'd come back and order something with caffeine so I can keep lying to myself that I am NOT in fact exhausted and that I am in control of my own life!" My mouth snapped shut and my hair fluttered out of my face with the unintentional huff of air. That last part came out a little snappier than I'd meant and every muscle seized into stillness as my eyes went wide.

I wasn't prone to outbursts! I didn't cause people trouble or do anything that anybody anywhere might be offended by or accidentally misconstrue as rude. Hell, most of the time I didn't even talk that much to keep the chances that I'd say something wrong or silly or stupid down to a bare minimum. Now, here I was being outright rude and insulting in the one place that I'd probably want to frequent most in the whole town.

"I'm sor-"

"My favorite this time of year is a sweetened cold brew with vanilla cold foam. It's deep enough to keep your feet on the ground but sweet enough to encourage your hopeful expectations." She raised an eyebrow again and I was beginning to think it was a habit of hers. As it should have been. Her whole energy changed when she did that, like she could see through your absurdity and still stand her ground against whatever you were trying to get away with. I preferred that gumption in her over the weariness I could see creeping into the depths of her eyes. And here she was, letting me off the hook for my short response like she knew the ropes holding back my emotions were more frayed than whole.

"This one is also higher in caffeine than a regular coffee. So it's not as boring as vanilla sounds. How's that?"

"Perfect. That's perfect, thank you." I knew my smile was weak at best, but I was still thrown a little off kilter by my own behavior. *I really need this coffee to kick in fast,* I thought with a wince.

My barista wrapped her knuckles on the counter like a bartender might do on the bar top and motioned her hand to the other end, silently instructing me to move along down the line with her. "I'm Sarah. This happens to be my shop and believe it or not that is the first time anyone has ever asked me to fix them MY favorite drink without knowing what it is first." She turned her back long enough to gather materials before glancing at me over her shoulder with a slight smirk. "It'd have been a good pick up line too, but I don't get the feeling that's what you were aiming to do. Unless I misread the fidgeting as embarrassment and it was actually nerves."

A genuine smile teased across my face. *Burn.* I'd always loved a quick, witty comeback but I didn't often allow myself a good verbal sparring match. It was better to not participate than to accidentally take it too far. Wasn't it? Maybe my conversational skills needed an overhaul like my coffee order.

"Pure, oversharing honesty? I'd just decided on the spot to shake up some habits, to feel like I could regain some control over my life. But my go to coffee order truly is a black regular, so I didn't even know how to begin to order anything else. Your menu is visually stunning, if a bit overwhelming, and I panicked. Thanks for helping me branch out. I'm Mabel by the way. You have a lovely little shop."

Something flickered across her face that looked an awful lot like deep understanding before her eyes shuttered away any tangible emotions. With a quick nod, she put my now finished drink on the counter and waved over it like Vanna White. "Survey says?"

"Mixing up your vintage game shows there, but I'll allow it." I took a hesitant sip and then sighed in pure bliss. "That is perfection. Thank you."

"No problem. Are you staying in town long? If you have time to come back in, I'll make you something else. We'll work on that new coffee order repertoire that you so desperately need. Sometimes change is good. Hard, but good."

While I was grateful for the banter and a potential friend close to my own age, I wasn't ready to answer questions about how long I was going to be around, especially since I wasn't too sure myself. "I should be able to stop in again. I have a meeting this evening though, could you please tell me how to get to," I pulled a business card out of my tote as if I couldn't remember exactly where I was headed, "The Law Office of Mr. Findley and Co.? I'm parked on the other side of the pet shop."

If I hadn't been looking for it, I never would have seen the mischievous glint in her eye as she answered me with a completely straight face. "Sure thing. Just head back out onto Spruce and then take a right on to Main Street. Off of Main Street, you'll turn onto Mountain View and it's the second little house on the right with a parking lot. Just look at the road signs and you can't miss it."

"Main Street, road signs, sounds simple enough. I'm sure I'll be able to find it. Thank you!"

"Yep, just follow Main Street and you'll be fine. Stop back in if you have the chance."

A soft giggle sounded from the front door, and I turned to see Dottie just coming in the shop. I grinned at her and picked up my cup to leave. Giving her a swift hug on my way by, I said, "I'm late for my meeting, Dot, so I can't stay, but I'm so glad I got to see your face. An unexpected treat."

"Don't even worry about it, sugar. I'll stop by the cottage tomorrow and check how you're settling." I could see Sarah's face over Dottie's shoulder as I gave her one last tight squeeze. Some mix of indignation and respect. A warm tingle filled my whole body and I felt alive in a way I hadn't in a very long time.

"You know about Main Street." Not a question and just barely not an accusation

"Well of course she knows about Main Street," Dottie replied as she made her way to the 'order here' sign. "Mabel used to spend weeks here with Constance during the summers."

At the mention of Gram, Sarah's head snapped up. Her eye caught mine with new interest and I could see all the questions swirling there. With a wink in Sarah's direction, I backed into the door to open it and blew her an exaggerated kiss as I flipped my sunglasses back over my eyes. Dottie's big belly laugh was the music that followed me out onto the street.

Maybe a little change CAN be good, I thought to myself as I sauntered back to my car. I felt lighter than I had in a few weeks and more playful than I had since I was a small child. I grinned like a Cheshire cat all the way to Mr. Findley's office as I drove down Stone's Throw Road.

FOUR

AS I TURNED off of Main Street and onto Mountain View, my good mood slowly started to slip away. Where my new coffee had given me a comforting buzz just moments ago, it was morphing in my gut into a distracting case of the jitters. "Okay, Mabel, maybe cold brew is too much caffeine after all." After getting stuck in my seat belt, forgetting my purse, and dropping my phone in the parking lot, I finally made my way across the side walk to the front of Mr. Findley's office.

I can remember when Mr. Findley bought this little house two streets over from Main and renovated it into his office space. It was my last summer here, and Gram and I had giggled at his exterior paint choice of peach which really turned out to be more of a sickly salmon color. He had quickly repainted it a respectable, if not slightly depressing, gray. Since coming to town, he'd assembled a limited staff that offered legal council to the small population of Painted Creek. Approaching the house turned office now as an adult, I wondered what had brought Mr. Findley to land in Painted Creek and stay all these years.

As I pulled the front door open, a whoosh of sweet smelling, air conditioned air hit me in the face. I could smell peppermint, but that wasn't all. It was so intricately intertwined with some other things that I couldn't make them all out. The end result was somehow revitalizing and calming all at once.

"Good evening," the secretary called from behind her desk as she stood up. "You must be Miss Morrison. Mr. Findley has been expecting you." She wore a cute swiss dot dress in a navy blue that highlighted her blonde wavy hair and striking blue eyes. Somehow, she reminded me of a bubble that was tethered to the ground instead of being free to float away. Or maybe Glinda the Good Witch, if she wore anything but pink.

"Goodness, I hope I'm not too late! I told him I would be driving in today but maybe I should've left earlier..."

"Oh, nonsense, I just meant that he was excited to see you, that's all. He's on a call, so just take a seat and I'm sure he'll be out soon. I'm Ms. Barnett, you just let me know if you need anything."

I ungracefully plopped into one of the chairs in the lobby, then quickly straightened my posture when I realized she was still watching me with a blazing smile. "It smells wonderful in here. I suppose that's your doing?"

"Oh, yes! Thank you for saying so. I always tell Mr. Findley that the smell of the lobby is the first thing potential clients will notice once they make it inside. I can't make him change that drab gray on the *outside* and Lord knows I've tried. So I figure the second first impression better be double good!" Her head bobbed animatedly as she talked, her earrings swinging from her ears like hula hoops.

I'd meant the compliment of course, but I was glad she took my blatant subject change and had quit staring at me like an animal in the zoo. "Well, you've done a great job. What is the scent exactly? I can't place it."

"Oh, that's my own blend! I love to dabble with essential oils, you know. I have them in two diffusers running by the air vents to help the smell get all around the building, and I have them on these cute little air fresheners all throughout the offices, too." She looked so proud, I couldn't help but smile at her. "Oh I've named this one Legal Ease and I only use it here. You know what with it being a lawyer's office and all," she giggled. "And the oils I used are meant to help calm and focus. Oh, it can't hurt what with some of the things that bring people in and all."

"Essential oils, that sounds fun. I'm not very familiar with them, but it does smell divine in here. Maybe I'll look into it." I gave her another genuine smile. It did smell fantastic in here, and I'd swear I could feel my mood changing, the foreboding and anxiety I'd felt in the car being replaced by a calm sense of purpose. I had the same hurdles to get over in this meeting, but now I felt as if I was equipped to deal with it. *I wonder if she sells her blends,* I thought to myself. *If I could literally bottle this feeling, I'd be unstoppable.*

"Oh!" I think that must've been her favorite word, like she couldn't start a sentence without it. "You should absolutely look into it! It's so much fun! And there are so many health benefits and so many ways to use them, too." She started to ramble on about, well everything essential oil related, and I tried to keep a pleasant, interested expression on my face. I didn't want to seem rude or hurt her feelings, but I did hope Mr. Findley was about to wrap up his phone call.

"Oh, and even jewelry!" My brain snapped back into the conversation as she waved her arm toward me in excitement. How long had I zoned out? I caught a slight whiff of a different smell, something almost effervescent that somehow was the woman personified in scent. "You can make essential oil diffusers in JEWELRY! Isn't that just FABULOUS?"

"It is absolutely fabulous, you're right. Maybe sometime, when I'm not here for a meeting, we can chat about it more." I hoped she wasn't offended by my trying to steer the conversation back to the real reason I was here.

"Oh my, oh my, I forgot to even page him that you'd arrived. I'm so sorry! Oh, I just get so excited talking about my oils! Let me page him now."

"Oh, no worries!" Great, now I was doing it. I cleared my throat, "It was delightful talking to you. Thank you for keeping me company while I waited."

She scurried back into her chair and pressed a button on the phone. A second or two later, Mr. Findley was walking down the hallway from the back offices, a warm smile on his face.

"Mabel," he said in a rich voice with something close to affection in his eyes. "It's so good to see you again. And I'm glad you took my advice and will be staying in your grandmother's house for awhile to sort everything out. Come on in to my office. We have some things to go over before the end of the day when Ms. Barnett will run out of here like the place is on fire and leave me to fend for myself." He shot a look at his secretary, but there was absolutely no heat in it at all, at least not from a reprimand anyway.

She blushed and lowered her head all the same. "Not like the place is on fire, sir, more like quittin' time means 'me time' and I'm excited for it."

"Now, you know I'm just teasing you. Best secretary I've ever had. And doesn't my office smell wonderful, Mabel?"

"I believe that's the exact word I used when I walked in," my grin slipped out unbidden across one side of my mouth at their banter. How nice to have a conversation with someone without worrying you've offended them. They must know each other well. Ms. Barnett looked Mr. Findley in the eye and said "You best get on to your meeting, sir, or you'll be locking up yourself. I have plans."

"Yes, ma'am" he winked and turned down the hallway. With a full blown grin of my own, I followed him to his office.

MR. FINDLEY'S OFFICE was a lot like the man himself; stoic, patient and sincere. I didn't know him well, but every time our paths crossed when I was younger he had a kind word for me and Gram, and he'd been nothing but patient and understanding since Gram had passed away and he'd had to deal with me.

I could see the difference the years had made for him, he was a little softer, a little grayer, but his eyes still shone with an intelligence that said he didn't miss much and put up with even less. His posture still spoke of a man that had pride in his job and knew he was good at it, and he carried himself with confident ease. You'd almost miss the slight set of his face that closed him off to others as he slid into his desk chair, if you didn't utilize the move yourself. Maybe, for him, it came with the job description.

Everything about the room, including the man, made you feel at ease, like together any problem could be tackled and overcome. Unlike the dreary outside of the building, the walls were painted a soft blue that really made his deep cherry desk stand out. Little knick knacks on the bookshelves built in to the wall behind the desk gave me something to look at instead of him when I needed a distraction or to think. But there were no personal photographs of any kind and once I again I wondered what Mr. Findley's story was, and if maybe his next chapter would include Ms. Barnett. I'd poke my nose where it didn't belong another day though, today was already stressful enough.

Once we both settled, he jumped right in. "Mabel, I know I briefly mentioned that Constance had left you some things, like the cottage, in her will. Thank you for agreeing to stay in Painted Creek for awhile as we sort through Constance's estate. We don't have time to go into great detail about all of it today, so I'd like to just give you the Reader's Digest version and we can meet again Monday morning once you've had time for it all to sink in. We can discuss all the ins and outs and what not then."

"All of it? You mean there's more than just the house? Even that was more than I expected." I don't really know why I was surprised. I knew I was Gram's only living relative so it made perfect sense that everything would fall to me. I guess I should've just been thankful that she had someone employed to help with all the legalities and paperwork.

"There's quite a bit more actually." His tone was brisk and business like, and it was obvious this was just another estate conversation to him when I felt like my whole world had tilted once again with the expectation of managing everything. "There's her estate, which was pretty substantial, some properties other than the cottage, investments and standing donations and the like, and some personal items she kept on file here with me in case anything ever happened unexpectedly."

Ms. Barnett's oil blend began to fail me and a wave of insecurity tightened my stomach. "That's.... that's a lot to think about." My voice quivered, even though I'd tried to lock it down.

Mr. Findley's face softened into understanding. "I know it's a lot, Mabel, and I know you're still grieving. We all are." I pulled my gaze from a particularly interesting carved figurine of a wolf on the shelf behind his head to the left and looked him in the eye. I saw nothing but complete sincerity and willingness to help, and I felt my rigid posture slump just a little with the unexpected comfort. "That's why I said we'll just briefly go over a few things today and I'll give you a packet to take back to the cottage to look at this weekend when you're ready. We'll meet again on Monday and you can ask me any questions you've come up with and I'll explain everything else until you're confident you understand." He sat completely relaxed and waited while I took a few deep breaths. When I nodded, he continued.

"You already know about the cottage. There are also two buildings in town that Constance owned, and your complete inheritance that's more financial in nature. We'll worry about all that on Monday. There's also this," he paused as he pulled a manila envelope, stuffed near to exploding, out of his desk drawer and plopped it in front of me. "To the best of my knowledge, this is all personal in nature. I don't know what's in here, only that Constance wanted me to have it here in the event of a tragedy. I think some of it at least is family history and the like, and it's possible that all of it is just copies and you'll find the originals in the house. Constance always did like to have a backup plan."

I full on smiled at that. She absolutely did always have a back up plan, even if it was just a second favorite ice cream flavor in case they were sold out of the first. 'Managing expectations', she'd called it.

"This much smaller, but probably more intimidating, set of papers is all of the legal stuff we'll need to go over Monday. Make some notes, but don't worry about it too much for right now. I just wanted you to have some time to prepare yourself before we went over all the details. Now, here's the keys to the cottage. You'll find I already took over some groceries and things so you don't even have to leave the house all weekend if you don't want to. There are neighbors down the way, but everyone's got a big yard and even bigger property so it'll probably still feel pretty secluded and quiet. I suggest you take the weekend to settle in, get reacquainted with the house, and go through the things in the packet."

I finally picked up the package and flipped it over letting the keys fall to the desk. On the other side, in my grandmother's whimsical handwriting was "Painted Creek Cottage". My head snapped up to Mr. Findley so fast I startled him and he jolted a bit in his chair. "Painted Creek Cottage?! You mean like the name of the town Painted Creek, Painted Creek?"

"Well, yes Mabel. Didn't you know the town was named after your family property?"

My eyes bugged out. "Family property?!" I think my voice was getting shriller by the second if the concerned look on Mr. Findley's face was any indication. I took in a deep lungful of the essential oil heavy air, hoping desperately to get some of the magic calmness I'd felt earlier back. "I guess I just always assumed that Gram bought the cottage at some point. She may have mentioned a story a time or two about her momma and the house, but I just assumed she meant the house she'd grown up in. I didn't know they were one in the same."

A deep sadness washed over me that no magically scented air could fix. Oh how I wished I would have paid more attention to Gram's stories! The sadness was followed swiftly by anger. Anger at Mother for keeping me away after Dad died and even more anger at myself for being scared to stand up to her when I was an adult and allowing her to keep me from coming back. I should have just come back home.

This was home after all, or at least it contained the feelings that

I associated with home. Mom and Dad were always happy when we were here and there was never a shortage of love and security and fun with Gram, with the whole town really. Even just driving down Main Street, I'd felt a deep sense of homecoming that I had been missing since I was eight years old. It's a different feeling, driving through when you know you'll be headed back out the next day, and driving through when you've come to stay. At least for a little while, anyway.

Mr. Findley cleared his throat, and I realized I had been staring blankly at the shelves behind him once again, lost to my own inner turmoil. "I don't know what nonsense you were telling yourself just then, sweetheart, but everything works out as it's meant to be. If I knew Constance at all, I'm sure the answers you're looking for will be found somewhere, whether in this packet, the cottage, or the town itself." He watched me for a moment before asking softly, "Is there something else, Mabel?"

"It's just..." Pausing, I sighed, trying to get my thoughts in order, and maybe muster up a little courage too. "I was thinking on the drive down here, and then had a little moment at the coffee shop that I'm sure you'll hear about by Monday." He narrowed his eyes at me and cocked his head in question. "No, not a moment that would require bail or legal counsel. Just, I've spent a really long time doing things just so, just the way they should be done, should sound, should seem, should look. Maybe I'm just done 'should-ing' on myself."

My eyes widened as I realized what I'd said. Out loud. At a professional legal meeting. He was still just watching me, waiting for me to get to the point I guess, I wasn't sure. I continued on anyway, maybe even trying to get to the point for myself.

"I guess I mean, this is a lot, and there was a lot that I wasn't expecting or prepared for. But if I've decided to handle my life the way that I want to handle it, to really live it, then I might as well loop in all these big huge scary changes and handle it. Or at the very least fake it until I make it. Right?"

I straightened in my seat a little and offered him a fake, bright smile I absolutely did not feel. Something flickered across his face so quickly I wasn't able to pin down the emotion before he straightened in his chair too and looked at me with something like pride.

"Right. And like I said Mabel, I'm sure you'll find everything you're looking for... Painted Creek seems to be magic like that, showing people what they need. Even when they're too stubborn to look. At least it was for me once."

He went over a few smaller things, reminded me again to take notes and jot down questions, and then he stood to see me out. I smiled weakly and thanked him, promising to be back at 9 AM on Monday morning.

He'd given me some great reassurance and guidance. Now, I only wished I could believe him.

FIVE

I THINK THE revelations in Mr. Findley's office had short circuited the part of my brain that thought all the thoughts. There wasn't a single solitary thing in my head on the drive to the cottage. Eerie really... normally there were at least song lyrics or a commercial jingle from the 90's taking up space in my brain.

It didn't take long, because really it didn't take long to get anywhere in Painted Creek, but before I knew it I was turning on to the long gravel driveway. I saw a beautifully painted sign off to the side that said "Painted Creek Cottage" that I didn't remember from when I was younger, or in any of the quick visits I'd had as an adult. Maybe it had been there all along and I just didn't pay attention.

Pondering the sign had taken all of my mental attention, and all of a sudden I was in park in front of the house. I turned the car off, but didn't get out. I just sat and stared up at the house that was such a huge part of my early childhood.

I had always loved Gram's house. It reminded me of a doll house. Not in the cheesy Hansel and Gretel way, but in the best way, like everything could be fancy without being ostentatious. Painted a soothing denim blue gray, the arts and crafts style trim stood out in its vanilla marshmallow cream color, making the whole place look cheerful and comforting. My favorite part was the trim along the dormer windows. I'd always felt like the house was winking at me when I came back for a visit, like it had a secret to share with only me, or it already knew about all of the mischief Gram and I would stir up on my visit.

The gray stone base around the house was the perfect backdrop for the landscaping I knew Gram was responsible for. She loved to dig in the dirt. My younger self was less interested in that and more interested in fabricating excuses to walk by the ice cream shop when we went into town. I'd found an appreciation for gardening though as I got older, but yard maintenance at my apartment was obviously taken care of, and there was no room anywhere for even a porch garden. At the time I was thrilled; I didn't have to worry about cutting the grass, trimming hedges, or keeping anything green alive and thriving. But looking at Gram's rose shrubs, lambs ear, and the rest of the flowers, I wondered what it would be like to paint a beautiful picture with living plants in the yard and not just paint on paper.

The house was nestled into the tress like a lush, green blanket surrounded it and it was just poking its nose out from under the covers. Tears sprang to my eyes as a deep sense of peace washed over me. *This* was home. "How can I ever walk away from here for good? How can I leave and never come back?" The house seemed to shudder, as if it couldn't bare the thought of me leaving either. I shook my head, and got out of the car. I grabbed the bags with my clothes, food, and toiletries and left the painting supplies for tomorrow. I didn't feel much like painting right now anyway, the weight of loss and responsibility making my fingers stiff and my limbs feel like lead.

Walking up the stone paver sidewalk, I started to notice the little things that must've been new editions since I last came to visit. New outdoor lighting lined the sidewalk from the driveway to the front door, and string lights with Edison bulbs dotted the expansive front porch like fairies were hovering around, waiting to be asked inside. All of the outdoor lights, and some of the indoor lights too, must've been turned on by Mr. Findley when he dropped off groceries since they were already glowing softly against the fading sunlight. It was a thoughtful gesture I'd need to remember to thank him for on Monday.

Off to the right at the very end of the porch was a porch swing, framed by the house and one of the massive sturdy columns of the front porch. I could picture Gram there, waiting for someone to come up the long driveway and visit, and my shoulders slumped as another wave of guilt and sadness crept over me. I took a deep breath that didn't quite reach all the way down to the bottom of my lungs, as if something was squeezing my chest. As I turned the key in the lock, a strong breeze stirred through the air. I could've sworn I heard someone whisper 'welcome home' as I stepped inside for the first time without Gram waiting on the other side with open arms.

A SMELL THAT was just so Gram hit me full force when I opened the door. Gram had been gone for a little over a month, and Mr. Findley told me there was a cleaning crew that had been through once a week and right before I came to make sure everything was fresh and cared for, but the house still smelled like Gram and her hugs and her love. It was the unmistakable scent of roses and a hint or two of something else I was never able to put my finger on as a child, but the combination would always be Gram. I idly wondered if Ms. Barnett could copy and bottle it for me.

Slowly starting to look around, it seemed as if the whole house had gotten a face lift since I'd been here last. The walls in all the rooms were still painted in their individual muted colors, all different earth tones that seemed to compliment each other seamlessly from room to room, but the paint glistened as if it were new, not dulled by age and wear. The trim on the doorways was still a beautiful, rich natural wood color and buttery soft to the touch when you grazed your fingertips along it lovingly as you walked by, but it sparkled and shined with the light as if it had been buffed and polished. Even the furniture was new, not many of the pieces holding memories of snuggles or movie nights or blanket forts. I made a mental note to ask Mr. Findley or Dottie about the changes; why and how and when.

The cottage was mostly a bungalow kind of floor plan with open sight lines through the main parts of the house. Gram always said it was made that way so the eyes in the back of her head didn't have to look through walls to see what I was up to while she was cooking dinner. I just liked that no matter where I was I could holler out a joke or question and Gram would holler back in response. The cottage was so quiet and still now, still comforting and calm but missing her steady presence, like the heartbeat of the home was gone.

I realized I was still standing right in front of the door and unceremoniously threw my bags to the floor. Walking through the foyer, I turned right into the dining room and put my purse on the shiny wooden table. The walls were painted a buttery yellow. It was a nice yellow, not too bright or obnoxious, mostly tan really, but unmistakably yellow somehow. Gram used to say yellow was good for digestion, so what better color for the dining room? I always thought that was especially funny because we rarely ate in the dining room... the table was always covered in a puzzle or craft or experiment and we ate at the bar in the kitchen instead.

I was just happy to be surrounded by color again instead of drowning in a sea of beige. *If I ever buy a house,* I thought, *there will be color and life in it like this one.* I pulled aside the curtains on the huge bay window in the middle of the wall to let in the fading light, and turned to face the heart of the house. Standing here I could see no less than four different paint colors on the walls, the foyer, dining room, kitchen and living room, but they all lived harmoniously like the colors in a matching paint pallet. The colors also reminded me of being outside, like the cottage and the nature surrounding it weren't different spaces, but a continuation of each other. It was grounding and peaceful.

Bypassing the hallway to the guest bedrooms on the left, I headed into the living room. The gray stone fireplace that took up the entire left wall of the main living area accented the theme of bringing the outdoors in, and I wondered how Gram had found stones for the sidewalk to match the fireplace so perfectly. Briefly, I considered that maybe Gram didn't match the stones. If this house had been in our family for a few generations as I had just learned, that wouldn't have been on her list of responsibilities.

The big TV still mounted above the mantle, however, was all Gram, although I think it had grown a few inches. Small, framed photos of our family lined up in layers across the mantle and I smiled as I remembered Gram saying she liked to see what was really important while she was watching junk on television. It was always such an enigma to me that my sweet, stable grandmother loved to watch *The Bachelor* and all the spin off shows that came after.

I wandered into the kitchen and true to his word, the pantry and fridge were stocked with a few staples from Mr. Findley. I snorted at all the new, unopened items in the refrigerator. Every time we would come over my mother would complain about all the expired condiments and things in the kitchen. Gram would just smile sweetly and say, "No one's died yet." As soon as she would be busy with something, my mother would throw it all out and drag Dad to the store to replace it all.

I think Gram did it just to aggravate her honestly. I vowed to myself, no matter where I lived, to always have a pile of ketchup packets in the refrigerator door... especially if my mother ever came back to this house. I wasn't hungry yet, so I pushed on through to the back doors that led to the patio. The door to Gram's suite was off to the right, but I just couldn't face opening that door tonight.

The back patio was amazing; an open, almost cavernous space

protected from the elements by a covered roof. With several porch fans, string lights around the perimeter, and lots of comfortable rocking chairs and other seating, it was obvious this space was meant to be used by residents and friends alike. The wind chimes hanging from the soffit around the edges of the roof broke the stillness as the early April breeze blew through the yard, making the space feel alive with its own playful energy.

I could just hear the creek that was down at the bottom of the expansive back yard. I didn't remember much about the creek. Gram had only taken me to walk in it a few times when I was younger, and we'd no reason to explore it on my rare visits as an adult. After my Dad died, Mother was always worried I would fall in and drown somehow. She made Gram promise not to let me play there on our rare visits, and Gram always respectfully followed her wishes, even when she didn't agree with them.

I knew Gram loved that creek, and how it snaked its way through the end of the backyard. I was excited to go explore something she loved with new eyes. But the twilight was fading fast, and all of a sudden I was overcome with a bone deep tiredness that would not be ignored.

"Tomorrow," I whispered, glancing one more time in the direction of the creek. "Outdoor exploring tomorrow."

I sat in the biggest, overstuffed rocking chair and enjoyed the cooler night air and the sound of the wind chimes. It was more of a big rocking egg chair really, the edges rising up slightly to reach for each other, and I could bury down into the middle and curl comfortably into a ball while rocking gently. "This is officially my chair now," I said aloud as I happily wiggled deeper into the chair. A bird hopped through the grass just past the patio and stopped to tilt its head at me, as if to say 'all of this is yours now, silly girl'.

"Yeah, yeah... let's just start with a chair, okay? I'll try and wrap my head around the rest tomorrow." He chirped at me, one staccato note that sounded rather impatient in my mind, and flew away, leaving me alone with the breeze and the faint smell of roses.

I SAT OUT on the patio for over an hour, until the sun was

completely gone and the crickets became louder than the wind chimes. My tummy finally let out a loud protest at being empty, so I wandered back into the kitchen. Right as I closed the door, my phone chirped with a message from the dining room table. "Crap," I frowned as I hurried over to retrieve it.

I hadn't let my mother know that I was in and settled, and I knew that it was her as soon as I heard the alert. Guilt, like rocks in my gut, replaced the peace I had found out on the patio as I dialed her number without reading any of the four missed text messages that I knew would only make me feel worse. It rang twice before the call connected to silence.

"I know, I know, I'm sorry I worried you. I finally got to the house and lost track of time getting reacquainted with everything."

"Well, I don't know what there is to get reacquainted with..." She huffed through the phone, the long suffering sound of a person who was always disappointed. "It's just a house. You would think you could've spared ten seconds to send a text message to your mother and let her know you were still alive. Or maybe found a neighbor to send a smoke signal, I'm sure they still use those in that town."

I was so, so thankful I hadn't Facetimed her and she couldn't see me roll my eyes. "I'm fine, Mother. I was just distracted. There are a lot of memories here after all."

"Yes, there are..." Her voice was unusually soft as she trailed off. I wondered once again what had happened to cause her to keep me from coming here, from visiting Gram and this town, after my Dad died. Sometimes she said things that made me think she missed coming here too. Other times she sounded as if she despised everything south of the Mason Dixon line.

"When do you meet with the lawyer?" Whatever vulnerability I'd thought I'd heard was gone.

"Monday morning at nine. But it's just the first meeting, Mother. I don't know how much I'll be able to settle right off the bat and I don't want to leave until everything is taken care of." It was a gentle reminder that I would be here longer than she liked. But I knew it wouldn't stop her from hounding me about coming back.

"Well, make sure you tell him you're on a tight schedule and you can't stay there forever. Honestly it was a little forward of him to suggest you come stay in town in the first place. Unless he's never heard of DocuSign and is still doing everything on paper."

I didn't justify any of that with an answer, and after a beat she moved on.

"Have you checked your web page to see if you've gotten any new commission requests? Don't slack on the business you worked so hard for just because you've gotten distracted by the past."

Quietly, I tried to pull in a calming breath without giving away my irritation. "Mom, I told you I just got here and got settled. I haven't even unpacked the car yet. Mr. Findley was kind enough to stock the house with some groceries so I don't even have to go back into town until Monday. I'll check my inbox tomorrow morning and then get right on the paintings I have already accepted. Nothing but commissioned hyper focus all weekend, I promise."

Unlike what I had just done, Mom didn't do anything to quiet her long sigh through the phone. "I know you will. You love to paint. I'm not really worried about your business, I just miss you. Tomorrow will be the first Saturday night dinner we've not had together in ages." I tilted my head the same way the bird in the yard had. It never once, not one single time, crossed my mind that my mother's attitude about my decision to stay awhile in Painted Creek came from a place of loneliness.

"I think I saw a package of noodles in the pantry. How about I'll throw together some noodles and cheese and Facetime you at five? We can still eat together." The beginnings of warmth bloomed in my chest at the thought my mother was going to miss my company. I'd just assumed she'd miss having someone to give orders to.

"That would be nice, Mabel. Just make sure you check all the expiration dates of everything in the refrigerator before you cook. You never know how thorough those cleaning companies are and your gram never did care about the chance of E. Coli food poisoning. And throw out all those tacky fast food packets!"

"Yes, Mother. Chat tomorrow. Love you, bye!" And just like

that, the warm fuzzies disappeared as I hung up on my mother for the second time that day.

I was definitely carving out a permanent place in the fridge for condiment packets.

SIX

DARKNESS HAD WELL and truly fallen outside, but all of Gram's lamps cast a cozy glow throughout the cottage. Gram LOVED lamps. She didn't discriminate on size or brightness or even if it fit in the space. If she saw one she liked, she brought it in and found it a home. The two end tables by the couch and love seat held traditional lamps and accounted for the majority of the light in the main living space. The shades were a soft dusty pink and Gram had taped cut outs of the silhouettes of rose blooms to the inside of the shade, creating a negative space design in the light that shone through. I loved it. That kind of simple touch was just so Gram; it didn't matter if it was 'proper' or made sense, if it brought her joy, she did it.

Sprinkled throughout the dining room, living room, and

kitchen were various types of Himalayan salt lamps. Gram had given me one for Christmas one year, explaining something about the ions in the air and boosting mood. I'd kept it by the dining room table in my apartment where I did all my painting. I didn't know if it was the negative ions or knowing it had come from Gram, but I did feel happier when it was on. It would be one of the first things I would dig through all of my boxes for when I settled somewhere permanently, wherever that would be.

For now, I was happy to get to enjoy all of the salt lamps Gram had placed lovingly around her home. My favorite was on a drop leaf side table in the small nook created by the fireplace and the wall as you came in from the foyer. It was a crackle glass dome filled with Himalayan rock chunks, a string of copper fairy lights tangled all inside. *I'll leave that on as a night light,* I thought.

Tiny little decorative lights were scattered along the mantle mixed in with the picture frames. Almost all of them were tea light size and barely emitted a soft glow here and there. A quarter round table in the landing from the attic stairs held a darling turtle lamp, his body made of brass and his shell beautiful green stained glass that let the light shine through, with a dried flower arrangement in a vase. Soft down lighting was coming from underneath the upper kitchen cabinets, and an owl shaped wax warmer was glowing from the outlet in the corner.

Maybe my favorite of all though was the hedgehog lamp in the dining room. He sat on the serving cart under the window, his cute little face watching over the whole house as light poured through the cutouts in his ceramic quill covered body. I loved him instantly and fiercely; maybe a little concerning since we were talking about a lamp, but love was love I suppose.

Not for the first time I wondered if all these lights were on a timer or if I'd need to wander around and turn them all off before I went to bed. It would be quite the bed time routine, but it occurred to me it would be like tucking the house in for bed too, and then I kind of didn't mind.

I still hadn't eaten, so I rummaged through the food I'd brought from home and the things Mr. Findley had left and put together a little snack plate of sorts. Maybe not a very nutritious dinner, but I had done enough adulting for today and just wanted comfort food. I put my plate and glass in the middle of the bar so I could reach it from all directions and then began to spread out everything I'd been given at Mr. Findley's office across the rest of the bar top.

The pile of legal papers he'd given me were stapled neatly into three different stacks. I laid them all side by side and put the envelope with Gram's handwriting very last. I'd go through the legal stacks first and take notes while I nibbled and save the ominous envelope for last.

The three legal stacks weren't as bad as I was preparing myself for them to be. It seems Gram had left everything to me free and clear, as Mr. Findley had said. One stack held information on the cottage that I just barely skimmed over, things like warranties and maintenance and a copy of the title which now held my name. The second stack seemed to be investment accounts and life insurance policies and the like. I wasn't exactly sure what to do with all of that but I knew I would find out Monday, so I decided that was a future me problem.

The third stack, simply labeled 'Real Estate', talked about two buildings in town somewhere that Gram had purchased. It seemed she was renting out one of them to someone while the other remained empty. I wasn't super worried about either... I assume the tenants could just stay on until their term was up and I'd deal with that one then, and an empty building was easy to sell as is.

I didn't even flip through all the pages of legal notes and details. After jotting down a few questions to ask on Monday, I neatly stacked all the papers together and moved them to the end table behind me by the couch. I wanted to have full use of the island to spread out whatever was in that last envelope.

As I slid the envelope over to me, my finger tips began to tingle. It was a sensation I wasn't unfamiliar with, although it had been awhile since it'd happened. In my early painting days as a child, when I would paint whatever struck my fancy, I used to get tingly fingers when a great idea crossed my path. Inspiration was everywhere, whether it was someone talking, a sound from outside, or even an ad on TV, I would pay attention to those tingles and paint the first thing that came to mind.

Over time, the tingly fingers grew into whole body tingles and goosebumps, a phenomenon called frisson. Technically defined as a response that occurs to a moving experience such as music or art, I felt like my frissons were backward somehow, as if I was being encouraged to create the thing that would give *someone else* aesthetic chills.

By the time the chills had brought goosebumps across my skin, a picture would form in my mind and I would feel such a strong pull to paint whatever it was that I usually couldn't work on anything else until I had a least jotted down the idea. Sometimes, the painting I ended up with had nothing to do with whatever had caused me to perk up and pay attention in the first place. It never really made sense to me, but as a child those were always some of my best paintings.

It was a frisson painting that had first gotten me noticed by a major art gallery in Columbus, which led to my first gallery showing when I was only sixteen years old. I'd kept painting whatever I felt called to paint while I finished high school and was lucky enough to have several showings in a couple of years time. Sometime during college though, I'd started taking commissions.

My mother had a friend who wanted a painting of her home to hang on the wall in her downtown Cincinnati office. She offered me a ridiculous amount of money to paint to her specifications, and I'd agreed. There were so many things that she wanted, or didn't want, in the painting, and I'd followed her instructions down to the tiniest detail, even when I felt like the painting had lost its spark. She was thrilled with the end result though, and told everyone she knew and every person that stepped foot in her office about how pleased she was by my professionalism and attention to detail. It snowballed after that, and before I knew what had happened I had a thriving commissioned art business.

I'd become very good at painting precisely what my customer wanted, even if it meant ignoring my artistic instincts on what the painting *could* be. I had a waiting list, and was fortunate enough that I could pick and choose clients based on time and subject matter. I knew how lucky I was to have a steady income doing something I loved that was so far outside the realm of a 'real job'.

But I didn't listen to the frisson anymore.

I tried to ignore them now as I unwound the string on the closure. Carefully sliding everything out, I scooted down to the end of the island. I figured I'd start at the top and lay things out as I got to them. If anything felt like it went together, then I'd put it in that pile. If not, it got its own pile. "Sounds simple enough," I puffed my cheeks out on a long exhale. Hopefully I wouldn't run out of island space.

There was an envelope of baby pictures of my father, and another of baby pictures of me. I decided to go through them later and add one of my dad to the photos on the mantle. He was a cute kid. There was another envelope that seemed to have photographs from multiple decades. Scanning them briefly, I didn't recognize anyone in the photographs, but I knew they must be family. I flipped a few over, hoping to find dates or names, only to find them all blank. It would have to be a research project for another day.

The last envelope had my name on the front in Gram's handwriting and a longing to be close to her had me ripping it open.

Mabel,

It's cliché sure, but if you're reading this then something has happened to me. Now all my contingency plans, the ones all y'all always picked on me for, are a necessity and I hope a blessing for you. Didn't I tell you girl, I'm always right!

Everything I have is yours, Mabel, and I want you to behave like it is. Don't stay out of my room, child. Go through every nook and cranny and snoop like you never did when you were little. Keep what speaks to you and get rid of the rest without a lick of guilt. Make this cottage your home. Make it everything you've ever wanted it to be.

And what do you want it to be, Mabel? It would make me so happy to know that you settled here in Painted Creek in our family home, but this is your life, sweetheart, and you need to put yourself at the top of the people-to-

please list. If what you want it to be is a distant memory, all I ask is that you take all the journals with you, to remember me and our family.

I never told you that did I? Painted Creek Cottage has been in our family for a few generations now. I sure wish I had had more time with you to tell you all the stories of our family, all the stories of me. You'll find some things in with this letter and I'm sure all the rest you'll figure out in your own time. Maybe you'll settle here and maybe you won't. This place will be a part of you no matter where you go.

I love you, sweetheart. And I'm with you still, no doubt about it. I'll always be around. Find your own path, tell your own story, or maybe paint it, hmm? Keep that spark of yours that shines so bright and feed it every day. You're made for beautiful, magical things, Mabel, it's in your blood. Trust me, I'm always right, remember?

> *All my love,*
> *Gram*

I must've read her letter three or four times, savoring her last words to me each time. Even writing a goodbye note she never knew if she would need, she did it with humor and only wanted me to be happy.

I was curious about the journals she'd mentioned, but I just couldn't take anymore tonight. It was after midnight anyway and I hadn't had a day this emotionally taxing in a long time. Turns out, all the lights were not on a timer, so I spent a few minutes tucking the house in for the night and turning them off, all but the crackle salt lamp on the table and the one in the kitchen. I made sure the doors were locked and whispered, "Goodnight, house," as I picked my bags up off the floor and made my way back to what I always considered 'my room'.

Off to the left of the foyer was a little hallway that led to the guest bathroom and the two guest rooms on the main floor. My parents would always take the room on the left, where the window faced the front of the house, and I would take the one to the right with two corner windows. Gram had added a papasan chair for me in the corner, and I would open both windows and listen to the birds and paint or read on a plastic lap desk. Tonight, I hefted my duffel with my clothes in it into the middle of the chair and left it to unpack tomorrow.

The room wasn't decorated as a 'kid's' room, but I always thought of it as mine. The walls were a light sky blue that was calming and restful, and I'd never appreciated it more than I did tonight.

Hanging on the wall was one of the first paintings I had done during a summer visit that was actually *good*, although Gram always pointed out something in everything I did that was done well, along with asking if I'd like her to tell me if she saw anything that could be improved. The day I painted this painting, Gram had shown me a photo of a Mabel flower, the Ixia Mabel to be exact, and I sat down and stared at that picture until I had my version just right. Looking at it now, the painting looked more like a hyacinth than a Ixia Mabel; the red flowers too close together and shaped like the soft end of a q-tip instead of the star-shaped cluster of flowers it should've been. But the color and shading was good, and at least it didn't look like a blob.

Then there was a painting I had given Gram for Christmas one year when I was an adult. It was of a Mabel Grey flower, a type of lemony scented geranium. It was a little surreal to see them side by side on the wall, to see just how far I had come in my painting abilities and styles. You could even see the almost fuzzy texture of the leaves, and the darker strokes of purple through the lilac colored flower petals were crisp and precise. I'd had a real Mabel Grey in a pot in my kitchen until I had packed to move, and I'd given it to Mom so she'd still have a Mabel nearby. She was not amused.

The paintings were just another reason this was my room. Gram also had Mabel Morrison roses planted outside my window, but even if it was my actual full name, I never liked them as much as her rose shrubs. The smell wasn't as strong and didn't remind me of her. I never painted that one, namesake or not.

After putting my other bag in the bathroom, I dug out an oversize t-shirt and some soft flannel shorts to sleep in. My favorite quilt in the whole world waited for me on the bed. It was made of flannel and velvet and bamboo and everything else you could think of. It was complicated, functional chaos and I loved it. Slipping underneath, I turned the light off and drifted quickly to sleep, my dreams smelling of roses and lemony geranium and something uniquely *home*.

SEVEN

GRAM DIDN'T HAVE a coffee pot. I knew this. I remembered every brief Christmas visit where I would tease her about not allowing coffee into the house and she would laugh and make me a cup of tea instead. All those times it was fine, a way to connect with Gram even. But this morning, the lack of my favorite small counter top appliance was *painful*. I'd slept better than I imagined I would with all the new information rattling around in my brain. But good sleep or not, there would be no proper human functioning without coffee.

I sang to myself as I bumped into the kitchen island on the way to the pantry. Spacial awareness really wasn't my thing, which was crazy since I made my living painting incredibly detailed and life like paintings. Somehow it didn't translate to real life. I stared blankly into the pantry hoping coffee would suddenly materialize and I wouldn't spend the next two days as a zombie. Too tired to even sigh in resignation, I turned and shuffled back out. It was going to be a long day. After a quick, coffeeless breakfast and a fantastically soothing hot shower, it was time to get my paint supplies out of the car.

While I had chucked all of my personal bags in the car all willy nilly, I had painstakingly packed all of my paint supplies and placed them gently in the back seat. It wasn't just that I'd need them to continue working while I was here, it was how I always treated them. They were like an extension of myself and I treated my paints with a kind of care I just didn't have for most things. Not that I didn't respect and appreciate everything I had worked for, that wasn't it. It was just that I was usually moving fast or twitching nervously and I sometimes came across as careless or fidgety. I had a kind of focus when I was painting that eluded me, well, in everything else.

Mother always said it was a choice, that if I would just slow down or just concentrate or just not worry so much I wouldn't seem so skittish and klutzy. Like I could control those things. I never considered myself to have a lack of concentration, it was more like I could focus on several things at once and so I seemed distracted to others. I think it was part of what made me such a good painter, that ability to notice *everything* about what I needed to paint. It's what made my commissioned paintings look so familiar and lifelike to the people that ordered them.

Whatever it was, I was excited to get all my supplies out of the car and into the house. It seemed like the right thing to do to spread them out all over the dining room table, to have it covered in crafts once again. "No eating in here for awhile, as it should be." I nodded once and made it so. In no time at all, the only visible spot of wood was in front of the one chair I'd left at the table to sit in. It was time to get to work.

I scrolled through the list of commissions that I had already accepted. I was so fortunate that I didn't have to take every request that came my way anymore. I had done some really crazy paintings in the beginning and I learned quickly that just because I was capable of painting a 'centaur with great Grandpop's face and beer belly' didn't mean that I should. The customer was thrilled, but I think I died a little inside every time I thought about that one.

I had also learned rather early on that I needed to give myself a huge deadline buffer. Even if I thought I could finish the painting in three days, I often forgot to account for real life and I would have to ask for an extension if something came up that took away my painting time. Now, I told everyone a minimum of four weeks. Even though I usually had it finished and delivered in two or less, that just meant my customers were thrilled with the time line and I wasn't as stressed out. It resulted in more word of mouth business and recommendations, which was nice too.

The painting someone had requested of the porcupine they worked with at the zoo reminded me of the hedgehog lamp that was now cheerfully looking over my shoulder, so I started with it. I got out my heavyweight paper, taped it down, and wet my watercolors. The next time I glanced up, four hours had passed. Stretching out my neck and shoulders, I slowly stood from the table. "It's so quiet here, Hedgie," I said to the lamp. "I'll have to set a timer or something from now on."

While my old apartment wasn't exactly loud, it definitely wasn't an only house on a country road level of quiet either. Sometimes I could hear the neighbor's car beep when they locked the door, or the kids that lived next door yelling when they got off the bus. It was always just enough to break my painting trance, and I'd get up and grab a snack or stretch or spend a few minutes on my stepper.

Don't judge a stepper until you've tried it! For someone who is not very athletically inclined, and by that I mean not at all, it was perfect. The fact that I could do it in the living room with no one gawking at how awkward I looked while watching half an episode of *The Gilmore Girls*? Priceless.

But none of those distractions existed here. The occasional music from the wind chimes would break through, but it was a welcome melody within the silence, not a staccato note that didn't belong. I glanced down at the porcupine that looked up at me from the paper. He was almost done, only lacking a few of the ultra fine details that would make him undeniably Mr. Harpoon, porcupine of the Zoo of America. I moved the mat over to the serving cart so that I could start on a different project and finish him later. "Watch over him, Hedgie. I'm sure you'll be great friends."

I'D ALWAYS WANTED to get a studio space somewhere in Columbus instead of painting from home. At first, when I still lived at home with Mother, I had a desk in my room that I would use. It was also a functional desk for school though, so I was constantly putting my paints away and moving things around.

When I got the apartment, I didn't have an extra room there either, so I painted at the kitchen table. But that meant that every time someone would come over I would have to pack it all up and hide it away. While I had gotten very good at moving it all, it was tedious and I hated it. I had tried leaving it all out when I first moved in by myself, but my mother commented on it every single time she came over, which was often. It was easier to put it away and make her happy than it was to listen to the passive aggressive comments.

If I was being honest, I wanted more than just a studio space. I wanted a shop; real, live, brick and mortar shop that people could stroll though and browse at their leisure. I could paint anything I wanted and watch as people fell in love with something unexpectedly. I loved my commission work, truly I did. It challenged me in a way I craved and was certainly never boring. But I missed painting just because I loved to paint. Somewhere along the way it had become nothing but a job, not a passion.

I glanced over at the painting of the porcupine again, and the hedgehog lamp sitting next to it. My fingers started tingling and I wanted nothing more than to sit down and paint the little lamp. Or maybe just a hedgehog. Maybe a glowing hedgehog? I wasn't really sure honestly, and that's how the frisson paintings tended to work. I just got this feeling like I had to paint, and a slight image in my head. I would sit down and get to it and usually be just as surprised by the end result as everyone else. I hadn't had a frisson vision in a long time. Ha... frisson vision. One hundred percent what I was calling them in my head from now on.

A knock on the door startled me, and I jostled myself into the kitchen island once again. "Smooth..." Murmuring under my breath I went to answer the door, already having a pretty good idea of who it was.

"Hey, Dottie," I grinned as I opened the door wide and rushed to hug the woman that was a permanent fixture of all my time in Painted Creek.

"Oh, sugar, what a greeting! I'll come over unannounced more often!" She laughed and I stood back to really look her over for the first time since we'd lost Gram.

Her hair was a cinnamon and sugar halo of permed curls all around her head. Dottie always looked so put together, the perfect outfit with matching shoes, not a wrinkle to be seen, on her clothes at least, and I don't think I'd ever seen her without the same pair of small diamond stud earrings in her ears. I guess she was your stereotypical southern little old lady.

I smirked as I remembered her and Gram wreaking havoc all over town. Gram was tall with deep dark hair only slightly sprinkled through with starry silver. She always dressed more like a gypsy than a proper lady, the kind of carefree I wish I could grow up to be. Gram and Dottie had been complete opposites and utterly inseparable. My very own Laverine and Shirley.

"What are you smirking at, honey, while you've left me out here on the porch?"

"Oh Lord, I'm sorry, Dottie. Please do come in! I'm so happy you're here." I shut the door behind her and headed into the kitchen. I filled Gram's kettle and put it on the stove so we could have tea. It was so second nature I didn't even think about it. If there was company in this house, there was tea.

"I just wanted to see how you were getting on. I know you've only been here a day, but I thought you might be right bored here by yourself. I should've known you'd already be painting. Is this one for fun?"

Dottie had wandered by the dining room once she'd dropped

her bags on the floor right where I'd plopped mine when I came in last night. I wondered if I had seen her do it so many times in my life that it was an unconscious response to coming in the house with bags.

"No, not for fun. I have a list of commissions I've already accepted before I open my books back up. That little guy is one of the animals my customer takes care of at the Zoo of America. Hedgie is watching over him while he dries."

"Hedgie?" One perfectly drawn on pencil thin eyebrow raised in my direction. "How original."

"Hey! No insulting Hedgie. He's my new best friend and I love him with all my heart." I pouted playfully back at her, watching the smile slowly overtake her face.

"Maybe we should get you a pet. Unless you think the lamp would get its feelings hurt. We wouldn't want that."

"Har har. I'd love to have a pet someday… I've always wanted a cat. As much as I love Hedgie there, I don't think I want a real hedgehog. A dog feels too demanding, but a cat feels more like a roommate that might snuggle now and then." I shrugged. "I'll get one someday. When I settle into a place that I know I'm going to stay."

Dottie's nose wrinkled like she smelled rotten eggs. "Well, isn't that something! Since it sure looks like you've got yourself a nice place right here. And speaking of, I brought you a house warming present. Don't worry, it's not alive, at least not anymore than your lamp over there, but you can give it a name too if it'll make you feel better. And we'll add a real live pussy cat to the list for one day," she waggled her eyebrows, "and maybe a man, too."

"Oh, Dot. You didn't need to bring me a thing, I'm just happy to visit with you. Plus, I think a house warming present is typically for when someone moves into a house and plans to stay. I'm just visiting while I sort through Gram's affairs. And I'm not justifying the man comment with a response, thank you very much."

With her hip propped on the edge of the table and her eyes narrowed in my direction, all five foot nothing of the sweet old lady in front of me seemed to morph into a formidable opponent. She

51

studied me for a beat that didn't make me uncomfortable at all, a lie, it totally did, before cocking her head to one side to glare at me.

"Baby, you know as well as I do that you're staying here. That there isn't another place in this whole wide world that would ever suit you like this very house in this very town. But if you want to keep lyin' to yourself and everyone else a little while longer, then you can consider this something to remember me by when you go instead of a house warming gift." She pushed off the table and picked up the bag at the door that she'd left with her purse. Walking over to join me at the island, she set the bag on the counter and sat at one of the bar stools across from me.

I slowly peeked in the canvas bag, like there could actually be something in there that might bite me. Reaching in, I gasped as I pulled out the most beautiful French press I'd ever seen. The thin glass was covered by a beautiful sage green metal with delicate herbs and flowers cut out, creating an intricate picture in the metal. The empty glass beneath almost seemed to sparkle, and I could imagine how the feel of it would change when it was full of dark, rich coffee. Also inside was a bag of coffee with the most adorable owl on the front. I couldn't tell if he needed more caffeine or if he'd had too much, his feathers sticking out everywhere and a disgruntled look on his face.

"Thank you, Dottie. In trying to get everything ready to come here I completely forgot Gram despised coffee. Until this morning of course." I winced, reliving my painful morning without my typical caffeine fix. "I've never heard of this brand of coffee. Is it good?"

"I got it at the Piggly Wiggly down in Asheville. I do believe it's my favorite brand now. They got all different kinds, too. Even that pumpkin spice nonsense you love so much in the fall." I blinked back a sudden rush of tears. Seems like I was doing that every time I turned around these days. Being back here in Gram's house with Dottie, I felt surrounded by unconditional love for the first time since, well, since I'd left here last.

"Dottie, let me just tell you again how happy I am to see you."

She seemed to be blinking back tears of her own as she replied, "You too, sugar."

Just then, the tea kettle started whistling and snapped us both out of our bittersweet mood. I rushed over and pulled out two hand thrown mugs and reached for a store bought box of spearmint tea that I'd found in the pantry. I assumed that Mr. Findley had brought it, along with a few other varieties, when he brought groceries. It would've been strange for Gram to buy any tea at a store unless it was black tea for sweet iced tea, but it was sweet of him to consider I might want to have tea while I was here, like old times.

I dunked a bag in each mug and wrapped the string around the handle. Passing one to Dottie, I came around the bar to sit next to her. I bumped her shoulder with mine and we sat in comfortable silence for a few minutes, sipping our tea. When she starting squirming in her stool, I giggled.

"Spit it out, Dot."

"Whatever do you mean?" Feigning ignorance. Nice play.

"You're talking to a master fidget-er here. I can tell you have something to say, so out with it."

"It's something to ask actually. I know you usually have a process for how you take on all those gorgeous paintings that you do. But I was wondering if I could get myself on that list somehow. I'm not in a hurry for it, mind. And I'm going to pay you same as everyone else so don't even try and say that I'm not." She set her mug back down and spun to face me like we might fight over her paying me right here and now. I'd let her think she won and come up with a work around later.

"I'd absolutely love to paint something for you, Dottie, you know that. Just get me some pictures so I have something to go by. What are you wanting?"

Her gaze went soft around the edges and she stared out of the glass doors to the backyard. "You know Constance and I would go down to Cherokee with the ladies every year." The ladies, as they all refer to each other when talking to other people, were a group of women that had been friends for almost fifty years. It was unbelievable for me to think about really, to have friendships so strong they still carved out the space to meet each other once a year after all this time.

"Yes, ma'am. I'm familiar with the old biddy trip. As I recall, y'all hadn't needed any bail money for the last few years or so..."

Dottie's belly laugh was the reaction I was hoping for. They were well behaved on their trips, Dottie most of all, but there was that one time with all that tequila...

"Hush now, sugar, you know we don't talk about that. Anyway, I want a painting of the cabin we would all stay in every year. Of course, I'll still keep on going until I'm not able. But it just won't be the same without your gram. I just thought if I got you to paint it for me now, I could keep her there a little bit somehow."

"That's a perfect idea. And my favorite commissions are sentimental ones, too. I'm honored to do this for you, Dottie, truly. Just send me some pictures and I'll get right to it." I looked down into my mug and swirled it a bit, focusing more on the tea bag being tossed about than my heart being tossed about by my feelings.

"Child, why did you use this store bought stuff and not your gram's tea?" She looked down at her own mug in front of her on the counter and eyed it suspiciously.

"Well, I used the last of it that she gave me at Christmas before she passed. I don't have any more. I wish I had known that the last bag was the last bag. I would have cherished it more or saved it or something." I looked outside, as if I could find the answers out there, or maybe just so I didn't have to see the look of pity that I was sure was on Dottie's face. I didn't expect the snort of derision.

"Lord, honey, you make it sound like Constance only made that one bag for you when you would visit and that's it. I'm not sure how far ahead she was in the mixing up of her tea blends, but there should still be some in the pantry. Didn't you find it?"

"Don't tease me, Dottie, seriously."

Dottie sat back in her bar stool and studied me again. Serious scrutiny twice in one visit, lucky me. "Mabel, I wouldn't tease you about something you thought you had lost. And I never tease about Constance's tea and her abilities to make the perfect blend for each and every person that needed it. She always kept a well stocked tea

54

arsenal in the cupboard in the pantry, in case she had trouble with her herbs or used more of one than she expected or something of the like. You know her and her contingency plans..."

"Dottie, I've been in the pantry several times since arriving, not to mention all the times I've visited in my life. There is no cupboard in the pantry and no extra tea at all." I'd swiveled in my bar stool side to side a few times trying to keep from jumping up and stomping my foot. Was I going crazy or was Dottie?

"Child, come here. And wipe that obstinate look off your face this second." She headed over to the pantry, pulling me by the wrist behind her. At least it wasn't by the ear. "I guess it's not a cupboard in the classic sense, not a big beautiful piece of furniture. But that's what she called it. See that door there, built into the wall? Didn't you think to open it?"

Sure enough, right there built in flush with the wall was a thin wood door with one tiny leaf shaped pull knob on the right side. It wasn't the height of the wall by any means, but still a good three feet tall and two feet or so wide, centered in the wall where the top wasn't too far above my head but I didn't have to bend down too far to reach the bottom either. I just stood there and stared at it.

It was me, not Dottie. I was definitely going crazy. How had I missed a whole other door in a wall? I wondered idly if lack of regularly scheduled caffeine was plausible cause for temporary insanity.

"How did I miss this?"

"Well I do imagine you have had a lot going on in that pretty little head of yours the last couple of months. And when you were a child, I imagine it looked like a boring electrical box or something that you never took note of. And what would a child want with a cupboard full of tea anyway?" She shrugged, patted me on the shoulder, and turned to leave the pantry. "Don't be so hard on yourself, honey."

"You and I are getting acquainted later..." Pointing two fingers between my eyes and the cupboard door, I slowly turned and followed Dottie to the living room.

EIGHT

DOTTIE HAD SETTLED in on the sofa, sitting sideways in the corner and wiggling herself in like she had done it a thousand times. She probably had.

"Dottie, when did Gram get all new furniture? I walked in last night and almost thought I was in the wrong house. She never mentioned it to me." Frowning slightly, I settled in on the love seat next to Dot's spot on the sofa. I always thought Gram and I were close in spirit, keeping up through text and phone calls. Finding out we perhaps weren't as close as I'd let myself believe was... uncomfortable.

"Oh a few months ago maybe, not too long after your Christmas visit. Said she was down right sick of looking at the old patterns and it was time for a change. I'll admit, I was surprised

Constance chose a plain, solid, non patterned soft gray," she giggled but then snuggled deeper, "but it sure is the most comfortable sofa I've ever rested my old derrière on."

"Derrière? Really?"

"Well derrière sounds a good bit better than what you kids are saying these days! I never."

"Hey! Don't loop me in with kids these days. You know I don't act like that."

I hadn't meant anything too serious with my response, but here she was, studying me again like I was a rare species in a zoo. Or maybe a flight risk.

"No, you certainly don't act like that. You've been closed up tighter than a drum since you were about ten years old. Most polite, grown, quiet child I ever did see." She curled her legs up underneath her and propped her chin on one hand on the arm of the couch, batting her lashes at me. "That is until yesterday in the Artful Brew. Whew honey, everybody is talking about how you got one over on Sarah. I'm honestly not sure if they're all impressed or a mite scared."

I laughed out loud, remembering the look on her face when Sarah had realized I was familiar with the town and its street names. "I'll admit, that was the most fun I've had in a couple months. I don't even know what came over me, I just decided it would be fun to play long. I had no idea you'd come in and help me deliver the punch line quite like that. I guess I kind of thought I would just go along playing tourist and leave, that it would come up some how later the next time I went in... I don't know."

"Well, it couldn't have worked out better if you ask me. I always did have a knack for being in the right place at the right time." She fluffed her perfectly shaped permed halo and lifted her nose in the air haughtily. "And Sarah needs someone to shake her up every now and again if you ask me. Just like you, that one, all grown up too soon and no fun."

"Well, Dottie, I promise I'll un-grow up when I'm in my seventies and get arrested with my friends when we—"

"WE DON'T SPEAK OF THAT!" Dottie was hiding her face with

both hands and I was laughing so hard I had tears in my eyes. At least it was the good kind for once.

"Lord, child, you behave yourself now! While it was good to see you havin' a little bit of harmless fun and maybe double good to see Sarah caught up in it, I have to ask, sugar, are you doin' alright? Not that you did a blasted thing wrong, of course not. But add that to up and gettin' out of that apartment of yours and coming on out here to stay a spell, which I'm selfishly grateful for, mind you, it was just out of character for you, that's all."

I glanced across the room at the three paintings hanging in a line over Gram's drop leaf table. They were all frisson paintings, from the era of once I'd really learned how to paint but before I only took commissions and stopped painting what I'd felt called to create. They were a riot of color, three separate bouquets of wildflowers and herbs all tangled together and tied with a silk ribbon. The fill color didn't go all the way to the edges of the, seemingly scribbled, flower outline and in some places it spilled right over as if the joyfulness of the color couldn't be contained. The color palette in each painting was different, but they all matched in a way that made the hanging arrangement its own focal point in the living room.

I had loved them before they were dry properly and knew they were meant to live here with Gram, though I didn't imagine she'd display them quite so prominently. The free, flowing style had felt like a breath of fresh air at the time, since I had really started focusing on the hyper realism style I had perfected now. I'd felt inspired to do more, but Mother had encouraged me to work harder on the 'normal paintings', as she called them, saying branching too far from what everyone accepted would only hurt my brand new business. I guess she was right, since my realism paintings and portraits paid all my bills and then some. But it did make me wonder what other styles of art I had given up to please everyone else.

"I'm fine, Dottie. But that may be the problem. I'm *fine*. Not happy, not miserable, just existing. I think when I decided to come and settle Gram's affairs, I initially thought of it as an extended vacation and an excuse to find a new place in Columbus that suited ME better. But then I realized I'm not quite sure what that would be. I'm not quite sure who me actually is. Like maybe I've been so caught up my whole life making other people happy I forgot what makes me happy, too." I frowned down at the throw pillow I had pulled into my lap as we were talking. My new emotional support pillow. "Can someone act out of character if they aren't sure what their character is?" I asked quietly.

When I glanced up at Dottie, she was doing that thing again, head tilted to the side and eyes narrowed, like if she could just get the angle right she could read everything written in my heart that maybe I didn't even know myself.

"I swear, Dottie if you don't stop studying me like that today I'm going to kick you right out of this house!"

A slow grin spread across her face and her eyes lit up with a twinkle. "Well, I guess you're going to be fine aren't you, Mabel? Good for you, sugar."

"Wait, what?"

She just laughed as she slowly unfolded from the sofa and stood. "I guess I best be going now. Thank you for agreeing to do my painting. You just let me know what I owe you and when you think you'll be done. No rush now."

I stood and gave the tiny older woman a tight hug. It was so good to spend some time with her again. It was so good to be back in Painted Creek. At Painted Creek Cottage. Who knew?

"I'll start on it as soon as you text me those pictures. I'd imagine I can have it finished for you in a few days. I truly am honored you asked me to do it, Dottie. It'll be good for both of us I think."

She picked up her tiny little purse from the floor by the front door. How anyone carried everything they needed in a bag that small was beyond me, although I suppose most people didn't carry around a whole watercolor kit in case they got bored.

"I'll send them tonight. It sure was good to visit with you, honey. I'll come by again soon. You keep on settling in. As a matter of fact, you settle in so deep you can't find your way out again, you hear?"

I smiled wryly, "I'll settle what I can and we'll see. Love you."

"I love you too. Bye now, sugar."

She softly closed the door behind her, and I sank back down onto the love seat. I had plenty of painting to do, and I'm sure my little porcupine friend was dry enough to continue working on after my extended tea break. I'd get up and get to it. In just a minute or two probably.

Maybe.

TWO HOURS LATER, I woke up from a blissful, accidental nap. "Whoa, this really is a comfortable couch. I'd have bought it, too." Standing up and stretching, I realized I felt actually rested for the first time in a long time. "Magic couch..." I murmured as I made my way into the kitchen, stumbling slightly as I went. My grumbling tummy reminded me I hadn't eaten since breakfast, and it was creeping up on dinner time now.

Pulling out a pot for noodles and setting the water to boil, I sent my mother a quick text.

Still up for a noodle Facetime date?

I am. I thought you'd forgotten.

Rolling my eyes knowing good and well she couldn't see me but probably knew anyway, I texted her back politely.

It's still ten till five Mother. Let me finish up my pasta and I'll call you.

Placing my phone on the counter and heading into the pantry, I grabbed the angel hair pasta and the bottle of white wine Mr. Findley had left with his 'welcome home' groceries. Turning, I glanced at the tea cabinet. I wanted so desperately to open it, but I decided to save that as a reward for finishing the call with my mother. I'd probably get distracted and lose track of time when I opened it anyway. Better not to be late for our phone date.

It wasn't that my mother and I didn't get along, we did. And more often than not, we even had a wonderful time together just shopping or doing things around her house in Columbus. It was just stifling sometimes, the way she wanted to have everything on the outside appearing just so, including me. Didn't mean the inside wasn't an all out mess. But I knew she loved me and I loved her and wanted to make her happy more than most anything. So that's what I did. Always. I sighed at the cupboard door and headed back into the kitchen.

Luckily, angel hair didn't take long to cook, and while the noodles boiled I made a quick sauce from the white wine and lemon juice I found in the fridge. There was a container of shakey Parmesan cheese too, so I was all set. I made a mental note to find a gift to thank Mr. Findley. Maybe a painting. "Future me problem," I said matter of factly. "Current me problem is calling Mother." Propping my phone on a pile of cookbooks, I slid my plate around to the other side of the bar and sat.

The Facetime call connected and I smiled as my mother's face filled the screen. "Hi, Mom! Miss you." I meant it. While I was enjoying the idea of figuring out who I was on my own during my extended stay here, I couldn't deny the jolt of homesickness when I saw Mom on the tiny phone screen.

"Hi, Mabel. Miss you, too. Although, this was a lovely idea. Thank you. What pasta did you make? Did you check all the labels and expiration dates?"

"Yes, Mother. Mr. Findley left me some groceries, remember? All perfectly fine and safe and not expired."

There was a slight pause. Then my mother said very quietly, " I just want to make sure you're safe."

"I know, Mom, but I'm fine. It has been nice to paint here in the quiet. I've almost completely finished one commission already today, and it's darling." I carried the phone over and showed her the painting before coming back to my meal. We chatted while we ate and it was a comfortable conversation. When we'd both almost finished eating, she surprised me by hanging up first. I'd told her I would call her again tomorrow, and that was that. I cleaned up my dishes and went straight back into the pantry.

Really looking at the cupboard door, after the shock of learning about it had worn off some, I could see how I never noticed it as a kid. It was painted the same color as the walls, a lovely soft lavender gray. The only distinguishing feature was the one knob on the right. It was a beautiful, intricately carved leaf in brass, and it didn't stick out very far either, just enough to get your fingers around to pull open the door. As for missing it as an adult, well I never really came in the pantry much anymore. I may have helped Gram put things away after a big meal or something, but my days of foraging for snacks were long gone. Not understanding the butterflies that were whooshing around in my stomach, I took a deep breath and opened the door.

The inside wasn't very deep, maybe a foot or so, but it was absolutely packed with shelves. Bottles and jars of all sizes, ranging from tiny to maybe eight ounces, were sitting neatly filled and labeled along the top half of the shelves. The bottom half held sealed bags of loose leaf blended tea, just like what Gram would give me when I came to visit. Tears sprang to my eyes and I felt such a deep relief to still have this connection to her for just a little while longer.

I noticed the bottles were labeled based on what herb was inside, like peppermint or lavender or catnip. The cellophane zip bags, however, were merely labeled with a single word, like "sleep", "sorrow" or "determination". I assumed that these were the names Gram had given her tea blends, but I had no idea what was in each. There was no list on the back of the door or labels on the back of the bags. And I had no idea what my blend had been.

Dottie was right, it looked like there was a pretty good stock here. I didn't know how often Gram made her teas, or anything about them really. But if she made her own, it stood to reason that there would be some sort of herb garden somewhere, at least for some of the herbs. I clicked the cupboard door shut and hustled to the kitchen door. It was time to explore the backyard.

NINE

APPARENTLY GRAM'S NEW love of outdoor string lighting had spilled over into the backyard. I could see them strung through the trees and down toward the creek in the fading light. I started with the light switches closest to the door on the patio and just started flipping on and off and on and off and... finally! Everything came to life and was bathed in a warm, twinkling light.

There was a nice expanse of backyard before it veered off into the creek. It was obvious Gram had planned out the landscaping back here too, and I vaguely wondered how I would learn to take care of it all. "Hope you're all hearty plants. Green thumb I have not." Wincing slightly to myself, I ran my fingers through some of the bushes as I walked on farther toward the creek.

I didn't have too many memories of the creek honestly. I was never really allowed out this far alone, and once Gram realized I didn't have the same love of caring for plants that she did, we didn't spend much of our time together in the backyard. But I was all grown up now, at least that's what people kept telling me, and I could go wherever I wanted to. At heart, I still felt like I was fifteen and looking for an adult to oversee my life.

I followed the stone path to the cutest little foot bridge I'd ever seen. I wasn't even sure if you could call it a bridge in the strictest sense of the word. I probably could have walked through the creek right next to it and not had water past my ankles. But it kept my shoes dry and put me right in the middle of the creek. Like so many other things since I'd come back to the cottage, I loved it instantly and fiercely.

The portion of the creek that flowed through Gram's yard rippled from the forest upstream and into a wooded area downstream at the end of Gram's property. It gave the illusion that the cottage and this part of the creek were isolated from everything else, even though I knew I was only about five minutes from town and Mr. Findley had said there were neighbors. Instead of feeling uneasy at being so alone, I felt a sense of peace. Like I could breath properly down deep into my lungs and just be. Maybe it was the fresh air, or the sound of the running water. Whatever it was, I liked it.

A little ways down from the foot bridge there were posts on each side of the creek connected by a third sturdy beam at the top that held up a single rope swing. It dangled out over the water, and I imagined that my feet would just skim the surface while swinging. The rocks in the landscaping had been expertly placed underneath so you could get to the swing without tripping or stepping in a particularly deep spot. I couldn't wait to try it out.

Leaving the foot bridge, I went back to the house side of the yard to follow the creek down to the wooded end. I was still searching for an herb garden that I knew had to be here somewhere. There were countless different plants and shrubs and vines, but nothing that I thought were herbs growing along the side of the creek. Just as I began to turn back toward the house to go scout out the side yard, I heard a faint shout from the trees.

"Hello? Is someone there?" My heart rate jumped and I took an involuntary step back toward the house. I was so not a runner, hopefully I wouldn't be making a mad dash across the yard tonight.

"Hey! Oh wait don't go! I came to say hello. Almost there!"

Just as the voice became clear enough to make out the words, I began to see the silhouette of a young woman coming through the trees. She wore a shin length skirt and button up blouse tied at the waist. Her deep ebony hair almost seemed to shine with purples and blues like a raven's feathers, but I figured it was a trick of the beautiful sunset throwing colors across the sky behind her. She moved toward me through the yard and waved enthusiastically.

"Hey there! Heard you had arrived and wanted to come see for myself. Hope I didn't scare you." She stopped about three feet away from me, feet planted firmly shoulder width apart like she was sure of herself and this conversation and her place in the world. I was instantly envious and in awe. I wanted to be this lady when I grew up.

"Well, I didn't expect someone to come through the woods into the yard at dark, so I'd say you scared me a little. But that's okay. I'm Mabel, and you are?"

A glint in her eye that could've been disconcertment or maybe mischief flashed briefly before she reached out a hand and said, "I'm Charlotte." The smell of what I assumed was her perfume washed over me as we shook hands, crisp and clean and refreshing. "I have a little place just down the way there. Walking through the trees is just quicker to get here than taking the road, but I won't do it again if you ask me not to. How are you settling in?"

I probably should have been a little more wary. After all, this complete stranger came into the yard like she'd done it a million times and acted about like she had more right to be here than I did. Then again, maybe she had done it a million times for all I knew and had regularly visited with Gram. And I sure did still feel like an impostor being back here now anyway.

"I seem to be settling as well as could be expected I suppose. I appreciate the neighborly call." I decided it might be nice to have a friend that lived so close by while I was here. "Did you know Gram well, come visit often?"

"You could say that. Constance was special and I sure was lucky to have her in my life."

My earlier envy was starting to turn a little green around the edges, and I found myself jealous of this stranger who was about my age and who had obviously gotten to spend time with Gram that I hadn't.

But I had no one to blame but myself for that.

"Well," I said with a smile that I'm sure didn't quite reach my eyes, "I'm happy to hear it."

"Are you, now?" She tilted her head to the side and cocked one hip out. She wasn't being obstinate, more asking a genuine question that most polite strangers would steer clear of. "I reckon I'd be a mite jealous myself if I'd missed out on some visiting time like that. But I suppose it is was it is now, isn't it?"

"I suppose it is," I answered quietly.

I wasn't sure how she'd known where my thoughts had gone just then, but I nodded absently and wandered closer to the creek's edge. Next time I came out in the yard I'd wear flip flops so I could put my toes in the creek and play in the water. For a moment, I simply watched the water flow before I glanced back at Charlotte. She was just watching me. Not the close studying that Dottie had been doing earlier, just... watching.

"Well, anyway, I guess it's best to just keep moving forward now. Are you? Moving forward?"

I didn't know how to answer her. I wanted to be moving forward, but the truth was I don't think I'd been moving forward for some time now.

The wind shifted then and blew down over the top of the house, through the yard and past us, rustling up the plants on the other side of the creek. I caught a slight whiff of a lemon drop, the scent of the Mabel grey geranium, even though I hadn't come across any planted in the back yard up by the house.

"Hmm, seems like the house thinks you're gettin' on just fine."

She smiled at me, but I just blinked at her, slightly confused.

"I'm sorry, but what?"

"Seems like the house suits you is all. Or you suit it. Either way, happy to have you in Painted Creek, Mabel. I'll pop in and say hello again. We'll be fast friends, I know." With that, she turned and strolled back into the trees, jumping over sticks like a fairy dancing in the night. I watched her go and shook my head before heading back up the long back yard and into the house. *Small country towns can be so weird,* I thought to myself as I turned off all the yard lights and locked the door for the night, but I was smiling the whole time. I didn't even notice the overpowering smell of roses that had greeted me in the house when I arrived now smelled like a sweet blend of lemons and roses and something vaguely familiar as I walked back to my room to go to sleep.

SUNDAY PASSED QUICKLY in a blur of painting and snooping. I finished the painting of the porcupine, Hedgie was lonely now, and one other painting off of my already accepted list. I was even able to start on Dottie's painting since she had texted the photos to me Saturday night. I was happy with how it was coming along, but the emotional connection made me want to make sure it was absolutely perfect. Perfect meant extra slow and tedious.

That's where the snooping came in. When I became frustrated with the shape of the trees or the exact color of the cabin, I'd get up and go open a drawer or a cabinet. Gram had so much stuff. Not an excess of clutter per se, but every nook and cranny of every space was full to the brim. It made me realize how easy it had been for me to pack up my personal belongings from the apartment and just leave. Even if I decided to sell this house fully furnished, it would take weeks just to get all the extra stuff and personal effects sorted and taken out. I sighed. This painting/snooping cycle was just the beginning.

After I'd finished the porcupine, I'd found a stash of fabulous gauzy blankets in the basket under the end table between the couch and love seat. Perfect for couch naps! During my lunch break, and a break from painting someone's beloved dalmatian, I discovered a whole set of hand thrown pottery mugs in the bar service cart underneath Hedgie. They matched the ones I had used when Dottie visited because they were all pottery, but all the colors and glazes were different. I'd set them all along the kitchen counter and the picture they painted together was a kaleidoscope of swirls up against the white back splash that made me smile every time I passed through the kitchen. They would look so good hung from hooks underneath the upper kitchen cabinets. Maybe I'd add them, if I decided to stay permanently. But I wasn't really considering staying here, was I?

Mid-day, I put one of those mugs to good use as I tried out Dottie's gift. The French press really was stunning, unlike any other one I had ever seen, and it made the coffee taste extra special. While I'd waited for the coffee to 'perk', I'd gone back and poked through the tea cupboard again. I still wasn't ready to make myself a cup of anything. It seemed wrong somehow, like I didn't have permission. Besides, I still didn't know what was in the blended bags on the bottom shelves. Plus, with Gram's sense of humor, the blend labeled 'sorrow' might induce a good cathartic cry instead of soothing raw emotions. After a good deep sniff of the jar labeled peppermint, I went back out to finish my coffee and get back to work.

I kept up that pattern all day, a little paint here a little snoop there, until it was dark out and time to tuck the house in for bed once again. It had only been two nights, but I found I enjoyed the ritual of turning off each light in all the corners of the rooms and making my way to bed. I still hadn't gone in Gram's suite, but I slowed as I walked by the closed door during what was quickly becoming my nighttime routine.

"Tomorrow... I'll at least open the door tomorrow. Probably. Maybe."

As I turned off the lights on the patio, I realized I hadn't stepped foot outside today. Frowning, I looked out over the yard and peered at where I knew the creek was waiting in the dark. "Fresh air tomorrow, too." I nodded definitively to myself as I walked back toward my bedroom.

"Goodnight, house." I called out as I shut my bedroom door. Outside, the wind blew across the yard, caressing the house in what sounded like a contented sigh.

TEN

I HADN'T SLEPT all night. It didn't really matter what I did or didn't do to try and settle down or get comfortable or relax or meditate or whatever, I just couldn't sleep. Some time around three in the morning, I idly wondered if Ms. Barnett had an oil blend for sleep. That was a thing, right? I made a mental note to ask her while I was at Mr. Findley's office for our meeting.

The meeting was the true reason I couldn't sleep. I knew that, but it didn't make the tossing and turning any less frustrating. In the wee small hours of the morning, thank you Sinatra, I finally gave up and got out of bed. I shuffled to the bathroom without ever fully opening my eyes and splashed some cold water on my face. Instead of waking me up, it really just soured my mood further and the woman looking back at me in the mirror didn't look like she was capable of seizing anything, much less the day that was going to get started without her if she couldn't wake up.

Deciding a hot shower was better for my mood, I took a long, steamy one and took my time getting dressed. "Good morning, house. Good morning, Hedgie." I began walking through the house to the kitchen and it dawned on me maybe Dottie was right, I did need a pet. I glanced at the gorgeous French press and sighed. Shaking my head, I picked up my keys and headed out. Some mornings just called for a coffee shop brew, and this was one of them.

I PARKED JUST off the other end of Main Street from the coffee shop, deciding it would be nice to walk the long length of the street while it was still early and not too many people were out and about. I'd walked the street many times with Gram, a few even with Dad and Mom in tow, but never at this time of day. There was an energy to the air you could feel, like as soon as the day really got going, anything was possible. It was potential energy.

I'd barely made it around the corner onto Main Street proper when I caught movement low to the ground. I could have sworn a huge tortoise just walked into the bushes on the edge of the square. I mean, a HUGE tortoise! I blinked a couple of times, thinking I had to have been mistaken. "I know I didn't sleep well, but that's a stretch even for me." Not being able to resist, I jogged over to the square and walked around to the other side of the bush.

Peeking back at me from underneath the leaves were two slow blinking eyes. "Well, I'll be." I stood up and looked around. What does one do exactly when they find a boulder sized tortoise in the middle of town? If I left it here to get help, it couldn't go too far before I came back, right? But what if I found someone to help and it *was* gone when I got back? Then I'm the crazy new girl in town that sees imaginary large tortoises under bushes in the town square. Before I could argue with myself any longer, I saw a man running toward me from the direction of the coffee shop, or more likely I supposed, the pet store.

"You aren't by chance looking for a tortoise are you?" I waved high in the air and talk-shouted at him.

His paced slowed as an even slower grin broke out across his face. "That's an oddly specific question for six-thirty on a Monday morning."

My face froze into a polite smile, but inside I was mentally cringing at myself. Crazy new girl title it is. "Oh, well I just saw you running from the direction of the pet shop and you aren't really dressed for running and since I just discovered this tortoise the size of a small horse I took a guess." The sarcasm sneaking its way into my voice didn't match the customer service smile on my face. Honestly, I wasn't sure which personality was going to win at this point.

He blinked as he came to a stop in front of me, and the slow grin bloomed into a full mega-watt smile. *Whoa.*

"Well, let me rephrase then. Your deductive reasoning skills are absolutely on point for six-thirty on a Monday morning. I am in fact looking for a tortoise, but I also already knew she was under that bush. But thanks for keeping an eye on her. Hi, I'm Elliott Scott, I own The Pet Parlor down the street." He reached out to shake my hand, and when I shook his back I swear my heart stuttered as it said 'oh there you are, finally'.

"What is this town doing to me?" I murmured under my breath.

"Sorry, what did you say?" He leaned a few inches closer as if to hear me better. I don't even think he realized he'd done it.

"Nothing, sorry. Nice to meet you, Elliott, I'm Mabel." Hey look, Ms. Manners is still in there somewhere! Yay. "You said you knew she'd be here? Not the first time you've lost a giant tortoise then?"

"A) I didn't loose her, she escaped. Again. And B) yes, I knew she'd be here. She found a huge watermelon slice here once during a town festival and has never forgotten. I think she thinks this a watermelon bush. Every now and then, I guess when she feels like I'm withholding the good treats, she Houdinis out of her enclosure and comes to check for watermelon. Mabel, meet Turtle."

At hearing her name, Turtle walked out from under the bush and bumped into Elliott's leg. My tortoise reading skills were sub-par at best, but I swear she looked dejected at the lack of watermelon under the bush. "A tortoise named Turtle huh? Well Turtle, nice to meet you as well. I'm sorry there's no watermelon." She reached her long neck toward me. How do you greet a tortoise? Do they sniff you like a dog?

"You can scratch her shell if you want, she likes it."

I stepped to her side and leaned over to run my nails across her shell. It was smooth and bumpy all at the same time, my nails getting stuck in some of the deeper ridges. I didn't know how to tell if a tortoise was happy, but she didn't pull away either, so I kept petting her. After a second, she started moving her cute little rear back and forth against my scratches and I giggled.

Looking up at Elliott, I asked, "Does poor Turtle have identity crisis, what with actually being a tortoise and all? Please tell me you aren't responsible for her name."

"Would you prefer Shelly? Or perhaps Pokey? You know, she did dress as Rocky once for Halloween, is that better?" he deadpanned.

"I don't know, maybe. How about Speedy? You managed to lose her after all. She must really be able to move." I finally crouched on my knees on the side walk to give Turtle my full attention. "Sweet baby aren't you? Don't deserve this whole existential crisis caused by your name, I know!"

Shoulders shaking with silent laughter, Elliott cocked his head and looked at us. "It's been awhile since I've used the psychology portion of my degree on a human, but that sounds like projecting to me. Tell me, Mabel, what about your beautiful name causes you stress?"

Standing, I grinned. "Deflecting from the true topic at hand. Nice try, Dr. Scott. Seriously, who named this sweet girl Turtle?"

"I used to work at a big zoo that will remain nameless, protect the innocent animals and all, and I was Turtle's keeper. She already had her name when we met thank you very much. Personally, I think she finds it ironically funny since most people don't know the difference between a turtle and a tortoise anyway." The playfulness on his face was contagious and I was grinning back at him as he said, "Are you a turtle lover at heart, is that how you knew she was really a tortoise? You can tell us, we can take it."

Laughing, I said, "Nothing like that. I'm an artist, so typically I have an eye for detail and I tend to retain useless information that I'll probably never use again. In this case, I painted someone's beloved pet turtle for them which led to a lot of research on species, shell types and shapes, and what not. Sometimes the picture in my head doesn't match the reality of what I'm trying to paint, and researching both things makes it easier to classify and picture what I *do* want to paint. This may be the first time in real life that my research for a painting showed up later with a practical application. I'll take the win, thank you."

He'd listened politely while I rambled. No, that wasn't quite right, he actually seemed interested in what I was saying. Habit won out though, and I found myself apologizing. "I'm sorry, that was a very long answer for 'I'd researched the difference between turtles and tortoises for a project.' I tend to over share."

"And yet, I much preferred the over sharing to the short, polite answer. Thank you for telling me." There was a quiet moment where we simply looked at each other. Time seemed to stop, or expand maybe, and my usually very loud mind was quiet as I looked in his eyes. Turtle smacked her big mouth, can tortoises smack?, and broke the silence that had wound around us.

I cleared my throat and said quietly, "Well, thank you."

He glanced down at his shoes and rubbed the back of his neck. Sheepish was cute on him. "Hey, did you say artist? You're Dottie's friend aren't you?"

I groaned. "Whatever you've heard, it's not true."

Turtle shuffled her feet at the sound of his loud laughter. "I could see why you would say that. But that woman loves you to death. Do you think you'd be interested in doing a painting for Pet Parlor?"

"Oh, don't feel like you have to ask me to…"

"I don't feel obligated. I'd be honored to have an original painting for the store. Maybe one of Turtle, but dressed in a turtle onesie instead. What do you think?"

"I would never offend Turtle that way." Smiling, I scratched her shell one more time and then backed away. "I'm headed to the coffee shop, do you need help getting her back? Wait, how *do* you get her back?" I'd never mention this to Turtle of course, but she looked really heavy.

He pulled some leafy greens out of his pocket and waved them in front of Turtle's face. She perked up and started following him down the sidewalk at a reasonable clip.

"I feed her, I swear. But she's a beggar and she definitely loves treats more than real food."

We continued to chat as we strolled along the sidewalk of Main Street that wasn't really Main Street with a giant hundred pound tortoise named Turtle. This town was weird, but that was the magic of Painted Creek, and I was loving every second of it.

"About the painting. You really don't have to ask me to do one. Plus, just because Dottie says I'm good doesn't mean I am. You could be getting a commission from one of those impressionist painters, and I'll paint you with three ears and half a nose or something."

He laughed, a deep rich sound that I was becoming obsessed with. "Who said Dottie said you were good?" He winked and kept walking as I stopped at the coffee shop door. "Swing by the store when you can and we'll talk about the painting." Turning to walk backward, he said, "It was really good to meet you, Mabel. See you soon."

I held up my hand, I'm sure a goofy grin on my face, and my body stumbled into Artful Brew feeling like part of my heart was already following along to the pet store two doors down.

ELEVEN

THERE WAS A pleasant bustle that you can only find in a coffee shop in full swing when I stepped in. I saw Sarah behind the bar straight away and hid my grin when I saw her smother a scowl. She looked up at the sound of the bells on the door to greet the new customer, only to realize it was me. Holding slight grudges then, got it. Hopefully I hadn't really made an enemy so soon and I could smooth over any rough edges that I'd created on Friday.

I walked over to the order here sign and waited patiently while I browsed the menu. It was still overwhelming. I guess it showed on my face, Sarah smirked as she walked over to take my order.

"Are we still working on that coffee repertoire? You look confused by my menu."

"It depends, do you suddenly have a secret menu that includes a lovely arsenic latte?"

She pretended to ponder it for a second, looking toward the ceiling and tapping her chin with one finger. Her nails were neat and short and painted a gorgeous metallic mocha color.

"Well, that seems a little harsh. Could I interest you in my vanilla eye-drop cold brew instead?" She smiled sweetly and I couldn't help but outright laugh.

"I'm sorry, Sarah. I honestly can't tell you what came over me Friday night. It's truly not like me to play jokes on people, especially someone I don't know. I sincerely apologize and hope that we can start over." She smirked, and I winced. "Hi, my name is Mabel and I'm back in town for an undetermined amount of time and I would love it if someone knowledgeable about all things coffee could help broaden my horizons while I'm here. Without poison. That'd be great."

She raised one eyebrow at me without moving another single muscle in her face, at least that was the same, and my shoulders slumped slightly. As I was about to order a plain black coffee that I would honestly probably be too afraid to drink and would throw away as soon as I escaped the shop, someone yelled from the other side of the room.

"Sarah, let that girl off the hook! Good Lord woman I think you got her back."

Slightly mortified that anyone had been listening to our exchange, I turned slowly to see who had spoken. Two women were sitting together at a table in the corner, chairs pushed together, coffee on the table, and huge grins on their faces. I turned back to look at Sarah, who now wore a matching grin with her raised eyebrow as if to say 'gotcha'.

"Welcome back to Painted Creek, Mabel. How about a mocha to add to your list this morning?"

"You're not mad?" I kept glancing between her and the other women, still not sure what was going on.

"I'm not mad. You were dealt a great hand and it was well played." She paused, and her grin turned slightly wicked. "And now we're even. Those two crazies over there are my friends. Go introduce yourself and I'll bring you your latte when it's done." She made a shooing motion, just as the other two women waved me over. I took a deep, fortifying breath, squared my shoulders and walked over to their table.

Peopling hadn't really been on my to-do list this morning.

"Hey, Mabel, I'm Alex. This is Heather, and we're already in love with you for pulling one over on Sarah. Not many people can do that."

Alex was curvy with deep red hair that she had braided over one shoulder. Her grin was infectious and I couldn't help but love her back. She was a little too loud and a little too forward and a little everything I wanted to have more of in my life. Heather was smiling at me too, but in a more subdued, almost apologetic way. It's as if she was saying she knew the other two were too much but there was nothing she could do about it. I gave her a genuine smile.

"Nice to meet you both. Thanks for letting me off the hook earlier. She had me convinced I'd never have coffee here again."

"Nonsense. Her bark is worse than her bite. Usually. Anyway, would you like to join us? We actually don't have too much longer before we have to run off to work, but it's better than nothing!" Alex scooted over another chair as if I had already said yes, so I sat down. I could feel my posture was rigid, my back ramrod straight with my hands folded in my lap, and I'm sure I looked completely out of place with these two who were relaxed in their chairs. Some habits were too hard to break easily.

"Thank you. Where do y'all work? Here in town?" I tried to relax without fidgeting. Fail.

"I own the bookshop over on Lively Street; The Secret Book Garden," Heather said. "I technically don't have to open until later, but these two keep such early hours that now I'm up in the mornings like they are." Her bright blue eyes shone with kindness through her deep purple glasses. The combination with her dark, chocolate brown hair made her seem sweetly enchanting.

"She's still not happy about it though!" Alex laughed at her friend's expense and Heather smiled back while rolling her eyes.

"I'm not a morning person. Like, at all. But when one of your best friends gets up before the sun and is incapable of making her own decisions, you end up awake whether you like it or not."

"Listen," Alex had completely turned in her chair to face Heather and was holding up her hands in front of herself, "I needed immediate feedback on the menu in case it needed extra baking or rising time, which it did thank you very much." She crossed her arms and blew her red side bangs out of her face.

"Menu? Do you own a restaurant?" I asked, genuinely interested. I loved that these women seemed to be just exactly themselves. It was refreshing.

"Bakery! Oh, I make a little bit of everything so I don't get bored. I guess people in town have gotten used to never knowing what they'll see at my shop. This morning it was cronuts." She grinned and did a happy wiggle in her seat.

"Alex, let's just assume from now on that if there's ever a menu question, the answer is always cronuts." Heather looked dreamily at the ceiling and I laughed.

"They must be good then? I don't know if I've ever had one." A gasp sounded from behind me, and I turned to see Sarah walking over with my drink.

"Well that's a travesty. Alex, hold one back for her to come pick up later."

"Oh, you really don't have to…"

"Sure thing! I made a triple batch this morning so Heather could freeze some." She bumped her friend with her shoulder. "I don't know when I'll make them again."

I wrinkled my brow a bit and asked, "But don't you worry your customers will be upset that you don't always have the same menu? What if someone is unhappy when they come in and their favorite is missing?"

"Then they can take their sad, pastry-less ass home and try again another day. I'm grateful for my customers, I am. But I don't bake for them. I bake for me." Alex looked me dead in the eye and shrugged like it was the most normal answer in the world while I felt like she'd dropped a bomb in the conversation. All I could manage was a weak "Oh," in response.

"I'll save you a cronut though, Mabel. Just come on by whenever you can today. You'll love it, it's like a cross between a croissant and a donut." She winked and settled back in her chair. "And Heather, yours are put back too, love."

"Thanks, Pookie," They both dissolved into giggles and Sarah raised an eyebrow.

"Behave yourselves children or you'll scare off Mabel."

"Yes, mom!" The other two said in sing-song unison. At the same second, another small voice called out "Mommy!" just as a flying whirl of hot pink ruffles and sparkles hit Sarah square in the back of the knees.

Sarah's hand went to the back of the little girl's head. "Becca, say hello to Mabel. Mabel, this is my daughter Becca." Becca's small face peeked out from behind her mother's legs. She waved shyly and I smiled back.

"Hello, Becca. It is absolutely lovely to meet you. And I think I'm rather jealous of your fabulous dress!"

At this, her little eyes lit up and she stepped out from around her mother. "Thanks! Look, it's swirly too!" She immediately began pirouetting around, showing me how her dress flowed out around her. On the third spin, she bumped hard into the table and my still full mocha spilled out all around the mug and into the saucer underneath.

"Becca, are you okay? You've got to be a little more careful of your surroundings, honey. Maybe no more swirling in the shop, okay?" Sarah's tone wasn't angry or reprimanding, more like resigned to the whirling dervish that must be spinning through the coffee shop all the time.

"I'm okay, Mommy. Sorry 'bout your coffee, Miss Mabel." She fidgeted a toe along the tile floor, still not completely motionless but trying her best, and a light sheen of tears covered her eyes.

"That's alright, sweetie. Hey, did you know that not every accident is bad?" I leaned in my chair so I could look her in the eyes. "Sometimes, something beautiful can come out of a mistake."

Her little mouth formed the perfect 'o' as she watched me pull a paint brush and piece of watercolor paper out of my bag. I never went anywhere without a brush and scraps of paper and a small pan of travel paints, just in case I got bored or needed to sketch something out before I forgot it. But I wouldn't be needing the paints this morning.

Looking over at Alex, who was watching me closely, I glanced at her almost empty cup. "Were you drinking black coffee by chance?" I asked her.

"Espresso, why?" she answered.

"Perfect. May I pour a little out on to your saucer, to match mine?" She nodded, so I poured some out and then sat her saucer next to mine on the table above the paper. Angling everything where Becca could see, I began to paint. The color of my mocha was lighter than the dark espresso from Alex's cup, and in no time at all I had a fluffy long eared bunny painted on the paper, completely out of coffee for paint.

It was monochrome, of course, and with a start, I realized I'd forgotten how much I loved doing monochrome paintings. It was amazing the amount of detail, variation, and contrast you could accomplish using only one color. I used to paint monochrome pieces all the time when I was in art school, but had stopped when I got so busy with my commissioned paintings. There weren't many people that wanted an all blue painting of Great-aunt Sally or a strawberry toned portrait of their smoke colored cat.

"We all make mistakes sometimes. It's what you do after that counts. Do you like bunnies?" She nodded her little head vigorously. "I think we should name him Mocha, what do you say?" I handed her the painting to keep and she took it with both hands like it was a priceless masterpiece. She looked up at Sarah and simply said "wow", but the smile that broke out across her little face was all I needed anyway.

"Baby, why don't you take that painting up to your room real quick like a bunny and then Auntie Alex will take you to school, okay?" She bounded off, slightly more carefully, to the back of the shop and up the stairs that I assumed led to an apartment above the shop.

As soon as she was out of earshot, Alex exclaimed, "That's it, we're keeping you!" She had a huge grin on her face that was mirrored on Heather's as well.

"That was awesome, Mabel. We'd heard you were an artist, but the way you made Becca feel like she could turn an accident into a blessing was really something special." Heather shook her head as she stared at the saucers like she couldn't believe it.

"It was nothing really. I'm glad I made her feel better. I hope I didn't overstep, Sarah." I glanced up at her, noting she hadn't really moved or reacted the whole time. "I just couldn't stand to see her little face crumple like that."

She regarded me with a blank face for a minute, and then replied, "Can you stay for a few minutes, Mabel? These two are about to run off, and Alex takes Becca to school for me so I can regroup after the early morning rush. I'd like to talk to you."

"Sure. No problem." The smile on my face was brittle. I felt a little like I was being asked to stay after class, but Heather's reassuring smile made me feel a little better. "It was lovely to meet you both. Thank you for asking me to sit with you."

"Oh, I was serious earlier." Alex broke in as she stood and started gathering her things. "We're keeping you now. We have coffee together every Monday, Wednesday, and Friday mornings at seven. Please join us any time you can. And don't forget to swing by later for your cronut!" She bustled over to the stairs to wait for Becca. A moment later, the little girl came bounding down the stairs, hot pink sparkles flying. Sarah gave her a hug and a kiss, and then she waved enthusiastically to me as they headed out the door. Sarah headed back behind the counter and I turned to tell Heather goodbye.

"Have I been called to the principal's office or does she really just want to chat?" I asked before I thought better of it.

"Just a chat I'd say... although with Sarah you never know. She can be a bit hesitant to trust, but once she lets you in she's in your corner for life. And no one is as fierce as Sarah." She hesitated as she stood to gather her things. "Hey Mabel, that really was pretty awesome, painting with coffee like that. You know, I think I have a book in the store on homemade inks from things like flowers and herbs and vegetables. Would you be interested in it?"

"Sure! I'll take a look. We covered that briefly in school, but I haven't used it since then really. That could be an interesting method to rediscover now." She was so sweet to think of something I may be interested in reading about for my art. I didn't have the heart to tell her that I'd probably never use the information in the book, if I even read it. "Thank you!"

"Great! I'll swing by Alex's and leave it with your cronut when I go pick up mine." She winked at me, shouted a goodbye to Sarah, and was out the door. I took my time to gather my things and finish my mocha, which was delicious if a little sweet for first thing in the morning, before heading up to the counter.

I waited by the end of the counter closest to the front door as Sarah finished up with a few customers. By the time she finally walked over to me, I had knots in my stomach. The best defense is a good offense right? Or was it the other way around? Whatever, I decided to talk before she could say whatever had her face filled with tension like that.

"Sarah, I'm sorry if I overstepped with Becca. It won't happen again."

"It's not that, Mabel." Her lack of raised eyebrow made my stomach twist even more. Whatever she had to say she was taking very seriously. "In a way, I'm actually incredibly grateful for what you just did with my daughter. But it's complicated."

"Is it prying if I ask why? I know everyone here seemed kind of stunned, but I just painted her a bunny. I'm a painter, it's literally in the job description." I was trying to lighten the tone a little, to ease whatever had caused this tension for her, but she just shook her head.

"It was more than that. You saw her. She's such a good kid but she's everywhere all the time and never ever slows down. She's a lot. And because she's so wide open all the time, she's just so accident prone... walking into things or people, knocking stuff over, blurting things out. I try so hard to let her be herself while still explaining 'societal norms'," she said the last words with air quotes and an eye roll, "but I can see how hard she is on herself every time something happens."

She paused and took a shaky breath. "In one little bunny painting, you showed her that not every mistake is a disaster. Not every mess is a cause for shame. And maybe sometimes being a little different can turn out beautiful."

By the time she stopped talking, I had tears in my eyes. "She reminds me of myself, honestly."

Sarah snorted and raised one eye brow. I was happy to see the familiar gesture. "Right. You're the exact opposite of Becca. The perfect picture of calm and polite."

"That's the thing about pictures, they only show you what they want you to see. My mother preferred for things to appear a particular way to others at all times... I became very good at portraying a certain image. I guess I've never stopped."

Sarah frowned. "I'm not sure how to respond to that. But I'll swap deep dark secrets with you. Becca's dad left about a year ago. Said it was just too much, we were too much, the shop was too much. So it's just me and her now, and I'll do anything to protect the little bubble we have going without racking up any more losses."

The message was clear. If I didn't think I was going to stay in Painted Creek, she didn't want me getting close. To either of them it sounded like, although I doubt she realized it. "Well, I think you and your bubble are doing a great job. And I appreciate the help branching out on my coffee ordering skills."

She nodded once, as if silently agreeing to my change in topic. "Any time. And take Alex up on the invitation to join us on coffee mornings, if you'd like."

I thought the offer was generous, especially since she knew I wasn't staying in town long. "I may take you up on that. Thanks, Sarah"

"I should get back to it. My next rush will be soon. I call them the second breakfasters...too late for the early birds but too early for lunch." She got a wistful look on her face. "Honestly, I wish I could be a second breakfaster. I'd love to sleep until 9 or so."

Laughing, I agreed with her and waved on my way out. That

unscheduled meeting with Sarah turned out to be not so bad, just like Heather said. Now, it was time to face my real meeting and hope that it went just as smoothly.

at (chedule a meeting with ... when turned out to be none so bad, just like Heather said. Now, it was time to do away with the meeting and hope that I wouldn't be as smooth.

TWELVE

I'D BEEN SITTING outside of Mr. Findley's office for ten minutes. I'm not sure why. This was just an in depth discussion of things I already knew now, right? How bad could it be? I shook my head like an Etch-a-Sketch... wasn't that a question you were never supposed to ask out loud, like a challenge to the universe or something?

But I hadn't said it out loud, I'd only thought it in my head. So it'd be fine, right?

Probably. Maybe.

"Get out of the car, Mabel. You're being ridiculous." I squared my shoulders and headed inside.

Sure enough, the same scent enveloped me like a calming cloud when I opened the door, and I felt a little of the tense anticipation for my meeting melt away. Ms. Barnett stood and greeted me with an enthusiastic wave and I couldn't help but smile back at her.

"Good morning, Miss Morrison. Oh! How was your first weekend back in Painted Creek?"

"It was lovely, Ms. Barnett, thank you for asking. I did think about your fabulous oil blend often. You made quite an impression on me for sure!"

"Oh, dear, please call me Carol. I'm not usually so formal with my friends. Oh, I do hope it was a good impression!" Her smile was kind and warm, and I felt myself relaxing even more, the maker of the oil blend having the same effect on my nerves as the oils themselves.

"It was, for sure! And please, call me Mabel." I was quick to reassure her, although it seemed like she was fairly confident that it had been a good impression and wasn't all that concerned. "I kept thinking about how you'd made a blend just for this office, and then I wondered if you made custom blends for people. And also, when I couldn't sleep last night, I wondered if you made a blend to help people sleep..." I realized I may have been rambling and trailed off. Carol's eyes were a little wide and hesitant.

"Oh, well, I haven't really thought about making a custom blend before. Well there's an idea isn't there?! Oh, I will think about that, Mabel, I sure will. Oh, I am sorry you didn't sleep well, though. I may be able to make a blend for that with no problem!"

"Not sleeping well the night before a meeting with her lawyer? Why I can't imagine you're the first or the last, Mabel." Mr. Findley had entered the lobby from the hallway and Carol and I had been so busy chatting we didn't even notice. Actually, I think Carol was already busy planning custom essential oil blends in her mind and trying to decide if that was something she wanted to agree to do. "Ms. Barnett, I imagine if you made a sleep blend and sold it here in the lobby, you'd make more than I did by the end of the week." He winked at her and she blushed scarlet.

"Oh, do you think so? You'd let me sell them right here in the lobby at work?" Her eyes were still open wide, and I briefly wondered if they'd be stuck like that until she made a decision. Was there an oil for that, too?

"Of course I would. As long as you promised not to get too successful and leave me." He cleared his throat and looked away. "Your job. Leave your secretary job I mean."

"Oh. Oh no, I love my job, Mr. Findley. I would never." Ah, there. Her eyes were no longer wide with shock and overwhelming possibilities. Now they were scrunched with her pleased grin.

"Perhaps it's about time you started calling me Phil. After all, you've worked here seven years now, and if my ears don't mistake me, you aren't that formal with friends?"

Oh, there was totally something here! I was thrilled that I was here to witness this moment that seemed to be about seven years in the making. I wondered what had finally prompted Mr. Findley to do something about their obvious feelings for each other.

"Friends. Yes. That's right."

There was a pause, and then another, and another and suddenly we were in one of those awkward moments where no one said anything. I was worried that I had celebrated the moment too soon. Would they spend another seven years on a first name basis and nothing more? Ugh.

Looking slightly dejected, Mr. Findley cleared his throat and said, "Well, Mabel, are you ready to get started?"

I ping ponged a look from one to the other several times. When Carol didn't speak again, I said "Yes, I suppose I am." Turning to Carol, I brightened my voice and said a bit louder than necessary, "Carol, please do call me if you decide to make a sleep blend. I'll be your first customer."

She startled slightly at my volume, and then called after Mr. Findley and me as we made our way down the hallway.

"Oh! Please do call me Carol, Phil!" Her large earrings danced in her ears with the movement of her small body leaning to see around me in the hallway. A different pair from the other day, but still happy and whimsical.

Mr. Findley had stopped walking and I saw his shoulders relax slightly. I stepped to the side as he turned to look over his shoulder down the hallway. "Gladly." He said simply and turned back to continue to his office.

I shot Carol a discreet thumbs up, at which she giggled like a teenager, and scurried to follow Mr. Findley to his office.

I TOOK THE same seat that I had last Friday across from Mr. Findley's desk. I waited until he sat down and looked at me expectantly before I poked the bear.

"So..." I was failing miserably at smothering my grin. "Phil Findley."

"I don't know why you're acting so surprised Mabel, it's on my business card and every correspondence you've ever gotten from me," he said dryly.

"Oh, I know. Just hits a little differently doesn't it? Hearing it out loud?" I'm full on grinning now, and I see his lips twitch in response.

"I could say the same for you, Miss Mabel Morrison."

"I'm not talking about alliteration and you know it." He wasn't wrong there either. I guess my parents had had a sense of humor. Although, it did kind of roll off the tongue nicely I guess.

He sighed in resignation. "You said something on Friday that made me think long and hard all weekend about my own life." He paused and looked me in the eye, and I could see the vulnerability swirling in his eyes. It was obvious that he didn't want to share, but it was somehow overridden by the determination to do so anyway.

"I have been 'should-ing' on myself, as you so eloquently put it, for a long time now. And when I stopped to really examine the reasons why, it wasn't to make me happy, it was to hide. I think I'd like to be done hiding now and see what it's like to live."

I got little chills over my arms. I wanted that for him, this man that I really didn't know well at all but was beginning to care for. He had always shown me kindness, and more so, like recognized like I suppose. I wanted him to find his happiness and stop hiding behind whatever it was he felt was holding him back. I wanted the same thing for me too.

"Well, Phil, maybe we can both figure out how to do that for ourselves." I scrunched my nose up and shook my head. "Nope, definitely sticking with Mr. Findley." He laughed and then began pulling things out of his desk drawer.

"Let's get to it then. Did you bring any notes or questions from reading over things this weekend? Would you like to start there, or just get to them as we go?"

"May I just interrupt you as we go along? I brought my copies of what you gave me, and I'll make notes around the edges. I'll stop you if I don't understand something."

"That's a good plan. Lets start here." He pulled out the sheets that explained all of Gram's investment accounts and things like that. Her financial planner had been notified that all holdings were now mine, and I could call to set up a meeting with him at my convenience.

Side note: I now had a financial planner?! Excuse me, but that sounds like something for an adultier adult. Good news was there was someone who knew what they were doing that could continue to handle all of that for me. I'd save the investments research for another day.

We went through all of that fairly quickly, along with the other small wishes in Gram's will that didn't have to do with her estate. He'd already taken care of these, but I was thankful he went over them with me. It would be nice to continue some of her donations in her memory, and she'd definitely left me enough to be able to do so.

"Now that brings us to the big stuff, the house and the buildings." He tapped the few stacks of paper we'd finished together and set them off to the side. Glancing up at me, he asked, "House or building first?"

"I choose house for 500, Alex." I was deflecting with humor, poor humor maybe but still. I winced internally, making a mental decision to try and show that I was taking the situation seriously. I straightened in my seat a little and settled my nervous fidgeting.

"Oooookay." He studied me for a second but kept going. "House it is. How closely did you read over the pages on the house and the buildings?"

"Honestly, I didn't read them verbatim, but I probably got the gist."

"Okay. But you saw that the house has been in your family for several generations?" He cocked his head to the side, probably waiting to see if I cared at all about family history and heirlooms, even if the heirloom was a house.

"I didn't see that in the printed pages, but Gram eluded to it in a note she'd left in the packet. I had no idea. I had no idea about a lot." I frowned and started tapping my pen on the notepad in my lap.

"That's okay, Mabel, you know now. And it may change how you feel about some of these options. It may not. It's your choice, and I will help you through the legal side of whatever you choose to do." I simply nodded, but that settled me enough to stop the tapping, so he continued.

"Of course, one option is to sell the house. There's a substantial bit of land with it as well, so I'm sure you'd fetch a fair price. That's the most final option, in my opinion, but it is an option."

I sat with that for a second. I knew it was what my mother wanted me to do though for the life of me I didn't know why. It probably was the easiest option logistically. I could go back to Ohio with Mother and find a place of my own and everything would go back to the way it was. But it just didn't feel right. My gut tightened uncomfortably when I thought about not having the cottage to come back to anymore.

"I don't think that's the right thing to do at this time. I'd like to explore other options first." Look at me, sounding like I had any idea what I was doing. Point one, Mabel.

"I agree it's best to think of all your options before you make a decision. If you know you want to keep the property, at least for now, there are a lot of things you can do with it. It may seem a little overwhelming, but you've got time. The house is completely paid off and in your name, and there's more than enough in the estate to continue paying the taxes and insurance and any up keep you may need to do to the place. Although, if I'm not mistaken, Constance had done a lot to the property and cottage recently and it should be in tip top shape."

I was absently nodding my head along with what he was saying. It did seem like Gram had been busy at the house, not just new furniture but all the new twinkle lights outside and I thought the roof even looked new. It was almost as if she knew something was going to happen. Or maybe it had just been time for updates, like Dottie had said.

"You could rent the cottage out on a permanent basis, open it as a BNB, rent it for weddings... I'm sure we could come up with an exhaustive list, but really, Mabel, this is something you'll have to decide on your own regarding the house and you've got all the time you need. The buildings however..."

I'd kind of zoned out again and was staring at a pair of bronzed baby shoes on the shelves behind him. He glanced over his shoulder and sighed.

"They were mine. My mother kept them and then wanted me to have them in my office to 'show how far I'd come'. I'd humored her at the time, but now I think she was right. Sometimes it is nice to remember how far you've come and the people that helped get you there." He paused and leaned back in his chair, flipping one elbow over the edge. "Do you need a break, Mabel?"

"No. No, I'm sorry. Let's finish all the piles so I know everything I need to think about. I'm sure I'll have more questions but I'd rather do everything we can now." I turned my attention back to him and leaned my forearms on his desk. "Why are you implying I don't have as long to make a decision about the buildings?"

"Ah, you were listening. Very well. Did you read about the buildings at all over the weekend?"

"That was one of the parts I just briefly skimmed. Honestly, all I retained is that Gram owns... owned... a couple of buildings somewhere in town and one has a tenant. I just assumed the rental agreement would still hold until the term ran out and I didn't need to worry about it."

He sat back straight in his chair, and I thought I could hear his foot tapping on the carpet under his desk. "Well, for starters, she didn't just own some buildings in town. She owned two of the buildings right on Main Street."

I froze, my eyes slightly widened in disbelief. "Main Street? That had to cost a fortune. How did Gram... when did she... wait, what now? You mean Stone's Throw Road right? Like, that Main Street?"

Two buildings on Main Street I didn't even know she had. Yet another thing she just never even mentioned. I'd assumed it was just some little tiny shop along a side road. Painted Creek had those all along the side streets. They were almost no more than shacks, but they were perfect for little artisan shops and most of them were decorated with a theme. But a building on Main Street was different. She must have gotten it sometime in the last ten years or so, since she'd never mentioned it on our walks down Main Street and around the square. Guilt about not visiting more often or for longer hit me again.

"The buildings are two separate stores that share a connecting wall and make up two thirds of the entire structure as a whole. They both fell into disrepair years ago when the previous owner retired and moved to Florida. They had left the buildings in the care of a property management company and unfortunately got swindled. By the time they found out about the neglect, they didn't want to deal with repairing the considerable damage, so they decided to just sell the two stores as is. It was still expensive, mind you, being prime real estate and all, but Constance knew about it before it was listed somehow and snatched it up. She brought one side back to life and rented it out, but she never got around to the other."

I just blinked at him a few times. I think there was a buffering symbol on my forehead. "How did I not know this? How has Dottie not mentioned this?" I could hear my voice getting higher and higher. "Dottie mentions everything, to everyone!"

"She may not know, Mabel. Constance hired a reputable property management firm that handles a lot of the cabins and other rental properties around Cherokee and even into Gatlinburg, Tennessee. She handled all of the business for the building through them. The rental agreement has the property management company listed as the landlord, so it's possible her tenant didn't even know she was the owner unless she'd told them herself. She never said why she did it that way, come to think of it..." He had the grace to look a little puzzled. "It makes good business sense I guess in a town this small. I'd imagine it was another type of contingency plan for Constance... if anything went belly up no one would know she'd been involved the whole time."

Okay, now that sounded more like Gram. "What a huge secret though. And right on Main Street too. Wait..." I sucked in a sharp breath and fought the urge to bang my head on Mr. Findley's desk. "A building on Main Street, two of the three stores and one is empty." I had a fifty fifty shot, but I just knew in my gut how this was going to play out. I closed my eyes as I asked, "The tenant is the coffee shop, isn't it?"

He smirked at me. Actually smirked. "Yes, ma'am. Have you met Sarah yet?"

"Har har. I know you and everyone else in town already knows I've met Sarah. Well, this is just peachy."

"Let's put aside who is renting for now and talk about the options for the building the same way we did for the house." I managed a nod again, so he continued. Non-verbal communication for the win. "It's basically the same options without the emotional attachment. You can sell the buildings outright, and again it's prime real estate so you won't have a problem selling and should get a good price, even with one building still needing a lot of work. You can leave everything just as it is, renting just the half with the other half remaining empty. You can continue to rent the one and fix up the other half to rent eventually as well."

His voice had started to take on a rambling quality, and when I tilted my head with a wry expression on my face, he cleared his throat once. "You get the idea. You have a list of options to choose from. The only pressing matter is that the lease agreement is up on the rented half of the building in sixty days. If you choose not to renew the lease, you have to notify the tenant within thirty days. So, you have to make a decision in that regard in the next four weeks at the most. The sooner the better honestly."

"Sure. Three weeks or so for all the decision making. It's nice to have a good solid deadline, I suppose."

"Mabel, I know it feels like a lot right now. Just take some time to think about it and see what feels right. You just have to do what's best for you."

I was back to wanting to bang my head on the desk. "Why do people always say that like it's the easiest thing in the world to do?"

He leaned forward in his chair and put both elbows up on the desk to look directly at me. "I don't know. But maybe it's time we both figure it out, hmm?"

His look was so open and earnest, I decided it was as good a time as any to stick my nose where it didn't belong. And change the subject. More the latter than the former.

"Whatever did bring you to Painted Creek all those years ago, Mr. Findley? I can remember laughing with Gram when you had the outside of this place painted in that awful salmon color." He winced, and I laughed again at the memory.

"Divorce." He said it plainly, like every other word, but my laughter dried up pretty quickly. Some wounds still hurt, even if we spoke about them flippantly.

"I won't go into the details, but it was nasty, and when I saw the building available here in Painted Creek, I decided it was as good a place as any to start over. I bought it while I was here on a weekend get away, trying to clear my head and all that nonsense, and began moving my practice here as soon as I went back home. When I finally made it back to town, Constance was one of the first people to stop by and welcome me. She brought tea."

He was gazing over my shoulder now, as I had been doing to him the whole meeting, seeing nothing in front of him and too much from the past. I straightened a bit, hoping he'd go on with his story, especially now that it included Gram.

"I had just corrected my misstep with the paint color, you're right it was dreadful, and I was trying to settle into my office. I had put out adds for help, secretary and the like, so when the bell rang for the front door I thought maybe it was someone who wanted to apply for a job. Then I walk around the corner and see Constance standing there with a travel tea service and a kind smile." He smiled fondly at the memory and brought his eyes to mine. "She was my first client in town. She hired me on the spot, and I've taken care of her estate and really everything else since that day. She was my first friend, too."

My eyes misted as I pictured the story he was telling. It was just so Gram to show up with tea to welcome someone new to town. My fingers started to tingle, the frisson slowly working it's way through my body as a picture popped into my head. I itched so badly to sketch it out on something before I forgot it. But I didn't want to be rude to Mr. Findley and interrupt his story. I tried to take a mental snapshot of sorts so I wouldn't forget it, and I'd sketch it out as soon as I got to the car.

"I know we've been over a lot, and once again you have a lot to think about. Take a few days and see what questions you come up with. There's no reason to rush into anything right now. Just be aware of the time limit on the first building. I'm assuming you want to keep it quiet that you're the owner?"

"Yes, definitely. I don't know that I'll be staying in town long term and I don't want to have to manage anyone's expectations on the buildings either." I frowned. I was already thinking ahead about the conversation I'd need to have with my mother about extending my trip. I don't think I could handle anyone else's expectations for me, too.

"Understood. Just call when you're ready to go over anything and we'll set something up. In the meantime, get to know Painted Creek again. If nothing else, treat it like a vacation, or maybe an artist's retreat?" He raised both eyebrows like it was a wonderful idea and I couldn't help but smile.

"An artist's retreat sounds lovely. And speaking of, I do still have a list of things to get painted so I better be going." We both stood and he walked me to the door of his office. As I turned to shake his hand, I said in a hushed voice, "I hope things work out for the best." I glanced over my shoulder toward the lobby and winked.

He shook his head slightly at my antics and said, "Me too, Mabel. See you soon." He walked back to sit at his desk, but I didn't miss his glance toward the lobby before I'd made it half way down the hall.

THIRTEEN

AS SOON AS I got to my car I pulled out one of my ever present pieces of scrap paper and did a quick sketch. The frisson was long gone and I was just hoping I could remember all the details of the picture that popped in my head while talking with Mr. Findley. I jotted some notes along the side, and then set off for the bakery. After all, there was a cronut and a book to pick up with my name on them. As I drove, I thought about getting a frisson vision, I giggled with the name again, while listening to Mr. Findley talk about meeting Gram.

It had been a long time, years even, since I had crafted a painting from a frisson like that. They were unpredictable, and I'd built my business around giving customers exactly what they'd asked for. My specialty had become hyper realism which was as predictable as you could get. People loved to see their cherished photograph turned into a beautiful painting.

Often times it happened just as it had with Mr. Findley; by the time I was able to rough out a sketch and make notes, so much of the detail that had come to me with the frisson was gone. I couldn't always get the level of realism that I could achieve with my other paintings. Not knowing why I was painting the thing I was painting added another level of instability too. I was often left wondering if the person would like it, if they would even know what it was or if I would just seem like a crazy person giving them some random watercolor painting.

Driving home from the bakery didn't take long... driving anywhere in Painted Creek didn't take long. So I took the time to make a quick snack plate to go with my cronut before I started painting. The odds were good that I would get lost in the colors and the way the paint interacted with the water on the paper, and I would forget to stop until well after dinner time. I threw together some baby carrots and a little roll up of turkey and cheese, still running on the welcome groceries from Mr. Findley. I really would have to go get my own groceries soon.

I sat down to look over my list of paintings that I still needed to begin. Even after adding Dottie's painting and the one I wanted to do for Mr. Findley, the list was nowhere near as long as I usually kept it. "Maybe this *is* like an artist's retreat... or at least a lighter load. I may even be able to actually read this book from Heather," I murmured to myself as I tossed it onto the end table. *Probably not*, I thought.

Painting with watercolors involves so much drying time between layers that I developed a habit of working in stages on multiple paintings at a time. Not only did it allow me to keep working on one painting while another was drying, but it gave my brain a break. I chose one painting off my commission list to begin working on, a portrait of a blue ribbon winning show horse turned family pet upon his retirement, while simultaneously working on Dottie's painting and Mr. Findley's thank you painting as well.

Painting in such excruciating detail was sometimes exhausting, especially if I couldn't connect to the subject matter. I tried to always do at least one painting per batch that I was really excited about, and I saved it for last in the rotation as a reward for myself. Yes, I still had to trick myself into doing the things I *had* to do, but hey, whatever gets the job done.

Cronut finished, it was one hundred percent worth the hype the ladies had given it, I started with a quick sketch on Mr. Findley's project. I refined what I had laid out in the car on a nice piece of watercolor paper with crisp, taped off edges and then started painting. Once the first layer of paint was down and drying, I did the same for the horse. Since I had already started on Dottie's painting, I dove right into some of the detail work that took up the majority of the time I spent on my paintings. After one rotation through all three of them, I was restless.

"I didn't expect to need a break, Hedgie," I said as I stood and stretched. "But, since I'm talking to a lamp, maybe a break is a good idea. No offense."

He took no offense and carried on casting a soft light on the paintings drying on the bar cart. I moved Dottie's to the end of the row and turned back to the dining table. "Not a terrible mess, all things considered." I decided a quick tidy of the room might help when I came back in to paint some more.

The bar cart was the perfect drying place, so I decided that was it's new permanent job. I stacked all of my new materials in a spare chair next to the china hutch, and made a mental note to order more paper. The extra large cork board that I used to hang finished art work was propped up on the opposite wall, looking pretty sad and empty with only the painting of the porcupine on the top left corner. The sound of my phone ringing from the kitchen island made me stop rearranging paints for the fifth time as I scrambled after it.

"Hey, Dottie!" I was happy to see her name on the screen before I picked up.

"Well hey, sugar. You sound chipper. What have you gotten in to?" I could hear the smile in Dottie's voice through the phone, and it made mine grow.

"Nothing too much. I've been painting and rearranging the dining room a bit to suit while I'm here."

"Glad to see some crafty stuff back at that table, that's for sure." There was a pause. No doubt we were both thinking about all the fun we'd had at that table with Gram. She cleared her throat. "I'm actually calling about your paintings, honey. Did you get my photographs?"

"Yes, ma'am, I did. I have actually already started on the painting, too. I think it's going to be so special."

"Everything you paint is special, girl, but I can't wait to see it. I told you not to rush on that though... I could have waited my turn on your never ending list."

I laughed in response, "Since when can you wait your turn, Dottie?"

"Oh, you hush your mouth!" She was laughing now too, and I realized how much I missed cutting up with someone and enjoying it. I didn't leave behind many genuine friends in Columbus, certainly none that would call just to chat and share a laugh. I'd need to be careful or I'd get used to having people around.

"Kidding. But believe it or not, my list is shorter than normal, and it means a lot to me to do this for you so I got started on it right away. I should have it done in a day or so."

"Oh honey, that's just wonderful! I can come pick it up Wednesday. Does that give you enough time to finish it?" she asked.

"Yes ma'am, it sure does. But let me bring it to you. It's been ages since I've been to your house, and I will desperately need real grown up groceries by then." I had wandered over to the pantry while we chatted and was poking through what I had left. I could get away with being a hermit for another two days.

"That sounds like an excellent plan. Can you come around noon? The quilting group will be here and I just know all those old ladies would love to see you. And I want to show off my Mabel Morrison original!"

Dottie and I chatted for a bit longer before saying goodbye. I wasn't ready to sit down and paint more, and it wasn't quite time for dinner, so I decided to go through all the information from Mr.

Findley again. After a quick text to my mother to say hello and tell her the meeting had gone well without giving her any details, I spread all the papers across the island once again.

I got out the stack regarding the building and rent agreement first. I really hadn't paid close enough attention the night I arrived. I'd blame jet lag. *Can you get jet lag from driving?* Shaking my head to clear the random thoughts, I focused on the rent agreement.

I didn't know much about leases, but I thought that Gram had been more than generous with the monthly rent, especially considering the apartment that was above the coffee shop was included. I smiled sadly to myself, thinking of Gram and how she always liked to look out for other people, even if they didn't know she was doing it... especially if they didn't know she was doing it. It was probably another reason that no one knew Gram owned the building in the first place.

I know Mr. Findley had encouraged me not to think about who the tenants were while deciding what to do with the building, but I couldn't help it. I know Sarah was anxious about Becca getting attached to anyone who wouldn't stick around, but *I* was already kind of attached to *her*. And I could see all the work that Sarah had put into that coffee shop to make it successful and her own. How could I just end all of that?

"Maybe I just keep the building. After all, I can keep the management company and work through them like Gram did. I don't have to stay in Painted Creek to keep the building."

I talked to myself out loud all the time. It drove Mom crazy, after all what would people think if they heard, but I couldn't help it. Sometimes things just clicked when I worked it out out loud. I made a note on the side of the page to ask Mr. Findley if the other side could be rented 'as is', and the tenant could deal with construction to suit whatever they wanted in there. That would be double the income with minimal effort.

Feeling like I had made a some progress, minuscule as it was, I decided a little time outside sounded like a great way to end the day. I settled in the big comfy rocking chair and sighed. It was peaceful and the air was lightly scented with all the plants and flowers Gram had planted around the yard. I was thankful for the big porch fans that stirred up a gentle breeze.

It wasn't miserably hot yet in early April, but I knew the humid summer temperatures weren't too far away either. As the sun started to set, I took a stroll around the yard and by the creek. The sound of the water was soothing, and by the time I went in for dinner I felt like some of the stress I'd picked up during the day had been eased away.

After a quick meal in front of the big TV, I started tucking the house in for the night. I found the routine soothing already, and after just a few days I was really enjoying the few minutes it took to turn everything off and lock up. I glanced at Gram's door across the house as I turned the corner to my room. I still couldn't bring myself to go in her suite. As I got ready for bed on the other end of the house, I didn't hear the sound of the door to Gram's room as it creaked open a couple of inches.

FOURTEEN

I WAS RIGHT, my toes *were* happy submerged in the water flowing through the creek as I swayed back and forth on the rope swing. My toes were the only part of me that was happy though. After yesterday's productivity, today had been a long, frustrating day of painting.

The day had started off fine as I made my rounds waking the house up for the day by turning on some of the lamps and opening curtains. I put water on the stove to boil for the French press, and puttered for a bit preparing breakfast. As I headed to the patio doors to open the blinds, I noticed Gram's door was open a crack. I stopped walking and just stared at it, a mixture of curiosity and trepidation warring for dominance over my nervous system.

"Well... that absolutely wasn't like that last night. It must've opened when I shut my bedroom door. Some sort of vacuum or suction or something..." Hearing a somewhat rational explanation out loud, even if it was from myself, was enough to get me moving again toward the patio. It was not enough to get me to go in her room though. Nope. Not today. I flipped all the blinds open and went back to the dining room to start painting.

Waking up the house felt like it was my last moment of true, uninhibited productivity for the day. The truth was I'd made good progress on the horse painting and even Dottie's painting, but Mr. Findley's painting was giving me fits. I couldn't decide if the angle was right. Was the color just a little off? What had it actually looked like when it popped into my head? That line was too short, wasn't it?

It was awful. I hadn't second guessed myself like this in a long time. I had grown confident in my abilities as an artist. I was still humble but I knew my art was good. When I was unsure of everything else in life, I could rely on painting to be consistent and comforting. It was doubly frustrating to be doubting myself in painting now, too.

So here I was, swinging over a beautiful creek, surrounded by about a billion plants, okay not really but they were everywhere, and feeling sorry for myself and frustrated with my painting. I had hoped being out here would calm me the way it had the other night, but as I watched the sun sink lower in the sky, just short of sunset, that sense of peace still alluded me.

"Well, don't you look madder than a wet cat?"

The voice, sudden and close, made me jump. Nervous laughter bubbled out as I almost slipped from the swing, and I somehow managed to hear Charlotte's laughter over the sound of my hammering heartbeat.

"Jump scare. Not cool! Rustle some leaves or something next time, would you?!" I had wrapped my arms around the rope of the swing and was clutching my chest, but I couldn't completely stop the grin that was turning up the corners of my lips.

"Right... I'll be sure to walk through all the fallen leaves next time. In April. Good plan." She was smirking at me but I could see her holding in her laughter.

"Ugh, you know what I mean. How did you just pop up like that? Geeze."

"My friend, you were so lost in thought I could've come in with a big brass band and I don't think you'd have noticed 'till I was right up on you." She settled on one of the flat rocks close to the swing and took off her strappy leather sandals. Once her toes were in the water too, she looked up at me, cocked her head to the side, and simply waited.

"Just a little frustrated with my job today. I came out here to try and find some peace, or inspiration, or even just a break, but my brain keeps going over and over it trying to figure out what went wrong. No luck yet."

"Oh, the great Mabel Morrison is having trouble painting? Well, I never!" She placed a hand palm up on her forehead and fake swooned.

Giggling, I asked, "How did you know I was an artist?"

"You're kidding, right? The whole town knows. If they didn't already know from Constance bragging on you every chance she got, they know now from Ms. Dottie telling everyone that'll listen how fine her Mabel Morrison original painting is going to be."

I groaned. While I was confident in my painting abilities, I certainly didn't brag about them and I didn't like to be the center of attention either. I'd gotten over that really quickly during all the art gallery showings when I was younger. Center of attention meant praise, sure. But it also opened you up to scrutiny.

"Well, there's that, I guess." I felt like a petulant teenager. I could only imagine what I looked like.

"Oh, that's enough of that now. It's good to have people in your corner. Let them be proud of you." She paused a second and then frowned when my expression didn't change. "Doesn't sound like you're enjoying your job at all right now, not just this painting. What's going on?" She was drawing patterns in the water with her toes, not fully focusing on me and giving me the space to feel like I could talk to her about what I'd been feeling lately without feeling like I was under a microscope.

"My whole career has become focused around the hyper realism style of painting. It is incredible to see a photograph or an idea even come to life in a painting so realistic it seems to be alive, I know. And my mother was always so proud that I could make my watercolor, of all painting mediums, look so lifelike. So, I'd found a niche I was good at and ran with it. But lately I've realized that the only paintings I do are commissions, and people only want this hyper realism style from me. I can't remember the last time I painted in any other style. Hell, I can't remember the last time I painted just for fun." I paused and smiled. "Actually, that's not true. I painted a bunny yesterday for fun. Out of coffee."

She slow blinked at me. A couple of times. "Coffee?"

I launched into the story then, and told her all about Becca and creating a bunny out of an accident. She nodded along and by the time I'd finished, she was full on smiling.

"That's amazing, Mabel. I know that girl will never forget that," she said.

"I don't think I will either. You know, I used to paint all kinds of subjects using whatever I could find to paint with. Once when I was little, I painted a big purple dinosaur out of grape juice that I'd spilled on the counter... I haven't thought about that in years."

My mother hadn't exactly been as understanding of my spill as everyone was of Becca bumping into the table. She asked that in the future, I clean up any messes instead of painting with them, especially since I had such lovely proper paints to use.

"That certainly sounds like an excellent use of creativity. And fun too! Why don't you do more of that?"

I shrugged. "I don't know. I don't really have time. I usually keep my commission list so full that there's not enough time to paint anything else. And my customers only request hyper realism from me now. I used to do some other things, in the very beginning, but the results were never consistent enough to be marketable." At least, that's what the art galleries and managers and my mother had said. And who was I to argue when I was fortunate enough to be able to paint in a way that *was* marketable?

"Not everything is about what you can get out of it. Sometimes, you have to do things solely because it brings you joy and feeds your soul. Maybe you just need to remember why you fell in love with painting in the first place. Maybe you just need to remember what *you* love."

I glanced over at her and wondered, not for the first time, how old she was. She looked to be around my age, but definitely acted and spoke like she was decades older.

"And what do you do? Other than your mad ninja skills I mean. Wait... are you a ninja?" I grinned, deciding she was right. I'd done enough moping and having someone to banter with was too good an opportunity to waste.

"Ha. No, not a ninja. I make soaps and the like. I used to have a little sundry in town but that was ages ago." She peered up at me, and I couldn't quite read the expression on her face. "I used to come here and borrow some of Constance's herbs to go in my soaps and sachets and things. Her herbs are always the best I can find, I swear they're like magic."

I tried to sit up straighter in the swing, which had me flailing around for a minute again. I had totally forgotten to check the rest of the yard for the herb garden!

"What herbs? I mean, I knew there must be an herb garden somewhere, there's too many dried herbs in her cupboard. I mean, I guess she could've bought them in bulk on Amazon or something and then put them in the containers. It is pretty like that. But Gram loved to grow things, surely she did her own."

A very unladylike snort from Charlotte broke through my little tirade and made me stop. "Oh. I'm rambling." I cleared my throat. In my best fake, sweet voice I asked, "Charlotte, do you happen to know where Gram's herb garden is?"

"Wouldn't you know, Mabel, I do happen to know where her herb garden is!" Her accent deepened into a sickly sweet southern twang.

"Would you be so kind as to show me?" I was full on grinning now and swinging my feet back and forth on the swing, kicking up small bits of water.

"Why, I would be ever so delighted to show you." She stood

and picked her shoes up. "Right this way, please," she said with an over flourish of her arms, and she took off barefoot down the yard toward the trees.

Sliding my wet feet into my flip flops, I scurried to follow her. The yard was several acres, and while most of it was easily visible by just walking from the house to the creek, I hadn't done much exploring on the other side of the creek or close to the woods. Charlotte was headed in the direction she had come and left from last weekend when we'd met. She stopped by another flat grouping of rocks, much like the ones that made up the edge of the creek by the swing. Winking, she walked across them and parted some vines that were reaching out determinedly toward the water in the creek.

The vines, which I had seen during my quick once over of the yard but had paid zero attention to, were like a door. On the other side, a large circular space had been cleared from the woods that surrounded the opening all the way around. Three large raised beds were built in a spiral design right in the middle of the clearing. You could easily walk along the outside of the spirals and reach everything within the bed. I stood with the vines tickling my back as they danced in the breeze, my mouth open in wonder.

"I... I had no idea. I might never had found this if you hadn't shown me. Thank you." I took a slow step into the space, stunned. There were more herbs than I easily recognized, and everything looked so lush and healthy.

"Constance had a way with plants for sure. Probably even more than I." She looked around almost wistfully, and I wondered what was troubling her.

"You know, you can come clip some herbs any time you like. You don't have to ask. I'm sure Gram would love to know you still came by."

She smiled, but it didn't relieve the feel of melancholy that was floating around her.

"Thanks, Mabel. I will."

"I guess I need to find someone that can help me keep up with all the yard and plants. I've gotten better over the years, but there's no way that I'm up to this level of plant parenting." I was getting a little overwhelmed, honestly. This place was stunning, and I didn't want to be the one accountable for letting it all wither and die.

"Everyone is different, with different strengths and weaknesses. I'm sure you'll figure out how to keep up this place, even if it's not with your own two hands. Plus, maybe your two hands will be busy painting for fun, hmm?"

She walked back through the vine cover, but I took one last look about the herb garden. I pinched a basil leaf off of the closest plant, bruising it between my fingers. I brought it to my nose, breathing in the spicy scent, and I finally felt the peace I had been looking for in the creek. A sense of courage washed over me, and when I saw the smudge of green on my fingers from the basil leaf, I felt a soft, silent nudge toward my paints, the natural stain of the basil urging me to fall back in love with painting again. I rushed out to catch up with Charlotte, but she was gone; the faint sounds of twigs breaking let me know she was already on her way back home.

I walked slowly back toward the cottage, sticking close to the edge of the creek the whole way. By the time I reached the patio, the basil leaf was all but smushed into pulp from my incessant sniffing, but I walked straight through the house to the dining room and put the leaf on the bar cart next to Hedgie. I could've sworn the scent of basil filled the room from that one small leaf.

I looked at the table and decided Mr. Findley's painting could wait a while longer. I was going to paint something, anything, for fun.

BEFORE I KNEW it, every space on the table and my drying board was full. It was well after two o'clock in the morning, but I was full of the kind of energy that came from doing something that made one genuinely happy.

The first thing I'd sat down to paint was Hedgie. The painting was sort of a mixture of my hyper realism and the loose outlines I used to love painting. Hedgie appeared in the painting as the adorable little lamp that he was with his cute little nose lifted in the air and soft light pouring through his spikes. He was painted as realistically as I could manage, and you could even tell from the

110

painting that he was made of ceramic.

Instead of sitting on the bar cart in the painting, he was sitting among bundles of herbs. The herb bundles were painted with a loose outline, the color splashed over in free flowing, mixey paint swirls. The combination of the two styles shouldn't have worked, but somehow for this painting, it did. As soon as the paint turned opaque and crisp feeling, I hung it on the refrigerator door and giggled the whole time.

After that, I was a painting machine! Not all of them were good mind you, and some made absolutely no sense, but I was falling in love with painting again. I was rediscovering all the amazing things watercolors could do when you let them breathe instead of suffocating them with the rigidity I had been using for so long. I even managed to finish Dottie's painting somewhere in the middle of my painting frenzy. It was drying on the island, and I was incredibly proud of the detail it had and all the memories it represented.

I had also painted several floral abstracts that were similar to the ones that hung on Gram's wall in the living room. They had thick outlines with splashes of color that didn't give much regard to boundaries or rules. There were a few paintings of buildings, all different in their architecture and surroundings, but instead of concentrating on matching every single brick for brick, the paintings expanded and flowed in a way that my normal realism paintings never did.

When I finally took note of the time and decided it was probably time to stop, I looked around at all of the paintings scattered on almost every flat surface of the living areas. "What am I going to do with all of this?" My own voice startled me in the quiet and I laughed. "Yeah, definitely time for bed."

As I went around tucking the house in for the night, I made a mental list of things I would need to buy. I hadn't done a portfolio in ages, but I could always add most of these paintings into a new one and save it as a keepsake from my time here in Painted Creek. Some of the paintings were definitely still good enough to sell, and I could probably list them somewhere on my website as originals and get rid of them that way.

I know other artists didn't have a problem throwing things away when they were just playing with their mediums, but it has always bothered me. I didn't think everything I painted was worth an art gallery display, that wasn't it. It was just that I felt like everything was created for a reason, that even if I didn't appreciate it, it was possible that someone else would.

Not for the first time since I'd been back in Painted Creek, I thought of having a shop. It was great to get commissions coming through the website, yes, and I could imagine it would be fun to see originals there, too. But picturing someone walking into a little shop they'd stumbled upon, expecting nothing and leaving with a piece of art or trinket that really spoke to them? *That* seemed like magic.

Once all the lights were off and I was ready for bed, I spent a little time with my good friend Amazon. I ordered a portfolio, several frames, and more paper. I even threw in some easels and these really neat frames that opened from the bottom with a hinge on top, so that I could change out whatever I wanted to display without completely reframing anything. I figured I could hang them with command hooks and have a little more display area without messing up Gram's walls. My walls? The walls in the cottage. I sighed aloud at my thoughts, not really ready to face them.

I dropped my phone to the bed and rolled to my side. I wondered if I would ever stop thinking of this as Gram's house. I knew, technically, it was mine now. But I didn't feel any right of ownership to this place, and I still didn't think I was going to stay. A few more weeks at most. It was more like I was house sitting for Gram than anything. Sighing, I whispered "Goodnight, house," and snuggled in to sleep.

Outside, a branch softly scratched along the siding, creating a steady beat for the song of the cicadas, and I was asleep in no time. When I woke in the middle of the night to stumble to the bathroom, I heard the squeak of hinges on the other side of the house. My sleep addled brain didn't fully register the sound, but in the morning,

Gram's door was open another few inches once again.

FIFTEEN

WEDNESDAY MORNING CAME early, and I felt a little hung over from my painting bender the night before. Suzy Sunshine I was not, and I grumbled unintelligible nonsense to myself as I shuffled through the house to boil water for coffee. I pretended to completely ignore Gram's now halfway open door when I walked to the patio and stepped outside. Breathing in the fresh morning air, already slightly humid for the day, I stretched and began trying to clear the fog from my head. After a few moments of peace, I wandered back inside for coffee.

On the end table between the couches lay the book from Heather about natural inks. I carried it over to the island and flipped through it while I had my coffee and yogurt with granola. During art school, one of my teachers had done a few lessons on natural inks, and I had loved every second of it.

I glanced toward the pantry and Gram's tea cupboard as if someone had called my name. Vaguely, I wondered if I could make some herbal inks to use as watercolors. Not wanting to use up what was left of Gram's supply, I quickly added a few bulk herbs to the order I'd placed online last night. It would be enough to experiment with anyway.

I didn't spend much time getting ready, letting my light chocolate brown hair air dry and holding it back with the sunglasses I knew I would need later in the day. Packaging up Dottie's painting was easy, and I finished the mailing label for the porcupine painting, too. I could swing by the post office on the way home.

All my paintings were packaged the same way when I sent them off to their homes, either in person or by mail. The paintings were sandwiched between two thick, sturdy cardboard sheets to prevent creases and bending. Then painting and cardboard went inside a self-sealing plastic bag, and a sticker with my logo was placed over the seal. I always added a handwritten note to the customer, and my business card of course. The process had become kind of methodical, but I enjoyed it, too. It was a ritual for a fond farewell to the paintings and stories that went with them.

On the back of my business card were the tags for all my social media outlets. Sometimes, customers would post photos of their paintings framed and in their new homes, and they tagged me in their posts. I loved getting to see the entire process, from inspiration photos to framed art. Reading what people chose to share about the stories behind their requests in their posts was always a delight for me. Sometimes it was more information than I'd gotten in the commissions form, sometimes less, but I loved it each time.

I gathered up both paintings and my bag and locked up. I meandered through the front yard a bit on the way to the car, simply enjoying the sunshine and the clean, sweet smelling air before heading off to Dottie's house.

It had been years since I'd gone to Dottie's house. Gram and I used to stop in all the time when I was younger. But as an adult my visits were so short, and usually during holidays, so sometimes I never even got to see her at all, much less make it over to her house. I pulled into her driveway and smiled. It was nice to see that some things never changed.

The little white vinyl sided house seemed small and demure from the outside, but I knew that it stretched on like a labyrinth inside with a basement level that couldn't be seen from the street. Much like its owner, a ton of love and personality was wrapped in its seemingly small package. The house looked well loved the way a child's favorite stuffed animal did, but it was still well maintained and cared for.

I giggled as I walked up the sidewalk to the door. The landscaping was fabulous and flourishing, and I knew that Dottie had absolutely nothing to do with it. It had all been Gram. Actually, looking around, I remembered helping plant some of the now larger shrubs while visiting one summer. I'd have to ask who her yard crew was, now that her go to landscaping help was gone.

"Right on time, I'd expect no less!" The door opened before I could knock, and Dottie snatched me inside for a big hug. I stumbled over the threshold laughing.

"Dot, don't break my neck! Don't you want your painting?"

"Oh, I'd just go through your bag and get it." I blinked at her, mouth open and all. "What? I'd call an ambulance first of course." She couldn't keep up the fake pretenses and was smiling broadly as she turned toward the kitchen. "Well, come on in now. Everyone else is downstairs, but I want to see this painting first up here. A private showing, if you will. Want anything to drink, sugar?"

"No, thank you." I walked over to her kitchen table and set my bag down. Pulling out her painting, I placed it on the table and firmly laid my hand on top. "I'm sorry to have disturbed quilting. I could have come any time you know."

"None of that now, honey. I told you all these ol' girls will be thrilled to see you. Betsy and Nora are here this time too, and I can't wait to see how jealous they are of my painting." She clapped her hands and rubbed them together in undisguised, rotten glee.

"You know, I can make artist's prints if you want to give them a copy. Then they can enjoy it too, but you'll have the only original." I knew having a copy of the painting of the cabin would mean something to Betsy and Nora too, since they were the other two original members of the ladies group. I also knew that Dottie would absolutely want them to have copies, even if she tortured them about it first.

"Well, now there's a nice thought. Maybe so! But that one right there," she gestured to the painting I was now pushing down on in case she tried to swipe it, "that one is mine. Gimmie!" She made grabby hands like a toddler, and the twinkle in her eye made her look twenty-five years younger.

"Oh, no you don't! This is my moment, too. I don't get to witness when a customer lays eyes on their painting for the first time very often any more. Let me have this." I knew they were totally unnecessary, but I gave her my best puppy dog eyes anyway.

She narrowed her eyes at me, ending with an eye roll a teenager would've been proud of. "Fine. Shall I close my eyes then?"

"Yes, please!"

She crossed her arms, but closed her eyes and settled. I lifted the painting from the plastic cover and stood in front of her a couple of feet away.

"Ta da! I hope you like it, Dottie."

She opened her eyes and froze. I could see a million memories flit behind her eyes. They misted over as she let out a slow breath.

The A-frame cabin was set back into the trees along what appeared to be a dead end road. In real life, there were cabins to either side, all with their own ample yards, but they were out of the frame of the painting and it really made you feel like you were looking at a place removed from time. The fire pit out front, surrounded by Adirondack style chairs, was painted in such detail that it seemed if you blew on the painting just right, the sparks would catch and the whole thing would go up in flames. The lights strung around the fire pit and around the frame of the cabin itself practically glowed with real light, as did the lights shining through the window to the right of the door.

I was really proud of this painting. Not only was it my typical hyper realism style, but something about it almost seemed ethereal too in the way the light played within the painting. I had varied from the inspiration photographs Dottie sent slightly, taking a few artistic liberties that just felt right to me at the time. No one would probably even notice but me anyway.

"Oh sugar... it's perfect." Her voice was barely audible as she continued to stare at the painting. I took a step closer so she could see it a little better.

"These trips have always been such fun, just the ladies. I'll be honest with you though, Mabel, I have been dreading going this year. It just won't be the same without Constance. But looking at this, I can see clear as day that she'll still be there with us.

"I don't know how you did it, but the way you stacked the wood in the fire pit... that's the same way your gram would do it every time, insisting that it was the best way for the fire starter to really catch. And that window you painted there with the curtains flung plum wide open? That's the bedroom that Constance and Betsy would share. Betsy always would come in first thing and shut the curtains, saying she didn't like feeling like someone was watching her. Your gram would come right behind her and open them every chance she got, just to piss her off."

She paused and chuckled, though it didn't quite chase the sadness from her voice. I don't think she even noticed that I was standing slack jawed, staring at her as she shared memories with me that I'd never heard. She had no way to know of course that they matched perfectly with the things I'd chosen to change from her pictures.

"I don't know how you did it, sugar, how you put your gram into this still life painting of an old cabin. But you did. And I know she'll be there for all the rest of our trips too." I just barely had time to raise the painting out of the way of her big bear hug. We stood quietly for a moment, taking comfort in each other, before she pulled away, squaring her shoulders and wiping at her eyes.

"Whew. No more of that. Honey, that painting is a masterpiece for sure. I can't wait to have it up on the wall where I can see it every time I walk past. Probably going to put it right here, what do you think?" She gestured to a small divider wall that separated the living room and kitchen. Dottie's house was mostly an open floor plan, and if she put the painting there she could see it from everywhere in the house except the bedroom.

"That would look nice, Dot. You could even make a collage hanging with photographs of y'all on trips or other artwork. I could help you, if you'd like."

"That's a right nice idea, Mabel. I'll take you up on that. We'll go shopping next week for frames!"

I cringed inwardly. Shopping with Dottie was always an all day marathon affair. When I was younger, I was always cranky and exhausted by the time Gram would excuse us to go home after the hundredth store or so. At least that's what it felt like. "Can't wait."

She smirked at me as if she could read my thoughts. "Come on, sugar, let's go show these other biddies what a beautiful painting you made me." She took off down the stairs, not a doubt that I would be trailing behind her with the painting and a smile on my face. I felt a little like a show pony, but for Dottie I didn't mind.

"LOOK WHO'S HERE!" She singsonged as she walked around the corner downstairs. There was a little entry way of sorts at the bottom of the stairs that led to a garage on the left. Turning right though, that put you in the middle of a quilter's paradise.

The finished basement was divided into two large rooms. In the first room, it looked as if an entire fabric store kept their overflow inventory here in Dottie's house. The walls were lined with six foot tall bookshelves that held nothing but fabric, folded perfectly and stacked according to color family. Stuck in the middle of the room like its own island sat at least a six foot long table that was the 'cutting table'. Self-healing cut mats and rulers were attached to the tabletop ready at a moment's notice to cut pieces or make alterations to patterns.

Instead of table legs, cube storage shelving held up the table top and was stuffed to overflowing with everything from scrap fabric pieces to interfacing to any kind of sewing notions you could imagine. Dottie had always said that buying sewing supplies and actually using them were two different hobbies. She was a master at one and incredible at the other.

The second room had comfy couches lining two walls, and three folding tables put together in the middle of the room. Ladies sat around the edges of the table, hand quilting various projects, some times working on the same one together. The couches were for the friends that didn't quilt but wanted to sit and visit. I had taken many a nap on those couches. Several quilts hung on the walls, a combination of actual wall hangings and real quilts, making the room feel cozy and colorful.

After a quick scan of the room, I said, "What, no snacks today? What kind of quilting group is this?" Everyone saw through my fake outrage and giggled.

"Ladies, you all remember this little thing here! And look what she painted for me!" Dottie was bouncing on her toes like an excited child and I laughed.

"Dot, let that poor girl all the way in the room before you start parading her around to everyone. Mabel, come over here and give me a hug, baby! It's been too long!"

I crossed the room straight into the arms of Betsy Meyers, a founding member of the quartet of best friends that was now a trio. "Still keeping Dottie in check I see?" I breathed quietly as I hugged the woman tightly.

"I heard that." Dottie said.

"Of course you did you old bat, you hear everything. Butt out and let me have my happy reunion moment." Betsy replied with absolutely no venom in her voice. She held me at arms length and sighed. "My how you've grown. I know you're supposed to stop saying that after your little one turns into a full blown adult, but really Mabel, you look incredible. It's so good to see you."

"It's good to see you too, Betsy. I'm sorry it's been so long."

"Oh, none of that." Her eyes went a little glassy and she swatted me toward Nora, who had put her quilting down and was making her way around the massive table to hug me, too.

"It's my Maybe-baby! Oh, you best have a hug for me, too!" She gave me a shockingly strong hug for an older lady and I choked out a laugh at the old nickname. I was not decisive as a toddler, and where other young children would answer a question with a loud, resounding 'yes', 'no', or 'gimmie', my favorite response was always 'maaaaaaybe'. Nora had called me Maybe-baby once and I'd laughed so hard I fell down. After that, the name stuck and sometimes she even just called me Maybe for short.

"Hey, Nora. Still not sewing I see." I glanced over at her little spot on the table and saw that the seam ripper was right on top. It was a running joke that Nora spent more time ripping stitches out than putting them in.

"Well, you know, best to make sure it's perfect. Even if that means redoing a bit or two here and there." Her cheeks pinked, ever the more sensitive of the group. I always wondered how she'd survived being friends with Gram, Betsy, and Dottie for all these years.

"And that's why your quilts are always the best." I whispered, kissing her on the cheek.

I greeted the few other people in the room that looked vaguely familiar with a brief wave and generic "Hi, everyone'. The quilting group didn't really have a set list of members. It was very fluid in who showed up each week and how often they came back. But it was nice to see that the weekly meeting carried on after all these years and they were still having a good time doing it.

"Okay okay, that's enough. Can you pah-lease show them that masterpiece you're hiding now? I just can't stand it, sugar!" Dottie's impatience was mostly put on, but I knew that deep down she was wanting to share the painting with Betsy and Nora and was close to bursting with the surprise.

"Yes, ma'am, I sure can." Crossing to a section of the table that was clean, I pulled the painting from the bag and held it up. The other four ladies in the room oohed and ahhed with various 'that's so pretty' comments, but I was too busy watching Gram's best friends to really notice.

Nora's hands came to cover her mouth, just as Betsy reached

out a hand for Dottie. They stood in their own little huddle and privately relived whatever memory the painting brought up for them, alone in their memories but together in their grief for a lifelong friend.

"Well, I never..." Betsy finally broke their silence and looked at me with wonder on her face. "I don't know how you do it, Mabel. It's like looking at a professional photograph, but with more soul." She went back to studying the painting, shaking her head slowly from side to side.

"This is exceptional, Maybe. So special." Nora had wrapped one arm around Betsy and glanced over her head to Dottie. "I'm jealous." She said.

"As you should be. As anyone should be when they see a custom Mabel Morrison painting." She looked downright smug, and I couldn't hold in the laugh that bubbled up at the looks of indignation on her two friend's faces.

She laughed then, too. "Oh, don't even look at me like that you two. I'd never leave you out of this. Mabel says she can make artist prints from this one, and that way y'all will have a copy too." Dottie had already started to walk away to another member of the quilting group at the table, who was looking particularly frustrated with her paper piecing.

"Well I guess that settles that then?" Betsy chuckled, shaking her head. "Mabel, I would love a copy. I think I know just where I'll put it at home, too. I can't wait!"

"Oh, me too, right by the big window in the dining room where my plants are!" Nora said, clapping her hands. "I've still got a Christmas cactus that your gram gave me when we were in our thirties." She grinned at me and I felt the love from and for these ladies wrap around me. Neither my mother nor father had siblings, so I didn't know the feeling of having lots of family around, but I imagined it must be something like this.

"That's pretty and all, but don't you paint anything normal?" The voice popped my warm fuzzy bubble.

"Bea, I don't know what could be more normal than a cabin. What in the world are you going on about?" Betsy had turned to address a woman that I didn't recognize at the other side of the table. Her quilt was all dark blues and navys and blacks, which could have been very pretty, but somehow it was reading as depressing.

"I just mean, nobody would want that painting but the three of you. Do you paint anything like flowers or animals or something?"

"Now see here..." Betsy somehow grew a couple of inches from her just over five foot frame as she puffed up to defend me. Dottie was the louder, outspoken one of the group, unless someone was attacked. Then Betsy came out swinging before anyone else had processed what had happened. Metaphorically of course.

Well, usually.

"Anyone with an eye for art, color, and composition would want this painting. Just because you can't see the emotional value in it doesn't mean it doesn't have value at all."

I looked over at her, slightly panicked, and tried to smooth out the situation. "It's okay, Betsy. I understand what Ms. Bea is saying. She's just asking if I have anything that might appeal to a wider audience."

"Of course that's what she's saying, Betsy, because Bea here would never insult our Mabel... isn't that right, Bea?" Dottie had chimed in with a steely look in her eye and the other quilters had gone quiet waiting to see what would happen.

"Why of course that's what I meant." Bea huffed. "Just a little sensitive aren't we?"

Deciding to jump in before anyone else could, I answered "Funny you should ask, Ms. Bea, because as a matter of fact I happen to have several new paintings of all different subject matter, colors, and styles." I smiled sweetly at her, but I knew it didn't reach my eyes, and for the first time I wasn't sure if I cared.

"What now? What's this? Are they all commissions? Goodness you have been busy!" Dottie whipped around to face me so fast I felt the breeze from across the room.

"No, actually. These were all just for fun." I gave her a cat-ate-the-canary grin.

Her grin matched mine as she said, "Well, I think I'd really like to come see those, sugar."

"Oh, count me in!" Nora said. "Maybe I'll get me a Mabel Morrison original painting, too." She stuck her tongue out at Dottie behind her back, and I laughed.

Betsy chuckled and said, "Me, too. I'd love to see what you've been up to since you've been back in Painted Creek."

"Sounds like a plan. Y'all just let me know when is good for you and we'll make a date of it!" I turned to address the rest of the room. "If any of you would like to come with these crazy ladies here, I'd be happy to have you." I looked right at Bea as I spoke, but she just 'harumphed' and looked away. Hopefully she wouldn't come, and I'd be able to enjoy the experience without worrying about an octogenarian cat fight.

SIXTEEN

I WAS FINALLY able to sneak out of Dottie's house a couple of hours later. Those ladies could carry on for hours, and they did almost every week, but when I told Dottie I was out of food in the cottage, that instinct to keep me fed kicked in and she sent me on my way.

I did have to go to the grocery store, but I decided to stop in the pet store first. I hadn't stopped thinking about Turtle and Elliott since Monday morning, mostly Turtle of course, and I was anxious to pop in and say hello.

A tiny little bell with the clearest chime rang out as I opened the door to The Pet Parlor. It was your perfect little small town pet store, with everything you would need to care for your furry or scaly or feathered best friend. Small animals like ferrets and hamsters had a focal spot in the middle of the shop and seemed to greet me when I walked in. Just as I rounded the corner to visit the wall of fish on the left hand side of the store, Elliott appeared from the back of the shop.

"Oh, hey, Mabel! What brings you by?" Elliott leaned against the wall that led back to what I assumed was the alley. In jeans and a t-shirt, he really was pulling off the whole care free pet shop owner vibe perfectly.

"Hey," I smiled at him and I could feel my face beginning to turn red as he smiled back and dimples appeared. "I was just out running errands and thought I would stop in and say hello. I came to see Turtle, of course. Is she available?" Batting my eyelashes at him, I clasped my hands together in front of me and scrunched up my shoulders, trying to be cute.

"Oh, you wound me. And so soon after stopping by, too." His fake pout was possibly cuter than his dimples.

"Kidding. I wanted to say hello, and if you were serious about wanting a painting, I didn't want to keep you waiting. We didn't really set up a firm meeting time to discuss it. I hope it's okay that I stopped in." Suddenly, I felt unsure. I could feel the slight sheen of sweat across my forehead as my nerves began to get the best of me. "Actually, it's pretty presumptuous of me, I'm sorry. I'll let you get back to your day."

"Hey, don't do that. I'm glad you stopped by." He walked toward me and put his hand on my shoulder. "I would've been asking Dottie about you soon if you hadn't." Nothing but sincerity shone from his blue eyes, and I relaxed a tiny bit under his gaze. He smiled and said, "Plus Turtle would be so sad if she found out you'd stopped by and didn't say hello. Come on, I'll show you where she stays... when she's not out looking for watermelon that is."

He headed back down the hallway he had just come from, and I followed behind trying to take everything in. There was what looked to be an office on the right, a door to the alley that was propped open at the end of the hall, and a staircase to the left.

"Do you live upstairs?" The question was out of my mouth before my brain caught up, and I cringed. "I'm sorry, that was very forward of me and I shouldn't have asked. It's just that Sarah and

Becca live above the coffee shop and all these buildings are set up similarly so I just assumed..." I trailed off, and when I finally looked up I realized he was looking at me, slightly confused.

"Why do you do that?" he asked.

"Do what?"

"Immediately assume you've behaved inappropriately or need to apologize?"

"I... I don't think I've behaved inappropriately, just maybe not professionally." I frowned. It was good to appear professional, right?

"Do you always have to be professional, Mabel?" He kind of jolted back then, as if a new realization had physically hit him. "Unless of course you really are only here for a painting commission. Which is fine, don't get me wrong, I want a painting for the shop for sure. I just kind of thought... uh well..." Now *he* was back pedaling and stammering. Maybe it was contagious.

"Ugh. Let's try this again. Hey Elliott, I noticed the staircase, do you also have a second floor in your building or is it a roof top garden?"

A shy smile stole across his face. "No roof top garden I'm afraid. But I do have a potted basil in my kitchen, which is on the second floor of this building. Does that count?"

"It absolutely does. And basil happens to be a new favorite of mine."

"Well, now that that's cleared up, come see Turtle." He pushed open the door to the alley, only it wasn't really an alley anymore. Behind his shop was a full blown tortoise retreat, complete with cameras pointing down at the enclosure and the back door of the store. The shop next door, now my shop I realized abruptly, still had an accessible alleyway that was empty. Next to that, I saw a small patio set and sidewalk chalk drawings on the pavement. Sarah and Becca obviously used their alley as a kind of outdoor living space.

Looking back to Elliott I asked, "Y'all don't need to use the alley? I guess I don't know a ton about owning a business in a brick and mortar building. I've always run my business online."

Cue the small internal panic. How was it that I now owned the next two shop buildings and I didn't even know if they needed alley access. I'd have to add it to my list I guess. But only if I planned to keep them I suppose. I shook my head, trying to clear it and stay in the moment. I was getting ahead of myself.

"Not really. Since my store is an end, my supply trucks can still wheel in the carts with boxes on them. I've made sure to keep enough space to get to the door. The next store is empty and has been for quite some time. Sarah gets most of her supplies in through the front door since it's never really anything big. We all just have our own systems I guess." He shrugged like it was no big deal, and I guess it really wasn't. At least not to a normal person who didn't freak out about suddenly owning a building or two.

"Oh." Weak response. But my brain was otherwise occupied with the downward mental spiral I created for myself. I tried to pull it together, and what better way than to pet a giant tortoise. I turned to look in her enclosure and saw her munching on some lettuce.

"Hi, Turtle! Nice to see you again." Turtle didn't seem to care that I was there, so I turned back to the other human in the alley, who was watching me.

"What?"

"Nothing. Just nice to see someone else talk to her too," he replied.

"Oh. Well. Actually maybe don't celebrate too soon. I've also been talking to a hedgehog shaped lamp since I got into town..." His mouth dropped open slightly in surprise before he grinned. "And now I just look crazy. That's nice. Can we go back to me talking to your tortoise?"

"Nope. Not a chance. Tell me about this lamp? Does it talk back?" His eyes sparkled with humor and I almost didn't mind that he was making fun of me. That was a first.

"No. Hedgie is more of the strong, silent type." I crossed my arms and looked away, trying to seem aggravated but I couldn't fully stop the grin that was fighting for control of my face.

"Oh, he has a name too, does he?"

"Hey, how'd you know he was a he?!" I was giggling now, and it felt nice to be silly with someone.

"Lucky guess. But seriously, it's nice to see how you act with Turtle. She's just a tortoise, sure, but she's still my pet and a living thing."

"Of course she is. I guess tortoises don't come across as typical fuzzy pet material. Especially one her size. Did you know in some places it's even illegal to have them as pets?"

"Is that more useless artist research knowledge?" He'd remembered what I'd said a couple of days ago.

"Yep. But judging by the look on your face it seems like maybe there's a story there for you..."

He looked back at the tortoise and just watched her for a few moments. When he started to talk, I couldn't help but lean closer, drawn into the story and the man telling it.

"I guess there is a story there. And it's the shop's origin story, too." He leaned against the side of the building and watched Turtle walk around her enclosure, body angled toward mine to include me in the story without actually looking at me.

"I think I've already told you I was a zoo keeper once. I loved my job. I mean what animal lover wouldn't, right? Getting to be around these magnificent creatures of all kinds and cultivate special relationships with them. But none of them were as special as Turtle...

"For whatever reason, she and I bonded. I was obviously her favorite keeper, and really who could blame her," he threw a teasing wink my way, "but I loved her back just as much. Then my mom got sick, and I decided the right thing to do was to quit my job at the zoo and move home to help my dad. They're both a little older, had me a little later in life, and my dad was lost without my mom running their lives." He smiled a sad smile, the mixture of a fondness for his parents and the hard memories of her illness.

"So I said goodbye to Turtle and all the other animals and people and moved back here to Painted Creek. I'd been gone about six months when a good friend from the zoo called me and said they were canceling the tortoise exhibit to make room for some big expansion with 'more exciting animals'." The air quotes weren't necessary as the disdain dripped from his voice.

I gasped in, only slightly put on, outrage. "Rude! Turtle is perfectly exciting! Just look at her!" Turtle took one... single... slow... step as if to back up my claims of excitement. I frowned. "Well... solidarity sister. I'm not exciting either." Glancing up at Elliott, I waved one hand in a small circle. "Continue, please."

A crooked grin had him looking down right sinfully delicious, leaning against the wall the way he was. At some point, I had come to rest on the wall beside him, close enough he was looking down at me slightly. He closed his eyes and with a small shake of his head, he finished his story.

"Well, in certain cases, when animal exhibits are deleted from a zoo, a zoo keeper can petition to care for the animals themselves. I knew I wanted to keep Turtle... there was no telling where she would end up otherwise. I told my friend on the phone to start the application paperwork for me there at the zoo, and I would work on things here to have a place to keep Turtle permanently. There are more permits required than you might imagine to own and transport exotic or wild animals. But I hired Mr. Findley and we made a plan."

My fingers started to tingle. I stood up straighter as the frisson worked its way up my arms and down my spine, and a picture started to form in my head. I saw it clearly, maybe more vividly than the others I'd had recently, but it didn't make any sense. Elliott must have interpreted my change in posture as investment in his story, because he started talking a little faster, gesturing with his arms as he spoke.

"At the time I was renting this tiny little cabin. I'd wanted my own space instead of staying with my parents when I moved back. There was no way I could create a temporary habitat there for Turtle, so I knew I would have to move also. Mr. Findley came up with the idea to let Turtle be an ambassador animal; people could come and learn more about her species and interact with her a little bit. Opening a business of some kind seemed to be the best way to do that and have some sort of steady income at the same time. After all, Turtle is cute, but she's not cheap."

"No woman is. Then what happened?" I circled my hand in the air again, slightly faster this time, urging him to continue. The more of his story he told me, the clearer the picture in my head became.

"I liked the idea, and decided a pet shop would fit into Painted Creek nicely. Everyone had been driving over to Asheville for the specialty items they needed and couldn't find at the grocery store here. It felt like a pet store would allow me to continue helping animals and the people that cared for them, just in a different way than I had at the zoo.

"I had a reasonable little nest egg saved up, so I began looking for something close to town that would work as a business and home for Turtle. Mr. Findley called me one night, so excited about a building he'd heard had just been listed. It was in my price point and had a lovely apartment on the second floor, so I would be saving the money I was currently paying on rent too. Fast forward through all the blood-sweat-and-tears parts, and here we are. The pet shop brings in a somewhat steady income, tourists are thrilled for an 'exotic' animal experience right here in town, and most importantly, Turtle has a forever home."

Turtle had wandered over to us at her measured, tortoise pace. She head butted Elliott in the leg, as if she'd understood the story and was thankful for everything he had done to bring them together again and give her a good home.

"That's amazing. You must really have a special bond." I leaned down and scratched Turtle's shell. "And you, you didn't tell me you were a celebrity! The famous Turtle the tortoise, animal ambassador of Painted Creek." She raised her head higher, as if to keep up an imaginary crown, and I laughed.

"Oh, don't make her ego any bigger than it is. She'll demand the good treats in her next contract negotiation." He smiled down at me, a full on mega-watt smile, which caused my face to fall as tension to pull my shoulders in tight.

"Hey, what's wrong? I'm kidding of course, she gets the good treats now."

"That. That's what's wrong. I mean not that you do that, it's actually wonderful, but that you're not being weird about it. About me."

He blinked a few times. "Mabel, I'm going to need you to use full sentences please."

"Pretty sure all of that could be considered proper English."

"Deflecting."

"Ugh." I huffed out air through my nose and looked at the ground. He just patiently waited me out while I tried to sort what exactly I wanted to say. "I love the witty banter... the silly stories, the embellishing reality. But I've never had the opportunity to talk with anyone else like this. In the off chance that I ever did play around like this, people would just look at me like I was weird or unstable. Or, at least they did. I was taught early there was a certain way to interact with others, to behave in public, to project myself to the world. And then once I really grew a client base and a following in the art community it became even more important, my public persona. I guess it's just nice to be myself for a change and have that accepted without question or judgment."

I could feel him study me, and I was in no hurry to look up or hear his response. He reached out a hand and lifted my chin.

"I'd never want you to act like anything you aren't. I think I like the girl who looks after escaped tortoises, talks to lamps, and embellishes reality a little." His thumb was gently tracing my jaw, and I couldn't think of a response. I couldn't think of anything.

He stepped back suddenly, and his shoulder bumped into the wall and jostled him, and I giggled. He shook his head and sighed, looking chagrined.

"Come on, say goodbye to Turtle and we'll go in the store and talk about what I'd like for the painting."

"Goodbye, Miss Turtle. I'll come see you again soon." She blinked up at me with her big, luminous tortoise eyes and I decided that meant she wanted to see me again, too. I turned away and followed Elliott back inside.

WE WALKED BACK through the store to the front counter and I looked around a little more closely than I had when I arrived. The shop seemed to be organized like your standard pet shop; dog, cat, small animals, aquatic and exotic. Instead of items being lined up on shelves in neat little rows, there were stacks of bins in neat lines along the aisles, and the items for sale were all piled into the bins.

"I like the bin system. Makes me feel like I'm digging for a prize instead of just picking something off the shelf." The tingles in my fingers returned gently, and suddenly the painting in my head made sense and I smiled.

He smiled back at me, but it was small and somewhat bashful, which didn't make much sense to me but was adorable all the same. "Thanks. It works." He moved behind the counter and pulled out some paper. "Let's talk about this painting. What do you need from me?" Randomly evasive. Filing that away for later...

"Well, filling me in on what you'd like the subject of the painting to be is always a good place to start." I smiled sweetly and twisted side to side. I wasn't sarcastic or baiting often, Mother had drilled into me that it was rude and would make my customers feel as if I didn't actually care about their business, but I felt safe with Elliott and knew that he would just snark right back.

"Har har. Also, good point. I think I would like to have the store front, maybe with the sidewalk but not the street or the building next to it. And then, down in a corner as a little bubble or something somehow, Turtle's enclosure. I don't really know how that would come together..." He trailed off and frowned, staring at the paper with his very precise rectangle and circle that I think was supposed to represent the building and Turtle's space.

Suppressing my giggle at his look of concentration, I said, " It's okay, it's my job to figure that part out. It'll be great."

"Great." The wrinkles between his eyebrows smoothed out and he relaxed against the counter, leaning toward me. It would be a great painting, and I loved the idea of having Turtle's enclosure overlayed on top of the building, as if it represented that she was the main focus behind the whole place. But I couldn't let go of the picture that I'd seen in my mind as he was telling me his story. I still didn't understand it or how it had anything to do with the pet store, or Elliott. Maybe I'd paint it just to get it out of my head...

"Let me just take some reference photos before I go. I've really cut back on the number of projects I'm agreeing to right now, Mr. Findley says I'm on an artist retreat, so I should be able to get it done by this weekend probably." I was walking away as I was talking, and had already reached the back door to the alley.

Punching through, I snapped a couple of quick pictures from all angles of the whole alley and Turtle's fancy set up. Before I went back inside, I got a few close ups of Turtle herself. Scratching her shell one more time I said, "I promise I'll make you look good, gorgeous girl." She kept munching on her greens, uninterested in my promise. "You weren't worried were you? You know you're the prettiest tortoise in town. Love the confidence, Turtle!" I blew her a kiss and went back inside.

I was making a bee line for the front door for more pictures when Elliott called out, "Hey Mabel, I was thinking...."

"Hold on, let me snap these pictures real quick. Be right back!" I walked right by the counter and out the front door without ever slowing down. When I came back in, he was shaking his head.

"What?" I asked, finally stilling.

"Nothing. Only just, you know the outside of the building would've still been there when you left, right?" He was teasing me, but I could feel my cheeks turning red anyway.

"Oh, well, you're right of course, I'm sorry. I guess I was just excited about the project." I fidgeted with my bag strap and frowned when I realized the seam was unraveling. Again. "I go through more bags..." I said under my breath.

"What?" He cocked his head to the side and was looking at me, amusement apparent on his face.

"Nothing. Anyway. Um, I have all the pictures I need and like I said I should be able to have it done by the weekend. I can bring it by Monday morning, if you'd like." Suddenly, the floor was the most interesting thing in here, and I was giving it all my attention to avoid looking at Elliott after I'd embarrassed myself.

"About that, uh, instead of Monday, do you think Saturday is doable? And then, ah, maybe I could get it from you when I take you home from dinner?"

My head snapped up. "Dinner?"

"Yes."

"With you? And me?"

"Well, Turtle doesn't have very good table manners, so yes, with me. And you." He gave me a full, bright smile again, and as distracting as his dimples were I could read the apprehension behind his eyes.

"Elliott..." I saw him flinch ever so slightly and rushed to get out a whole sentence. "It's not that I don't want to, I would love to go on a date with you. I enjoy our conversations. It's just that I don't think I'm staying in town long term. I mean I'm not really living here permanently and I don't know if it's a good idea to get involved with someone when I'm not staying. Probably not staying. I mean, I don't think I can stay. Ugh I don't know what I'm doing with my life and I don't want to drag someone else into that!"

I stopped. My eyes widened slightly and I just looked at Elliott. To his credit, he didn't look ready to run away from the crazy woman that just spewed a bunch of verbal nonsense all over his counter. So there was that.

"Well, somewhere in all of that I think you were trying to tell me you were apprehensive about getting involved with someone when you didn't know where you would be in say, six months?"

I just nodded, eyes even wider. Best to keep my mouth shut. Forever probably.

"Just dinner, Mabel. I understand anything more might feel like a commitment you aren't prepared for. I'd just like to spend more time with you. I promise not to ask for your five year plan or anything. I just want to get to know *you*."

I still looked like a fish out of water, mouth gaping open and closed and all. I snapped my mouth shut finally, and nodded once. The smile he sent in my direction in response was next level, the same bright dimpled smile from a moment ago but all the anxiety was gone from his eyes. *I'm in so much trouble,* I thought to myself.

"Great! Here's my number. Text me so I have yours, and I'll pick you up from the cottage at seven on Saturday."

I blinked at him. He blinked at me.

Shaking my head like an Etch-a-Sketch, I reached for the paper he had slid across the counter. I sent him a quick text with my name, mostly to have something to do with my hands and to prolong having to, you know, speak.

His phone pinged and his smile grew even more confident. He typed out something, and a second later, my phone pinged.

See you at seven on Saturday. I can't wait.

"I'll... I'll call you if I have any questions about the painting. See you later, Elliott." I all but stumbled into the door in my haste to leave. I heard him call out, "Bye, Mabel," to my back as I practically ran to my car, eager to put distance between me and the possibilities swirling in the air of The Pet Parlor.

SEVENTEEN

I RAN ALL the errands I needed in record time. There really was something to be said for small towns. Everything in Painted Creek was so close together I was done and pulling into the drive at the cottage in the same amount of time it would've taken me to make one stop in Columbus. The change of pace was nice.

Unloading everything and putting the groceries away didn't take long either, and by the time I'd made a small lunch and cleaned up, I still had half of the day left. I glanced at the dining room, itching to sketch out Elliott's painting and the vision I'd had while in his shop. Lucky for me, it was still clear as day in my mind. I wasn't afraid the details would fade before I could get them down like I had been with other frisson paintings in the past.

I knew that once I got started, I would easily lose track of time, so I decided to call Mother and check in first. I groaned out loud when I realized I'd have to reschedule our Facetime dinner on Saturday. That was not going to go over well...

She answered on the second ring. "Hello, darling. How are you?"

"Good, Mom. Just thought I would check in and say hello. How are things at home?" I heard myself say home, and it struck me that Columbus didn't quite feel that way anymore. Maybe it was just my record breaking shopping trip, but Painted Creek had grown on me even more during the day today.

It had absolutely nothing to do with dimples or tortoises. Nope. It was the lack of traffic, I was sure.

"Oh, just the same as always dear, just the way I like it you know." She chuffed, not exactly a laugh, but I think it was meant to be.

I decided chatting about menial things for as long as possible was the way to go. As soon as someone brought up my business here in Painted Creek I had a feeling that I wouldn't want to talk much longer. After only about five minutes or so, she finally asked.

"So are you almost done wrapping things up there? I found the cutest little house for you and it's only about five minutes away from my house! Isn't that amazing? It even has a little Florida room that would be perfect for a studio space, that is if the pictures in the listing are accurate. You know how those things can be. Like a bad dating profile, but for houses..."

"Mom, what would you know about a bad dating profile?!" I was giggling but I wondered, not for the first time, if Mother was as happy with her 'same as always' life as she claimed to be.

"Oh, well, it's just a saying you know. Catfishing and all the things they warn you about. Anyway, Mabel, that's not the point. Should I schedule a walk through of this house? I don't expect it to be on the market for long you know. This neighborhood is such a desirable area. And it would be so nice to have you closer permanently."

My stomach tightened at the thought of moving back to Ohio. That was always the plan originally of course, to come here just long enough to sort things out and then move back into a place that was more 'me'. But as I looked around Gram's house with all the new furniture and old memories I wondered if I would ever find a place more me than this.

"Mabel, are you listening?" I had zoned out I guess and now Mother's tone was exasperated.

"Yes, Mother, of course. I was just thinking." I took a deep breath. "It's going to be a little longer here than I originally anticipated. There is some other, unexpected real estate that I have to get sorted, and I'm still not settled on what I want to do with Gram's house. You should see it, Mom. So much has been redone but so much is still the same. It's comforting really."

The complete silence on the other end of the phone prompted me to keep rambling.

"Plus, I've painted more this week than I have in the last three months. There was a slight break in my approved commissions list so I've been doing some other things and it's been really good for my creativity and focus. I'll send you a picture of a commission I just did and I swear it looks like the horse is actually breathing." I purposefully left out the other styles of painting that I'd been playing around with. She would see them eventually, but it didn't feel like now was a good time to bring it up.

"That's all well and good, Mabel, but don't forget about your local customer base here. And by moving closer I can help you with the packaging and shipping and save you some time so you have more time to paint. Just like old times." She grew quiet again and underneath the slight snarky tone, I swore I heard sadness.

"I know, Mother. I think I'll be at least another week here. I just don't want to leave until I feel like I have considered all my options and I've done what's best for Gram's legacy and my future. But I promise I'll let you know as soon as everything is settled. And if it will make you feel better, go ahead and go on a walk through of the house you found. But don't make any promises!"

I always hated leaving a conversation with my mom when I felt like she was sad. It wouldn't hurt anything to get more information on the house she'd found. Who knows, maybe it was perfect like she said, and then maybe I wouldn't feel so torn leaving Painted Creek and I could go back to being close by for her.

"I think that's smart, dear, which is why I already set up the walk through for Saturday. I'll have to reschedule our Facetime dinner, but I'll send pictures when I go. Stay safe, Mabel."

"I will, Mom. You, too. Love you."

"Love you, too."

We hung up, and I looked around Gram's house, sort of dazed for a minute.

"Well... at least I didn't cancel dinner. Ugh."

I felt a little like I'd been hit by a steamroller, as I often did with Mother, and I flopped belly first onto the couch with a huff. I had a few commissioned paintings left on my list, Elliott's painting, and Mr. Findley's gift to finish, but the mood to paint was gone. I glanced at the book on the end table that Heather had left for me.

"Side quest," I murmured, pushing off the couch and shuffling to the tea cupboard in the pantry. I looked longingly at Gram's blends, but settled for pulling out a hibiscus tea bag from a box in the corner. I decided it was the perfect time to curl up on the couch with one of the blankets I'd found the other day and flip through the book.

Luckily, the book was an interesting and well written read. There were things that I remembered from school and some new information too on the different processes for making your own natural inks. Some were simple and some were incredibly involved with a lot of materials that I didn't have already. As I placed my now empty mug on the end table, a zing went through my arm. Almost like the tingles I get from a painting inspiration, but closer to a shock from static electricity. I looked at the tea bag and the beautiful, deep pink color of the small amount of tea left in the bottom of the mug. Grabbing the mug and the book, I sauntered into the kitchen to experiment. *Side quest win*, I thought with a smile.

About an hour later, I had my first herbal ink. It was a little weak in color since I used the same tea bag I had used to make my tea, but it was enough to play with without feeling like I was being wasteful. I plopped down at the dining room table and stared at the

140

blank page of watercolor paper I had taped down to my mat.

"Well Hedgie, here goes nothing…"

Another hour or so later, I sat staring at a finished monochrome painting of a night sky with the Strawberry Full Moon. My first painting since school using natural inks.

"This is so freaking cool! To the fridge!" I laughed at myself, putting this painting on the fridge with the painting of Hedgie, like my own private art exhibit. But I was definitely keeping both of these forever. And I was without a doubt going to make more natural ink paintings.

I caught the time on the clock on the oven and realized the day was almost gone again. After a quick meal, I decided a stroll in the yard was a good way to stretch my muscles after sitting still all day before I started on Elliott's paintings. I'd decided to paint him two; the one he had ordered and the frisson vision. I had a lot to do in the next two days.

KITCHEN ALL CLEAN and paint supplies ready for the next project, I took my stroll around the yard. It really was beautiful in the layout and thriving plants, and I thought again about needing to hire someone to help me keep it all alive and happy. The twilight sky painted everything in rosey tones, and a warm happiness washed over me with each deep breath in the open air of the back yard.

Walking slowly along the edge of the creek, I wandered to the swing and ran my fingers across the ropes as I passed over to the other side. It was slightly more over grown here than the house side of the creek. Though still thoughtfully laid out, there was barely a walking path between the landscaping and the woods. I finally came across the hanging vines that I now knew hid the herb garden Gram cared for herself. I wondered if whatever company I found to maintain the yard would teach me how to care for the herb garden so I could do it myself, too. Parting the vines in the middle with one hand, I stepped inside and was met with a shriek.

"Mabel! You scared the tar out of me!" Charlotte was standing on the other side of the spiral raised bed with a hand to her chest and an over turned basket of clipped herbs at her feet. After the initial shock of hearing a scream wore off, I was laughing. After a beat, she was laughing too, although it seemed more like how a mother would laugh at the antics of their toddler, placating while still full of love.

"Boo-yah! Who's the ninja now?" A huge, self satisfied smile split my face in two as I danced around the raised bed toward her. "Here, let me help you pick all this back up. I'm sorry I startled you, although, what is it they say about turn about and fair play?" I tapped my chin as if thinking, but I couldn't quite smother my smile while doing it. I wasn't a very good actress.

Charlotte chuckled, "Fair, and thanks for the help. What brings you out here this fine evening?"

"Just a stroll. A good stretch before I sit down to paint again. What about you? What are you gathering for tonight?" The smell of rosemary was strong in the air, although I didn't see any rosemary clippings in her basket. I must have brushed it when I bent down to help pick up the clippings. Standing and brushing my hands together, I started running my fingers over various herbs in the circle while waiting for her answer.

"A little of this, a little of that. Thanks again for letting me continue to use the herbs. I've been using this herb garden a long time."

"Oh, don't mention it again. I'm truly happy for you to use the garden, and I'm glad someone is keeping an eye on it honestly. Someone is going to have to teach me to care for it properly if I stay here. I can hire a crew for the rest of the yard, but this I'd like to care for myself."

"If you stay. Hmm… this isn't a permanent relocation then?" She was moving among the plants like they were old friends, and I guess to her, they were. If I didn't know she was talking to me, it would seem as if she was carrying on a conversation with them instead.

"It wasn't meant to be. I was coming to stay a week or so and make sure Gram's estate was handled properly. It ended up being a little more involved than I expected though, so I'm staying a bit longer now. And I've really missed Painted Creek. It's been nice to be back."

She made a noncommittal noise and kept running her hands through the plants, and it almost seemed to me that the plants reached out for her touch as if they were as fond of her as she was of them. Various earthy smells floated through the air each time she did, and I started to feel myself settle, the pent up energy in my muscles from painting all afternoon dissolving into a pleasant warmth under my skin.

"Anyway, I'm glad you're here. I want to tell you thank you for the nudge to try and paint something just for fun. I went in that night and have practically re-wallpapered the whole house with new paintings." I smiled at her warmly and waited as she rounded the last stretch of flower bed to stand in front of me again.

"Well, I'll be. Must've been good for the soul then."

"I think you're right. I actually spent this afternoon painting with a homemade ink of sorts from my leftover hibiscus tea." I laughed when she straightened from the flower she was inspecting and scrunched her eyebrows. "Crazy right? One of the ladies in town gave me a book on natural inks after the impromptu coffee painting. I was reading it while I had an afternoon tea and thought I'd just try it out."

"So what I'm hearing is you only paint with leftover beverages now. How niche." Her eyes twinkled and I knew she was teasing though the rest of her face gave nothing away.

"Yep. My branding will be something like 'spill the tea and paint'." I waved one hand over my head like reading a banner and giggled. "Although, that sounds more like a gossip group than a recycled beverage artist..." I frowned slightly, and shrugged.

Charlotte rolled her eyes and said, "Have you made your own inks before?"

"We had to do a small project in school, but I haven't since then. I always got more consistent, realistic results with commercial paints, and that's always been my thing. So. Yeah." I wasn't sure why, but I was feeling... regretful? Nostalgic? Anxious? Something, I was feeling something about narrowing my art style so much over the years. I'd really had so much fun the last few days experimenting again, branching back out.

"You know," Charlotte's voice startled me as she gestured to the flowers she'd been messing with, "once upon a time, chamomile was used to make dye for fabrics. I bet you could make a pretty ink with it. Feel free to make a tea and drink it first of course. Don't want to mess up your branding." She smirked and then sobered and looked me dead in the eye. "But sometimes we find where we're really meant to be when we shake up where we've always been."

She turned and snipped a few sprigs of chamomile and handed them to me. "Here, this one needed a little trim anyway. And now you can practice. There's no rule that says you can't do more than one thing you know. Paint your photograph styles with the fancy commercial paints and then paint another style with your fancy homemade paints. Do both. Do you."

As I reached for the tiny white and yellow cut flowers, I said, "Thank you. I think I will give it a try. And I'll skip the tea step this time."

As she started to part the vines and leave, I called out, "Hey, Charlotte? Did Gram teach you how to care for the herbs here when you would come for some to use in your soaps?"

She looked back over her shoulder, and the scent of roses blew in through the crack in the vines, no doubt being carried on the breeze from the big bushes up closer to the house.

"You could say that I suppose. Why do you ask?"

"Do you think you could teach me how to care for the herb garden?"

She cocked her head to the side and regarded me for a minute before asking, "You mean if you stay, of course?"

I blushed, feeling like I'd been caught by my mother in a lie when I was a child. "Right, of course. If I stay."

"Well, I say we just cross that bridge when we get to it. I best be going now though. See you again soon, Mabel." She slipped through the vines and was gone before I could call out my own goodbye.

I looked down at the chamomile in my hands and decided that

even if I didn't stay in Painted Creek permanently, I was going to take these new painting styles with me into my future projects. Maybe some life lessons, too. With one more deep breath of fragrant air and a last look around the garden, I walked through the vines, letting them pull at me as I passed into the yard, beckoning me to stay. I'd spend some more time out here soon, but for now, I had ink to make.

I'D NEVER BEEN a wasteful person. Even as a kid, if there was a little bit of paint left in the pot, I would try and create something with it instead of throwing it out. Every plain scrap of paper was saved for color swatching or notes. Leftover food was saved and eaten later. Trash was recycled in some way. It was just part of who I was naturally.

Sometimes, it could cause me some trouble though, like when I had so much scrap paper I couldn't find the good paper. Or when I had so many tiny pots of paint left I'd have to spend entire days recreating them into a single color so that I could throw away ten containers that were only five percent full.

This was absolutely one of those times. I had made a few of my own inks and was so excited to sit and paint with them I almost couldn't stand it. There was an entire shelf in the refrigerator that now held nothing but little tiny bottles of homemade natural inks. The bottles themselves were a huge find, shoved in the back corner of the laundry room cabinet. Complete with corks and the perfect size, I had squealed when I found them, scooped them up, and ran to the kitchen so fast I clipped the corner of the island with my hip on the way by, almost dropping them all. I absentmindedly rubbed the new bruise while I stared at the current mess on the kitchen counter.

The easiest way to make a homemade ink with minimal ingredients is sort of the same process as making a reduction for cooking or baking. A mixture of plant matter and water is simmered at low heat for a long time and strained, creating a hyper pigmented ink. While I was waiting on the ink, I even had time to coat a few pieces of water color paper in an alum solution, so that the natural inks would be more color fast on the paper. They would be dry by the time the inks were finished. The whole process went off without a hitch. Until I got to the straining part.

The strained left overs were mushy, and most of the color had leached out into the water, but I still couldn't bring myself to throw away the flowers and materials that I had strained off of the ink. Since I had made a few, the chamomile, a lavender, one with avocado pit which I did throw out, one from rose petals, and even one from a blue pea flower tea I had found in the pantry, I now had four bowls of spent plant matter lined up across the counter.

"Just throw it away, Mabel. Really, what are you going to do with it?" I sounded like my mother, which may have had the opposite effect than I wanted from my little pep talk, because now I just wanted to find a way to use it even more. After staring at the bowls a little longer, I put lids on them all and put them in the refrigerator, too. I'd Google it later.

I grabbed all my new inks and headed over to the dining room table to paint. I sat down and glanced at the clean white paper taped to the mat. "It's mocking me, Hedgie... taped down in all its clean blankness..." I was outright glaring at the paper now. I decided to try another little trick we had learned in school. Sometimes facing a plain piece of paper when you didn't know what you wanted to paint caused the painter's equivalent of writer's block. Nothing felt good enough for that pristine piece of crisp, white paper. So, you dirtied it up first to take some of the creative pressure off.

I brushed blobs of color across the paper, leaving pale purple splotches from the lavender ink without really any thought about where or what or why. The color swirled over the paper, and like a switch was flipped, I wasn't stumped on what to paint anymore. After a few layers of pale to dark pink from the avocado and rose petal inks, streaks of yellow from the chamomile ink and a blue background from the blue pea flower ink, I had a beautiful sunrise skyline painting. It looked like a hazy dream, and I loved the whimsical feel of the whole thing.

Now that I was on a roll, I taped the next paper off into four sections so I could experiment more with the inks and have four smaller paintings when I was done. Before I knew it, I had four distinctly different paintings, a firm grasp of what I could accomplish with my homemade inks, and a big smile on my face.

"Well folks, I think that's a wrap for tonight." I stood from the table and stretched, finally aware of just how long I had been sitting at the table without moving much at all. Shaking out my hands, sometimes my fingers threatened to go numb from holding the paintbrush for so long, I cleaned up my paint supplies and put the inks back in the refrigerator before walking around and closing up the house for the night. As I walked by Gram's door I stopped, noticing that it was now practically half way open.

"I get it. I'm just not ready yet, okay? I'll go in soon. Probably. Maybe." There was no reply from the quiet house, so I slowly turned and went to bed.

EIGHTEEN

THE LAST TWO days had passed much like Wednesday evening had, in a haze of paint, ink, and happiness. I had found my stride with the natural inks and felt like I was really flourishing by having an outlet for the crazy creativity I had been keeping somewhat locked down while doing all my commissioned paintings.

And speaking of commissions, I had even finished two more paintings off of the list and accepted three more from the requests on my website. The finished portraits were beautiful, and I was proud of the details in both of them. Maybe even more so than normal, since I also had some very loosely structured paintings to compare them to now.

Sometimes, when you get so used to seeing something every

day, you stop appreciating it. Having this wide variety of art styles scattered all over the house had allowed to me appreciate my gift for hyper realism again. And that was a gift in and of itself.

My Amazon packages had arrived earlier in the day and the embarrassing number of boxes were now piled along the wall in the dining room, waiting for me to make sense of the chaos. That was a material gift, and a logistical nightmare.

Luckily, both paintings for Elliott had gone smoothly, and I couldn't wait to give them to him. Every time I thought about him seeing the surprise painting, my stomach erupted in butterflies. He would be the first one, since I was a teenager, to get a painting from me that wasn't hyper realistic and I was anxious. Excited, but anxious.

Elliott had been texting me on and off since I stopped by the pet shop on Wednesday, and it was nice. The easy banter we had in person flowed into our texts, and I found myself actually looking forward to spending some more time with him, at least until I thought about it too hard. I was still concerned about getting too attached when I wasn't staying in town permanently.

Because really, I couldn't stay here permanently! Every time I found myself thinking of the cottage as home, I thought about not being near Mom and it made me queasy. It had been just the two of us for so long. We have only had each other for most of my life, and I wasn't sure I could put so much physical distance between us.

Before I knew it, the day was gone and I was packing up Elliott's paintings in my tote bag. I smiled to myself as I remembered our text conversation yesterday. I'd panicked momentarily that he wouldn't be able to find the cottage to pick me up, to which he responded, "Mabel, everyone knows how to get to Constance's house. I'll see you at seven."

I wish I could have been around more to see all these people come in to visit with Gram. I did like knowing she wasn't always alone, but it didn't ease the ache of not being there to see her interact with all the people that loved her almost as much as I did. Before I could chase that train of thought all the way down, a knock sounded at the front door, replacing my melancholy with a fresh wave of nerves.

"Here goes nothing..." I murmured shakily as I quickly walked to the door. With one last deep breath, and a smoothing of my dress, I opened the door.

To a face full of flowers. Seriously, flowers everywhere. He must have had the bouquet pushed against the door, or it really was just such a huge bouquet that it took up the entire porch. Probably both. I gasped and took a step back, holding the door a little wider. At the sound, his blue eyes finally appeared over the top of the bouquet, twinkling in delight at my response.

"Hey..." I finally managed to squeak out.

"Hey to you, too. You look lovely, Mabel." I could feel his quick full body glance, and I was thankful that I had bothered to pull this dress out of the bottom of all my packed clothes. It was a sage green that complimented my chocolate brown hair well. It was so breezy and soft without looking slouchy that it was one of my favorites. Although my hair always kind of did whatever it wanted, I did have my make up done at a date worthy level, and sparkly rose pink toenails peeked through my strappy sandals.

"Thank you. You look... flowery."

He laughed and held the bouquet out to the side. "And now?" The twinkle in his eyes said he already knew my answer; the Henley t-shirt he had on was doing him all kinds of favors. I liked that he'd worn nice jeans and not anything dressier. It was easier to think of this as two friends getting to know each other than as a date. I needed to keep telling myself that.

"Ah yes, you look human now. Very good." I gave him a cheeky smile and gestured for him to come in the house.

He narrowed his eyes and said, "Hmm... I'll take it. These are for you."

The bouquet really was stunning. Flowers of all shapes and sizes came together in a riot of color. It was so wild it shouldn't have worked, but it did, and I loved it.

"These are very beautiful, Elliott. Thank you. You didn't need to do that though. Let me just put them in some water." I turned to the kitchen and started rustling around for a vase. "You can go introduce yourself to Hedgie. He's in the dining room."

The grin he gave me as he moved farther into the house showed both dimples, and I'm sure my answering grin just looked goofy. He moved slowly through the dining room and I knew he was sneaking a look at all the paintings that were, well, everywhere. He finally got around to the bar cart under the window and regarded the little hedgehog with more interest than was strictly necessary for a lamp.

"Nice to meet you, Hedgie. You're quite bright." I giggled from the doorway and he looked up to see me watching him. "I can see why you're taken with him. He's cute, I'll give you that."

Giggling again I shrugged. "I know… it's a little unhinged. But when I get all caught up painting, sometimes I don't talk to another human for days. He keeps me company." He looked between me and the lamp a few times, considering what I'd said.

"Must get a little lonely though. Unless he's started talking back?" He raised an eyebrow and waited.

"Still the strong silent type. I'll let you know if that ever changes though. You ready?" He gestured for me to go first, and locking the door behind us, we headed out for the evening.

ELLIOTT STAYED TO hold my door open for me, and then jogged around to the drivers side of his SUV. The car was nice. He must have turned on the seat warmer on his drive over, and I wiggled cozily down into it since it was still warm now as we pulled out of the driveway. Even though it was pleasantly warm outside, it was a sweet gesture.

"Where are we headed?" I asked as he turned on to the main road.

"Depends. Are you in the mood for fun, food, or both?" He shot me an adorable grin and I felt a shy smile steal across my face as I looked out the windshield into the night.

"I'm always in the mood for food. And I could go for some fun. But, like, low key fun."

"No mountain climbing. Got it." He winked and steered the car toward the highway. "We're headed to the next town over. Not too far away, but hopefully what I have in mind meets the good food and low key fun requirements."

We chatted easily on the drive, and by the time Elliott parked the car in a lot next to an unmarked building, I was relaxed and happy.

"Where are we?" I asked, looking through the windows. None of the buildings around us were marked, and none had windows so it looked as if everything on this street was closed for the night.

"You'll see. Come on." He jumped out of the car with lightening speed to run around and open my door, helping me out. He steered me toward the largest building on the block with a hand on my lower back that he didn't remove as we walked along the sidewalk. I felt myself leaning into him a little. He smelled slightly of cinnamon and something woodsy. Somehow, it felt like home.

He held the door open and gestured for me to walk in first, and as I stepped into the building, I realized not only was it occupied, it was a very busy restaurant. My eyes were wide as I tried, and failed, to take in everything all at once. I heard Elliott chuckle behind me and turned to face him.

"I kind of wish I had walked in first, so I could have seen the look on your face the whole time. Can we do it again?" His eyes were filled with warmth and joy as he teased me, but I couldn't banter back. The part of my brain in charge of bantering was still staring open mouthed at the beautiful surroundings.

"What is this place?" I asked a little breathlessly.

"It's a fondue restaurant!" He exclaimed excitedly, which was adorable. "They decorated it as a speak easy, so it's moody and dark and private. But the menu is amazing and what's more low key fun than fondue?"

"This is amazing! It's perfect, Elliott. Thank you for bringing me here." The awe was evident in my voice, but I didn't care. He shot me a cheeky grin and a wink, but honestly he had done a great job picking this place and deserved to be a little smug about it.

In no time at all, the hostess was leading us off to a table. I'm glad Elliott was following behind me, again guiding me softly, because I was too busy looking around the restaurant while I was walking. I was paying absolutely no attention to where I was going.

The booths were tiny, probably only meant for two people, but each side was just large enough you could be cozy together in one seat if you wanted to. The tables had a built in fondue pot in the middle that seemed to be split into two separate sides, each with a lid. *Oh, please let there be chocolate fondue* I thought to myself as we settled into our booth.

The waiter came over to take our drink orders, and as he walked away I continued my visual perusal of the restaurant. There was a bar along one side with mirrors all along the wall that made the space feel like it went on forever. The ceiling was guilded tin tile, which I loved maybe more than any other architectural feature in the history of ever, with beautiful elaborate crown moldings. The chandeliers were glitzy and sparkled like diamonds in the sea of black and ruby red decor. As my gaze came back around, I accidentally met Elliott's eyes. He was sitting quietly, just watching me look around the restaurant.

"Sorry," I laughed nervously. "I've never been anywhere like this. It's incredible."

"I've actually never been here before either, but it seemed like the perfect night to try it out." His smile was a little shy, and I thought I'd caught a hint color creeping into his cheeks, but it was hard to tell in the dim lighting.

"Well, thank you for bringing me with you. How does it work?" I wiggled happily in my seat, and he laughed.

"You can choose a hot oil and cook raw meat, or you can choose a cheese and dip cooked meats and breads and things."

"Definitely option B, please."

"Agreed. Then, you can also choose a dessert fondue. There are a few options, but they're known for their chocolate."

"Yes, please!" I was practically squealing with delight, and had to resist the urge to clap my hands and bounce in the plush leather seat.

Before I knew it, we had finished the cheese fondue portion of our meal, and the chocolate was on its way. As excited as I was for warm melty chocolate, I was almost sad that the evening seemed to be passing by so quickly. When I had agreed to go out tonight, Elliott had said he just wanted to spend a little time together and get to know me better. I certainly felt like I knew more about him now, and everything I was learning only made me like him more.

I started to worry again about getting too involved, with anyone in town really, not just Elliott. I had a lot of decisions hanging over my head, the biggest being my future living arrangements, and sometimes it felt like I just couldn't handle any more. Just as my thoughts really started to spiral, Elliott reached across the table and placed his hand over mine.

A warmth crept all the way up my arm and settled in my stomach. Looking in his eyes across the table, it occurred to me that I didn't care about any of the decisions I still had to make, or my uncertain future. I could mentally put that in a box and close the lid for tonight, and enjoy the company of the extremely handsome, kind man in front of me. Probably anyway.

Maybe.

"Where'd you go just then?" Elliott asked. It wasn't a thinly veiled reprimand for spacing out on him. He seemed genuinely curious. Which made me even more determined to convincingly lie, or try to anyway.

"Oh, nowhere really. I have something for you and I'm a little anxious about it is all." After all, the best lies often hold a little truth.

"Well, I can't imagine what you would have that would make you nervous. But you don't have to give it to me, you know."

"Well, you ordered it from me, so I kinda do yeah."

He sat up straight so fast I startled and laughed. But it put enough distance between us at the table that his hand had pulled from the top of mine. I missed it immediately.

"You brought the painting with you?! That's exciting!"

"No actually, I haven't." I pulled the paintings from my bag, and placed them face down on the table in front of his ridiculously adorable, confused face. "I've brought two."

I'd stacked the paintings so that when he flipped them over, the one he ordered would be on top. It was just exactly what he said he wanted and painted in my typical hyper realistic style. The pet shop stood proudly in the middle of the page, all of the letters painted on the windows legible and shiny with opalescent paint.

In the bottom left corner of the painting, the sidewalk and street faded out to leave a little bubble of space that held part of Turtle's enclosure, with the tortoise herself taking center stage. I was so proud of the detail on Turtle's shell and skin. I had probably spent the most time on those two parts alone.

"Mabel... this is incredible. I can't believe how much detail you are capable of capturing in your paintings. I've never seen anything like it."

I could feel myself blushing. I was never very good at taking a compliment anyway, but somehow coming from him, it was even more difficult. Somehow, it meant more.

"I'm glad you like it. I should warn you though I suppose. The other painting is nothing like that, so try not to be disappointed."

I had lowered my gaze while I was talking without realizing it. Elliott's hand over mine again, drawing circles with his thumb, brought my eyes back to his.

"I don't think I could ever be disappointed with you."

My breath caught, and for a moment we just sat looking at each other. Finally, with a small shake of my head and an even smaller smile, I nodded toward the other painting.

"Go on then."

The second painting was of the inside of an old fashioned hardware store. Aluminum bins sat stacked on the aisles, holding nuts and bolts and other vaguely hardwarey things. Spinning racks held various tools, and you could just make out an old coffee station on the back wall.

It was painted very loosely, some of the detail that I would usually add was lost to the color and emotion. Some parts were left uncolored while other colors splashed outside the lines, but it all worked together to make you feel as if you'd stepped into a small town hardware store; dependable and gruff and strong.

I couldn't watch his face as he pulled the second painting in front of the first and began looking it over. The sparkly mosaic tiles on the bar held my attention instead, and I told myself I was waiting for him to break the silence.

But he didn't, and I had zero patience, so I peeked.

His eyes were actually misted over, and his throat bobbed up and down as if he were swallowing hard.

"Are... are you okay?" It was my turn to reach for him, and I placed a hand on his forearm, squeezing softly.

"You couldn't possibly know what this means to me. And how did you know about the hardware store? Did Dottie tell you?"

"Um... well... no, no one told me. And I'm actually not even sure why bins from a hardware store would mean anything to you, although I have a guess since the bins in the pet shop are the same, but that doesn't mean that I know why you left them or if they're even the same ones in the first place. I mean, I guess you could have just liked the design element. After all I did think it was a cute design choice when I first saw it in your store and that was before I saw it in my head.... and I should stop talking now. I'm sorry."

My brain hears my stupid ramblings as I'm halfway through them, but it always takes me another minute or two to actually just. stop. talking.

Elliott's eyes were a little wide, in word vomit shock I think. I recognized the look, as I tended to do it to people often when I was younger. I wasn't sure why the hold-my-tongue training seemed to leave me around him.

He shook his head slightly and closed his eyes. "I'm going to tell you what I got out of that, and then hopefully you can explain."

"Okay."

"You gave me a painting of the bins from the hardware store that was in my building before I bought it."

I nodded my head slowly.

"But you didn't know that it used to be a hardware store."

I pursed my lips and shook my head no.

"And you don't know why I care that it used to be a hardware store."

Still a slow shaking no.

"Uh huh. Okay. Right."

He sat there for a minute, looking deeply off into the middle distance. It would have been cinematic gold if someone were filming him. I just sat still and let him process.

"Yeah, okay no, I've got nothing. You have to explain. Mabel, how did you do this?"

I sighed. This could go one of two ways. Either, he would take everything in stride and just accept it. Or, he would think I was some kind of freak and politely request to never see me again. *Sounds like a fun game to play, why not,* my inner snarky self questioned.

"Sometimes, usually when I'm talking to someone, I get these tingles in my fingers. It kind of feels like when your hand falls asleep because you've been sleeping with your wrist bent and crammed under your chin, just not as intense. Have you ever done that? Slept like a T-rex?"

"Mabel, I'm really going to need you to focus until you finish explaining this to me before I go crazy."

"Focus. Yes. Sorry." Deep breath, Mabel. "After my fingers tingle, I guess as a little warning to pay attention I don't know, chills kind of creep across my body, like when you hear a really powerful symphony play or a deep bass drop in a souped-up sound system, and then a picture sort of pops into my head. Sometimes it's fuzzy, but yours was as clear as a photograph in my mind. I don't usually know why I'm seeing what I'm seeing, sometimes I don't even really know what I'm seeing."

I'd moved my hand from his arm and was now rolling the edges of the cloth napkin in on itself only to unroll it and then roll it up again.

"It used to happen all the time, and I'd paint what I saw. But the results were never really consistent since half the time I didn't understand the subject of my painting. I could never quite make them work with the hyper realism painting style, and that was the direction I ended up moving my painting career in, so I quit doing them. And then the tingles didn't really come all that often anymore, at least not until I came back to Painted Creek."

I was frowning, I could feel it. But I was confusing myself I think, as I tried to give Elliott an explanation. What I'd said about quiting my frisson paintings was feeling like a poor excuse to quit doing something that came so naturally to me. I scrunched my eyes closed and shook my head rapidly. I'd self analyze that later.

"Anyway, this picture came to me so strongly and so clearly, that I felt like I had to paint it for you and take the chance that it would mean something to you. Does it? Mean something to you?"

I was leading him to explain his side to me now. And hopefully distracting him with his own story so he wouldn't be freaked out by mine.

"It means so much to me Mabel, you have no idea." He looked back down at the painting, and when he looked back at me his eyes were glassed over again.

"I told you the other day that Mr. Findley was helping me with all the paper work and permits and things to get Turtle and that he'd heard about my building being listed for sale."

"You did, yes."

"The previous owner of my building had decided to sell when his sister had her first baby. The baby had special needs, and she was a single mother and the only living family he had left, so he decided to move closer to her, so he could lend a hand whenever she needed it."

"Well that's a great reason to move. Family is important. I believe I know another kind man who moved home to help family." I smiled at him, and his eyes softened as he looked at me.

"Yes, well. This man was also a client of Mr. Findley's. When he called him to ask for help on the legal parts of selling the building versus selling the building and the business together, Mr. Findley told him my story. Probably a huge breach of client confidentiality but if he'd had time to ask my permission first I would've said yes in a heartbeat.

"I guess our somewhat similar situations, as you pointed out, meant something to him too, and he agreed to let Mr. Findley show me the building, upstairs and all, before it was listed on the market.

We closed that same week. Until I bought the building, it was a small town hardware store. Complete with nuts and bolts bins and a coffee pot full of burnt coffee in the corner."

"That's a lovely story."

"I've always been so grateful to that man. Without the building, none of the rest of it would have been possible."

"I'm sure you would have found a way."

"Yes, but this way," he pointed down to the painting, "this building with the space above for me and the space out back for Turtle, was always the *best* way. I kept the bins in the store to honor its past, in some small way. But this painting, this I'm going to frame and hang right behind the counter. Thank you."

Now my eyes were a little misty, too.

"You're welcome, Elliott. I'm glad you like it."

The beautiful thing about a fondue meal, other than the delicious melted chocolate, was that it stayed in a constant, warm, melty state in the pot on the table. We'd become distracted by our conversation for awhile, but with the paintings tucked safely back in my bag, we finished our dessert.

As we reached the bottom of the chocolate fondue, I realized that Elliott had never commented on my explanation of the hardware store painting. I wasn't about to bring it back up. Either he didn't want to talk about it or it just didn't bother him, and I didn't want to potentially ruin our evening by finding out. Turns out, I wouldn't have to be the one to bring it up anyway.

NINETEEN

"IN THE RESTAURANT, when you told me not to be disappointed in the second painting, was it because of your tingles?"

We had been driving along back to Painted Creek in an amiable silence before he spoke, and the noise and words spoken caused a sudden, unpleasant jolt to my nervous system.

I wanted to giggle at the way he said tingles, but suddenly I was too anxious. I sat up straight in the car seat and crossed my feet at the ankle. I saw him shift his gaze to me from the road briefly, but he didn't say anything.

"No, it had nothing to do with that. It was the style of painting I was referring to."

"What do you mean? The painting was beautiful."

"Thank you. But it was not my normal style, too loose and not

160

enough detail. Some people would say that it wasn't up to my standards, I suppose. I didn't want you to expect something of the same caliber as the first painting and be disappointed."

He was quiet, but when I glanced over at him from the corner of my eye, I could see the muscles in his jaw working, washed blue from the lights of the dashboard.

"There's so much there to unpack."

I blinked. "I didn't realize Dr. Scott was driving me home. I'll watch what I say I suppose."

"You already are, Mabel, I can see it in your posture. But I apologize, I shouldn't have said it that way. I just meant that there is so much I want to say in response to that and I don't know where to start."

I remained silent, and after a minute he sighed.

"Do you remember my reaction to the first painting? My emotional reaction, not necessarily my words."

"Yes."

"And do you remember my emotional reaction to the second painting?"

I squirmed a little in the seat. "Yes, I do."

"How can you possibly feel like the second painting was worth less just because it was painted a little differently? Especially when it obviously meant so much to me."

I frowned down into my lap, spinning the ring on my finger around and around but I didn't answer.

"There's no question that you're remarkably talented at that first type of painting, Mabel. I know nothing about art and even I can see that. But I can't believe anyone would tell you that anything else you do isn't up to that standard, because it's still incredibly beautiful in its own way."

I wanted to believe him, but it was hard. And it seemed easier to try and sabotage this conversation than to convince my brain that he may be right, so my tone was baiting when I replied.

"You've not commented on the fact that I basically pulled the entire second painting out of thin air. Doesn't that bother you, me knowing things I couldn't possibly know?"

"Everyone has a gift of some kind Mabel... a way with animals, the ability to put together the perfect culinary experience, a mind for numbers. The way I see it, you just have more than one gift. I'm sorry that anyone, anywhere has ever made you feel like it's anything less than that."

He said it so simply, like that was the one and only possibility and I was being ridiculous over nothing. And maybe I was being ridiculous, but I was also scared. How could he really be this calm? And accepting? And perfect?

I decided to ignore the subject of the frisson vision, which was kind of an asshole move since I had just called him out for doing the same thing, but I really didn't know how to respond to that right now.

"Since I've come back to Painted Creek, I've been playing around with a lot of different painting styles again. I think I'd lost some of the joy in what I did, but I'm slowly finding it again. It's been nice."

"That is nice."

The tension in the car dissipated a little, and I started to relax again in the seat. When he reached over the middle console to put a hand on my knee, I felt hopeful that I hadn't ruined the entire night. We rode in comfortable silence once again the rest of the way back to the cottage.

WHEN WE CAME to a stop in the driveway, Elliott turned the car off and turned in the seat to face me. He looked a little hesitant, but determined, and it was so adorable I couldn't stop the small smile that played on my lips.

"What?" I asked.

"Can I come in?"

"Wait, what?"

"That's really forward of me and it would be even worse if I meant anything by it, which I don't. Mean anything by it that is. I mean, not that I didn't think about it, but I'm not expecting anything of course, you said you didn't want to date so I guess that means you also don't want anything else. Which is fine of course, and I mean, this was a date, don't get me wrong, but..."

"Elliott!" I sounded loud even to myself in the tight space of the car, but I recognized a word vomit spiral when I heard one, as I was quite prone to them myself. I was trying to stop him before it got any worse.

"Maybe take a second to collect your thoughts and try again?" I mimed a deep breath in and out, gave him a small smile, and simply waited.

He looked so bashful, a small smile on his face as he ran a hand through his hair, and I knew I was in seriously big trouble. Bashful Elliott was right up there with playful Elliott and adorable Elliott and really all of the sides of Elliott I'd seen so far.

He gathered himself slightly and said, "Mable, may I please come in a have another look at all the art work I saw sprawled about the house? After our conversations this evening, I would really like the opportunity to look at them more closely and talk about them with you."

He was completely serious. He just sat, looking in my eyes and waiting for an answer. He really just wanted to know more about my art, about me.

I wasn't just in trouble. I was a goner. How freaking inconvenient is that, when I still didn't think I could stay?

After a shuddering breath, I simply nodded, and got out of the car. I heard him scrambling behind me to get out and follow me up the walk, and it calmed my nerves a bit, thinking that maybe he was as off kilter as I was. I was especially thankful for all of Gram's lights. Wandering around and turning them all back on gave me something to do as he came in the house behind me.

"Make yourself at home. Would you like anything to drink? Wine? Tea?"

He had been slowly moving in from the front entry toward the fireplace until I said 'tea'. At that, his head whipped around to look at me in the dining room.

"Do you make tea like Constance did?" He sounded utterly surprised, and I wasn't quite sure why.

"Well, I mean, I boil water and add dried herbs and flowers, so.... I guess so?" All the lights had been flipped back on, and I came to a stop next to him in the living room. His face fell a little, and I was even more perplexed than before. Although, when I thought about it, Gram's tea always was exceptional compared to anything I'd ever found anywhere else.

"I guess I know what you mean. Gram could make a mean cup of tea."

He chuckled a bit and shook his head. "I'm sorry, Mabel. I didn't mean to imply that your tea making skills were sub-par. But Constance was definitely known for her hot tea. Maybe that was her gift. Although, I think the conversation that went with the tea had a lot to do with it too."

"Well, I can certainly offer conversation to go with the tea. Come on, you can pick your mug."

I led Elliott into the kitchen and gestured to the mugs, now hanging from underneath the cabinets from hooks. I had finally decided that the change was small enough that it wouldn't bother anything, and it would bring me a lot of joy to see all the mugs out all of the time.

"This is clever. And they're all so unique. It's like another form of art work for your kitchen." He brushed his fingers across a few mugs before selecting one and handing it to me. "This one reminds me of your dress tonight. Beautiful."

I knew I was blushing but there was nothing I could do about it. My arm brushed his as I put the tea pot on the stove and turned it on. He leaned into me slightly, I think unconsciously, before taking a step back and then walking to the bar stools on the other side of the counter.

"Thank you. It probably is my favorite dress. And this is a very pretty mug." Lame.

He smiled a shy one dimple smile and glanced at the refrigerator over my shoulder.

"Hey! It's Hedgie. Is that a self portrait?" His grin had turned teasing, but I was thankful some of the electric charge was fading from the air.

"Har har. Not a self portrait, no, but it is the first painting I did here in the cottage just for fun. Just for me." I looked over at the painting too and couldn't help but smile. I loved that the herb bundles were a match for the framed art hanging across the room that I had painted years ago. Mixed with the hyper realistic painting of Hedgie, it was kind of like my past and present were coming together to make a beautiful piece of art. I should probably frame it properly. Maybe I'd wait to get a frame that would match wherever I settled. Whenever I settled.

When I looked back, Elliott was studying me now instead of my refrigerator and I fought the urge to fidget.

"What?" I asked, losing the battle and rubbing two layers of my skirt together between my fingers at my side.

"I was just thinking about what you said in the car, about how you didn't realize you had lost some of the joy of painting... I'm glad you found it again." He glanced around at some of the other paintings in the dining room just as the kettle started to whistle.

I poured the water into a large measuring cup I had set up with two tea bags. As the steam rose into the air, I took a deep settling breath and turned back around to face Elliott.

"I am, too. I didn't realize how much of the spark I had lost until I started experimenting and playing with painting again."

"That makes sense." He said, nodding slowly. "You can't keep doing the same thing in the same way over and over without getting bored or burnt out. Or both. Honestly, I'm surprised you didn't struggle sooner. Though I'd imagine having different subjects to paint each time probably helped."

I laughed and said, "Could you imagine only ever painting one thing over and over and over?" I fake shuddered, but the realization was creeping over me that he was one hundred percent right. I had gotten bored in my work and didn't even realize I was slowly burning out on the one thing I had always loved doing.

"There are studies on it. We learned a little about it in my psychology classes, both for humans and animals. Boredom can effect not only your mental health but your quality of work, too."

"Ah yes, the psychology degree again. I really should be more careful about my behavior around you. My mother would be appalled to hear you know I talk to Hedgie."

He threw his head back and laughed. "I wouldn't worry too much. That degree is awfully dusty. Plus, normal, socially acceptable behavior is boring. Didn't we just learn about the dangers of boredom?" He winked at me, smiling, and though I knew he was just playing around, I felt a peaceful feeling of belonging and acceptance wash over me, and I decided I wouldn't worry so much about appearances after all.

For at least the next five minutes or so.

"Let me pour these up and I'll show you some of the other paintings. It's an absolute mess in there, so don't judge. Hedgie is a slob." I winked at him and just barely caught the surprised, amused look on his face as I turned to finish the tea.

I hadn't even asked what kind he wanted, I just picked what felt right from the collection of store bought tea bags. I'm sure it would be a far cry from whatever tea he'd had with Gram, but I was too anxious about showing him all of the other art to care too much.

"Here, it's a mix of chai and chamomile. Sounds weird maybe, but I like it. If you don't I can fix you something else." I handed him his mug over the counter and waited as he took a sip. He stared down into the mug for a beat too long and I winced.

"I'll make you a peppermint or something, I'm sorry." I put my mug down and was reaching for the pot to refill it when he got up and came around in to the kitchen.

"Mabel, stop. There is nothing wrong with the tea." He put his mug down next to mine and placed both of his arms along mine, holding me still so he could look at me. "I was just surprised, that's all. It's actually a wonderful blend, and perfect for tonight. Warm and exciting, but comforting and familiar all at once." He'd begun rubbing small circles on my biceps, and I wasn't sure he was even aware he was doing it. I, on the other hand, was hyper aware of the small touch, and had stopped breathing.

"You may have more of your gram's tea making abilities than you think. Gifted girl..." He had taken half a step closer, and was tall enough that I was now looking up to see his face. He studied me for a half a second before shaking his head, as if to clear his thoughts, and said, "Please don't remake the tea. It's perfect. Will you show me your art now?"

Clearing my throat I said, "Uh huh," because I'm super articulate and elegant like that. He dropped his arms from around mine, but I grabbed one hand as it slid away. Tugging on him, I led him into the dining room and laughed as he tugged me back so he could grab his mug and take a huge gulp as we were walking.

I saw the chaos in the dining room through new eyes, and was immediately embarrassed at the disorganization. It certainly wasn't dirty, more like overwhelming with art on every surface and then some, the collections having no regard for matching colors or styles.

"Whoa..."

"I know... it's kind of a lot." I gestured to the boxes on the floor. "I ordered some stuff on Amazon to organize things and display it all better but it just came today and I haven't had the chance to do anything yet or put all this stuff together. I haven't wanted to make any changes to Gram's house by putting nails in the walls or anything so I've been trying to just lay stuff around, but since it's just me I haven't worried about it be overwhelming for anyone else to see or anything so it's just all over all higgledy-piggledy and why are you looking at me like that?"

Throwing my arms up in the air with my rant, I had turned back to face him and Elliott was just standing at the archway of the dining room, eyes slightly wide but amused, and leaning a few inches backwards, away from me.

"Oh, so. many. reasons." My mouth snapped shut and he started laughing. "First, that was all one breath, which was impressive and also terrifying. Second, I'll help you put all this Amazon stuff together if you'd like, but if I understood everything you said at dinner correctly, this is your house now so you can put nails in the wall if you want to."

"Yeah but I..."

"Also," he said loudly over my interruption, "and maybe most importantly, higgledy-piggledy? Really?"

"Yes. Really. Unless you'd prefer willy nilly. Either way really it translates to a big freaking mess." I'd gone from embarrassed, to indignant, to a complete loss of steam, and it showed in my posture as I hung my head.

"Hey... Mabel, I was just picking on you. I'm honored that you're showing me the mess behind the perfectly put together girl I just drove home from dinner. Now," he clapped his hands once and rubbed them together, "what's in these boxes that we need to tackle? I'll help put things together, and you can tell me about each piece of art as we un-higgledy-piggledy this dining room."

I looked up at him through my lashes, and he put a finger under my chin to raise my head. We just looked at each other, and for one terrifying minute I thought I might cry. I had never felt so safe, so seen in another person's presence, and it was like all the weight I never knew I was carrying was laid to rest all at once, the overall effect a strange mixture of relief and complete loss of control over my emotions. Instead, I simply nodded once, and he let me go.

"Thank you. We don't have to go through all this tonight though. I can get to it over the next few days."

"Do you have any pressing engagements for the next couple of hours, Miss Morrison?" He was smiling at me, and the playfulness was driving away the last of the embarrassment.

"Why no, Mr. Scott, as a matter of fact, the rest of my evening is wide open."

"Let's get to it then." He sat in the floor and pulled over the first box, ripping it open with ease.

"I was going to offer you scissors, but I see that's beneath you."

"Far, far beneath. If I ask for a pair later, it's only to protect the feelings of lesser mortals." He started pulling pieces out of the box and laying things out on the floor. "What is all this stuff anyway?"

"It's mostly display frames and easels for art work. I got a few portfolios too, but some pieces I like to look at for awhile after I've finished them. Like this one." I picked up a painting barely peeking out of a pile on the end of the table and handed it to him.

It was one of the natural ink paintings, and completely

monochrome. The painting was a beautiful snow owl, the negative space making up the majority of the owl's body while the blue ink from the pea flower created the snowy night background and shading. I loved how the layers seemed to change the color in some places, and the play on light and dark gave it almost an ethereal vibe.

Elliott took the painting from me and went still as he studied it. Just when I started to shift my weight from foot to foot with nerves, he looked up and handed the painting back to me.

"Mabel, that's really special. I have never seen a painting in all one color have so much complexity and depth. I think it's really great."

I blushed, but looked at the painting again as I answered him.

"Thanks. This is one of the paintings I've done in the last few days from the inks I made myself. That's what all those dried herbs are for, too," I gestured to the bags he'd tossed aside out of one of the boxes, "so I can make more ink when I run out. It's been such a fun process, I'm just not ready to pack them away yet." I frowned down at the painting. I could suddenly picture it in a beautiful vintage white frame, and it made me sad to think that it would end up in a portfolio or, at best, I would sell it as is and never see it framed as art.

"Honestly?"

He glanced up at me briefly before returning his attention back to the assembly instructions for one of the easels. "Always."

"I've always wanted to have a little shop. Not an online store but like a real store where people can wander in off the street and find something that really speaks to them. I want to display all these beautiful pieces and watch someone's eyes light up when they find an unexpected treasure."

He stopped, and gave me his full attention. He looked adorable, slightly ruffled and now surrounded by pieces of wood and screws and tiny rogue pieces of Styrofoam. Unconsciously, I reached down and brushed one out of his hair.

"You absolutely should do that. Seriously, Mabel, that would be amazing. You could even offer spots for other vendors if you didn't want it to feel too much like an art gallery. I think it would be really successful, especially with that kind of passion behind it."

I smiled, but shrugged. "Maybe someday, when I come across the right place."

He looked at me for a beat without saying anything, but I could see the muscle in his jaw tick as he nodded before he lowered his head and reached for the screwdriver.

THE REST OF the night passed quickly in a blur of laughter and the easy familiarity you usually only get after knowing someone for a lifetime. I told him a little about a few different paintings while he worked to put together several easels and the cute little display frames. Once everything was assembled, he asked more questions about my painting process while we sorted and organized paintings around the room. I didn't miss the little touches and brushes all night, and when I walked Elliott to the door a few hours later, I couldn't have stopped the long, lingering good night kiss even if I'd wanted to. And I most certainly did not want to. Each time we touched, my heart fluttered while my brain cringed, worried about the future.

After he left and I walked back through the kitchen, I realized I never drank the tea that I had made when we first got back to the house. I reheated it in the microwave, deciding to enjoy it while I tucked the house in for the night. Once it was hot again, I took the mug and stood in front of Gram's bedroom door. I took a deep breath, pushed the door open the rest of the way, and took one single step over the threshold.

Nothing happened. The house still stood, time kept moving forward, and I still felt the empty space in my heart where Gram should be. I missed her fiercely, and I knew that would never fade, but I was hoping the guilt would eventually, even if it hadn't lessened yet.

I took one more small step, and then another, tightly clutching the warm mug until I was finally standing in the middle of the room. Looking around, I realized that nothing much had changed in here from my childhood memories. While the rest of the house had undergone minor touch ups here and there, Gram's room remained the same cozy, comforting space I always loved. Even though the door had been opened, it still smelled of roses in here, and I randomly thought I'd need to ask Carol for some rose oil to keep the smell strong in here always.

Absentmindedly, I took a sip of the tea and froze. I'd had this blend a million times, always preferring to cut the chai with the softer chamomile, and it was delicious but not any different than drinking any other hot tea. My eyes darted around the room, trying to make sense of what I was feeling, landing on different personal effects with each sip; a handmade quilt on the foot of the bed, a journal closed on the desk in the corner, a fancy hair brush set on the dresser.

After a few minutes, I realized with complete clarity that this tea blend reminded me of Elliott. More specifically, it reminded me of me and Elliott. Not that there really was an *us* but that was the only way I could describe it. I couldn't help but feel like Elliott had thought the same thing when he'd had the tea, and I smiled at how he had described it. He had to have felt something when he drank his tea too, or he wouldn't have said that.

Looking down into the mug, I wondered if that's why he said I may have some of Gram's tea making skills. Her tea made you *feel*. When I drank a cup of my special blend from Gram, I always felt confident and loved and settled in my own skin. Whether I meant for it to or not, tonight had gone way beyond two friends getting to know each other. Feeling like we had a special blended tea now only confirmed that. And if I was being completely honest with myself, I knew from the moment we first shook hands that he was going to mean something to me.

Now, I just had to figure out what I was going to do about it.

TWENTY

SUNDAY WAS SPENT painting and arranging the dining room, and then rearranging the dining room again. And at least once more. I was so grateful to Elliott for the help in putting things together, but the organizing had gotten a little sloppy so late at night. The artist in me that had been drug over the coals in art galleries during showings was obsessing with the layout in the dining room, and I was about ready to lose my mind. By Sunday evening, I decided not to touch it again, even if I didn't think it was perfect. This wasn't a gallery after all, it was a home, and as long as I could see the paintings for the time being, that was enough.

I had managed a few more natural ink drawings, and most of them ended up being monochrome. I was really enjoying the play on negative space and the layering of the same color over and over, so I just kept making more until I had a whole section of the dining room wall covered in nothing but that. It was beautiful.

I'd also managed to finish the new commissions I had just accepted, and I'd sent text photos to my mother for proof of life, and to reassure her that I was still actually working. She grudgingly agreed that they were some of my best work, and chocked it up to needing a little time off. I wasn't about to tell her it was because I was playing around with some other styles and enjoying myself again. At least not yet. I accepted a couple of more requests, though, just to keep working.

I pointedly ignored all the photos she sent of the little house she walked through. She was right, it was probably perfect for me and what I needed on paper, but I just wasn't excited about it. Like, at all. So, avoiding a conversation about it was the only plan I had, and I knew that wouldn't work forever.

I was working on Mr. Findley's painting a little at a time, in between other things. I was still struggling, but it was slowly getting better. At one point, I was considering scrapping the whole thing and starting over, but I just couldn't bring myself to do it. Something in my gut said to keep going, so that's what I did. Hopefully it would turn out well and I would finish it soon. I wanted to take it to him sooner rather than later.

That evening, I spent a little time on the patio snuggled in the big rocking chair with a good book. I hadn't ventured out to the creek or into the secret herb garden since the last day I saw Charlotte. I'd been so busy, focused on the new inks and learning what I could do with them, I'd barely done anything else at all.

Looking around the yard though, it was past time for it to be cut. I'd need to ask Dottie about a yard crew again when she came over tomorrow afternoon. I'd ask her about Charlotte's house too. Maybe I could drive over one day and ask her again about teaching me to care for the herb garden. I wasn't exactly a stomp through the woods kind of girl.

I'd managed to drag myself in Gram's room a couple more times, each time stopping just short of standing in the middle of the room, to look around. I hadn't been able to snoop yet, like she'd wanted me to do in her letter and like I'd slowly been doing around the rest of the house.

I was completely comfortable in my bedroom and the dining room, slowly moving things and making sure the space suited my needs. And I had added the hooks for the mugs in the kitchen, which I absolutely loved. But otherwise, I still felt mostly like I was house sitting, and I couldn't bear to make any changes to Gram's home. I was even putting things back in the refrigerator in the same place, although I suppose that was Mr. Findley's doing and not Gram's, now that I thought about it.

"Fine. I'll rearrange the fridge, too. Baby steps." I shut my book and headed back in to the house, ready for the nightly routine of turning off all the lights and locking up. As I passed Gram's door, I stopped, not necessarily with determination but perhaps with a bit more gumption that usual, and went in again.

"What's it called, where you keep doing something and eventually it gets easier to do? I'll have to ask Elliott." I walked across the room to the bed and sat down, running my hands over the quilt folded across the foot. No doubt it was one from the quilting group, and I'm sure there was one hell of a story to go with it, but I didn't know what it was.

Grief is weird. After some time, it settles deep inside, like a small, heavy ball bearing that you always carry around so you almost don't notice it anymore. But every once in a while, something jostles you and that weighted ball moves around again. Maybe it would just roll around a little, or maybe it created a full on tsunami style wave that threatened to pull you under again.

Eventually though, the ball would settle and come to a stop again, the wave would subside, but inevitably at some point, you'd repeat the whole process all over again. Usually when you least expected it.

Right now my ball wasn't just moving, it was rolling around like one of those old fund raiser coin funnels. Remember those? You'd drop a coin through the slot and it would roll in a spiral, huge at first and progressively getting smaller as it went down until finally it dropped through the neck at the bottom and fell with a satisfying clunk into the jar.

Looking around the room, I saw the journal sitting out on the desk again. I didn't remember Gram keeping a journal, but that had to be what the little leather bound book was and what she had referred to in her letter. It looked well loved, the first three quarters of the pages wrinkled along the visible edges. I stood and crossed the room, almost as if pulled by a magnet. Tingles simmered pleasantly under my skin when I ran my fingers gently over the leather tie holding the soft chocolate colored book closed.

My smile was soft and more than a little sad, and I patted the book gently.

"Not tonight. Not yet."

As much as I wanted to know any of the stories I had missed, I didn't think I could handle it right now, not while my tiny ball of grief was still silently rolling in my stomach. But I knew without a doubt now that this was Gram's journal, and it would be there when I was ready to go through it.

I turned away slowly and glanced toward the closet door. I knew it would smell like roses and Gram when I finally opened it.

Suddenly, I had a memory from when I was younger, maybe seven or so since it was before my dad died.

Gram was in the closet and I came skipping in behind her so fast I bumped into the back of her knees. She laughed and ruffled my hair as my dad came running in behind me.

"Careful, Sprout," he said, scooping me up unceremoniously and swinging me out of the closet. I was laughing, reaching back over his shoulder for Gram while she laughed, pretending she was trying to reach me and couldn't.

"The closet is where Gram keeps all her best secrets. We don't want to mess around in there!"

"Secrets?" I was never one to snoop, but what seven year old wouldn't be interested in a closet full of mystery?

"Yes! Like her famous ice cream recipe."

"And Christmas presents? And dragons?" I asked, eyes wide.

"And Christmas presents!" my dad laughed, shaking his head. "And magic pressed flowers, and sparkly jewels, and maybe even a dragon to guard it all!"

Gram laughed then, shaking her head at the two of us. She shooed us out of her room completely, closing both doors behind her.

"I can't do anything about the dragon, but maybe we can make our own magic pressed flower?" Gram asked, smiling down at me.

"To the flower garden!" My dad yelled, carrying me through the house to the patio on a trot, laughing the whole way.

Gram had let me clip a beautiful purple flower off of the geranium bush and taught me how to press it using the microwave and a few heavy plates. I don't know what happened to the pressed flower, but the painting I had made for her after of a dragon wearing a jeweled necklace holding a purple flower was still on her nightstand.

I hadn't thought of that memory in years, but I smiled now, looking at the door and shaking my head.

"It's your fault, Dad." I whispered. "You created the magic. What if I open that door now and it's just a regular closet?" The weighted ball engraved with dad's name rolled around a bit, bumping into Gram's.

Wincing, I turned away and turned the lights off in Gram's room. Part of me wanted to slam the door closed again, to leave the feelings and the memories locked up tight where they couldn't hurt so badly. But that felt a little like leaving the good bits locked up too, and that thought hurt worse than facing the grief and sadness. I placed a little iron mouse door stop in front of the door to keep it propped wide open, and puffed out a harsh breath. Healing, moving on, *moving forward* was a choice, and it was hard.

I finished tucking the house in for the night, turning off lights and wiping down the kitchen one last time. Since Gram's door had been wide open, I noticed how the scent of roses would travel through the house on a breeze every once and awhile, as if Gram had just walked through the room. It blended well with the lemony scent that seemed to hang in the air in the house, and I took a deep breath that helped settle me as I walked toward my room.

"Goodnight, house," I said, clicking off the last light in the hall.

Outside, the breeze carried the scent of rosemary and crisp water from the creek, while the crickets did their best to sing me to sleep.

TWENTY-ONE

I THINK IT was a woodpecker. I had no other explanation for the tap-tapping that had woken me bright and early the next morning. I really wanted to be mad about it, I loved to sleep in after all. But something about it was nice, too, and I laid in bed awake listening for awhile. It was without a doubt nicer than that horrid blaring noise that came out of my old alarm clock, that was for sure.

When I finally rolled out of bed, I decided that coffee from Artful Brew sounded like a great way to start the week. Since Alex had extended the invitation for Monday morning coffee, I didn't want to be rude and blow them off. And it would be nice to have a little bit of conversation. I could still make it home in time to tidy a little more before Dottie and her friends came over.

Showered, dressed, and in desperate need of caffeine, I drove over to Main Street and parked next to the building on the side street. Walking past The Pet Parlor and sneaking a peek in the window to see if Elliott was awake was purely a coincidence. Yep. Definitely not on purpose. But the store was still dark, so I hurried past, barely sparing a glance for the empty building, my building, as I scurried by. That was a future me problem. Present me needed coffee.

There was nothing quite like the sounds and smells of a bustling coffee shop, and Artful Brew was certainly up and running this morning. It was around seven o'clock, and the place was packed, although it seemed most people were getting their fix to go. I spotted Heather and Alex at the same table across the room, and when they spotted me at the door they waved me over. Relieved that it was an actual standing invitation and not a pity invitation, I pointed at the order counter and then held up one finger, letting them know I'd come over once I ordered.

When it was my turn, Sarah came over to the register and bumped the other girl working out of the way.

"Hot or cold?" She all but barked out, looking at me.

"I'm sorry, what?" I just blinked at her, feeling like I had missed a conversation I was supposed to be paying attention to.

"Would you like your beverage hot or cold this morning?" She grit out through her teeth, as if the extra five seconds it had taken her to speak in a complete sentence caused her pain. "Are you still continuing your coffee house menu education or have you reverted back to your safe, plain black coffee so soon?" She arched an eyebrow at me and waited.

"Ah. That. Yes, um, hot this morning please."

"I'll make it a large, sounds like your brain needs the extra caffeine today. It'll be $7. Just put it all in the tip jar and I'll bring it over when it's done. Next!"

The guy behind me in line jostled me a bit so that he could order, and it shook me out of my apparent stupor. I turned to the table with the other ladies, who were both silently laughing. By the time I sat down, I was giggling a little, too.

"What just happened? I feel like I ran right into a brick wall I didn't even know was there." I settled my bag on the floor and turned to the other two women.

"Congratulations, you've officially just met rush hour Sarah; efficient, precise and kind of a bitch." Alex was laughing, love evident on her face as she bad mouthed her friend. Her red hair seemed to sparkle like there was glitter in it, but I think it was just her natural effervescence.

"She means the congratulations, by the way," Heather said as she leaned a little closer to me. "She only shows rush hour Sarah to people she's close to."

"I wouldn't say we're close." I glanced up at the counter and then back down at my lap. It would be nice to call all three of these women friends, but Sarah was still stand-offish at best. I guess I couldn't blame her though.

"Okay, maybe not close, but she at least trusts you enough to give you her true personality when it's hectic instead of her customer service persona." Alex had pointed her spoon at me, as if to accentuate her point.

I snorted, very unladylike but here we are, and glanced up when they both giggled.

"What was that for?" Alex's eyes were twinkling and she leaned forward like she wanted to be let in on a joke.

"Oh, well, nothing really." Now Alex snorted, but more in indignation than amusement as mine had been.

"It's just that you sort of implied Sarah's true personality was to be a bitch." As soon as I said the words I wanted to take them back. Both women were looking at me with straight faces and I couldn't tell if I'd offended them of if they were just trying to work out what I'd meant. I rushed to clarify.

"Sorry, I should've kept that to myself. It just struck me as funny is all. How you all are obviously so close that you're comfortable talking about her like that. It must be nice. But it wasn't my place to say it quite like that. I apologize." I was so worried that I had offended them, I kept looking between the two of them and never thought to look behind me for the cause of their straight laced faces.

"Damn it ladies, I can't leave you alone for five freaking minutes without you saying bad things behind my back. No more coffee for you, you're all cut off." I literally jumped in my seat when Sarah started speaking and the rest of the table broke into loud laughter.

Sarah arched an eyebrow at me as she handed me my coffee, but she must've seen the genuine worry on my face that I'd offended someone, and she winked at me.

"They're right. I can be kind of a bitch. But only when it's busy."

"Or you're hungry." Alex said.

"Or you're tired," Heather threw in.

"Or someone hurts Becca, but that doesn't count because then we're all going to throw down. Forget I said that one. When else Heather?"

"Oh, I'd say with any mild inconvenience."

"Definitely when she's PMSing"

"And when she's not…"

It was like watching a game of ping pong. They were both trying to keep a straight face, but the more ridiculous their suggestions got the harder it was.

"Do you ladies have something you'd like to tell me?" Sarah was trying to keep up her stern act but was failing.

"We loooooove yoooou!" Both Alex and Heather singsonged in unison, causing Sarah and everyone else within ear shot to laugh. I smiled but looked down at my lap again. I'd never had friends like this. Friends so secure in their relationship that joking and teasing was second nature, received without a bit of insecurity and delivered without any malice or ulterior motives. It was nice to witness, even if I wasn't a part of it.

"Try your coffee, Mabel." Sarah nudged my shoulder and gestured to the cup I had left sitting in front of me. "It's a café con leche. You were a little slow on the uptake this morning, this should help."

There was a twinkle in her eye under that arched eyebrow, and I wasn't sure which I should trust more; the challenge so obviously there or the amusement. After taking a tentative sip, I knew it was both.

"Holy crow that's sweet... but..." I took another sip, "I think I like it?" And another. I smacked my lips, pondered a bit, and took another sip. "Yep, I like it."

"Careful, Mabel, that shit's addictive." Alex said with a grimace.

"Only because you have a sugar problem." Sarah answered with an eye roll. "The rest of us normal people can stop at one just fine."

"What's in it?" I asked, staring at the cup like it held the answers instead of the lady who made it standing next to me.

"I make my version with strong, bitter coffee and sweetened milk."

"That's all? No, that can't be all."

Heather shook her head slowly. "The milk is sweetened condensed milk. I hope you can handle your sugar and caffeine, Mabel, or I hope you have a long to do list for today."

"She just gave you liquid crack. Have fun with that." Alex was laughing, actually all of us were giggling like crazy. It was at my expense, but for once I didn't mind. I didn't feel like they were trying to trick me or make fun of me. I felt included.

Looking to Sarah, I asked, "Is this on the menu?"

She looked slightly sheepish. "Well, not exactly. But we're broadening your horizons, remember?" She turned on her heel and headed back to the counter to help the other barista.

"I forgot one earlier... She's a vindictive bitch, too." Alex said.

"I heard that." Sarah yelled from across the room, and we all dissolved into giggles again.

"Aaaaanyway, what have you been up to, Mabel? I keep thinking I'll run into you in town, but I haven't. Are you settling in okay?" Heather had turned to look at me with genuine interest and a little concern.

"I am, thank you. I tend to hermit a little, especially when I have a big painting due or a new project I'm excited about."

"Which is it this time?" Alex asked.

"Excitement, for sure, which is a nice change. Actually, it all started the last time I was here with y'all and I painted that bunny from coffee."

"Which was a total badass move by the way. But please continue." Alex waved her hand in the air for me to continue as if she wasn't the one who interrupted me. Heather shook her head with a small smile.

"Well, I was finally able to sit and read the book that Heather lent me with my cronut, which was ah-mazing by the way-" Alex said 'thank you' at the same time that Heather said 'it was a gift', and then both of them looked at me expectantly waiting for me to continue.

"-and it had so much wonderful information on making your own natural inks. I had done a little back in school but, I don't know, I guess now was just the right time for me to really get in to it. I messed around a little with some leftover hibiscus tea and that was fun. Then I ended up talking with a neighbor about it and she recommended trying chamomile flowers to make an ink."

They were nodding along, and I started to wonder if I was boring them and they were just being polite.

"I'm sorry. I'm rambling on. You guys don't want to hear all the details."

"Um, yes we do. That's why we asked?" I was noticing that Alex was always the one to speak first and think later, and I kind of admired that about her.

"What she said. This is super interesting stuff. Plus, I get to take credit for whatever comes next since I gave you the book. Carry on." Heather grinned at me and I smiled shyly back, appreciative of the reassurance.

"I ended up making several natural inks from various plant materials. I've been sort of obsessed and have been locked in the cottage learning how best to use them and trying some different art styles. It's actually been a lot of fun."

"That's so cool. I love that feeling... you know when you finally try something new or unexpected and it kind of brings back the spark to everything else again." Alex's eyes were wide and bright and she was wiggling a little in her seat as she talked, which made me smile. I did that too, sometimes, at least when my guard was down.

"I had gotten in a rut at the bakery. Not the business, mind you, but mentally I guess?"

"It was a dark time. She stopped making my favorite cookies. Because she was *bored*. Lousy excuse, but whatever." Heather rolled her eyes and rested her chin on her wrist, waiting for Alex to finish her story.

"*Like I was saying*, I was in a rut. The business was doing well, but I was so worried that people would get tired of or unhappy with what I had to offer and stop coming in to the bakery. I spent hours scrolling Pinterest and other sites looking for a recipe I hadn't tried, or a flavor combination that was exciting. In my head I was so convinced that I had to make everyone else happy that I forgot I opened the bakery because *I* loved to bake."

She was slowly rolling the layers of her napkin into a skinny napkin snake, frowning slightly. It was odd to see Alex so somber. I hadn't spent much time with these ladies, but every time I had been around them, Alex was the boisterous one, stirring up everyone else.

"I can see how hard that must've been to go through. I think I can relate, too. I was feeling that way with my art. People request paintings from me because I can provide them with such realistic detail. I've been doing only that for so long, it's like I'd forgotten that I actually love to create art, that it's not just a job."

Alex was nodding along as I spoke, and I knew that no matter where my relationship with these women went, if I stayed in town and we became fast friends or if I left and we never spoke again, she and I understood each other in a way that maybe not everyone could.

"People recognize passion though. And just because one person can't stand the texture of oatmeal cookies doesn't mean there's not someone else out there who loves them because of her grandpa." Heather patted Alex on the shoulder, the gesture half mocking and half genuine comfort.

"Yes, yes. And thank you for letting me use his recipe, by the way."

"Thank you for making them so I don't have to." Heather turned to me. "I can't bake."

"Or cook. Or boil water."

"That was just that one time!" Heather pouted for a second before a grin split her face. It was so obvious they had been friends forever, and I was happy to be allowed to see in to some of the inside jokes.

"So, tell me then, how did Alex get her baking groove back?" I asked.

"I think, after a few weeks,"

"Months..."

"Whatever. I think after a few months, I had just had enough. I had never really been a people pleaser before, and I was sick and tired of worrying about whether or not every single person that came into the bakery would love every single item I had to offer. Late one night I came across the recipe for the cronuts, and I tried it, just because I wanted to."

She stopped fidgeting with the napkin and looked right at me. I was grinning at her, and I could see the transformation in her demeanor back to the Alex I had met for the first time in the coffee shop.

"I made a few batches, a few tweaks here and there, and loved every second of it. I was baking and creating and making the whole thing mine. It was probably partly because it was a new recipe, something I'd never done before, but it reminded me of the joy of having all the different ingredients come together to make something delicious. Ever since I added them to the shop menu, I sell out within a couple hours of opening. Every single time. But I'd still make them even if I didn't sell a single one... because *I* want to."

"Well, I want to be more like you when I grow up. My people pleasing is deeply ingrained I'm afraid."

"You're a people, too." Heather said quietly. I snapped my gaze to hers, but she was looking down at her lap. I don't think she meant for me to hear her.

"I'm sorry, I took over the conversation. So what's happened with your natural inks? Are you happy with the results or has it just been fun to play with them?"Alex asked.

"Both, actually." I huffed a laugh and rolled my eyes a little at myself. "There's one ridiculous part though... I hate to waste things, I mean like even things that should probably be trash. I just always feel like maybe there's a use for it that I just haven't discovered yet. So now, I have a refrigerator shelf full of slimy, boiled plant goop that I strained off of the ink and I can't bring myself to throw it away. I mean really, how ridiculous is that?!"

I cringed inwardly at myself. Definitely not proper conversation to share with others, how I can't throw things away. They were probably picturing the cottage full of trash and clutter and junk. Ugh.

Heather sat up straight so quickly it jostled the table and scared both me and Alex. Good timing for me though, as it derailed my inner 'you're so weird and stupid' monologue.

"I think maybe I have a book for that..."

"You maybe have a book for everything. A book for what though, letting things go?" Alex asked.

"No. Well, yes I have one for that too if you need it but I don't think you do. I think I have a book on handmade jewelry."

I blinked at her, then looked at Alex. She blinked at me, then looked at Heather.

"We're going to need a little more to connect the dots, babe."

"Handmade jewelry, like making your own beads and stuff." The blinking and looking and blinking some more continued as Alex and I tried to figure out what she was talking about, and Heather struggled to get the words out to tell us.

"Ugh. Hang on." She took a deep breath with her eyes closed, and tried again. "Mabel, I think I have a book somewhere that you might want to look at. I'm pretty sure there is a chapter in this handmade jewelry book about how to make beads from clay that you've made from flower petals. Like keepsake jewelry. Originally, it was used to make rosary beads out of rose petals."

I tilted my head, and as I thought about what she said, I got the slightest tingle in my fingers, but the frisson didn't continue from there, and no image came to mind. Weird, I must've been sitting funny or something. I moved my hands from my lap to the tabletop and crossed my fingers together.

"Well that's really freaking cool." Alex said, leaning back. "I bet if you can make them out of flowers, you could make the clay out of your leftover goop too. Although, we might need a new name for it. Goop beads isn't all that appealing."

"Goopy beads?! I want some goopy beads! That sounds awesome!" Becca had come bounding up to the table and skidded to a stop in front of Alex, bouncing on her little toes. "What is goopy beads Auntie Alex, are they squishy and squeltchy and slimey?"

Heather shuddered across the table, and when I glanced at her, she mouthed 'texture issues' and shuddered again. I snickered under my breath but nodded emphatically.

"Fair," I mouthed back. She smiled.

"No, kiddo, we were just being silly grown ups. But now, it's time to be serious grown ups and get you to school!" Alex said, booping her on the nose.

"I don't want to be a serious grown up." Becca pouted.

"Neither does Auntie Alex, squirt, but we all do what we have to do." Sarah had walked up and ruffled her daughter's hair affectionately. "Thanks for taking her to school."

"Best part of my Monday! Let's go, kiddo!"

"Bye, Mommy, bye Auntie Heather, bye Miss Mabel!" She waved enthusiastically and then skipped off toward the front door, Alex hurrying behind her.

"Y'all good? Refill?" Sarah asked.

"No, thank you. I think a refill of this requires a prescription," I said, grinning. Sarah snorted.

"No, thanks," Heather said, too. Sarah nodded and turned back to the counter.

"I'm going to head off to the store. Mabel, I'll look for that book and give you a call if I find it." She started gathering her trash and then paused.

"I don't have your number do I?" she said.

"No, I don't think so. But I can text it to you, if you'd like?" Rationally, I knew she was asking for my number. My brain though was telling me that she was just being nice.

"Oh my gosh, I can't believe we haven't all traded numbers yet! It's almost like we've known you forever. Yes, please text me and then I'll do a group chat so you have everyone else's numbers, too."

"Oh, you don't have to do that. I'm sure they don't want..."

"Hush, of course they do. Alex says we're keeping you remember? In case you haven't noticed, Alex usually gets her way. Best not to fight it."

Heather rattled off her number and I sent a text with my contact card. Her phone pinged from the depths of her bag, almost as big as mine and undoubtedly more full, and she nodded as she stood.

"Great! I'll text you soon! Don't throw out that goop until you hear from me!" She was laughing as she waved goodbye to me and Sarah in turn and left the coffee shop.

I gathered up my trash and bag and headed for the front of the store. As I reached the door, Sarah called out, "Have a great day, Mabel!"

"At warp speed, I'm sure!" I called back.

She threw me a Vulcan salute, and I laughed all the way to my car.

TWENTY-TWO

I MADE IT home from Artful Brew in plenty of time to clean and rearrange again before Dottie showed up with her friends. After talking with the ladies this morning, I grouped the paintings more by feeling than application or style, and while it seemed like it was a little scattered, I think it actually made more sense from a shopping stand point. If this were a gallery showing, I would've had little cards describing what style painting they were and other things like that.

"Maybe if I ever have a shop..." Hedgie seemed to twinkle extra brightly, so I decided he agreed with me, and left it at that. About fifteen minutes past noon, I heard the cars pull into drive.

Opening the front door, I waved, and waited for all the ladies to get out of the two cars they'd carpooled in and make their way up the walk.

"Fashionably late again I see," I teased Dottie, pulling her in for a big hug.

"Sugar, you know the party don't start 'till I get here anyway." She did a little shimmy and breezed past me into the house. "Come on ladies! Come see how brilliant my Mabel is!"

They all filed behind her in a single file line like little ducks, and I giggled as Betsy and Nora reached me last.

"Hey, Maybe-baby." Nora kissed my cheek as they stopped on the front step before going in the house.

"Thank the good Lord it's finally Monday. She hasn't talked about anything but this for five whole days." Betsy said with an eye roll.

"Yeah… we love you too, Maybe, but if we hear your full name followed by painting one more time, I think we may finally disown her." She looked down right serious but I knew there was nothing that would ever come between these women.

"Well, I'm so sorry that you have been tortured with tales of my masterfulness, and now you have to witness it for yourself. How ever will you survive?" Eyes wide with fake concern, I looked from one to the other as they stared at me in surprise. Betsy broke first.

"Sarcasm. From Mabel." She cocked her head to the side a moment. "I like it. Come on Nora, let's go try and reign her in."

I grinned at Betsy as she walked by, Nora gave my hand a little squeeze on her way in, and then we were all finally in the house and a captive audience for Dottie, who was actively singing my praises from the entrance to the dining room.

"Ladies, I just can't wait for you to see. I mean, I haven't seen either, but I just know that everything is going to be so fantastic." She caught us walking in out of the corner of her eye and turned. "Oh good, Mabel, there you are. Take us in, sugar. We were waiting for you to come show everything off."

I sighed. I truly hated this part of creating art. It always felt so salesy and egotistic. Like, hey look at me, I painted this stuff now please tell me how pretty it is and how special I am. Blah.

Nora heard my sigh and squeezed my hand again. I looked down at her and gave her a genuine, grateful smile before replacing it with my public relations smile.

"Thanks for coming everyone. I hear that Dottie has been talking about my paintings nonstop for a few days, so I hope your visit lives up to the hype." Dottie huffed, and everyone else chuckled politely.

"Just go on in and get a better look at everything. There are several different styles of paintings in there, so if you have any questions or anything please don't hesitate to ask and I'll answer them to the best of my ability."

"Meh meh me meh meh meme. Lord, honey, you sound so up tight." Dottie had walked over from the entry to the dining room and was standing with the three of us, letting the other five ladies that had come along look around without being crowded.

"That was certainly a far cry from the sass out on the porch, that's for sure," Betsy chimed in.

"Now don't you two go ganging up on me. This is my job and my livelihood. A bit of professionalism is expected and required."

Well, I just opened my mouth and my mother came out. That's great. Good times.

"Whatever you say, darlin'." Betsy was patting my arm as if to soothe me. "We just want to see what you've been up to."

"When you were over at Dottie's house, you said you'd been painting some just for fun. Are some of those in there too?" Nora was glancing in to the dining room at their other friends who were ooo-ing and ahh-ing at something over in the corner.

"Why don't you go see?" I nodded my head in that direction and gestured for them to go in ahead of me.

I had no idea I would be this nervous! Showing the paintings to Elliott was hard, but I think since they had come out one at a time and he was so busy helping me put together displays, it didn't feel quite as intimidating as this did. Almost all of the work I had done in the last week or so was out and proudly displayed, well, at least displayed, and there was no hiding from the fact that they were all different styles and vibes. Come to think of it, the only paintings in my normal hyper realism style that were displayed were the commissions that I was getting ready to package up and mail this week. I guess I'd done so many in that style, it didn't qualify as painting for fun now.

All the sugar and caffeine I'd had at the coffee shop was turning to an electrified ball of lead in my stomach. I pushed a hand against my belly trying to get it to settle a little.

"Mabel, are any of these for sale?" I vaguely recognized the woman that called for my attention near the china cabinet, but didn't really know who she was.

"Well, I hadn't really thought about it, but yes I suppose some of them are. Which one are you interested in..."

"Oh goodness me, sorry dear. I'm Gertie. Nice to finally meet you."

Gertie looked like Mrs. Claus, and I liked her instantly.

"Nice to meet you as well. Which painting are you interested in? I can tell you a little more about it."

She gestured to one of the monochrome natural ink paintings that I had painted just yesterday. It was chamomile ink, and the bunch of lemons in the middle of the page stood out in soft, golden yellow. They didn't look real, in the strictest sense, but they were cheerful lemons all the same.

"The paint used here is actually a natural ink made from chamomile flowers. I made the ink myself."

"Now I didn't know you were doin' all that, sugar. How interesting!" Dottie wandered over from where she had been examining one of the commissioned paintings of a vintage bicycle with a puppy hanging over the edge of the basket.

"Yes ma'am. It's one of the things I've been dabbling with since I got in to town." I walked around the room and pointed out the other paintings that were done with natural inks, and I could feel my shoulders relax down from my ears when everyone seemed to receive them well.

"I would love to have this painting for my kitchen, if you can bare to part with it." Gertie said. "I have lemons all over, but none quite as cheerful as these."

"Why lemons, Ms. Gertie?" She had a wistful look in her eye, and I couldn't help the question from bubbling out of my mouth. Stupid brain to mouth filter malfunction again.

"Because of my Alfred. When we were dating, I would make him lemonade. He always said it was the best he'd ever tasted, so I made sure that I had a big pitcher full every time he came over. I never even had any myself, I had tea instead, because I was saving the lemonade for him. I thought he liked it so much that I was giving him a special treat each time.

"After we'd been dating several months, my momma came out on the porch after pulling weeds in the back yard and poured herself a glass of Alfred's lemonade. She spit it right out all over the porch! She said 'Gertie! Why didn't you use sugar in this lemonade, child? I've never had anything so sour in my life!'"

We were all invested in Gertie's story, and several ladies were looking more closely at the lemons in the painting while chuckling softly.

"Well, I didn't know you were supposed to add sugar to lemonade! I thought it was just lemons and water, and since I never had any with Alfred, wanting to save it all for him, I never knew how sour it was. That sweet man was drinking this horrible lemon water with a smile on his face, for months mind you, just to keep from hurting my feelings. I turned and looked at him, and I knew right then that I was going to marry that man. And I did. And I've had lemons in our kitchen ever since."

"Thank you for telling me your story, Ms. Gertie. I'm used to hearing the story first and trying to paint to match it the best I can, but knowing that this reminded you of something special, just by happenstance, well... that means a lot to me." I could feel that my eyes were actually a little misty as I reached out to pull the painting off of the stand.

"Let me wrap it up for you."

"Only if you'll let me pay for it, dear. Really. This means so much to me. Something about the way you captured the lemons, or how plump they are, I don't know. But it just reminds me of my Alfie and I love it."

I considered it for a moment, having not really been prepared to sell anything today, and turned to her to say, "If you insist, twenty dollars will be more than fine, Ms. Gertie. I'm honored you love it."

"Whooo boy, that's a steal!" I wasn't sure that it was such a steal. After all, I felt like all these paintings were things I had done just messing around. They weren't really anything special, were they? And they certainly weren't the same standard of my normal paintings if you were judging strictly by proper technique and composition. But it undeniably meant something to her, and that meant something to me.

"I'm glad you think so. Thank you again for sharing, and for the purchase." Impulsively, I gave her a quick hug, and pulled back to see her wiping a tear from her eye.

"You know, dear, it's so funny, every time I came to visit your gram, she would always fix me lemon tea. I don't think I ever told her that story though, I guess lemon was just her favorite." She paused for a second and then laughed. "You know, on the days when I'd visit, and Alfred was on my ever loving last nerve, that lemon tea would be a mite bit more tart than other times I came for a visit. And I'd always think of him drinking my sour lemonade, and I'd be a bit less mad at him when I left here. I never realized that before now. Lord, I sure do miss having tea with Constance though."

I was having trouble speaking around the knot in my throat.

"So do I, Ms. Gertie."

After handing her the painting, safe in a little plastic bag with my sticker holding it closed, I wandered in circles around the dining room, talking with the others about the rest of the paintings. I realized that Nora had been quietly staring at a watercolor of a wildflower bouquet for some time. It was a riot of color, and glancing over her shoulder I realized it was similar to the one that Elliott had brought me on Saturday night. I had painted it the Thursday before. *How funny,* I thought to myself as I put my arm around Nora's shoulder.

"You're going to stare holes in this painting straight through to the wall. What are you thinking about so hard?"

She smiled wistfully but never took her eyes off of the painting.

"This reminds me of a bouquet I got once. It was a first date. I was so sure that he was all wrong for me, and really, it was more of a pity date if I'm being honest."

"Nora!" I gasped. She turned and saw the look of complete shock on my face and giggled.

"What? Just because I'm soft spoken, Mabel, doesn't mean I'm all sweet as pie on the inside you know."

"I'm pretty sure you're the sweetest, most pure person here. But finish your story anyway."

"Well, like I said, I was sure that this date wasn't going to go anywhere. And for awhile, it didn't. I had a reasonable time, but he never came calling again so I just let it go. A few months went by, and he finally came calling again, although it didn't look like him at first. Turns out, his brother had gone and joined the Civilian Conservation Corps, the CCC, and he was trying to help out as much as he could at home. He sure had filled out in those few months, grown into a young man instead of a boy."

She was lost to the past, still staring at the painting but eyes unfocused and a little sad. I had a feeling now she was talking about her late husband, Theo, but I didn't want to interrupt her and ask.

"Anyway, he came calling again, and it wasn't just his looks that had matured, but his behavior too, and I was smitten. We ended up getting married, and had a wonderful life, you know. But part of me always wishes that I had something left of that first ever bouquet. Some sort of physical proof that he always did know best." She took a calming breath before she continued, and leaned into me a little where I still had my arm around her shoulder.

"It's amazing that you painted those others from ink from a flower, Mabel. What a wonderful way to create art and preserve a memory."

"Oh how wonderful to phrase it like that. I never thought of it that way." I looked around at the natural ink paintings and realized that a whole other reason for painting them was opening up before me. True, my commission paintings were also a way to preserve a memory. But I really liked the tangible connection to a memory, like ink made from flowers. It gave me the warm fuzzies.

"I'd love for you to have this painting."

"No, Maybe-b..."

"Don't you no Maybe-baby me. Not on this. You just gave me a wonderful gift, a more positive way to look at these paintings that until now I thought I was just messing around with. But now when I look at them I see value in what they are. Let me return the favor, and you take this painting home. Please. I don't know how close it is to the first ever one you got from Theo, but if it's close enough to remind you so strongly, I want you to have it. Please."

She looked at me with watery eyes and nodded. "Thanks, Maybe. Love you, doll."

"I love you, too." I gave her a proper hug, and then packaged the painting for her.

BEFORE I KNEW it, most of the ladies that had come today had a purchase, and most had a story to go with it. Not all of the stories were as sentimental as Gertie's and Nora's of course, but it was still a really amazing experience for me. It must've shown by the huge smile on my face as I packaged up the last painting.

"You look happy, sugar." Dottie said as she gave me a sideways squeeze.

"I am, Dot. This was fun. Thank you for bringing your friends."

"Thank you for sharing your talent with us! It was so good to see what you've been up to since you got back to the cottage. And I'll admit, I liked seeing some paintings that look a little more like the stuff you used to do. Not that I don't love your style now, not many people can paint like that. But it's nice to get a glimpse of little baby Mabel too."

She was pinching my cheeks now and shaking my head back and forth, laughing to herself.

"Betshe..." I yelled through smooshed lips, "come get wor fwend pweesh."

Everyone was laughing as Dottie let go of my face and spun me back toward the dining room.

"Say goodbye to your adoring fans, honey, and we'll get out of your hair."

"Y'all aren't in my hair. This was fun. Thank you all for coming."

"Where can we see your work again, Mabel?" one of the other women asked.

"Oooooh yes, I'd like to know, too. I would love to get some paintings as gifts before Christmas this year. But I'm sure you don't want us traipsing through your house every time we need a little gift." Gertie was almost bouncing on her toes with enthusiasm, as if she wouldn't mind traipsing though my house, but I wasn't sure how to respond.

"Oh, well I don't really have a place for them. I mean, I don't have a way to... that is that..." My brain was not brain-ing, and I didn't sound like a very competent human, much less like a successful business person.

"Mabel, you should open an art gallery!" one of the ladies by the door called out.

"No," Gertie interrupted, "art galleries are just for displaying art, not buying gifts, right Mabel?"

"Oh, well, actually..."

"That's foolish then. The girl's gotta make money too, not just show off, if she's going to stay in town," someone else piped in from across the dining room by the window.

"Uh, I'm actually not..." This is what a fish feels like out of water, right? Trouble breathing, mouth opening and closing but no apparent sound coming out?

"She makes money now, Stella. Didn't you see all those beautiful photograph looking paintings she said she's already sold?" Gertie was glaring at the other woman, her stance slightly defensive as if she was insulted on my behalf. The image of an angry Mrs. Claus, ready to throw down, came to mind, and if I was having trouble responding before, it was hopeless now.

"Lord Gertie, you know I didn't mean anything by that. You get so upset so easy, bless your heart."

"I'll show you upset..."

"She should open a gift shop!" Betsy's voice was loud, and the rest of us quieted down a bit. The others out of something close to respect for what she had to say and me from utter bewilderment at not knowing what to say in the first place.

"That's actually a wonderful idea, Mabel," Nora said quietly. She just looked at me, waiting for me to gather my thoughts, and luckily everyone else was so curious about what I was going to say that no one else chimed in for a blissful moment of quiet.

"I... well actually, I've always wanted a little shop. Somewhere that people could browse just like y'all did today, maybe find a little something that spoke to them."

There were various remarks of encouragement, things like 'oh how darling' and 'wouldn't that be nice' and 'sounds like fun'. My head was spinning a bit. Can you get vertigo from a conversation? Or maybe it was just the possibilities swirling in the air.

"Do you make anything else?" It was the same woman by the window, Stella I think? I heard Gertie harumph in her direction and she was quick to stammer, "Not that the paintings aren't lovely on their own, I was just curious is all. Sachets, or jewelry or little whatnots and the like. You know."

My hands tingled briefly along with the side of my face and neck. It didn't feel quite like a frisson, and maybe it wasn't vertigo, maybe it was a stroke. Surely the stress of this conversation was causing a mini-stroke. At least I had a new ally in Gertie. I could feel how wide my eyes had gone, and I felt a little like my breathing was coming too fast. When my gaze landed on Dottie, she took pity on me and took charge like only Dottie could.

"Okay ladies, enough! Thank you all for coming out here with me today so I could show off my girl a bit. Glad some of you found some hidden treasures, but leave Mabel alone. I'll let you know if she does another showing in the future and I'll drag you all out here myself. Now vamoose! Let's skedaddle!" She threw me a quick wink and started literally shooing her friends out of the front door.

"I'll call you later, sugar!" she yelled from the front porch, followed by a "Come on you old bats!" and a loud cackle as she walked to her car.

"We've been summoned," Betsy said dryly with a roll of her eyes. "Love you, honey. I'll see you soon I'm sure."

"Love you too, Betsy." I gave her a hug and walked with her and Nora to the door.

"Just breathe, Maybe-baby. Everyone was just trying to be supportive."

"I know. I just wasn't prepared for anyone to like the new paintings, much less want to purchase one or come back for more later. I was caught off guard."

"Did you mean what you said about always wanting to open a shop?" Betsy asked.

I hesitated. I had only told Elliott about that particular dream, and I was worried the more I said it out loud, the more power it would have. That wasn't necessarily a bad thing, but it was scary.

"I did. I've always thought it would be fun. Someday, maybe."

"Someday, Maybe-baby, you have to grow out of the maybes." Nora shrugged like she hadn't just given me some next level advice, kissed me on the cheek, and then walked to the car where Dottie was furiously motioning them to hurry up through the window. Betsy blew me a kiss and hurried to follow her.

I stood on the porch, watching the two cars full of supportive friends and strangers drive away and shook my head, trying to clear the thoughts that were still swirling around. Could a quaint little gift shop really work? Was I capable of taking that leap away from what I knew I was successful at and trying something new? All of a sudden, I really wanted a nap. I'd think about the shop again later.

Probably.

Maybe.

TWENTY-THREE

THERE WAS SOMETHING about a mid-day nap that made you feel like all was right in the world. I woke up feeling refreshed, and I knew it was one of those nights that I would work well into the early morning hours and love every second of it. Perks of being your own boss.

I sat up on the couch slowly and stretched, taking my time while my eyes wandered around the main space of the cottage. I wasn't really sure what I wanted to do with the rest of my day, and it was the first time since I'd been back at the cottage that I felt a little rudderless. The sun was just getting ready to set, so I decided a little stroll through the yard would be nice.

Grabbing a water on my way through the kitchen, I stopped at Gram's door. It was easier now to go in her room, but I still hadn't done any snooping. My nap had left me almost overly revitalized, and I was buzzing to get in to something. Walking to the dresser, I opened the top left drawer.

"See? I'm snooping. Snoop snoop snoop."

I poked around a little, still feeling like a little girl that was going to get caught at any moment. There wasn't really anything earth shattering, which I was thankful for honestly. Some beautiful old leather gloves caught my eye more than anything, and I realized they must've been Gram's from the 1950's or so. I wasn't sure why, but they called to me, and I couldn't bring myself to put them back in the drawer. After poking through everything else, I put it all back save the gloves, shut the drawer and left the room. I knew the day would come that I would have to go through all of it and get rid of things. But that day was not today.

I carried the gloves out into the living room and arranged them on the mantle among the picture frames. I loved the little kiss of vintage flair it brought to the room, and a little romanticism too.

"You live there now. Good change." I made a mental note to try and find a picture of Gram from that era to put with them. Maybe I'd get lucky and find one of her actually wearing the gloves.

The sky was finally a beautiful purply-pink, and I headed outside to enjoy what was left of the light. As I got to the little stone path across the creek where the swing was, I realized it would be the perfect place to set up a little travel easel and paint outside.

I didn't do too much of that, painting outside. Watercolor required so much drying time between layers that I usually didn't have the patience to literally sit and watch paint dry. When I painted inside, I could get up and bustle around for a few minutes, or make it dry with my little heat gun. But looking at the beautiful sunset and the tranquility of the creek and swing, I decided it might be worth the effort to set up another evening.

"Cottage bucket list. I should start one, just in case." I murmured to myself quietly, staring at the swing moving gently in the evening breeze.

"I think they say only crazy people talk to themselves."

Charlotte's voice didn't startle me this time, although I did grin at her choice of words.

"Good thing I'm talking to you then. Your ninja skills are getting rusty."

She snorted, and took a seat on the rocks crossing the creek. As she dangled her toes in the water, I noticed her sage green skirt and grinned.

"I love your skirt. I have a dress in almost the exact same shade. It's my favorite. Mine's all breezy feeling." I did a little hula shimmy dance move.

She nodded slowly. "It's a good color, my favorite."

We sat in companionable silence for a while. I was just enjoying the fragrant evening air, and she seemed content to have a quiet moment by the water. After a few minutes, though, I got curious.

"Did you say you had a sundry in town once? What a lovely word, by the way. Sounds so much more delicious than store and more vintage than shop." I giggled.

"I did."

"What was it like? To run the shop I mean. Like, you said you made soaps right? Was it just a shop full of soaps or did you make other things, too?"

She smiled the way one might at a child they were placating by playing twenty questions.

"I did make a couple of other things, salves and the like. But that wasn't all that was in the store. I had other things made by other people to round it all out."

"Oh! Like a little consignment store. That sounds like fun!"

"For a time, it was." She was smiling, but it was far away looking, like her smile got lost in a memory on its way to her lips. She turned her head to look back at me where I had settled on the swing. "Why do you ask?"

"Um... well, Dottie brought some of her friends over today..."

"Lively bunch, those girls."

I burst out laughing. "Yes, they sure are. But several ladies bought some of the paintings I have been playing around with the last week."

"I bet that felt good."

"It did. But the topic of a gift shop came up, and I just can't see a shop full of nothing but paintings being very exciting or successful." I scrunched up my nose a little, and reached out a toe to drag patterns through the water of the creek.

"Do you really think so little of what you create? Or have you really become so bored with what you do that you just can't see the value in it anymore? Or is it both?"

I slow blinked at the back of her head. "Wow. Solid burn. And you didn't even look me in the eye while you said it."

She turned her body sideways on the rock to face me. "Shall I say it to your face then? Or would you like to just answer the questions?"

I should've stopped talking at solid burn. Having her full attention on me was definitely worse, and I started squirming around on the swing.

"I see value in my established business. And some of the paintings I sold today undoubtedly had some value in the memories that they represented to the people that bought them."

"But..."

"But... I don't know. I think I've been conditioned to feel that if it isn't the style art I'm known for then it isn't worth my time. When I first really started focusing on that style but I hadn't completely cut out everything else yet, people would say things like 'oh my why do you waste your time painting that when you could be painting this' or 'well that's cute but this is spectacular'. I think after so long, I started thinking it, too. And since my established business brings me such a good income, it's hard to value things that are just for fun and not monetary gain. Ugh. That sounds awful when you say it out loud doesn't it?"

She sat quietly for a moment and I couldn't tell if she was collecting her thoughts or letting me collect mine.

"Let me ask you this; is joy worth your time? Is a hedgehog less than a porcupine because it's cute instead of intimidating? Is reading a good book less worthy of your time than something else because you can't make money off of doing it?"

I snorted. "Actually, believe it or not, I've painted both of those animals recently and I can say I preferred the hedgehog hands down."

She chuckled and shrugged. "Not the point, but good to know. Mabel, if you don't see value in what you do, no one else will either. Think about that the most. But if you still don't want a store full of paintings, then put other things in your store."

"You say that like it's obvious and simple."

"Because it is."

I sighed. A gift shop was something that had always appealed to the part of me that loved to find those special treasures unexpectedly, like at a thrift shop or antique store. *Or a grandma's dresser drawer*, I thought to myself as I remembered falling in love with those leather gloves just a while ago. The commissions that I took on were special because they were designed to be special. The paintings I sold today were special because they invoked a memory without being a direct replica of that memory. I liked that.

Charlotte startled me a little when she stood.

"I'm sorry, I got lost in my thoughts there for a minute... But maybe you're right, and it is just that simple."

"Oh, I'm always right." She winked at me and crossed over the creek and settled on the bench that was along the waters edge but far enough away to stay dry. As she was wiping the water from her feet with her hands to put her sandals back on, she stalled and looked up at me, one soft leather sandal dangling from a finger.

"What else would you have in your shop then?"

I thought it over for a second, chewing on my cheek. "I'm not sure. I think I'd like to stick with handmade things. Or maybe even nature inspired things. Handmade nature things?" I rolled my eyes skyward, frustrated with myself.

A great idea hit me, and I sat up straight so quickly that I wobbled in the swing just as I had the other night. *Have got to stop doing that before I end up in the water one of these days*, I thought to myself, taking a settling breath. Charlotte was watching me, quietly laughing, and I smiled in spite of myself.

"Hey, you could make soaps for the shop! You said you enjoyed having the shop, and this would be a little like doing that again, but you'd only have to worry about what you wanted to sell."

Her look was somewhat guarded, and I couldn't figure out why. I found myself back pedaling, worrying I had offended her or brought up bad memories. Maybe she had gotten tired of making things in wholesale batches or something. Just as I opened my mouth to apologize, she spoke.

"You think about if you want other people in your shop, and maybe we'll talk about that again another time. Be picky, Mabel. Don't let just anyone put anything in your store. After all you'd be the one to take the loss if it doesn't work out."

I narrowed my eyes a little and frowned. I'd definitely hit some bad memories, but I wasn't about to pry any further. I'd put my foot in my mouth enough for one night, and all she was trying to do was be a helpful friend.

She surprised me when she laughed out loud. I glanced up, and she was standing again, getting ready to leave I assumed.

"Mind sharing with the rest of the class?" I asked.

She shook her head slowly, closed her eyes briefly, but answered me. "I had one young vendor who tried to make her own jewelry from clay beads she'd made herself. She said she boiled roses to make the clay, which was the craziest thing I'd ever heard. They weren't very good either, especially not at first when they were always cracking and falling apart. But she was very convincing in her sales pitch, so I let her put a few pieces out. Eventually she moved on to offering something else, which worked out better for both of us for sure."

I was gaping at her, and she cocked her head as if to say 'what?'.

"That is the second time today someone has mentioned handmade beads to me."

"That feels like a stretch. Even more than a porcupine painting."

"Fair. But also, it's the truth. It's a long story, but a friend at the coffee shop this morning mentioned a book on handmade beads."

"Well. It's been my experience that when the universe wants

you to know something, it'll make it pretty hard for you to miss it. Best make sure you're paying attention."

"Ooooooo… she's a ninja and a sage." I was grinning, and some of my earlier energy was coming back, making me wiggle in the swing again.

"You forgot never wrong, too. I best be getting back home. I'm going to snip some lavender on the way out, if that's okay."

"Of course, Charlotte, you don't ever have to ask. Me casa es su casa, or herb garden I guess." I giggled and leaned back in the swing, pumping my feet a little.

"Good to know. Don't fall out of that swing now. Ninja skills are leaned not inherited, and you don't have the training not to fall out right on your tail." Her voice was stern but her eyes were twinkling.

I laughed and threw up a hand, my elbows were still around the swing rope because she was right, I was not a trained ninja or naturally coordinated enough to let go AND wave goodbye.

"See ya around, Char!"

She just shook her head and kept walking away toward the hanging ivy door.

Later I'd find that while we were having this conversation outside, inside my phone was pinging with a new text from Heather, saying she had found the book and there was indeed a chapter on the ancient art of rosary making, in which you made the beads from rose petal clay.

"Okay universe," I whispered. "Can't say that I'll follow directions, but I'm listening…"

TWENTY-FOUR

THE BURST OF energy I had from my nap on Monday followed me into the next two days. I spent Tuesday in a steady rotation of painting and snooping and texting.

My phone had never made this much noise in its entire existence, and I don't think I had smiled this much either. Not only had Heather texted about the book on Monday night, she had started that group chat with me and Alex and Sarah. They texted about everything, and nothing, and memes, and gifs, and pictures of squirrels outside bookshops. It was slightly chaotic, sometimes unhinged, and always a distraction. But I was loving every second and still a little shocked to be included.

I was proud of myself for slowly going through some of the things in Gram's suite, although I still couldn't bring myself to go in the closest or read her journal. Honestly, I should be more thankful that I didn't have to clean *everything* out. Since it seemed like my two main options for the cottage were to rent it out, either as a B&B or a rental house, or to live here myself, almost all of the furnishing and whatnots could stay. I had a few small boxes and trash bags set by the front door to take to the donation center when I went out today. But that wasn't the delivery I was most excited about.

The painting for Mr. Findley was finally done, and I was exceptionally proud of it. I started this painting for him before I rediscovered my love of some different styles of painting, and I think that's why I had struggled with it so much in the beginning. Yesterday, I just allowed myself to go where the subject was taking me and follow the vibe of the painting instead of trying to make everything look 'real'. After I'd quit fighting it, the whole thing came together beautifully and I was excited to give it to him.

In fact, Monday and Tuesday had been so productive, I was taking today off. I wanted to spend the whole day in town, getting groceries and wandering Main Street like Gram and I used to do. I was looking forward to my day, so after a quick shower and breakfast, I was on my way.

Mr. Findley's office had to be the first stop. His gift was metaphorically burning a hole through my bag, and I knew I wouldn't be fully present for anything else until I had delivered it.

I pulled in to the few spaces out front of the little house turned office and sat looking at it for a few moments. I don't know how I hadn't realized it before, but there were a lot of similarities between the current office and the subject in the painting. I had no idea what the story was behind what I'd painted, but I was more curious than ever now, and I hoped he'd share his story with me.

I was anticipating the lovely smell that would greet me when I opened the door, and I wasn't disappointed. It was amazing how quickly your brain could associate smells with people or places or feelings. That had to be a psychology thing... I made a mental note to ask Elliott.

"Oh, hello, Mabel! What a lovely surprise! Although I am so glad you stopped in, I have something for you!" Carol's genuine enthusiasm was infectious, and I kind of bounced across the lobby to her desk.

"How kind of you! Completely unnecessary though, I hope you know." I was grinning at her, but her matching grin was much wider and the look on her face screamed *proud*. I certainly didn't know what she was about to give me, but I knew that I would make a big deal about it no matter what it was.

"Oh, well, I couldn't help thinking about what you said last week about making custom blends. While I do have this one here for the office and one I created for myself at home, I just wasn't sure I knew how to make blends for other people or for specific reasons. Oh, I've just been going with my gut mostly until now. This week has been... challenging." She was drumming her fingers on the desk, unconsciously I think, and I could see her reliving whatever small personal journey she'd gone through in the last week.

"I understand that. I've been changing up my painting style a little lately, too. It can be scary doing something differently at first. Like being on a first name basis with people for the first time, hmmm?" I raised my eyebrows and winked at her when her gaze snapped to mine, a surprised look on her face.

"Oh my, well, we aren't talking about that right now!" She put a hand to the side of her face, trying to calm the blush there. "We're talking about my oils!" Her blush deepened as she grinned at me anyway and said, "Oh, but yes, Mabel, sometimes change is good."

I scrunched my nose and gave her a satisfied smirk. "Good to hear. Now, what's this surprise!"

"Oh, yes," she reached into the top desk drawer and pulled out a little organza drawstring bag. "Here you go. Oh, please do open it while I explain!"

Her earrings were jingling, literally as there were the most darling tiny bells on today's pair, as she bounced on her toes in excitement, leaning toward me. Each new encounter I had with Carol made me feel a little more like I wanted to be her when I grew up... she seemed so carefree and whimsical and just perfectly herself.

I opened the dark sapphire colored bag and pulled out a card with a tiny vial attached to it. The card was hand written with the word Slumber across the top in a vintage style calligraphy. The bottom of the card had a lovely little description of the scent notes and properties of each oil used in the blend.

"Carol, this really is beautiful! Are you selling these?" I kept sniffing the card, trying to get a feel for what the oils in the vial smelled like.

"Oh! Oh no, not yet anyway. I just wanted it to look nice when you opened it. Check the bag though, there's more."

At the bottom of the bag was a tiny plaster rose, a string running through the top for hanging. It too was vintage looking and delicate and beautiful, and my breath caught a bit as I ran my thumb over the surface.

"This is lovely." My voice was quiet as I still studied the small rose. "What is this for?"

"It acts as a diffuser for your oils. You can put a few drops of oil on the rose and hang it near the bed. Oh, the scent will last all night that way instead of rubbing off of your skin onto the covers."

"This is an amazing gift, truly Carol, I love it." She beamed at me. "But please, please let me pay you for it. I am the one that asked in the first place, and I'd love to support you if you are considering making these to sell."

She shook her head hard, and the little tinkling bells were the only sound in the office for a moment. "Oh no, no way. This is a gift. I loved every second of creating the blend, and it was more fun than I anticipated making the card and packaging it all up. Thank you for requesting it. It was the little nudge I needed to make something new."

She was looking at the card and rose in my hand with pride, but I could still see the doubt behind her eyes. I got it. It was hard to put something out there when you didn't fully believe anyone would like it. I had done it once when I started my business years ago, but I was doing it again now that I was exploring other styles.

I guess this is what Charlotte was talking about last night, I thought to myself. It was so much easier to see when it was someone else.

"If you insist, but only this time. This is absolutely worth paying for, and as soon as you start selling them please let me know." I leaned in to hug her, and she squeezed me back a moment longer than I expected.

"Oh thank you, Mabel. That's very kind. Let me know what you think."

"I will for sure." I packed everything back into the small bag, and put it carefully in a pocket inside my tote bag.

"Oh anyway, I suppose you're here to see Phil. Is he expecting you?" She had flipped right back into secretary mode, and her confidence level rose with the switch. I genuinely hoped she could transfer some of that over into a new essential oil business one day.

"Yes, I am, but no, he is not. I understand if he is busy and I can come back any time today. I just thought I would stop in and take my chances."

"Now should be fine. He loves when people stop in. Especially when they don't have a problem." She laughed, but then sobered very quickly. "Oh, you don't have a problem do you?" She asked hesitantly.

"No, not today." I giggled a little and pointed to my bag on my shoulder. "I actually have a gift."

"Oh, then he'll definitely want to see you!" She winked at me and made a shooing motion toward the hallway. "Go on back, just knock on the door a little before you go in."

"Thank you!" I headed down the hall, and as I knocked on the door, the nervous butterflies decided to come back and go with me.

"MABEL! WHAT A nice surprise! Come in and have a seat." Mr. Findley stood and gestured to the chairs in front of his desk. His smile was warm and welcoming, and while the butterflies didn't leave, they at least landed, softly opening and closing their wings instead of swarming. I took 'my' seat, and set my bag on the floor.

"Thank you. I hope I'm not interrupting. I should've called first I suppose."

"You're not interrupting at all. That's the beauty of a small town isn't it? People just drop in on each other and no one bats an eye." He winked, and leaned back in his chair completely at ease.

"Now, what can I do for you today?"

"I'm actually here because of everything you've already done for me." He cocked his head slightly but didn't interrupt, so I went on.

"From the day Gram passed away, you've done everything you can to help me through the process. From things that needed to be done immediately, to things that could wait, to things that I know didn't even fall under your job description like stocking the house with groceries... I just wanted you to know that I've recognized it all and that I'm incredibly grateful for your guidance. And friendship?"

The last part came out as a question, and though I hadn't really meant it that way in my head, it was probably better to phrase it that way. I took a deep breath and held it. Not really in anticipation of what or how he would respond but more to keep myself from rambling on until he did.

"You don't need to thank me, Mabel. Constance was a dear friend, and she was here for me when I first moved to town in a quiet way that I didn't even know I needed at the time. I'm honored to be able to return the favor by being here in the same ways for you. It's been amazing to watch you grow through the years, and I'd be delighted to call you friend the way I did your gram."

I didn't expect my eyes to mist over the way they did, and I smiled at him a little shakily.

"I... I have something for you. Just a small way to say thank you for everything you've done. I can't really explain, so I'll just say I hope you like it."

Reaching into my bag, I pulled out the painting. Not only had I packaged it in plastic with my sticker like all my others, I wrapped the bag in tissue paper like a gift. I passed it over the desk and then sat back in my chair and waited.

"Well now, could this be a Mabel Morrison original?" His grin was genuine, if a little teasing, and I just nodded sharply in answer. As he pulled the tissue paper away, the grin slid off of his face and his entire body went still.

I watched his face closely, trying to determine what he was

thinking but I couldn't. His face was completely devoid of all emotion as he stared at the painting. I could see his eyes moving, taking in all the small details. That was the only movement in his entire office. It seemed even the air was completely still, waiting for his response. I was too terrified to even blink myself, and for once the urge to ramble and fill a silence was missing, too.

Finally, after what felt like an eternity, he cleared his throat and moved his eyes to meet mine. I could see pain, and acceptance, and a quiet strength all swirling there, but I still wasn't sure what it meant.

"How?" He said simply. His voice was scratchy with emotion.

"How what?"

"How did you know about this place?" His eyes had gone back to the painting, and I could tell that his mind was revisiting whatever memory it brought back.

The only thing I knew for sure about the building in the painting was that I personally had never seen it before with my own eyes, only as it popped into my head during our last meeting. It was a beautiful antique building, all glass front with the striking architectural details that no one bothered with anymore. All the trim and molding was painted in a rich deep cream, and it accentuated the terra cotta color of the main structure perfectly.

A large iron clock stood off to one side, keeping watch over everyone's time, while a matching filigree iron sign stood out from the front of the building. There were no plants in front, the door leading straight to a sidewalk, but big flowering bushes grew down either side of the building, barely seen yet somehow still softening up the overall visual.

Gold lettering was displayed proudly across the windows. What the lettering was, however, was known only to Mr. Findley. The words never came to me, and so I had painted them onto the windows in a dream like way, alluding to the fact that they were there without solidly defining what they were.

It was part of what had made me so uneasy about the painting in the first place, the inability to lead the audience in a solid direction, to make it a concrete *something*. I still had no idea what the building was; grocery store, laundromat, ice cream parlor, it could be anything. But once I thought of the building as if it were appearing in a dream or memory, all fuzzy around the edges and soft, it was easier to finish it. I was still proud of how it had come out as art, but was feeling less confident at how it was as a gift now.

"Um, it's kind of hard to explain..." I was fidgeting with one of my rings, spinning it around and around on my finger. I actually, foolishly, hadn't thought about this part of the conversation, having to actually explain why I had painted this particular building that I'd never seen and didn't know anything about.

Mr. Findley's eyes met mine again, and he simply waited. I didn't see any anger or fear or anything else that would cause me to want to keep my big mouth shut.

So I told him the truth.

"Sometimes, when I'm talking with people, a picture just pops into my head. Sometimes, it's related to what we were just talking about but sometimes it isn't related at all. This was for sure one of those times that I had no idea why this particular picture appeared in my head, but it was clear enough I could paint it, and it felt strong enough that I thought it might mean something to you..." I swallowed anxiously as he just blinked and continued looking at me.

"I apologize, Mr. Findley. I'm not sure what I was thinking..." I could feel heat creeping over my entire body, the embarrassment of having given him this gift that seemed to so obviously be upsetting him causing my whole body to feel flushed. I looked down at my lap and kept spinning my ring.

"Mabel."

"I'll see myself out. Again, I'm sorry for any bad feelings I've caused."

"Mabel."

"Let me know something else that you'd like a painting of, and I'll be happy to do it for you in my standard style."

"Mabel McGillicuddy Morrison!"

I startled at his raised voice, and my brain shut off at his poor attempt at my middle name. Which come to think of it, I'm sure he knew after all of the legal paperwork we'd been filing.

"McGillicuddy?"

"I was keeping up the alliteration theme we seem to have going. Do I have your attention now?"

"Yes, sir. I'm sorry."

His long suffering sigh reminded me a little of Gram when I apologized for something like spilling the flour when we were baking cookies.

"You have absolutely nothing to apologize for, Mabel. Nothing at all. But I may owe you an apology if you think for one split second that I don't love this painting."

I looked to him, ready to see the lie written plainly on his face, but there was nothing but earnest gratitude.

"Let me guess, did this picture come to you during our last meeting?" he asked.

I nodded.

"When we were speaking about my dreadful design choices and my first encounter with your gram?"

I nodded again, but snorted, too. Encounter could be a pretty spot on word for an interaction with Gram, if she was in rare form.

He took what I imagined was a settling deep breath, and leaned back in his chair.

"Do you have time for a story, Mabel?"

"Yes, sir," I said quietly. I tried to appear more comfortable and at ease in my chair, but it was a lie. I still wasn't sure that he actually *liked* his painting, but I was more intrigued now that he guessed exactly when I had the vision of the building.

"Picture it; Sicily, 1910..."

"What?!" I sputtered a laugh.

"Just seeing if you were paying attention." A twinkle had come back into his eyes and his mouth turned up into the barest of smiles.

"Oh, don't think we won't circle around to the fact that you watch *The Golden Girls*. But please, do carry on."

He chuckled and shook his head. "I'll give you the Reader's Digest version, hmm?"

Nodding quickly, I actually did relax some into my chair, looking forward to his story.

"I was on my honeymoon in a quiet little seaside town. We were staying a week, not really doing anything but wandering and exploring and enjoying each other's company. At the time, I had just started working at this large firm in this big city with plenty of potential to work my way up. My then wife was working at a similarly competitive marketing firm. Between our two jobs, we really seldom saw each other, so the week together should have been wonderful."

I cringed a little at the words should have been, but kept quiet, not wanting to interrupt the flow of his story.

"One of the days, we were strolling along their Main Street, not much different from Painted Creek's Main Street, although I think the actual name of the street was Main..." He smiled fondly at the inside joke of this little town.

"We passed by this," he held up the painting, "and I stopped walking right in the middle of the sidewalk. My wife jolted to a stop next to me, having no clue what had caused me to stop. It was a small law office, just exactly as you have it painted here. No big huge sky rise building, no people bustling in and out, no expensive cars lined up in the parking lot. Just a quaint, antique, well loved, beautiful old building in the middle of a small town."

His expression had turned a little wistful, and I was completely drawn in to his story, wondering how just passing this little building could have such an effect on him all these years later.

"Well, that was the beginning of the end of my marriage I'm afraid, although I couldn't see that then. I explained to my wife that I always wanted to work in a little place like this and help people. Truly help real live people, not slosh away at some of the things that came across my desk where I was currently working sixty plus hours a week. She laughed, thinking I was joking, and then scoffed when she realized I wasn't. She always wanted more... more money, more status, more stress if you ask me. I never did.

And, well, you know how the story ends. I ended up here, in my own little small town practice, and I can honestly say it's the best thing that ever happened to me." He smiled, reassuringly at me, but I frowned back at him.

"Not to pry, but that doesn't sound like a moment that I would want to have memorialized forever and hung on my wall." I cringed a little at my own emotional visual. He just chuckled.

"That's where Constance comes in. In the beginning, you would've been one hundred percent correct. I was bitter and sad and angry and throwing myself head first into creating the life I wanted without any respect for the events in the past that got me there."

"....Oh...kay?"

He laughed. "When Constance showed up with her travel tea, I'll never forget it was some kind of lavendery, basily, minty concoction, she brought some excellent advice with her, too. She told me healing isn't just moving on and moving forward. It was being able to appreciate all the good things that had happened without being blinded by all the bad. In my case, it was recognizing that I could appreciate all of the good lessons that had come out of my marriage, all of the good moments I'd shared with my ex-wife while we were together, even though it ended badly and there were some awful moments, too. It was being able to forgive myself for things I didn't know in the past, and take all the new things that I had learned with me to the future."

I was unconsciously nodding slowly, like I got it, but I was still processing. He shifted in his seat, leaning over his desk with his elbows bent and hands clasped in front of him. It was a move I could imagine him doing countless times in meetings, when his client needed to really hear whatever he was going to say next.

"If I hadn't had the pain of realizing our desires and ideals weren't aligned, I may not have realized what was most important to me in my career and what direction I wanted to take with my job, my life. I needed to learn to appreciate the pain for what it taught me, instead of being angry I was in pain at all." He gazed off over my shoulder. "I don't know that I would've learned that lesson so quickly if it hadn't been for your gram. She blew in here with her tea and tough love, and I was a changed man when she went back home. I sure do miss having tea with that woman."

He said the last bit quieter, like it was tough to get the words out, and I could feel the grief and love that he had for her as clearly as my own. That lead ball in my gut with Gram's name on it rolled around a little, but it somehow felt smaller, as if knowing that maybe Mr. Findley had a ball with her name on it too made it slightly easier to bare.

He cleared his throat and brought his gaze back to me. "Thank you for this painting, Mabel. Truly. It will always remind me of what I want out of life, like that old law office did. And it will always remind me to appreciate the moments of my life, both good and bad."

And now I was blinking back tears. Truly did not expect to cry this morning, but here we were.

"I'm glad you like it." It was too simple, but I couldn't think of anything else to say. Until...

"Mr. Findley... did you originally paint this building that horrid salmon color because you were trying to recreate the color of this building?" I gestured to the painting on his desk.

"Yes." His mouth twitched with a suppressed grin.

"You missed."

"Well, we can't all be a color composition genius, now can we?" He said wryly.

"No, I suppose we can't." I was grinning at him teasingly.

"Speaking of buildings, Mabel, have you put any more thought into what you are going to do with the buildings *you* own now?"

The grin slid off my face, and I suppressed a very unladylike eye roll.

"Oh, now don't you give me any of that. Almost two weeks of your four week deadline are gone. It's reasonable for me to ask."

I sighed and crossed my legs, sitting up straighter. Mother always said that your posture portrayed your feelings to others. I was trying to create a sense of calm, or maybe control. Confidence? Something like that. Then maybe I'd believe it, too.

"I know. I know I need to make some kind of decision. My mother is expecting me back soon, too."

"Did you have a concrete return date in mind? Or is that flexible?" he asked.

"It's flexible I suppose. Although she hasn't exactly been subtle about feeling like I've already spent enough time here."

"Could you stay two more weeks? I can meet you at the building Friday morning and we can walk through it so you really have an idea of what you have. I know you've already been in Artful Brew, so you know what that building is like and you have an idea of what you could do with it if you decide not to renew her lease." I repressed a shudder. Definitely didn't want to think about that right now. Or maybe ever.

"If you stay for the remainder of the term, you can sign all the papers before you go. You won't have to make a return trip. " He rapped the desk with his knuckles like it was a done deal. And I suppose it was. It was a good plan after all, and if I found the strength to leave town again, I knew I couldn't face coming back only to pull myself away after only a day or so. It was getting harder to face ever leaving again at all.

"I can stay. I'm still getting a fair bit of work done while I'm here, so there's really no reason not to. And I suppose you're right, actually walking through the building would be helpful."

We made arrangements to meet Friday, and it was time for me to go. He thanked me again for the painting, I waved at Carol on the way out, and then I was off to face the rest of my day, feeling slightly more settled with my painting choices and slightly more unsettled with the rest of my future choices all at once.

TWENTY-FIVE

COFFEE CALMED YOUR nerves, right? Wasn't that a thing?

"Lies I tell myself..." I muttered under my breath as I pulled open the door to Artful Brew.

I wasn't nervous exactly, more like anxious. I'd have to tell my mother that I had decided to stay in town at least two more weeks, and I really would have to buckle down and make some decisions about what I was going to do with these buildings and the cottage, too. But for the moment, I was just going to grab a coffee and enjoy it.

"Morning, Sarah," I said as I walked up to place my order. I glanced up at the menu, simply admiring the detail that had gone in to making it, the lovely handwriting and embellishments in the corner.

"Morning. Planning on ordering for yourself today?" She arched an eyebrow at me but it wasn't in a challenge, she was just waiting for my answer.

"Nope. You pick. Iced, please, and maybe a tenth of the sugar as last time. Although, I did get a hell of a lot done in the last two days. So thank you for that I guess."

She laughed, a genuine laugh, and I was surprised at how much it changed her features. Some of the stress and sadness slid off of her face, if only for a moment.

"Got just the thing. Going to sit or take it to go?"

I looked around and noticed the place was practically empty.

"Fancy some company? I missed morning coffee date today, so I'm behind on my socializing quota..."

She looked at me skeptically, and I was sure she was going to say no.

"Sure. I'll bring your coffee over. Grab that seat close to the counter." She gestured to the small table for two right behind me and turned on her heel without another word.

"What was I thinking again?" I muttered under my breath as I pulled out one of the chairs and settled in to wait. I was too far in my head when I walked in and thought some conversation might be a nice distraction, but now I was wondering if 'nice' had been the right adjective.

I pulled out my tiny pallet of travel paints with spray bottle and a piece of scrap paper from the little container I kept in my bag. Without really thinking about it, with a few quick swirls of the brush I painted a little coffee mug.

Steam was coming from the top, swirling through the air above the mug. Sparkles crackled off of it, as if the fragrant water vapor carried magic within the steam. I kept the color palette to dark blues and chocolate browns. Potentially boring and drab, but in this case it worked, giving the painting a dark and mysterious edge. The coffee visible in the top of the mug had swirls through it, left by the white paper, and it almost looked like it was actually shiny with spots of whipped cream.

"I was gone like three minutes. Damn Van Gogh."

Sarah plopped down into the chair in front of mine and was openly admiring the tiny painting. She slid the iced coffee over to me, and I slid the painting over to her.

"Careful. It's still wet."

As Sarah turned the tiny painting right side up and studied it, I took a sip of my new iced concoction. Ours eyes met as we studied each other.

"Well?" she asked.

"Smooth, not too sweet. Refreshing?" I took another sip. I couldn't place it, but I think I liked it.

"Huh." She studied me mildly.

"What is it?"

"Coffee cola. Equal parts bold cold brew and cola, with whipped cream and cardamom on top."

"Shouldn't work, but it does."

She nodded in agreement. "Not a lot of added sugar, but something about the cola and the coffee together packs an unexpected punch. I hope you have a big to do list for the next couple of hours." She raised that one eyebrow like she was daring me to react, but I just laughed.

"I do indeed. This is perfect, and maybe my favorite yet."

She glanced down at the painting again and her fingers twitched on the table, like she wanted to touch it but knew she couldn't.

"Well?" I asked

Her lip raised slightly, fighting a grin, as I tossed her own question back at her.

"Dark, but alluring. Simple, but that's what makes it complex. Second favorite to Mocha the bunny."

"Huh."

"Why'd you paint it?" She asked.

"I don't sit still very well. And my thoughts were too loud. This helps. Why do you like it?"

This was the weirdest game of getting to know you I think I had ever played. It was so plain to see she didn't trust people easily, and

I was just so introverted that small talk was painful.

"It reminds me to keep looking for the sparks of light in the darkness."

"Whoa."

Her eyes darted up to mine, a hit of self consciousness there, and I scrambled to try and take it away.

"Sorry, that slipped out. Deeper than I expected, but I'm honored that it makes you feel something so... important."

She nodded once. "Don't get me wrong, I love my life. I have a great kid, a job I love that I literally started from the ground up, good friends." She glanced at me briefly before turning her attention back to the tiny painting.

"You can still love your life and feel like it's incredibly hard sometimes. And if it's too hard, you can change it."

"You sound like Constance. God how I miss having tea with that woman." She smiled softly. I slowly sat up straighter in my chair. "She said something similar to me once. I stopped in to have tea with her on a rare day off. It was the first tea I'd had over coffee in I don't even know how long, some sort of mint and fennel combo. She told me never to forget to count the stars in the darkness of my life. And if it was too dark to see them, move somewhere with less light pollution."

I laughed at just how much that sounded like Gram, the profound, solid advice almost hidden within her sense of humor. But Sarah just shook her head sadly.

"At the time, I think she was trying to tell me to leave my husband. Didn't matter though, it was just a few weeks later that he left us."

Yep, way deeper than I expected. But I saw an opening to learn a little more about her true feelings on this shop, so I took it.

"Do you regret staying here in Painted Creek? Or running Artful Brew? It can't be easy by yourself. I know I couldn't do it."

She snorted. "That's the thing. You could, if you had to. People don't really know what they could or couldn't do until they don't have a choice but to figure it out." She glanced down at the painting again, and this time she did lightly brush her fingers over the sparkles rising in the steam.

"I suppose that's true."

"As for the shop? There's nothing else I'd rather be doing. I love it here, and this town is the perfect quirky place for my somewhat quirky coffees." She gestured to the coffee cola. "Turns out light pollution wasn't my issue, it was just cloud cover. When the clouds moved on, all the stars that had been hidden put on quite the show…"

She slid the painting back to me, but I already had my hands out shaking them.

"Please keep it. Really. I'm happy it means a little something to you."

She regarded me for a moment and then nodded once. "I'll trade you for the coffee. I should probably get back to work though…"

"Of course. I'm going to take a little stroll up and down Main Street I think. Could you tell me how to find it?" I asked with mock innocence.

She kicked the feet of my chair and just raised an eyebrow. "Find it yourself. See ya later, Mabel."

"Bye."

I took a few minutes to pack up my little paints and sip my coffee. As I stepped back out onto the sidewalk from Artful Brew, I knew Sarah belonged in this town as surely as I knew I needed coffee every morning. Now, I just had to decide what my role was in keeping her where she was meant to be.

I TURNED LEFT on the sidewalk and moseyed toward the pet shop. I was walking at a leisurely stroll, so it didn't seem odd when I stopped in front of the empty building between The Pet Parlor and Artful Brew. The building I owned. One of two buildings I owned that no one knew about. Ugh.

I peeked in the window, but it was too dark inside to make out anything other than one massive space. I guess it was good I had scheduled a time with Mr. Findley to take me inside on Friday, or rather he had scheduled with me I suppose. I needed to start making some final decisions, and to do that I needed all the information I could get.

Moving on toward the pet shop, I noticed I was moving a little faster. I chuckled a little at myself and purposefully slowed my steps. I was excited to see Elliott again after our long date on Saturday. We had been texting back and forth non-stop ever since, but neither of us had mentioned seeing each other again.

Just as I opened the door, I heard Elliott yell, "Close that door fast!" I scurried inside and pulled the door shut, leaning back against it and looking around to take in the scene in front of me.

Don't laugh Mabel. This is one of those times where it's not nice to laugh. But oh, sweet mother of pearl was it hard not to! I tried to school my face in preparation for when Elliott turned around.

Chaos. Feathered chaos. The contents of the bottom shelf of at least two aisles were now on the floor, scattered from one end of the store to the other, some cans even still rolling on their side toward the fish tanks while dust and tiny feathers floated in the air. In the middle of it all was Elliott, with what appeared to be a very calm bird on his shoulder and feathers in his hair.

"Hi..."

"Hi." He sounded like a man who just lost a battle and knew the war was still to continue.

"I'd ask, but..."

"Maybe it's better if you don't. Mabel, meet Tina. Step up."

Pretty as you please, the gorgeous orange and green bird stepped up on to Elliott's fingers, and he walked over to introduce us.

"Nice to meet you, Tina. You're a very pretty girl."

Tina chirped in agreement, and I was surprised at how loud she was.

"That's quite a set of lungs you have there." I giggled.

"Oh, you have no idea. She's named after Tina Turner, and I think if bird Tina were at a concert with human Tina on a microphone with 100,000 screaming fans, you'd still be able to hear bird Tina over it all."

I laughed harder, but tried to look understanding and

supportive when he looked down at me.

"Looks like you've already had an interesting day. What happened?"

"Sometimes, I will bird sit at the store for a customer while they run errands. It's a long story, but Tina here doesn't do well when she's left alone. Since her owner works from home, that isn't often, but when she does have to be gone for most of the day, Tina here comes to bird day care at The Pet Parlor."

"Well, that's an incredibly kind service to offer for Tina here."

"Kind. Uh huh. Yep. Keep reminding me of that, okay?" He was looking at the offending little bird like he was rethinking the birdie day care package.

"What happened exactly?" I was almost afraid to ask, but I was having a hard time picturing how so much damage could be caused by such a tiny little creature.

"Conures don't talk as much as other parrots, but they do like to mimic sounds. Tina here loves bells. But she doesn't so much mimic them as she joins in on causing a racket." Tina ruffled her feathers. "I forgot to take the bells off of the back door before she got here this morning, and when I opened the door to check on Turtle, the bells chimed..."

"As they do..."

"Which made Tina squawk her peach colored little head off, while flying around my head like a dive bombing, tropical fighter pilot menace."

I snorted and slapped my hands to my mouth. Elliott glared down at me, obviously still too close to the situation to see the humor in it.

"Sorry. Continue."

"She scared the living daylights out of me, Mabel! I knocked into the shelves trying NOT to hit her with my wild swatting when I realized what was attacking me. Then you opened the front door and I was worried she would make a break for it while I was still slipping around on the floor."

"Tina, ma'am, I think maybe you deserve a time out." I reached out a finger to stroke her feathers, but she nipped at me. "Ah! Feisty feathered mango!"

It was Elliott's turn to snort chuckle as he carried Tina back to her cage. "I think I'm just going to keep her door closed for awhile..."

"Good idea. Let me help you clean up."

It didn't take long to set the store right again, it honestly looked worse at first glance that it actually was. We chatted as we cleaned, and once everything was finished, I inched towards the door.

"I'll let you get back to it. I just stopped in to say hello while I was strolling Main Street."

He leaned on the counter and smiled what was quickly becoming my favorite, one dimpled shy smile. "I'm glad you did. And thank you for coming to my rescue too, although hopefully next time I can make a better impression."

"I thought that only mattered on first impressions?"

"First, second, twelfth, whatever it takes..."

"Well, you rescued me from having to unpack and build all those art stands this weekend, so I'd say we're even." I realized we had both taken a small step toward each other unconsciously. He was like a magnet, and I wasn't sure how much longer I could lie to myself about resisting the pull.

"Could I call you later tonight maybe? Just to chat?"

"I think I'd like that."

We were standing close enough now his hand was on my waist, thumb sliding up and down my side. His fingers squeezed as he leaned down and kissed my cheek.

"Have a good stroll, Mabel. I'm glad you stopped by."

I smiled shyly, but I didn't trust my voice. With a small wave of my fingers, I left the pet shop without saying another word.

IT DIDN'T TAKE terribly long for me to make it all the way down Main and then back up the other side. I wasn't really in a shopping mood so I hadn't gone in many places, but it was nice to peek in the windows and just be out in town for awhile.

Heather's shop was across the street on the same end of Main as where I'd parked. So, when I reached the end of my stroll I was able to sneak right in the book store before I went back to my car.

The Secret Book Garden was everything I never knew I needed in a book store. The walls, what you could see of them anyway, were painted a deep rich green; not quite emerald, the shade was earthier than that. Sturdy shelving made from a medium toned, rich, warm wood ran along most of the walls, but didn't reach past what you could easily get to with a large step ladder, several of which I saw scattered around the store.

Frames in all shapes and sizes littered what was left of the walls, pieced together in groupings here and there. All the frames were slightly gilded, not just in gold but every metallic you could imagine, just enough that they sparkled with magic and mischief but not so much that the warmth and homeyness of the wood underneath couldn't shine through. The overall effect was otherworldly; comforting and inviting but with an undercurrent of enchantment. I never wanted to leave.

A grouping of tiny, hammered brass bells hung from the door and made the most beautiful tinkling sound when I came in. A small counter was off to the right, and I realized this store was set up a lot like Elliott's pet shop, minus the feathers of course. A beautiful vintage bell sat on the counter with a sign that said 'ring for service' and even the cash register looked like it was over 100 years old.

I slowly started browsing the store, my earlier indifference to shopping chased away by the sights and smells of all these lovely books in this enchanting shop. The children's section had the largest stuffed dragon I'd even seen, more of a couch really than a stuffed animal, with soft blue-green fur that looked like scales and shining emerald eyes that seemed to follow me as I walked by. I could picture the epic story times that must happen there, and I patted him on the snout as I passed.

"I see you met Marcus."

I jumped a little at Heather's voice. I'd been so enamored with my surroundings I never heard her walk up.

"Is the whole town full of ninjas?" I exclaimed.

"What?" Heather asked laughing.

"Nothing. Wait, Marcus the dragon."

"Yep." She popped the 'p' and shrugged. "Don't know why that's his name. Just is."

"Fair," I responded as I moved out of the children's section and back around toward the front.

"Oh, don't let me stop you from looking! I just wanted to say hello." Heather had walked behind the counter, and I realized her chair was wrapped in a deep purple velvet quilt. It made me think of a sorceress, which was fitting. This had to be the most magical place in town, and she was its keeper.

"Heather, I think if I started browsing, enchanted vines would grow from the gardening section, wrap around my legs, and I'd never leave." I was still looking all around the shop, mouth slightly open in wonder. "Seriously, this place is absolutely incredible. Did you do all this yourself?"

Her cheeks turned slightly pink. She looked around the shop as I did, and I wondered what she saw when she stopped to really *look*, after seeing it day in and day out.

"I did. Not all at once mind you, a little here and a little there. Sarah and Alex helped occasionally... we had an epic painting party once... but yeah, it was mostly me." She shrugged again.

"You're a genius. Magician. Sorceress. Marketing aficionado!" I was gesturing with my hands like I held a magic wand myself.

"No, none of that. Just a girl who fell in love with *The Secret Garden* when I was young. When I got this place I thought, how can I recreate that feeling in a book store? Now here we are."

I knew in my bones there was so, so much more to that story, but I didn't push. Some stories sounded worse to the authors when spoken out loud.

"Well, it really is magnificent. I don't know how you ever leave here to do anything else."

"Alex requires in person, proof of life meetings at least once a week. So. There's that." She was grinning fondly at the mention of her friend, but I got the feeling that it was also completely true, and if the extroverted Alex didn't drag her out of here on occasion she'd be perfectly happy staying in all the time.

"I just knew we were kindred spirits. Although, I don't have anyone to drag me out. I usually only come out when I've run out of food!" I laughed softly, but all of a sudden I realized how true my joke was. *How sad,* I thought to myself.

"Well, you do now. Better not miss more than two coffee dates in a row or there'll be a search party sent out."

"Aw, thanks."

I'd wandered closer to the front wall of the store and was examining some of the art in the frames hung there. All seemed to be book themed somehow, even if it was only that the art was painted on a book page.

"Now there's an idea. I wonder how well it would hold up to watercolor..." I was mostly musing to myself, lost in thought and the enchantment of the store, but Heather answered anyway.

"I keep empty frames for new art, if you ever want to give it a try." She smiled in a way that said she was completely serious but there was no pressure, and I was at a loss on how to tell her how much that meant to me. I just smiled back and nodded.

"Oh! Let me get you that book on handmade jewelry! It's in the back room, I'll be right back. Look around some more!" She rounded the end of the counter and practically skipped off to what I assumed was a back store room.

I moseyed in that direction, not really looking for anything but enjoying being in the store. Nestled between some shelves in the back was a charming little coffee station, built in to what looked to be an old TV cabinet with the doors removed. The back was now a chalkboard that read 'penny for your cup' in a speech bubble. A little Keurig was set off to the side, surrounded by all the necessary coffee fixings and accessories. A vintage piggy bank, standing proudly on a pedestal, was showcased on the other side with rows of neatly stacked to go cups in the middle.

"No better smell than coffee and books..." I muttered as I ran my fingers along the spines of the books next to the coffee station. Mixology and coffee recipes. How clever.

"Here you go!" Heather popped out of the storeroom waving

the book slightly overhead. She looked so proud, I decided I'd find time to read the book whether I needed to or not. *She was right the first time though, wasn't she?* I thought to myself.

"Thank you! I can't believe you remembered a single chapter in one book out of all the books in this place. Half the time I can't remember where I put my phone..."

She laughed. "I didn't really remember it so much as I had a feeling that I remembered it." She scrunched her nose. "That sounds weird."

"No, no. I understand completely." And I did. That's kind of what the frisson visions were like when a painting came to me in my mind. Kind of like what was happening right now.

Heather looked a little uncomfortable, and I realized I'd been standing still, sort of staring at nothing as the picture in my mind solidified. Either now she thought I was the weird one, or she was self conscious about what she'd said. I shook my hands at my sides a little and laughed nervously.

"Women's intuition, right?"

"Something like that, I suppose. It took me a little while looking through the database to find the actual book, but I knew it would be there somewhere."

"Well, I really appreciate it. I'll let you know if I end up with goop beads. What do I owe you?" I asked as I started walking back toward the front of the store. I was eager to leave now so I could get this painting out of my head and at least sketched on to paper.

"Not a thing. I hope it helps."

"Oooh, I don't think so, Tim." The ninety's TV reference slipped out as natural as breathing, but Heather snort laughed so she must've gotten it. "You've already gifted me a book. Let me pay for this one, please."

"How about we trade? A book for a painting? But only if you do it your way." She was looking at me pointedly, but I wasn't sure what she meant.

"ALL the ways 'round here belong to me!" I said in my best Queen of Hearts voice. Random classic book villain quote for the win. My pop culture references were on fire today! Must be the atmosphere in the book store; it was making me simultaneously smarter and more creative.

"Ha ha. But seriously. If you want to do your standard style because it makes you happy for this project, then that's great. But if you're called to some other way, even better." She shrugged. "Just enjoy the process, Mabel. I'll love it either way."

I must have looked completely shocked, because Heather literally pointed and laughed at the look on my face.

"Small towns, you know? Plus, you had Dottie and company over to see all your new paintings... that's more effective than a billboard." She was still grinning at me like I should've known better, and I couldn't help but grin, too. She was right, I should've known.

"Ugh. That woman. Anyway, I'm happy with a trade Heather, thank you. I should have it in about a week or so."

"Oh, no hurry! I'll just enjoy the anticipation until then." She giggled, and after a few more pleasantries and goodbyes I was on my way back to the cottage.

TWENTY-SIX

I WOKE UP to the sound of rain beating on the roof. It sounded like one of those spring storms that snuck up out of nowhere, unleashed an unholy amount of rain, and then took back off as fast as it had come. I laid in bed just listening to the sound for awhile. After a few minutes of listening and just quietly existing, I realized I couldn't remember the last time I was this relaxed or at peace. Normally, there was too much on my to-do list that I felt had to be crossed off to allow me to just exist in the moment.

Frowning, I got up. I still had things to do on the list here, too.

I knew I really needed to get serious about cleaning out the cottage, no matter what I was going to do with it long term. And I had to make some decisions about the buildings too. It was just going to get harder to decide the longer I let it go, and the more time

I spent with Sarah and the other people I was beginning to think of as friends compounded the problem. Remarkably, cleaning out the cottage felt like an easier task this morning, so that's where I started. Then maybe I'd earn the right to relax...

I pulled on some flannel pajama pants with my tank top, messy bunned up my hair, and shuffled to the kitchen. I still hadn't gotten a real coffee pot, but at this point I didn't think that I would. I loved the beautiful French press from Dottie, and if I needed anything more than that, Artful Brew was only a few minutes away. I'd managed to go twice this week and would probably go tomorrow too before my meeting with Mr. Findley.

"Becoming a bit of a habit it seems..." I mumbled to myself as I walked around waking up the house. Once the windows were open, lights on, and coffee poured into my mug, I stood facing Gram's room. I'd been leaving the door wide open, like maybe being able to see inside all the time would make it easier.

It didn't.

"Hedgie," I called over my shoulder to my little lamp friend, "I'm going in. And I mean business this time."

Side note, maybe I did need that pet that Dottie had mentioned when I first came back. Seems like I did things out of order... wasn't it supposed to be pet *then* man? I closed my eyes and shook my head slightly while my fingers rubbed together two layers of material on my PJs at my side.

"Aaaaanyway..." I rolled my eyes at myself and walked into Gram's room.

I quickly made good progress on the dresser drawers. The bedside tables were easy too, each only having one small drawer. The table on what I assumed had been Gram's side of the bed held books, which I had moved out to the coffee table in the living room. It seemed to me endlessly sad that she'd still had a side of the bed, the mattress dipping down noticeably even with the bed made, when her husband had died more than thirty years before. I'd never gotten to meet him.

The bathroom was easy, I pretty much just swept everything into a trash bag and tried not to think about it too much. There was a small half round shelf, the top a soft, worn wood on a black iron frame, above the towel holder next to the sink. It displayed a few bars of what looked to be hand poured soaps with darling little stamped labels. I left those, along with an antique perfume bottle made of blown glass and a silver hairbrush on another shelf across the room. I was beginning to think of my interior design style as comfortable cottage with a splash of vintage glam here and there. Pretty sure that wasn't a thing, but it was working for me. And it was a far cry from the beige of my old apartment, thank goodness.

After wasting thirty minutes or so just working myself up to doing it, I stood in front of the closet door.

"I was never really a snooper at heart..."

Without thinking about it much more, I yanked open the closet door and groped around the walls for the light. As my fingers flicked the switch on, I held my breath as I looked around.

Just a closet. No dragons. No treasure chest hidden in the back, at least from what I could see.

"Just a closet... right. Good. Okay."

I laughed nervously to myself. This was ridiculous. Of course it was just a closet. It would still be hard to go through though, emotionally and physically. Gram had a lot of clothes. And shoes.

Since I'd decided to work this morning, work I would. I started in the floor with the shoes. I'm not sure why... it seemed like the more obvious choice would be to start at eye level or at the top and work your way down, but here I was in the floor, chucking shoes out of the open closet door into the bedroom floor.

When the tenth pair went flying, I used a little too much oomph and it sailed all the way across the room and hit the bedroom wall.

"Oops."

It landed right underneath a picture of the women who had been in Gram's life for as long as anyone else on the planet. Suddenly, I felt horrible for not thinking of including them in this. I grabbed my phone from my pocket and called Dottie.

"Hello?" She sounded groggy and I winced. I forgot she was a night owl too but usually slept longer than I was able to in the morning. Too late now.

"Do you want any shoes?"

"Shoes?"

"Yes, shoes. Or clothes? Or things? I already cleaned out from under the kitchen cabinets, but I don't think y'all would've wanted any of that anyway. I'm sorry I didn't ask first."

"Sugar, what in the blazes are you talking about? Are you okay?"

Not only did I wake her up, I could hear the concern in her voice and I didn't mean to worry her. I took a long breath before I answered.

"I'm sorry, Dottie. I didn't look at the time before I called, and I'm fine. I didn't mean to worry you. I was just cleaning out some things in the cottage and it occurred to me that I hadn't offered to let you and Betsy and Nora come over, that there may be things that were important to the three of you. I apologize."

She sighed. "Well now, while that was easier to understand I suppose, I sure do hate when you button up like that."

"Wait, what?"

She ignored my confusion. "What's this got to do with shoes, honey?"

If she could ignore what she'd said, so could I. I was a queen of disregard, in fact.

"I was cleaning out Gram's closet and throwing shoes into the bedroom to donate."

"Ah. Well, set up a target next time and keep score. How's your aim?"

"Dottie..."

"Mabel!"

I just waited her out. I hadn't quite calmed my panic over potentially hurting their feelings yet, and she certainly wasn't helping.

She sighed. "Sugar, we're all old. We have plenty of shoes. Load 'em up and get 'em out!"

I still didn't have anything to say. I just sat in the closet floor, picking at a string in the carpet that had unraveled.

"Mabel, baby, really. We had practically a lifetime with Constance, and I'm thankful for it every damn day. It's awful sweet of you, sugar, to consider that we might want to hold on to some things, but our houses are already full of memories and mementos and gifts from her through the years. You can call the other two if it'll make you feel better, but I'm telling you, we don't need a thing."

"Okay."

"Constance would want you to make the place yours, I just know it."

"I don't know if-"

"I know, I know… you don't know if you're going to stay. Nonsense, in my opinion, but if you insist then she would want you to make that cottage whatever you wanted it to be. Even if that meant cleaning it up to rent it out or something equally ridiculous."

"Tell me how you really feel, Dottie. Please, don't hold back."

She laughed loudly through the phone, and I felt my lips twitch slightly in spite of myself.

"Now that's more like my Mabel. I knew you were in there somewhere."

I didn't respond again, and after a beat or two she asked, "Sugar, do you need help? The girls and I can load up and be there in a jiffy. We'll bring snacks."

I did grin at that, and I started to feel the panic subside just a little. I looked around the closet from the floor and realized that I actually did want to do this on my own, like a few more last moments with Gram to say goodbye.

"No, thank you for offering, Dot. But I've got this."

"I know you do, honey. I'll call you again later, okay?"

"Okay. Love you."

"Love you, too."

As we hung up the phone, I turned back to the remaining shoes on the shoe rack nestled up against the closet wall. Looking out into the bedroom and all the shoes already littered across the floor, I grinned.

"Red shoe is five points, blue shoe is ten points, and bright yellow pump is fifteen points. Aaaand go!"

I spent the next ten minutes playing rapid fire shoe toss and smiling ear to ear. By the time I'd made it through all the shoes and boots, I had five pair that I wanted to keep, and I'd lost track of my points. But I did feel a small sense of accomplishment looking at the empty space in the floor, and that in and of itself was a good start.

As I got up to walk out of the closet, an empty hanger on the lower clothes rack got hung in the shoulder of my tank top. I stumbled into the double rack of clothes and kind of bounced off the door frame.

I wish I could say this was unusual for me. It wasn't.

When I got my feet back under me, I reached for the offending hanger to move it to the top level where the other empty hangers were. If I didn't, there was a seventy-five percent chance that something like that would happen again. Sliding the clothes on the top to the right a little, I realized there was a shelf on top of the bottom rack of hanging clothes that was hidden by the clothes hanging from the top rack. Using both hands, I shoved at the hanging clothes on top and pushed them back into the closet as far as I could.

The shelf was full of clear plastic totes. Not huge, thankfully, but large enough to hold all of the books I could see inside. I bent down to see the label on the first tote more clearly, brushing my fingers over Gram's playful handwriting. It simply said '2010-2020', and I realized that they weren't books at all, but journals.

"Whoa." I stared at the tote for a second, and then looked at the back wall of the closet. There was a good fifteen feet between me and the back of the large walk-in closet. I walked halfway down, sticking my hands between the hanging clothes and looked in; more totes. I had no idea that Gram had even kept a journal, much less that there could be an entire lifetime of them.

I slowly walked over to the bed and plopped on to the corner. I had been so sad to have missed so much time with Gram, so many stories and things I'd never know. Was it possible that it was all right here for me to read?

"There was treasure in the closet." I whispered to myself. What must be story after story, written by Gram herself, waited for me, a glimpse into the life that she'd lived. I sat there in awe, feeling like it was almost too good to be true.

My stomach picked that moment to remind me loudly that I hadn't eaten breakfast yet, which was probably good because my brain was a little overwhelmed with possibilities anyway. Standing slowly, I tiptoed my way through the shoe land mines and out of Gram's room. The mess, and treasure, would still be here later.

AFTER A QUICK breakfast, I set up the dining room table for another painting. While the pull of the newfound journals was still there, I'd kind of slacked in the work department the last few days, which had been nice in its own way, but I really did need to keep up with my obligations, too. I pulled up the list of commissions, and settled in to knock some out.

The next painting on the list was a re-creation of an old family photo. The client had asked if I could paint the old sepia toned photograph of the family's dairy farm in vivid color. They'd also asked permission to make prints for their family members. This made me smile and think of the painting I just did for Dottie of the cabin. I was excited to take on this project, so it made it the perfect one to start with today.

Like always, before I knew it a few hours had passed, and I had a rumbly in my tumbly again. But laid out on the dining room table in front of me was a good start at an honest day's work, at least for an artist who worked for herself, so I was more than ready for a break and a change of scenery.

As I poked through the kitchen looking for something to fix for lunch, my mother's ring tone blared through the stillness of the cottage. I really should change it to something more soothing, so my nervous system wasn't already up in arms before I even answered the phone.

"Hello, Mother. Putting you on speaker so I can fix lunch."

"Hello, darling. Good to hear you're still capable of feeding yourself, since you seem to be incapable of responding to a message."

Wow. Two seconds in. I wish I could say it was a new record, but it wasn't. At least she wasn't mad enough that I'd lost the 'darling' in greeting.

"I'm sorry that I didn't touch base with you about the house. I received your pictures. You're right, it's a cute little place."

"But..."

"But there's been a slight delay here, and it looks like I will need to stay in town for another two weeks at least while we sort through some paper work and contracts."

Complete silence. Danger alert! I'd never been able to wait out my mother, and against my better judgment, I found myself filling the void now, too.

"It's just easier for me to stay, Mother. I have all my painting supplies out and have been doing really well on the commissions I've accepted on the website. Here, I'll send you a picture of what I started on today." I stopped crafting the perfect sandwich to snap a picture and text it to her.

"If you moved in down the street, Mabel, you wouldn't have to send me a picture, I could just come see it in person and visit with you while you paint."

"I know. There are just some things I still need to see to here. It's easier for me to stay. For now. It should all be settled in a couple of weeks."

My stomach flipped over, and now the fantastic sub I had been making for lunch somehow seemed to sit heavy in my stomach already, even as I looked at it still complete and sitting out on the plate.

My mother huffed into the phone. "I doubt this place will still be on the market in two weeks, Mabel. I'm surprised that it's still available now."

"Well then, I guess if I don't find a place to move straight into, I'd just have to come stay with you for awhile then wouldn't I? That's not so bad, is it?"

She sighed. A step up from a huff at least.

"No, I suppose it's not. I do miss you, Mabel, I hope you know that."

"I know. I miss you, too. It's not forever though."

Probably. Maybe.

"Hmm. Well, what is the delay anyway? You're being awfully tight lipped on any details."

"I have to decide what to do with the building that is being leased before the lease is up in two weeks. I also have to decide if I want to lease out the other building or just sell it. Not to mention figuring out what to do with the cottage. I would have to come back to sign papers for everything anyway, so like I said, it's just easier for me to stay. I can continue my painting streak, visit with people, and come back refreshed."

"You're still planning on letting it all go though, isn't that right?"

I paused. There was absolutely no way to continue this conversation without making her upset. Might as well rip off the bandaid.

"I... um well, I think I might keep the buildings. I can rent them through a property management company and have very little to do with it all. Unless I decided I wanted to stock a shop myself." *Stocking* a shop totally sounded better than *running* a shop, didn't it?

"Really, Mabel, we've discussed this multiple times. Opening up a store would take away some of the exclusivity that you've worked so hard to build for your business. Plus, shipping things in for inventory from here seems exhausting. You'd be better off not splitting your time and energy."

"I know. We'll see how it works out."

"Well, I can't tell you what to do obviously. You do what you want."

I was so glad this wasn't a Facetime call, the eye roll that little statement caused had a mind of its own and would not have been silenced. I couldn't remember the last time I'd just done what I wanted, save coming back here to Painted Creek for this trip.

"Yes, Mother. Look, I need to eat so I can get back to this painting. It's at a pivotal point and I need to add a layer before it completely dries. I'll talk to you soon."

"Yes, alright then. Love you."

"Love you, too." I managed to hang up the phone before I let out a half groan half scream. Every time we spoke, the guilt I felt about coming back here grew a little. Neither of us was used to being away from the other for this long, and I was worried that my mother was just sitting around, waiting for me to come back. But thinking about moving closer to her, and having conversations like this one practically every day for the rest of forever had me feeling like I was trapped under a weighted blanket. It was supposed to be warm and soothing, but I just felt like I was suffocating.

Grabbing the plastic wrap, I wrapped up my lunch plate and put it back in the fridge for later. I liked my subs cold anyway.

TWENTY-SEVEN

I HADN'T RAGE painted in a long time, but that's what I found myself doing for the rest of the afternoon. I used my regular watercolors and the first few paintings were nothing but angry splatters and vivid strokes across the page. Once I felt a little calmer, I pulled out an old trick that I used to use in art school to calm my brain after a particularly stressful test or an argument with Mother.

I took a waterproof pen and drew big sweeping, squiggly lines all over the paper. Every where the lines intersected and created a point, I colored the point in, making it into a curve.

"Rounding out the pointy bits, rounding out the pointy bits..." I singsonged to myself, letting my brain have a break by not thinking of anything else.

Once all the intersections were smoothed out, I got my paints back out and just colored in the sections. I paid exactly zero attention to whether or not the colors mixed or if the sections filled in completely or if I even liked it. I just watched the paint swirl around on the paper, and I felt myself finally settle into some semblance of calm.

I was thankful that art still did this for me. It was so easy to get bogged down in the business side of it all, and the perfection that I required from myself. If I didn't take anything else from my time back in Painted Creek, I was grateful to have rediscovered the magic of being present in the moment of what I loved to do. And I did love to paint.

I stood and stretched and decided that my sandwich sounded like a good idea again. I took it and the new book from Heather to the bar and settled in.

A jewelry maker I most certainly was not, but the book was interesting anyway. There were a few crafts that made me think of Becca, and I thought I might loan the book to Sarah if it was something she thought they might like to do together.

A chapter toward the end of the book laid out detailed instructions on how to make a clay from rose petals, along with a brief history of its origin and use in making rosaries. And I did mean detailed. It was a lengthy process that involved a lot of boiling the plant matter, blending it smooth with a blender and then boiling it again. For days. And it seemed like a whole lot could go wrong somewhere in the middle, especially for me. My attention span wasn't usually *days* long.

It was fun to read about it, but I still wasn't sure that it was something I wanted to try. Especially not as a way to preserve something special, like a wedding bouquet.

Even as I was telling myself no, I glanced over at the beautiful bouquet from Elliott and I thought about Nora's story about her first bouquet. I shook my head hard, like an Etch-o-Sketch; my go to you're-being-ridiculous reset button for a clean mental slate.

"Seriously, Mabel, don't you have enough on your plate now? No new projects."

My mouth was saying no, but my feet were headed to the refrigerator to pull out the containers of goop that I'd stored from making the inks. I pulled out the one that had been chamomile flowers once upon a time, took the lid off and peered inside.

"Well... this was boiled after all. Surely that counts as step one. Now where did I see the blender again?"

I never was very good at following directions for a craft project. I didn't have a lot of patience for things like ironing down seam allowances or letting things dry between steps... it really was a wonder that I could successfully watercolor at all. If we were being honest, crafting was probably the only place I *didn't* follow the rules. It'd worked out so far, so no reason to stop now.

The flowers had already been boiled to extract the color into the liquid to make ink, which also means that all the liquid had been drained off. I figured theoretically that draining off the water and boiling it off might be kind of the same thing. It was worth a try anyway, and it allowed me to skip several steps and save a few days of time.

Another thing the book mentioned was that you could add bentonite clay to your plant matter, and it would make it stronger. Luckily, I had some. I was allergic to practically every commercial skin care product that contained synthetic fragrance, which was almost everything, so I had been making my own face masks and other products since college.

So, I found myself sitting back at the kitchen bar with a bowl of chamomile goop clay in front of me considering how best to roll it in to beads. I was worried it was still too wet, but it held together, and at least I was giving it a try before I threw away the goop.

Alex was right, I needed to stop calling it goop.

An hour or so later, I had around fifteen beads, somewhat close to round, drying strung on a sturdy thick wire. I found a place out of the way in the laundry room to leave them be, and I'd try to remember to rotate them every now and then. I'd just have to wait and see if they turned out okay.

I glanced at the unfinished painting on the table, but I still just wasn't in the mood to focus on that amount of detail. Walking in the yard sounded like a much better option, and it wasn't long before twilight would fall and I could swing as the stars came out.

That was another thing that I was enjoying about my time here in Painted Creek. Columbus, Ohio wasn't a massive city by any means, but it was big enough that the light pollution still reached the sky and blocked out most star gazing. Here though, tucked away in the Appalachian woods of North Carolina, the stars were endless. I tucked my phone into the pocket of my pajama pants, another perk of being self employed was all day pajama days, and headed out to tromp through the yard.

EARLIER IN THE week, I had finally gotten around to hiring the yard company that Dottie had recommended, and I noticed what a good job they'd done as I walked around outside. It was kind of unsettling to think that people had been crawling all over the place while I wasn't here yesterday, but I was really thankful to have the help keeping up the yard and all the beautiful landscaping. I'd hired them for the whole month, and they'd come once a week until I decided if the upkeep of this place was still my responsibility or not.

Dottie was right on our call earlier. I was just lying to myself every time I thought I might not keep the cottage. This place was home and always would be. Even if I didn't live here, which I still wasn't sure that I could, I would keep it. It would be a fantastic rental property of some kind and I knew that Mr. Findley could help me figure all of that out. But for now, it was just mine, and I enjoyed walking around the yard and the silence of the impending night.

I had specifically asked the yard crew not to mess with the herb garden, or to cut the vines that made the makeshift door. The guy was super impressed with the layout and I told him I couldn't take any of the credit, but that I was learning how to care for this part myself. I was anxious to see if they'd left it all alone like I'd asked.

As I strolled along the edge of the creek, I noticed some of the soft, smooth rocks in groupings and little rock gardens scattered here and there. Some were submerged and some weren't, and the effect of the water splattering over them made it seem as if they were being painted with watercolors themselves. The water changed the color of the rocks, making them more vivid, and all of the piles seemed to dance and shimmer with their own energy as I walked by.

"Almost like the creek is painted... wait, painted creek... huh..."

When I crossed over the creek to go to the herb garden, Charlotte appeared at the edges of the woods. I waved and waited for her to meet me at the vine door. She looked like she was dressed to play in the dirt, capri pants and a soft white t-shirt with a gathering apron on top. Her raven hair was pulled back into a soft French braid, but it still shined in the fading light.

"Fancy meeting you here. Out for a stroll?" I asked.

"It appears so. And I wanted to see if any of the herbs needed to be pruned. You still don't have anyone to look after the garden, do you?" Charlotte regarded me with a completely straight face, giving nothing away. I wasn't sure if she wanted to continue working in the garden or if she was disappointed that I hadn't found anyone.

"No... I hired someone to help with the yard, but I was kind of hoping to learn how to care for the garden myself. At least while I'm here."

"Still thinking about selling then." A statement, not a question, but she still frowned as she said it.

"No, actually. I could never outright sell this place. It's too special. Not just the memories, but the feeling I get when I'm here... I'd be a fool to let that go forever." She was nodding slowly, walking among the herbs, touching them gently here and there. "I still don't think I'll be living here permanently, I'll probably rent it out somehow, I don't know. But it will be nice to be able to come back whenever I want."

"Makes sense."

As I watched her go from plant to plant, taking clippings from some and just looking over others, I realized I had no idea where she lived. She had to be close, since she always walked here, and it was so close to dark now I couldn't imagine her being out in the woods after dark alone. Suddenly, I felt like a horrible friend.

"It just occurred to me that I owe you an apology, Charlotte."

She snorted. "I can't imagine what for. But let's hear it."

"You've listened to me moan and complain for practically two weeks, I'm always sneaking in to what I would imagine is your quiet time in the garden, and I've never even asked where you live or if you might need a ride home. I apologize for being so self centered"

"Definitely an unnecessary apology. Feel better anyway?"

"Not really. I've not been a very good new friend. So tell me, if I'm out on the road, how do I get to your house, other than turning left out of the drive?"

"Turning left is a good start. Then just down a few klicks. Did you want to learn a little about the garden now? This plant needs a little help." She had knelt down next to what I thought was an oregano plant and was brushing her fingers through the stems.

"Yes, please!" I hurried over to the other side of the spiral and knelt next to her. "What's wrong?"

"Nothing too bad, just needs a little pruning. If an herb goes to flower, the taste of the herb can be altered and bitter. When you prune the tops, it keeps the plant from flowering and encourages it to grow out instead of up." She gestured with her hands as she spoke, motioning to how tall the plant could aspire to be or how much space it could grow to fill.

"It seems like I remember hearing that before."

She handed me the little pruning scissors that she had in her apron and encouraged me to snip the tops of the plant.

"Sometimes, branching out is a good thing." She said quietly.

I had laughed lightly but shook my head no at her musings. "I tend to branch out too much I think. At least in crafting. I see a new trend or something catches my eye on Pinterest and the next thing I know I've spent $100 in craft supplies that I'll probably never use again."

I handed her all of the clippings and she tucked them away in one of her pockets. The apron really was quite cute, made of linen worn soft with use, criss-crossed in the back with multiple pockets around the front. It was vintage in that way that was making a come back, and I was thinking of asking her where she got it so I could buy one to hang on the hook in the laundry room. It'd complement the whole vintage pop thing I had going on in the cottage.

She raised an eyebrow at me, and in that moment she reminded me so much of Sarah that I snorted and quickly covered my mouth with my hands.

"Never hurts to explore new things. What if you never tried anything new and then missed out on something that brought you great joy or helped other people?"

"Is this experience talking, oh wise Ninja Char?" I poked her in the shoulder as I fell ungracefully backward to sit on the ground instead of kneeling.

"Ninjas don't have nicknames."

"Fine, then I'm revoking your ninja status. Char suits you."

She narrowed her eyes at me briefly, but chose not to comment. "It's a little bit of experience I guess. I love making soap, but I had the best time when I first started experimenting with salves and other things. And when I could create something that someone needed, to heal cracked hands or help a baby sleep, well, that's the best feeling in the world."

I was absentmindedly drawing doodles into the dirt, but I looked up at the wistfulness in her voice.

"I'd love to see some of your soaps and things sometime. They sound lovely. Hey, maybe we could trade!"

She smiled. "Maybe some time we will. What's the most recent new thing you've tried?"

I laughed, and then told her all about the goop I had kept from making the natural ink, and that I had tried my hand at flower clay bead making.

"Luckily this time it didn't involve buying any new supplies, so there's that. We'll see how they turn out in a few days. Doubt I'll be making millions off of my new jewelry line any time soon." I shrugged and then stiffly got to my feet.

She'd been flitting around all the plants like a bumblebee, but stopped and came to stand next to me at the front of the garden.

"There's more value in things than money you know. What about the value of the experience? Of a lesson learned? Of putting something out into the universe that wasn't there before, that now exists only because *you* put it there. That's worth your time, too. At least to me it is." It was her turn to shrug, and I followed her out of the garden.

"You're right. I know you are. I guess after making a business out of my talent and passion at such a young age, it's gotten hard for me to remember that sometimes just doing the thing is reason enough to do the thing. I'm too afraid it won't be perfect or that someone won't like it."

"I can guarantee you someone somewhere won't. Who cares? When you do things with love and good intentions, other people, the right people, will be drawn to it. Forget the rest."

I looked at the sky and realized the sun was almost completely down, and soon the beautiful pinks and oranges on the horizon would be covered in the deep blues and purples of night. "Hey, would you like to come in for some tea? I can drive you home after."

Charlotte's eyes cut over to the cottage and back so quickly I almost missed it. I thought I saw a look of longing cross her face before she replaced it with a brilliant smile.

"That's a great offer, but I can't tonight. Don't worry about me though, these woods and I go way back. I'll be fine."

"Maybe next time then. My tea isn't as good as Gram's but it's better than muddy water I suppose." I gave her a goofy grin and a little finger wave and I started walking backward back toward the house.

"I'll see you around, Bell."

I stumbled in my backwards walk at the nickname. "Bell? Why, because my personality is so shiny?" I sang the last bit in my best giant animated crab impression.

"No, because you're always making loud and unnecessary noise. Usually in the form of an apology."

"Rude! Fair, but still rude!" I called to her retreating back.

She laughed, I wished she would do it more often, and threw up a hand in an almost wave as she disappeared into the woods.

I walked the rest of the way up to the house and flipped the outside lights off. I wanted to sit in the darkness when it well and truly descended over the backyard. The sound of the creek was gentle and soothing, and not for the first time I wondered how I was ever going to leave this place.

Charlotte's speech about finding value in things was making me reconsider my housing choices. There was value in being close to my mom, sure. We relied on each other for almost everything and we had for a very long time. But wasn't there value in building community, too? In having other people that would offer to bring snacks and clean out closets and trespass through your yard in the evening?

More and more it was feeling like I had to choose which I valued most, this new sense of community I seemed to be slowly building for myself, or the safe life my mother had built for us since I was young. It felt impossible.

The stars twinkled in the sky, and as the gentle breeze danced through the yard, the smell of rosemary calmed my racing thoughts. I still hadn't seen the hedge that had to be thriving nearby for me to be able to smell it so strongly so often. With one more deep breath, I drug myself in the house and locked up for the night.

I had a feeling tomorrow would be a long one, even if just mentally, so I was ready to head to bed. Tucking the house in as I went, I grabbed the new book from Heather off the bar on the way to my room. I glanced one more time at the flowers from Elliott. I was extremely tired all of a sudden, but I stayed awake long enough to place another online order. This one from a small Etsy shop full of jewelry making supplies.

Maybe branching out could be fun...

TWENTY-EIGHT

HELLO, MY NAME is Mabel, and I have an addiction to coffee from Artful Brew. It was rapidly becoming the only coffee I wanted, and I wasn't sure if it had to do with the new flavors and blends I was being introduced to or the company. Probably both.

This morning's meeting, for lack of a better word, was even better because Alex had brought an entire batch of cronuts just for us to have while we visited. I decided it was a really good thing she didn't make them every morning, or I would be gaining a lot more than a new group of friends to eat them with. The smooth espresso that everyone opted in on was the perfect complement to the pastry, and I was grateful to know such culinarily talented people.

Heather asked if I'd been able to look over the new book, and then squealed when I told her I had ordered some jewelry making supplies. The squeal was infectious, and by the time everyone went their separate ways I was in better spirits than I had been in for days.

I tried to hold on to that feeling as I got ready to face my meeting with Mr. Findley, and to see the empty building for the first time. I'd done a little shopping on Main Street while I waited for the time to come, and I swung by the car on the way. I'd walked down the other side of Main like I had the other day while I was shopping, and I'd parked at the end of Elliott's shop again too, trying to avoid the large front windows of the coffee shop. I just had to pray the small town rumor mill gods were on my side, and no one else in town saw me go in the empty building either.

Mr. Findley was right on time, and I couldn't help but grin at him when he checked his watch as he walked up to me.

"Exactly on time."

"I'd expect no less," I said.

"Shall we?"

"I mean we are standing here and all, so I suppose." I sighed.

"Come on, Mabel, chin up. It's a building, not a firing squad." I swear I thought I saw him roll his eyes, which seemed to be a very un-Mr. Findley-like thing to do, but he was turning away from me to unlock the door so I couldn't be sure.

As soon as we stepped inside, I knew I was in trouble. It was a mess, and it needed so, so much work, but it just felt right in a way I truly wasn't expecting when I'd agreed to the walk through. It felt like home in the way that the cottage had always felt like home, like some part of me recognized this place and could breathe a sigh of relief now that I was back. I gasped, and started walking in a slow circle trying to take everything in.

Mr. Findley must have mistaken my gasp for one of alarm, because he winced.

"Yeah, it is a bit of a mess. I don't know why she never started fixing this building when the other was rented out and bringing in an income. It was like she never really wanted to fix this one at all."

"What did this used to be? I'm having trouble placing it from when I was younger, but then so many of the stores are different now I suppose, and I probably only paid attention to the ice cream shop anyway." I was slowly making my way to the back of the store, careful of my step, but eyes wide with possibilities.

"When I moved to town, it was a pharmacy and that's still what it was when the owner retired. I think that it had been a pharmacy for around fifty years or so. I can dig into some old town records and try to find out more of the building's history if you'd like."

"Yeah, as an eight year old kid I definitely would have overlooked a pharmacy on the list of places I wanted to shop. Please do find out more, I'd love to know." I'd reached the back wall and was glancing down the hallway toward the alley access and what I assumed would be stairs leading to the second floor. "Are the stairs sound enough for us to go up?"

"Oh, yes. Structurally, the building is in great shape, just like the two on either side. That part at least had to be maintained for safety reasons. It's mostly cosmetic changes that the place needs."

"More like plastic surgery…" I mumbled.

"You may have a point. But we can go poke around upstairs safely." He gestured for me to go ahead.

We made our way up the staircase, which admittedly was a little creepy right now with plaster hanging off of the wall and creaking stairs under foot. The door at the top was much more charming that I expected, one of those old vintage kind of doors that was half glass in the top. I almost expected to see 'Private Investigator' written on the glass in gold box letters.

"Too many old movies." I rolled my eyes at myself.

"Pardon?"

"Nothing." I grabbed the glass doorknob, because of course it had a glass doorknob to pull on my vintage glam heartstrings, and let us into the apartment above the store.

There was so much light! I mean, so much that I just stood there blinking for a few moments, not really sure what else to do. The windows weren't even really that large, but the effect was as if the whole front wall was made of glass.

"How is there so much light?" I asked in awe.

"It's probably this way until the sun starts to go down. Just the right height I guess. I'm sure you could add curtains…"

"No! Never. It's an artist's dream. SO much light…" My sentence trailed off as I crossed the vast open space to run my fingers along the window sills. It was incredible.

"I think there are two other rooms, probably supposed to be bedrooms, and a bathroom over here."

"Are you here as a real estate agent or a lawyer today?" I teased him. There seemed to be all the necessary pipes and hookey-dos poking out of the floor for a small kitchen set up along the opposite wall, too.

"Well, Mabel, I'll be honest with you… I'd love to see you stay here in Painted Creek. So if I need to brush up on my sales skills and show this place off, I'm not above doing it."

I turned to face him and stopped my slow perusal of the upstairs apartment.

"Why?" I asked simply.

"Constance loved this town, and I think you do, too. Further, I think this town could be good for you, if you let it. And hell, you've been good for *me* since you got here, pushing me to admit something that's been right in front of me all along." He paused and I couldn't help but smile, thinking of Carol and Mr. Findley together was adorable.

"Tell Carol that her sleep blend works beautifully, by the way. She really should start selling her blends."

"I've already helped her set up an LLC and told her to start selling them in the office." You couldn't miss the pride and affection on his face, and I couldn't stop myself from poking at him just a little more.

"That sounds like an excellent excuse to celebrate. On a date. Together. You know, you and her?" I gave him a ludicrously exaggerated wink and giggled at myself. He rolled his eyes. For sure this time, I know because he made sure I saw it.

"Anyway. Mabel, I think sometimes the magic of a place isn't in the perfect location and big windows and good bones, it's in the people you'd be surrounded by. And rarely, maybe once in a lifetime, you're lucky enough to find it all. Don't let it slip through your fingers."

"Wow. Definitely a lawyer. A good one, too. Nice closing argument. Really hits you in the feels." I wasn't sure how else to respond to what he'd said, so I went with sarcasm. I knew I had so much to consider, now more than ever knowing what the building was like on the inside.

I still didn't think I could permanently uproot my life and leave Mom by herself in Ohio. After spending time with Dottie again and making some new friends, and maybe most of all finding Elliott, it was plain to see how lonely both Mom and I had been in our own little bubble, closed off from the world. She really would be all alone if I left.

My heart ached, torn between what I'd always known and what I'd always wanted. But deep down I knew Mr. Findley was right, this was a once in a lifetime chance that was literally being handed to me by the one woman who'd always encouraged every little whim and side quest and serious business venture without a single ounce of worry that I'd fail. I just wasn't sure I could take this big of a leap without her cheering me on.

We finished a quick walk through of a store room and bathroom downstairs, and then went our separate ways. Mr. Findley seemed to understand that I had a lot to think about and he didn't push me to set up another meeting. He did, however, remind me none to subtly that the deadline was fast approaching, and that I only had two weeks left to make a decision on the lease for the coffee shop.

I already knew, deep down, that I was keeping the cottage and the first building. There was no way that I could let the cottage go. It was where I belonged, at least some of the time, and I felt almost as strongly that Sarah was where she belonged too at the coffee shop. I'd keep her lease through the management company and no one would ever know that it was me behind it all, just as Gram had done.

But I didn't have a handle on this second, empty one. I certainly had enough money between my art business and my inheritance that I could afford to fix it up and rent it out as well. But I didn't want to rent it out.

Deep down, I wanted this little shop to be mine! I could already picture certain displays set up, and the entire upstairs would make the studio of my dreams. I wanted to fix it up and keep it. I wanted to turn it in to a thriving little gift shop slash art gallery of sorts, and I wanted to run it myself.

I just didn't believe that I could actually bring myself to do it.

I'd wandered the green in the center of the tiny downtown area, just trying to get out some pent up energy, when I realized all I really wanted to do, needed to do, was to go see Elliott.

I hadn't told him what I was doing this morning, I hadn't told anyone of course since no one knew I owned the buildings. But I figured I didn't need an excuse to pop in and see him, especially since he'd been a little preoccupied the last time. While he'd taken to calling me every night for a chat, I still missed him.

"How is that possible, Mabel? It's been what, two weeks? Get a grip, girl." My self pep talk was more like a scolding, and I didn't realize that it had the volume to match until a lady passing me on the sidewalk harumphed loudly as she walked by. Oops.

I pointed my feet toward the little pet shop, and with each step in that direction, I felt my shoulders sink down farther from my ears as the tension started to melt away. I'm not sure when it happened, but Elliott had become my safe place.

I OPENED THE door to the pet store hesitantly, remembering the rogue bird that was on the loose last time. I heard Elliott's laughter from the other side of the front counter before I had the door fully opened.

"You can come in. It's safe this time," His eyes were twinkling as he cocked his head to one side, "although I suppose you never really know."

"This is a dangerous place, Mr. Scott! One can never be too careful you know." I batted my eyelashes at him, thickening my fake southern belle accent, and he leaned over the counter for a quick, small kiss. My heart still skipped a few beats, not getting the 'small hello kiss' memo.

The phone rang, and after checking the number Elliott said, "I have to take this, and it might take a minute. Supply issues. Why don't you go keep the small furry animals company?" He answered the phone before I could answer him, so I gave him a quick thumbs up and went off to the middle of the store to find the critters.

I'd never asked for a pet when I was little. Before Dad died, we were always traveling and I never really felt the need for a companion when I had such great ones in my parents and Gram. And then after, well after I didn't want to add any stress to my mother, even if I was lonelier that I'd ever been in my whole life.

I watched the hamsters run on a wheel for a few minutes, giggling when one would go faster than the other seemed capable of. Mice had never really held my attention, even though I did think they were cute, and if I ever got a rat I knew that would be the end of my mother ever visiting my house ever again. Ever ever.

There were a few empty habitats, some reptiles I wasn't the least bit interested in, and some empty bird perches. I giggled when I thought about Tina… it certainly was a lot quieter in here today. I had just rounded a large pen with a couple of small, cuddly looking bunnies when Elliott came back in.

"Make any friends?" he asked.

"More like friendly acquaintances. All cute though."

"Just like you." He leaned in for a quick peck, and I realized that no matter what I had been telling myself, we were for sure dating. Before I could mentally pick that apart too much, he grabbed me by the hand and tugged me toward the back door of the shop. "Come on, come see Turtle."

We went out back to the alley, and Turtle came right over to see what was going on.

"I love how inquisitive she is. Hello, Turtle, happy Friday!"

"Turtle and I have a gift for you." Elliott said.

"Oh really, why is that?" I cocked my head to the side and peered up at him from where I was crouching next to Turtle.

"Why, not what?" He mimicked the head lean to the side. I giggled.

"Well, I mean, yeah. It's not a major holiday or my birthday, and I haven't done anything especially fabulous lately to deserve presents..."

"You exist? A happy Friday gift?" He shrugged. "I saw it in an antique shop when I was out with my mom and dad and it immediately made me think of you."

"Oh."

"Well, I mean if you don't want it..." He was taunting me now, and somehow it was just what I needed to get over the sudden bout of nerves and shyness.

Leaping from my spot next to Turtle, I walked over to him making grabby hands. "Well now I really want it. Gimmie!"

Laughing, he reached for my hand at the same time he reached into his pocket. He slid a beautiful bracelet onto my wrist and then lifted my hand to kiss the back.

The beaded bracelet was cool against my skin. Practically the whole thing was made up of light green beads, nearly sage in color if not a little brighter. There were a few dark, almost black beads in the middle like a focal section that didn't appear to be any kind of stone. After I stopped gaping at it, I look back up to see Elliott smiling at me.

"It's very beautiful, thank you. You know, I have a dress this exact color."

"You don't say! I bet it looks fantastic on you."

I made a noncommittal kind of noise in my throat as I slid the bracelet off to examine it better.

"The lady at the store told me that the green beads are green aventurine, and yes, it without a doubt made me think of you in that dress. That was a good night. The best I've had in a long time." He reached up and tucked my hair behind my ear to keep it out of my face and I found myself leaning into his touch.

"Did she say what these other beads are?" I was holding it up to the light now, enjoying the way the aventurine caught the light and the other beads seemed to absorb it.

"She did... I'd never heard anything like it though. She said they were actually old rosary beads, and were made of roses.

Something about how people used to make rosaries out of actual rose petals? I don't know. I would've bought the bracelet just for the green beads, but that was kind of cool, too." He shrugged like it was no big deal while I gaped at him like a fish. "Why are you looking at me like that?"

"Okay universe, you win."

"......what?"

"Nothing. The universe has been trying to tell me something, rather aggressively honestly, so I guess I better listen."

He was looking at me with this sweet sort of confused look on his face, like he had absolutely no idea what I was talking about but that it didn't really matter either. I just walked back over to Turtle and leaned over to talk to her again.

"Thank you for the bracelet, Turtle. It's beautiful, just like you."

I gave her shell some scratches and when she did her little wiggle dance, I smiled up at Elliott where he was watching me from the wall of the building. Without a word, he leaned down and pulled me to him, kissing me senseless. I knew I should stop him, stop whatever this was that had been growing between us before either of us got hurt when I decided to leave, if I decided to leave. But seconds after his lips touched mine all rational thinking in my brain cut off.

After giving Turtle an inappropriate show for a few minutes, I started to pull away.

"Elliott..."

"Don't. I know you're going to say you don't know if you're staying and that we shouldn't be doing this, whatever this is. But I want to spend every second I have with you to the fullest, not holding back. I really like you, Mabel, and if you leave tomorrow, I'd rather miss you knowing we made the most out of our time together than miss you and regret that we held back and missed out on something beautiful."

Well. If that didn't sound like a perfectly rational plan, I didn't know what did. And all of a sudden, I didn't want to hold back either. I would already miss him like hell, not to mention the other people I was getting close to, when I left town again... might as well make sure the pain was worth it.

"I was just going to say, Happy Friday, Elliott." Slowly, as if he were thinking over all the possibilities of my response and what it had to do with our time together, a grin crept over his face, and he pulled me close again, eliminating the distance that had crept between us while he was speaking. I laughed, but went into his arms willingly, and didn't try to stop the matching grin on my face that was pressed against his shoulder.

He flipped us so that I was pressed against the brick wall of the alley and placed an arm over my head, leaning over me. "Happy Friday, Mabel."

His voice had lowered a few octaves, and I fought the shivers that it sent down my spine, stronger than any frisson I'd ever had. Just as he leaned in to kiss me again, a loud wolf whistle sounded from down the alley. I felt my face flame instantly, but turned to face the noise anyway.

"Whew! Don't stop on my account. But maybe keep it to weekdays and school hours so Becca doesn't catch you." Sarah winked, shielded her eyes with one hand and waved with the other as she headed back in to the coffee shop.

"I'm mortified." I dropped my head to Elliott's chest, trying to hide completely between him and the wall. I felt his torso shake with his laugh, and smacked him lightly on the side. He kissed me on the top of the head, and raised my gaze to his with a finger under my chin.

"I'm not. Not even a little bit. I'm glad that in approximately three point four seconds everyone in town will know we're dating."

"Uuuuuugh! Small towns are the worst." I covered my face with my hands and stopped just shy of stomping my foot like a child.

He laughed again, but took my hand to lead me back inside. "You love it here. Gossip line and all."

He was right. I did.

TWENTY-NINE

THE WEEKEND WAS passing in an exhausting blur of cleaning and trips to the donation center. Lucky for me, my strapping, handsome, heart of gold, almost boyfriend offered to come over and help. It certainly made all the time spent in the car driving back and forth more fun. He was shocked by my varied and wide musical interests, but would just shake his head good-naturedly and chuckle when something seemingly completely off the cuff would pop up next on my playlist.

It was amazing how much Gram really had updated things since I had last been here. In the four months since Christmas, she'd bought all new towels for both bathrooms, I think all the bed linens were new too, and the place sparkled from top to bottom. I supposed the sparkling could have been a cleaning company that came in before I got here, but either way, I felt spoiled that things were in such good shape. I wondered if Gram somehow knew something was wrong and did what she could to make things easier for me, just in case.

I wish she would have called and asked for a visit, just in case.

By the end of Saturday night, I was starting to feel like I had gone through, sorted, or at least touched absolutely everything in the cottage now, except for the totes in Gram's closet. Elliott had helped me with the rest of her space, save the desk, but I felt like the totes full of journals and the desk drawers were things I needed to do on my own. And I would soon.

Probably. Maybe.

But I just didn't have the emotional strength to go through anything else by the time Elliott left. It was late, I was tired and sore and sad, so I turned to my paints on the table, still too restless to go to sleep.

I really was tired though, and my already well established klutz status gets worse when I'm really tired, so almost as soon as I sat down I knocked my paper and, thankfully still dry, paints to the floor.

"Biscuits." Deciding that I was more likely to fall out of the chair if I leaned over to pick them up, I got up and gathered my scattered materials. When I went to put everything back on the table, the flowers that Elliott had given me a week ago caught my eye. The accent lights for the kitchen were shining down on them like they had been set up for a photographer. They were still stunning, not wilting yet, and I just stood looking at them for a second before I sighed in resignation.

"Ah, hell. Fine. Hedgie, we're making beads."

I took several pictures of the bouquet, in the kitchen and then in different places around the cottage for posterity's sake, along with a little note card that had the date and a summary of the evening of our first not-a-date date. Then, I picked out a beautiful, huge dahlia that was in the center of the bouquet and took pictures of it, too. If this worked, I wanted to remember it forever.

So far, it seemed as if my goop beads were turning out alright, so I decided to use sort of the same process with the dahlia. If the ink it threw off was pretty, I'd keep it too for painting. So really, when you looked at it like that, I was totally still working.

A couple hours, two *Gilmore Girls* episodes, and a bag of popcorn later, I was ready to be done boiling goop. I think the smaller petals of the dahlia worked in my favor, and it seemed to be finished. I strained off the liquid and then squeezed the ball of slimey flower petal goop inside a cheesecloth wrapped in paper towels to get all the water out that I could. When I finally dumped it all into the blender, I was a little surprised at the tiny ball it had made.

"I'm going to need to get a tiny personal blender if I keep doing this." I muttered.

Scraping out the blender after the contents inside were as smooth as I could get them, I finally sat down at the bar to play with my new 'clay'. There really wasn't much from one flower, but it was an experiment anyway so I only needed enough to see if it would work. I formed up six small beads and a single tear drop shape the same way I had made the chamomile beads and took them to the laundry room. too. Gram had part of an old accordion clothes dryer hanging on the wall, pottery style knobs placed at each intersection, that I assumed she'd used to hang herbs to dry. I giggled, thinking that I'd need to add some kind of bead drying station if I kept messing around like this.

Finally, kitchen clean-ish and house all tucked in, I fell in to bed. I texted Elliott one more time to tell him thank you again for the help, but I was asleep before his reply came in only a minute later.

I SLEPT IN Sunday, missing three calls from my mother before I woke and realized my phone had fallen off the bed and on top of a discarded blanket, muffling the sound. My heart pounded, worried something was wrong, but when I called her back she only wanted to discuss another house she'd found for me, just one neighborhood over from hers.

"You drug your feet too long on the other one, Mabel, and it's no longer on the market. This one doesn't have a studio space, but you'll just have to make do," she'd said. I'm actually not sure how I responded, it wasn't the kind of phone call I usually had before I'd had any coffee. Hopefully I hadn't committed to anything or been outright rude.

I knew I was going to have to tell her that I was seriously considering staying in Painted Creek sooner versus later. And that was exactly what I wanted to do. I was kidding myself every time I considered leaving and living anywhere else but right here.

Even though that's where my heart was, I actually didn't think I wanted to tell anyone what I wanted to do yet. It still felt like it was too far out of reach, like a pipe dream, living here. Telling people led to expectations and comments and horror stories disguised as well meaning advice. No, it was best to just keep my head down for now until I had everything sorted, including the buildings.

I bumbled around for a little, wandering aimlessly through the house with my coffee mug. I wasn't in the mood to paint, and I thought about cleaning things out but we really had accomplished so much yesterday that there wasn't much of anything left to do. As soon as the thought fully formed in my mind, I heard a soft thud come from Gram's room. I narrowed my eyes in that direction and huffed a strand of hair out of my face.

"Seriously, house?! I tuck you in every night and wake you up every morning. What more do you want from me?"

Another soft thud echoed through the house, and I straightened. "Char, I know you're a ninja and all, but if that's you, we're going to need to have a chat about boundaries…"

Outside, a bird twittered in what sounded like laughter, but inside the house was quiet. I slowly made my way toward Gram's room, taking my time and looking things over along the way, but I was just stalling. I knew the sound had come from her room and I'd bet money it had come from her closet. It was the only place in the cottage that hadn't been completely sorted, dusted, set up and organized.

I flipped on the light to the bedroom and just looked around. Everything was still as Elliott and I had left it yesterday. I'd rewashed the linens and changed up the bedding, opting to have the beautiful quilt fully covering the bed instead of folded at the foot.

I took a sip of coffee but it had gone tepid. I made a face and set the mug down on a coaster on the dresser. Gram had a stunning old sepia toned photograph of her and my grandfather on the dresser, and I picked it up and brushed my fingers along her face. She looked so familiar like this somehow, young and happy, yet not familiar at all. Almost like I was trying to superimpose this image of her into memories where it didn't fit. But I could see the Gram I'd grown up with in the photo too, in the set of her lips when she smiled and the hint of mischief always just barely there in her eyes. Some things didn't change with time.

I set the photo back down on the dresser and turned toward the closet. Propping the door open with a little cast iron mouse door stop, what was it with the doors in this cottage anyway, I flipped the light switch and found the cause of the mystery thuds.

One of the totes full of journals must have been knocked around as I was pulling out clothing to take to the donation center. It had landed on its side, the lid lying on the other side of the closet floor. Two journals lay directly under the bucket on the floor, and a third was dangerously close to falling out as well. I set the tote upright and returned the journals, making sure they went back in the same order in which they had fallen out. I still didn't know if they were stored chronologically or not, or even if they were labeled, and I didn't want to mess anything up before I really knew what I was working with.

The closet was mostly empty now, a far cry from the full to bursting state it had been in when I'd started. The only things left were the few shoes and clothes I had saved, a few decorative items I thought I might want to put out around the cottage, and the totes. I grabbed a huge, patchwork floor pillow and chucked it at the back corner of the closet wall, making my own little reading nook to settle in to. Studying the tote that had fallen over, the years read '1965-1970'. Doing some quick mental math, I guessed that my dad was a young child during the years contained in this tote. I pulled out the first one, the one that had made the first thud, and took it with me to settle on the floor in the corner.

I was met with story after story of my dad's early childhood, all in Gram's familiar handwriting. Every now and then, a photo was taped to the page at the end of the entry, and that felt like an extra gift. I was literally watching my dad grow up in snap shots and personal stories.

Some of the stories I had heard before, like the time he accidentally flicked a small green pea down the back of Gram's blouse at the grocery store and she'd screamed and carried on, thinking it was a worm. Some I had never heard, like when he hid the car keys in the dog food bag so his dad wouldn't have to go to work.

I sat there and smiled, flipping through the years and looking into the memories of people I loved dearly but knew in a very different way from what was portrayed in the journal. Sometimes, it seemed impossible to merge the two in my mind, these personalities and the ones I knew, almost like I was reading about the lives of strangers. Then other stories were just so *Gram*, I could see her in my mind plain as day, hacking down the grape vines that grew along the laundry line because of a little green snake.

Gram loved her flowers and her herb garden and her creek bed, but the woman hated snakes. As much time as she spent outside, it was a wonder that she didn't have more run-ins with the danger noodles... they must have had some kind of understanding with each other about who's side of the property was who's after the clothes line incident.

Standing to stretch, I gently put the journal back in the right tote and replaced the lid. For the first time, I noticed that there was a moisture trap taped to the lid, and I was thankful that Gram had thought of that, and that maybe some of the much older journals would still be legible too.

I ran my fingers along the totes, going back in time until I found the year 1960. Gram would've been around my age, and suddenly I wanted nothing more than to know what her life was like then, how it compared to mine.

I flipped through pages, not really reading much more than a word here and there, until I came to the first page with a taped in photo. Gram was stunning, posing in an over exaggerated way, like a movie star from the 1940's. I figured it was surely meant to be a joke, but she looked so amazing I'm sure the joke didn't land. I flipped to the beginning of the entry, and started reading.

My William and I are going on our last date as an engaged couple. I can't believe in just a week's time we'll be an old married couple, too busy arguing over the dirty socks in the floor to go out anymore!

Momma says I have to stay around the house next week until the wedding. She says it's to get all the last little bit of work out of me that she can, but I know it's because she wants to spend time with me. There's nowhere else I'd rather be. I know I'll still be over nearly every day to help with the garden and what not, but it won't be the same for either of us, I'm sure.

I make sure to make us both a cup of tea every day, and we sit and enjoy them together. I already have a blend planned in my head for each of us to have at night when I'm gone in my own house, and I even got cute little tins to put them in, too.

She went on to describe the rest of the date and how excited she was to be getting married after having to wait 'all this time'. I didn't know the story of how my grandparents had met and fallen in love, but I found myself looking at the totes in their straight line in the closet and wanting to read them all just to find out. It was amazing to read that Gram had been making up tea blends for practically her entire life, and I hoped that somewhere in one of these journals was the story of how she got started. No wonder they were so good... she'd had a lot of practice.

I looked back at the photo at the end of the entry and realized that Gram had on a pair of gloves. I laid the journal out as flat as I could without bending the spine too much and took a picture with my cell phone. It wasn't perfect, but it wasn't bad. I'd get a frame for it for the living room mantle as soon as I could. I should probably check in to some kind of photo scanning app too, if there were going to be journals full of photographs like this.

I spent the next several hours on the floor, flipping through random journals from random years and imagining my grandmother's life through her words. When I was too stiff and too full of pent-up energy to go through any more, I went back to my paints. In no time at all I was tucking the house in again for another night.

Monday morning girls' coffee came early for a night owl, but I found that I was looking forward to it and didn't want to miss it. It was shaping up to look as if waking up early, at least three days a week, was going to be part of my new routine in my new life.

I just had to be brave enough to truly accept this new life, and hold on tight.

THIRTY

I WAS LATE. Even though I anticipated having trouble getting up and I went to bed early, here I was rushing around like a crazy person trying to get ready and make it to the coffee shop by seven.

It was 7:05 now.

I threw on the closest clothes I could find, messy bunned up my hair, and flew out the door. By the time I got to Artful Brew I knew it was almost time for Alex to leave with Becca. Hopefully Heather could stay a few more minutes to visit.

As I pulled open the door, I regretted coming at all, much less killing myself trying to get here in a hurry. All three ladies, Alex and Heather sitting at the table with Sarah standing next to them, turned to face me and made loud kissy face noises.

I could feel my cheeks turn beet red, I hated being the center of attention and everyone was definitely staring now, but they were making such a spectacle that I could feel my lips twitch too, no matter how much I wanted to be mad.

"You're all the worst, and I'm sorry I came." I plopped into the empty chair at the table and just barely resisted resting my head on my arms to hide my face.

"You loooooove us." Heather singsonged through her laughter.

"Mabel and Elliott in a back all-ey…" Alex sang.

"K-I-S-S-I-N-G" Sarah added, with another kissy face for good measure.

"Hey, Mommy! I know what that is! That spells kissing!" Becca picked this exact second to come barreling into the seating area, and her volume one hundred percent matched her enthusiasm.

Sarah had the good grace to look a little embarrassed as a couple of other customers chuckled. "Yes baby, good job. You've really been working on those -ing endings, I know." She ruffled her hair affectionately.

"Come on, kiddo, let's get going. Ya'll don't forget to make plans for after the festival." She pointed at me. "You, too. And Mabel, I'll text you later. I don't feel like I've had an adequate amount of time to pick on you about the smooch fest."

"Auntie Alex, what's a smooch fest?" Becca's earnest little face peered up at Alex.

"Becca, did you know it's 7:32?" Heather asked in a calm voice.

"Oh! That's two minutes after my projected leave time. We have to go, Auntie Alex! Let's go!"

"Well done. And thank you." I heard Alex murmur under her breath as she gathered her things.

"Projected leave time?" I looked at Sarah.

Pinching the bridge of her nose, she closed her eyes and said, "I was trying to help her learn to be on time for things with reverse math. Like, if you have to be there at eight and it takes you ten minutes to get there then you have to leave by 7:50."

"Ah, yes. And if it takes you ten minutes to put on your shoes, then you have to start doing that at 7:40." I was nodding my head with all the sage wisdom of a person who had been reverse mathing her entire life for years. "Solid plan."

"It seems to be working well too, Sarah. You're doing a great job," Heather said.

"Ugh. Thanks. I just didn't expect her to remember everything I'd said and parrot it back to me with complete accuracy."

Heather giggled and said, "It's good for her to have a broad vocabulary. It'll be fine."

"I know. That's why I let her hang out with Alex." Sarah called out, laughing over her shoulder as she headed back to the counter.

I glanced after her, ready to get up and order a coffee. After the public humiliation and quick wit of my new friends, I felt like I was under prepared by a few milligrams of caffeine, give or take a hundred.

I scooted my chair back to get up, but Heather put a hand on my arm. "She'll bring you something in a second I'm sure. Plus, I have to fill you in on the festival."

I vaguely remembered Alex saying the word festival as she left, but I was most focused on the smooch fest portion. "What festival?"

"Painted Creek's May Day Festival. You don't remember it from when you were younger and visiting?"

"May Day... no, I usually came to visit in the summer, so I guess I've always missed it. I think Gram may have told me about a booth a time or two though." I could feel that my face was all scrunched up in confusion, and I worked to smooth it out. There went that lead ball rolling around in my gut again. I should've asked more about Gram's life instead of being so self centered when we talked.

"It's so much fun. They close the square, and it's a weird combination of craft fair, food vendor lot, and block party. There are tons of booth spaces that you can rent that are officially official from the town, but by the end of the day people come with their own tables and just put them all over the green. They don't sell anything, but there's lots of trading and bartering going on."

"Sounds... unique."

"It's awesome! And every year after the festival, we have a

ladies' night party as kind of a last hurrah. It's Sarah's turn to host this year."

I nodded slowly without responding. It sounded like they had a long standing tradition and not for the first time I was wondering if they were really interested in adding someone new or if they were still being nice out of obligation to the new girl in town who might not even stay anyway.

"Everyone brings a drinking food or two, so you best be thinking of what you're going to bring." I jumped at Sarah's voice next to me. She had one eyebrow raised, as per usual, and was holding out a to go cup for me to take.

"Wait, what?" Between the sudden startle, the smell of coffee tantalizingly close and my stomach picking this exact moment to growl loudly, I wasn't sure how to process all of that and what she'd said.

"You know, like pizza or chicken wings or brownies? Drinking food." Sarah shrugged.

"We would love it if you would join us, Mabel," Heather said softly. I cut my eyes to her, mouth open in surprise as I reached out for my coffee cup. I'm so glad she seemed to get me, that'd I'd need to hear an actual invitation, but I was still a little taken aback by it anyway.

"Oh, yeah well duh. I thought that was obvious." Sarah rolled her eyes and sighed.

"I'd never want to assume. But thank you for the invitation. I'd love to."

Sarah's eyes sparkled, and all the sudden I wondered what exactly I'd just agreed to. "Oh, I can't wait to see if you finally loosen up a little bit."

I almost spit the sip of coffee I'd just taken back into the cup, and gasped out a pitiful "What?" as she laughed and walked away again to help the customer that had just come in.

"I'll put all the details in the group text. It really will be fun, Mabel. I'm glad you're going to come. You should totally check on a booth for the festival, too!" She clapped her hands a little and bounced in her seat.

"I don't know. I'm sure all the booths are gone. And even if they aren't, I don't have the equipment and probably don't have enough merchandise either..." I'd started shredding my napkin unconsciously, and Heather placed one hand over mine to stop me and get my attention. The look on her face was kind and understanding, and I felt the slight panic I hadn't realized was creeping in start to fade away.

"It was just a thought. It might be a fun experience, but it would be fun to just walk around and enjoy it this year, too. There's always next year."

"Yeah... I suppose."

We chatted for a little bit longer before we both gathered up our stuff to go. Heather was holding the door open for me when I realized I'd never asked about my coffee this morning. It was sweet, and slightly spicy, and I had immensely enjoyed every sip.

"Hey, Sarah," I yelled back into the shop. "What was today's coffee?"

"It's a blend of cinnamon and vanilla with a small dusting of nutmeg." She answered me in her no nonsense, dry kind of way, but I nodded and smiled.

"I really enjoyed it. What's it called so I can order it again?"

"Love Potion #9." Laughter from both her and Heather erupted at the same time, and I was surrounded by their teasing.

But it kind of also felt like love.

AFTER A QUICK grocery run, I headed back toward Main Street to see Elliott. I had been thinking about what the girls had said about the festival, and I really wanted to get his opinion on the whole thing, or maybe at least some more information that didn't involve school yard teasing.

Opening the door to the pet shop, I poked my head in and looked around before I fully stepped inside. Immediately, I heard laughter coming from a few aisles over.

"It's safe to come in you know. You really don't have to peek in every time you swing by like there are monsters inside." Elliott called.

"Not monsters. How did you put it... dive bombing tropical fighter pilots? Where are you?"

"Fish."

I turned left and headed toward the sound of his voice and the dimly lit aquariums along the wall.

"I'm afraid Tina has put you off birds forever." He was stocking some shelves with aquarium decorations, completely at ease in his space.

"No, she was adorable. Totally worth the nightmares." I gave him a cheeky little grin and then started opening other boxes and passing him the contents. "Hey, I have a question."

"Shoot."

"What do you know about the May Day Festival? Specifically the actual rented booths. I'm a little fuzzy on how the rest of the day works... it might be above my Painted Creek visitor's status."

He frowned a little, but to his credit didn't comment on me still only being a visitor in town. I frowned a lot. I really needed to make some decisions and get out of this limbo I'd put myself, and those close to me, in.

"Well, I have a booth. I get one every year. It's just fun to be out and talk with people as they walk by and see all the other tables set up. Most of the other store owners around the square get a booth too, not to mention all the craft vendors that will set up. Why do you ask? Considering a booth?"

"I don't know. The ladies at coffee this morning mentioned it and told me I should consider participating, but I don't know that I'd have enough inventory to decorate a booth..."

"Mabel. I've seen the dining room, and that was a week ago. I'm sure you have more than enough by now."

He wasn't wrong. I was just... apprehensive? I didn't know if it was the fear of something new, the fear of failing, or the fear of falling more in love with this crazy town. Probably all three.

"Why don't you call Dottie? She's on the festival committee so I'm sure she can answer all your questions about the specifics."

He shooed me off toward the back of the store, saying I could talk in the alley and not get interrupted if anyone came in the store.

After a quick hello to Turtle, I called Dottie.

"Hey, sugar. What are you up to this fine Monday morning?"

"Hey, Dot. Not too much. I had coffee with Alex and Heather and Sarah this morning and they were trying to tell me all about the festival coming up. I came over to ask Elliott some more about it, but he said you'd be the one to ask."

"Well I suppose I would be, since I've helped spearhead the thing for the last ten years. What do you need to know?"

"I was kind of toying with the idea of maybe getting a booth, but I don't know that I would be ready in time, or if there's even any left to rent."

"Honey, I am just so happy to hear you say that. I already got you a booth." I could hear the barely disguised glee in her voice.

"You did what now?" There was barely disguised panic in mine.

"Now you hush. I already got you a booth, and then I fixed it to where it's right next to the pet store's booth so you and Elliott can spend the day together when you aren't too busy with people walking by. Constance should have all of the tables and tents and chairs and whatever else you might need in the attic-"

I smacked myself in the forehead and groaned out loud, interrupting her. "Oh my God, how did I forget to go through the attic? The freaking stairs are literately right in my face when I watch TV and I've just been completely ignoring them like they're behind some kind of cloaking spell or something! And I thought I was doing so good cleaning out the house, too!" Dottie was quiet while I ranted, even though I'd interrupted her. "Ugh, and attics are creepy. Any chance we can forget I asked about the booth?"

"Nice try."

"I don't really need a table then, right? I'll just set up on the grass..."

"Tables are required." She was beginning to sound exasperated with my whining but I didn't heed the signs.

"Well then, I can't go. I'm going to be too busy cleaning out a creepy attic to be able to adequately prepare. Thank you for your consideration though."

"And now that's quite enough of that young lady! Mabel, have you ever been up in the attic?"

"No." I kicked at a stray rock and watched it bounce off of the wall of the building. "I was never allowed to when I was young, and I seriously think there's a cloaking spell hiding it now. I never thought about it again."

"It's not actually an attic anymore, Mabel, it's a finished upstairs. Your gram always called it an attic because that's what it was when we were growing up. She and your grandfather closed it in and finished it when they moved back into the cottage... when your dad was a teenager, I think."

That didn't make any sense to me. I looked at Turtle and tossed my arms in the air, looking for a little solidarity. She just kept munching on her lettuce.

"Why wasn't I allowed to go up there then?"

"I don't know for sure, sugar, but you took a tumble down a few of the stairs when you were a tiny thing, and the upstairs was a no go area after that. I'd imagine it was a precaution from then on." I frowned, but that did sound like a decree my mother would make to try and keep me safe. "And I wouldn't feel too bad about ignoring it now. You just aren't used to that really being a part of the house."

I frowned down at my shoes again. Some great homeowner I was turning out to be. I'd missed an entire floor.

"Anyway, back to the matter at hand. I already have your booth. Just bring whatever you have or whatever you can get done this week and it'll be fine. I won't take no for an answer, so you might as well start looking forward to it, you hear me?"

"Yes, ma'am." I was trying not to sound petulant, but my shoulders rounded as I closed my eyes and sighed quietly away from the phone.

"That's my girl. Now, get that young man of yours to help you haul everything you'll need down the stairs, turn that frown upside down, and get to painting, sugar! We have a festival to get ready for!"

I laughed in spite of myself as we said our goodbyes. I gave

Turtle one more scratch before leaving her alone and then headed back inside. I was beginning to feel a little like I'd been played. Walking back to the counter, where Elliott was now typing what I assumed were inventory numbers into the computer, I crossed my arms and just waited for him to acknowledge me. When he looked up, the twinkle in his eye told me everything I needed to know.

"You knew."

"I guessed." He shrugged, grinned, and one dimple appeared.

"You may not have *known* but you totally knew. And yet, you still let me walk right into an ambush unarmed. Not very gentlemanly, Mr. Scott, I'm all aghast." I wanted to appear angry and stern, but I just didn't have it in me. It was much more fun to joke around with him like this and I didn't want to waste the opportunity.

"I may have known she was up to something when she came in Friday just before closing time because she just had to have the bird treats she was out of, and to confirm that I had my usual booth at the festival."

"Dottie doesn't have a pet bird."

"I know." Both dimples were out now, and I knew he was enjoying this immensely.

Blowing my hair out of my face, I huffed. "Well, sir, congratulations. You officially get to help me haul stuff out of the creepy attic that isn't actually an attic but an entire second floor in the house that I now own that I apparently overlooked and mentally decided somehow wasn't even there. I mean, there could be a dead body up there and I wouldn't have known. Or raccoons or… something. So. Just you keep grinning. Joke's on you." By the end of my rant, I was gesturing wildly, pointing my finger in his face.

"Mabel, I have no idea what you just said, but any excuse to spend time with you is well worth it to me. Creepy non-attic, here I come. I'll come over right after work with dinner." He reached across the counter and grabbed the back of my head to pull me in for a kiss.

When I left, I was grinning, too. But before I left the sidewalk in front of Elliott's shop, I sent Dottie a text.

Hope your pet yard birds enjoy their new fancy treats.

She'd sent back an entire line of spinning laughing emojis. I was still muttering about her under my breath as I unloaded the groceries from the car, but I was still smiling, too.

Once everything was put away and I grabbed a quick lunch, I told myself that I was going to go up the stairs. I stood at the bottom, in the little alcove that was mostly hidden by the fire place wall, and looked up the steep, straight staircase to the door at the top, but I couldn't even take the first step. Sighing, I decided it was okay to just wait for Elliott, and I could be productive doing other things to get ready for the festival.

I sorted through all of the paintings that I'd already finished. Elliott had been right this morning, I had more than I realized. I probably didn't need to panic about making a bunch of paintings, but I wanted to spend some time making little things like book marks or cards so that I would have a variety of price points and sizes. That was a thing, right? Pretty sure that was thing. I had a few hours still before I needed to stop and clean up, so I sat down with my supplies and got to work.

THIRTY-ONE

A KNOCK ON the door startled me. "Shit," I murmured as I realized I'd completely lost track of time. Again. "Shit, shit, shit." I looked around as if seeing everything around me for the first time, and leaned down to bang my head on the table. At the second knock, I groaned and drug my feet all the way to the door. Closing my eyes, I opened the door just enough to peek my face out.

"Hi."

"Hi."

"I lost track of time."

"And it affected your eyesight?" Elliott asked. I could hear the humor in his voice, but I still didn't open my eyes.

"No, it's more of an if I can't see you, then you can't see me kind of thing..."

"Ooookaaay..." there was a brief pause, "nope, still don't get it."

Sighing, I opened my eyes. He was smiling at me softly, more perplexed than anything I think, but he hadn't run away. And whatever was in the plastic to-go bags he was holding smelled amazing.

"I'm being weird."

"Yep."

"You're still here."

"Also yep."

I felt a grin pull at my lips. "I think that makes you weird."

"In definite danger of contamination at least. Possible starvation, too. Can I come in?"

I looked down at my feet and noticed for the first time my fuzzy socks didn't match. I felt my shoulders droop even lower. I was a mess.

"Mabel, short of you having a full blown zoo in the house, I'm sure it's fine. We're all a little messy sometimes." His voice was kind, if a little exasperated, and I pushed the door open the whole way so he could come in.

He leaned in to kiss me on the cheek as he passed, "Thank you," he said.

"I've always wanted a miniature donkey, you know. They'd fit in a house." I answered to his back.

"Noted. Now let's eat."

He walked right over to the kitchen bar to put the bags down, and I loved that even though it was only the third time he'd been here, he seemed completely at ease in the space. He must have felt me watching him, because he glanced up from unloading the food.

"Fuel first, then manual labor. Want to sit and eat or want to stand and show me what you were working on?"

He was just so earnest with his question, and I felt my shoulders finally sink all the way down away from my ears as the tension melted away. "How about sit and eat, then a brief tour of the dining room disaster, and then manual labor? Possibly with a side of psycho-analysis."

"Hmm... we took an entire class on that in school."

"On what?"

"How to never psycho-analyze your girlfriend. It's one of the top dangers of psychology." He said it with a completely straight face, and by the time I processed that he'd called me his girlfriend, he had already turned around to get plates from the cabinet.

Just gonna let that one go, I thought to myself. I walked over to the bar and sat down, letting him plate and serve everything. "This looks amazing."

"Jesse's has the best burgers in the whole county. We're lucky to have them."

"I haven't tried it yet, and it wasn't there when I was younger. Thank you for bringing dinner." I had seen the little diner when I was driving through town, but I hadn't stopped in. Actually, I hadn't eaten in any restaurant really, and I was genuinely excited to try it. As he slid my plate over to me, I did a happy wiggle in my chair. I caught his soft smile out of the corner of my eye and blushed.

We tucked into our food and chatted easily while we ate. It was a fantastic burger, and really hit the spot after I'd so completely lost myself in painting this afternoon. Once we'd finished eating, Elliott clapped and rubbed his hands together, which I was noticing was something he did when he was ready to get work.

"I'll let you clear the plates. I'm going into the dining room to snoop without you hovering and worrying and apologizing."

He was grinning, and I wasn't offended anyway. He wasn't wrong.

"Fair. Thanks again for dinner. I'll just be in here scrubbing these two plates until the finish comes off. You let me know when you're done."

His easy laughter trailed behind him as he playfully jogged into the dining room. I realized I wasn't really anxious about him seeing all the work I'd done, just like the first time he had come over. I was as comfortable having him in my space as he seemed to be in it.

Suddenly, I was more anxious to get these dishes done so I

could join him than I was for him to see my new work. I wanted to know what he thought about everything. I threw all the dishes into the practically unused dishwasher and crept into the dining room.

Elliott had his back to me, one hand on his hip and the other stroking across his chin while he looked down at the table where all the work was scattered. I ran my hand down his shoulder, and he jumped, making me laugh.

"Whoa, those must be some cheap plates if the finish is gone already. You snuck up on me."

"The finish lives another day. What do you think?" I gestured to, well the whole room really, and waited for him to respond.

All of the display stuff he'd help me set up before was still there, and it was completely covered. Paintings were on display everywhere, clipped to the top, stacked one behind the other and generally just overflowing from lack of display space. The bar cart with Hedgie was crowded with postcard-sized paintings in various stages of drying, and I even had things taped to the glass of the china cabinet in the last stages of drying, too.

The dining room table was barely visible under all the art. I'd started with bookmarks, and those were drying on one side. At some point, I'd moved on to greeting cards, although I'm not sure what made me do it. I made a mental note to buy nice envelopes before the festival.

I stopped glancing around the room and brought my gaze to Elliott. His eyes were a little wide, but I couldn't decipher why. Crossing my arms, I leaned one hip on the edge of the table, trying to seem completely at ease. Of course, Elliott's eyes went straight to my toes, where I was scrunching and unscrunching them against the floor at an obviously failed attempt at unnoticeable fidgeting.

"Nice socks," he said with a single nod of his head.

"My feet get cold when I paint from sitting for so long, and I've always felt like bothering to match socks was a waste of time." My tone came out a lot more defiantly than I'd meant for it to, and I shrugged as if that would make me sound less like an argumentative toddler.

"It wasn't a dig, Mabel." He reached out and tugged on one of my tightly folded arms, until I found myself in his. "It suits you. One somewhat respectable sock with polka dots, one somewhat wild sock with hippie flowers." He lifted my chin with a finger and kissed me lightly. "I like your socks, Mabel." He said softly against my ear.

I felt myself relax a little more, and I wound my arms around his back to lean into him completely. I felt safe, and accepted, and like I was finally *home*. "Thanks." We stood like that for a few moments, both likely lost in thought, before I started to wiggle free.

"Alright, Mr. Scott, what do you think?" I gestured to the room again.

"I think there must be three of you. Seriously woman, did you do all of this today?!" His eyes were wide again, but instead of feeling like he was judging the mess or the styles or anything really, I realized it was from some kind of mixture of wonderment and pride.

"Well, no, not exactly. Most of the larger paintings were already finished. But all the small stuff I did today, yeah." I shrugged, not really seeing what the big deal was. They were little paintings. I mean, there were probably thirty or so of them, but they were little.

"She shrugs." He sighed and pinched the bridge of his nose, which made me giggle.

"Psychology 101: don't analyze the girlfriend, remember?" I winked at him, but I wasn't prepared for the look on his face when I said it. Just like I hadn't commented earlier, he didn't comment on the 'G' word, although I'm sure he was ignoring it so *I* wouldn't get spooked, not because *he* was having an internal freak out. He just turned his attention back to the table.

"In that case, I'll just say that this is a really impressive day's work. I don't think you need to worry about having enough inventory for your booth at the festival..."

"Well, I doubt I'll be able to do this again this week, so I probably won't have much more to offer. And I've never done one of these things, so I don't really know how much I'll need in the first place. I mean, part of me thinks that I won't sell a single thing and will have to haul all this back here when it's over and I'll be super embarrassed. But part of me worries that I won't have enough somehow and I'll be sitting there with a lonely empty tent for half the day."

"Well, we can't have that. When you sell it all, I'll send Turtle over to your tent and we'll turn it into the 'Pictures with Turtle the Tortoise' booth." He smiled at me so sweetly that I swear my heart cracked open a little more, and it actually hurt. "Either way, my booth will be right next to yours, so I'm sure we can make the best of the day no matter what." He yanked on my arm and kissed my nose. "Now, I think I promised to do some manual labor. Or ghost busting? Something about dead bodies? Full disclosure, I didn't bring a shovel and I have a weak stomach."

I laughed and poked him in the stomach, which absolutely did not feel weak at all. "Gah, no shovel? Well you might as well go ahead and leave then. We may not be prepared enough."

"Ha. Good try though. Let's do this." He clapped his hands together once and I grinned in spite of myself.

"Okay, Captain. This way..." I grabbed his hand and linked our fingers. With a tug, I started shuffling toward the stairs as Elliott whistled 'Love Will Keep Us Together' while he followed close behind.

THE STAIRS LEADING up to the 'attic' looked the same as they had earlier in the day; just a normal staircase, if a little steep. I flipped the light switch for the wall lights, and with Elliott close behind me, I was able to take the first step up, then another, and another. When we reached the top, I hesitated, my hand in mid-air reaching for the doorknob. He gently squeezed my shoulder, so I took a deep breath and opened the door.

It was just one large, open finished room, ceiling slanting down toward the floor on the sides. No visible rafters or spiderwebs, no draftiness, and certainly no dead bodies. It was almost cozy in a way, though dark, and I patted around on the walls searching for the light switch I just assumed would be there.

"Huh. Rather anti-climatic." Elliott was peeking around my

shoulder, and I realized that I hadn't even come in to the room enough for him to get off of the last stair step.

"Sorry. I suppose you're right though. It's just a room."

I looked around again with the over head light on. Most of the middle of the room was wide open with a lovely room sized rug in the middle. It was a comforting soft sage color with flowers in the middle, corners, and all along the edges, connected by sweeping swirls and scrolls. The color reminded me of my favorite dress, and Charlotte's skirt from the other day.

The entire left wall of the room, which was massive since it ran almost the full width of the house, held sturdy looking deep storage shelves filled with plastic totes that looked suspiciously like the ones in Gram's closet. A single, comfortable looking chair sat opposite the door under the only small window with a blanket draped over the back, as if it were waiting for someone to come curl up and read.

On the right was another storage system that looked like it had been pieced together from wooden crates, half sets of shelves, tote storage, and really anything you can think of that could be put together to hold things. "Funky, but it works I guess," I whispered as I moved past it all toward the chair.

I ran my hands along the blanket, not surprised in the least that it was in fact a quilt, and I smiled to myself. "I'm so glad that Gram had such good friends," I said to Elliott. "She was never alone. Not really."

I saw him nod slowly in agreement as he ran his fingers over some of the totes on the the the shelves. "These are all labeled with years, I wonder what they are. Keepsakes maybe? Taxes?"

"I think I know." I walked back over to the shelves closest to the door and looked for the tote that would contain the year 1937, when Gram was born. I pulled the tote to the floor, yanked off the lid, and was met with the spines of leather journals, month and year marked as plain as day. I looked for the one marked 'May' and pulled it from the tote.

"They're journals." Elliott's voice was quiet, almost respectful, as he came to sit next to me on the floor. "How did you know?"

"Remember all the totes in Gram's closet that you offered to pull out for me so that I wouldn't have to haul them off of the shelf? They're all journals, too. Based on the dates of the ones in the closet, they're all Gram's. Based on *these* years, it's possible that this set is from my great grandmother or great grandfather." I sat with the journal in my lap, excited and scared to open it all at the same time.

"That's amazing. I could never keep a journal for more than a week or two before I gave up. There's a whole lifetime here." He glanced up at the shelves. "Maybe more."

"Yeah." I was just looking at the book in my lap, stroking the year along the spine. It was a little surreal honestly; I'd come to Painted Creek sad that I would never learn all the stories that Gram had to share, and now here were all the stories I could ever ask for and more, neatly marked by year.

"You don't have to open it right now, Mabel," Elliott said as he bumped my shoulder with his. "You don't have to open any of them ever if you don't want to. Just knowing that you can is a gift."

I nodded, but I opened the journal carefully and flipped just shy of midways through to where I imagined the right date might be. The handwriting was feminine and elegant, the margins straight and clear. After flipping through a few pages, I found an entry with the date I was looking for.

May 22, 1937

She's here, all 7 pounds of her with ten tiny toes and ten long fingers. Her name will be Constance Wren, and she will be steadfast and loyal and lucky and wise with a touch of wildness, just like her name. I just know it.

I want nothing more than to sit and watch her sleep in her peacefulness, but I had to take a quick moment to record the pure perfection of this day. I can't wait to watch her grow.

It was a short entry, but beautiful in its raw hopefulness. We sat in silence together as I blinked back tears. Gently, I closed the journal and put it back in order in the tote.

"Your great grandmother then. Do you know anything about her?" Elliott asked.

"No, not really. Gram would tell stories about her, well not really stories but quotes I guess. When I'd gotten so mad over something I'd done out of impatience, Gram would say, 'my momma would say, 'you can't un-pick a flower Connie so it's best to just move on now''. And I think I was just too young to piece together what kind of person she was from hearing things like that. But I know that Gram thought she was the strongest woman in the world."

Elliott returned the tote to the shelf for me, and then offered me a hand to help me up. "Well, now you can get to know her through *her* stories, if you want to." He smiled at me kindly and stroked a finger down my cheek. "But for right now, let's go dig over here and see if we can find the festival supplies. Dottie said your gram already had everything up here, right?"

And with that, we well and truly got to work. Gram did in fact have everything that I would need to set up a booth at the festival, which wasn't all that surprising since she used to set one up herself. We carried down the tent, folding tables, and several large totes of table cloths and other display items. I knew I would probably set it all up on the back patio, all but the tent that is, and change the layout about a billion times before Friday came and I had to set it all up for real.

When everything was piled by the back door, I thanked Elliott for all the help as I walked him out. After a lingering goodbye and promises to stop in the pet shop this week, he headed home and it was just me and the cottage once more.

I plopped unceremoniously down onto the couch and stared at the black TV screen. From here, it was easy to see how I could have just overlooked the stairs. They were completely hidden by the mantle wall, and it was such a narrow passage anyway that you didn't feel like there was missing space.

I shook my head, still upset with myself that I'd missed an entire floor. I don't remember falling down any stairs, so I must have been really young. And I definitely don't remember ever having gone upstairs or even hearing about an upstairs for my entire life. Briefly, I considered asking my mother, but dismissed the idea almost as quickly. I suppose it didn't really matter why I didn't notice before, only that I knew now.

Sighing, I got up from the couch, barely shuffling my feet I was so tired, and started tucking the house in for the night. Once all the lamp lights were off, I stood at the base of the stairs one last time, looking up at the closed door. Just as a wave of guilt tried to take me under, my fingers started to tingle... a light but steady whisper under the skin that turned to a wave of fizzy sparkles as it made its way up my arms and down my spine. Instead of a picture in my head, I could hear my grandmother's voice clear as day saying, "All in your own time." Closing my eyes, I took one big deep breath before I turned and headed off to bed, the scent of roses following along through the house behind me.

THIRTY-TWO

THE REST OF the week passed in a blur of painting, preparations, and panic. I'd like to think the alliteration made it less exhausting, but it didn't. It did make me wonder if I was about to crack though. *Good times.*

First thing Tuesday morning, I jumped straight on all of my open commissions and finished them all by Tuesday evening. I didn't want to let anything with my business slip through the cracks, but I wanted to be able to focus on the festival too, so that seemed like the easiest way to accomplish both. I'd briefly spoken to my mother a few times, mostly just to catch up and listen to her hound me about the house she'd found close by. I didn't tell her about the festival, deciding I'd rather send her pictures afterward and tell her it was a spur of the moment set up my friends had helped me pull off.

And I think I did have friends. Over the last week our group text chat had been blowing up with plans for the post-festival ladies' night and endless amounts of teasing. The menu was worked out, although I was sure Alex would change her mind another fifty times and surprise us with whatever she wanted to bring at the moment. All three women had already texted this morning with good luck wishes and promises to swing by my booth sometime during the day.

Elliott had been incredibly helpful, too. He came over again Wednesday night to help me package up paintings and had come last night to load all of the booth supplies in his truck. He was taking them to the town square for me and had graciously offered to set up the tent and tables before I arrived. All I had to take was my inventory, which by Thursday night took up the entire back of my car. There was no way I was going to need it all, but there was no way I was going to leave any of it behind now that it was all done.

As I drove toward Main Street, I realized that the panic I thought I had been feeling all week was really starting to feel more like excitement. Funny how they kind of feel the same, isn't it? I decided that meant I could choose what I was feeling, and I was choosing excitement today.

I had found a little cart of sorts in the outbuilding at Gram's and I'd cleaned it up to use today to haul everything from the car to the tents. By the time I got the cart loaded up, I got a text from Elliott.

Tent is all ready to go! Need help unloading your car?

*Yay! No thank you, I've got it. Setting up the tent was a huge help. What do I owe you? *winking emoji**

*I'm sure I'll think of something. *kiss face emoji**

I giggled as I put my phone in the back pocket of my jeans and grabbed the handle of the cart to set off down the sidewalk. I'd traded in my more formal looking regular clothes for what I was calling my craft fair look of jeans and a t-shirt with Van Gogh's Starry Night on it. It was a far cry from the little black dresses and pants suits of my normal business ventures, but the pockets were most certainly a plus. It was going to be a good day.

HALFWAY THROUGH THE official hours of the festival, I was tired, hungry, and astounded at the outpouring of love and support I'd received from the town and the tourists alike. Sitting in my little pop up chair in the back of the tent, I looked over the tables and easels for a moment and took note of what had sold and what I still had left.

I was shocked at how well the little things like bookmarks and postcards had done! They were fun to make, and I decided that when I needed a break from my big huge commissioned paintings in the future, I would make a bunch of those little items and sell the originals on my website. I snapped a couple of pictures of the bookmarks displayed on the table and posted them to social media. The caption read 'New inventory offers coming soon!', and I hit post without too much over thinking. Later today I would get someone to take my picture in front of the booth so I could post it, too. Mabel Morrison's first arts and crafts festival. It felt good.

The best part of the day though was without a doubt watching people come in and unexpectedly fall in love with something. One girl came in with her mom and was immediately attached to a painting of a park bench surrounded by a riot of wild flowers. As I was wrapping it up, the woman explained to me that they had just moved to one of the neighboring rural towns.

Previously, they had lived in a very urban city, where the girl and her best friend had been on a school beautification committee together. They planted flowers around school grounds and the city park. She went on to tell me how much her daughter had been missing her best friend, and the smile she saw when she laid eyes on the painting was the first real smile she'd seen since they moved, even if it had been a little wistful, too.

Another older gentleman had come in to browse, saying he was just trying to escape the crowd for a moment. I offered him my chair, and as we chatted he mentioned that the last festival he'd attended had been with his late wife. He said they used to go to all of them they could find that weren't too wild or too hot or too far. This year, his granddaughter had asked him to come to this festival with her.

As he was talking, my scalp and shoulders shook with frisson and I remembered a painting I had done just for fun this week. Walking over to the mid-sized paintings, I pulled out one of a cobblestoned street with a table for two set in a corner of a building. I told him I wasn't sure why, but I wanted him to have it. His eyes immediately misted over, and he told me about their favorite festival that happened once a year a few towns over. They'd always take a break in the middle of the day for Italian ice at a small café that had tables set out, just like in the painting.

He'd hugged me goodbye when his granddaughter came in the tent to pull him along farther down the sidewalk.

I had a handful of stories like these, and each time, I was more thankful for the break I had taken when I first got to town to just paint whatever my heart wanted. It turns out, sometimes they were good for someone else's heart, too.

Mr. Findley's voice startled me out of my daydreaming.

"Mabel! What a fine booth you have here! How are you doing? Enjoying the day?" He gave me what can only be described as an awkward side hug, as if halfway into the hug he realized he didn't know whether to treat me as a friend or a client.

I laughed and said, "It has been a wonderful day so far, yes. I never thought I would enjoy something like this, I'm really not a people person. But it's been a lot of fun to hear people's stories and see them enjoying themselves."

He was eyeing a bookmark on the table, and I tried to smother my grin before I said anything about it. "That would be perfect. Is she here with you? I'll wrap it up before she catches back up to you."

The bookmark was a cacophony of color. I'd put clean water on the paper and then just dropped every bright and beautiful color I could think of on top and let them mix and flow together. Once it was dry, I'd used a pen to draw flowers and doodles over the entire thing. It was happy and bubbly and perfect for Carol.

His cheeks flushed scarlet, but he nodded once, so I scooped it off the table and packaged it up.

"What do I owe you?" he asked, not quite looking at me. It was adorable, and I was secretly hoping that Carol would come in before he left so I could see them interact with each other out here in the wild and not in the office.

"How about you meet me early Monday morning and let me in the empty building again and we'll call it even?"

His eyes met mine, and I could see a brief flash of something like hope before his lawyerly mask fell back in place.

"I can do that. I'll stop by and let you in on the way to the office, say eight-thirty? And honestly, Mabel, I'll just leave you the key. It is your building after all. I don't know why I didn't offer before. Constance just wasn't interested in keeping up with it and left the keys and all the other things to me to deal with." He shrugged, as if admitting he didn't understand but also not being all that concerned about it either. "You come and go as you please. I apologize for not thinking of it sooner."

"Actually, it's probably better. I still haven't told anyone that I own both buildings, and I don't think I plan to, so it looks best for you to have to come let me in. Like, on behalf of the management company or something, I don't know."

"Uh huh... sure." He looked like he was going to let it go, but then his fingers twitched at his side and he said, "You know, Mabel, it's almost time to renew that lease on the first building anyway. You're going to have to make a decision sooner rather than later. Maybe it's just time to go all in, hmm? Forgive me for saying, but it sure seems like you've enjoyed your time here, and maybe you have a few new reasons to stay."

I followed his gaze and saw Heather in the booth next to mine laughing with Elliott. As if he could feel me watching him, he looked at me and winked. Heather laughed harder and then held up a finger to me as if to say she'd be over in a minute.

I looked back to Mr. Findley and handed his bag to him. "Maybe. I'm just still not sure if it's something I can commit to, building or otherwise. And I've not discussed the idea of staying in town permanently with my mother."

"I see. Well, all I can say is that I'll be here to help you sort it all out when you decide. But off the record?" He looked at me intently, so I nodded once but swallowed hard. "Maybe that talk with your mother shouldn't be so much a discussion as it is informative. Sometimes you have to stop looking back to see what's right in front of you. Don't wait as long as I did to look toward the future."

As if summoned, Carol walked in the booth and as soon as her eyes landed on Mr. Findley her face split into a wide grin.

"Here you are, Phil! Oh!" She glanced around the booth, taking in the paintings and other things. "Oh Mabel, this is absolutely lovely! Look at everything. Oh, you really are so talented."

"Thanks, Carol! Maybe next year, you'll have a booth, too." I grinned at her mischievously and raised my eyebrows up and down.

"Oh my. Well. I don't know. I think I much prefer walking around with this guy anyway." She bumped Mr. Findley with her shoulder before winding her arm through his.

"I think that's our cue to go peruse a little more. We'll see you around, Mabel, and I'll meet you first thing Monday morning."

"Thanks! Y'all have a great time."

I watched them turn down the sidewalk hand in hand and felt a warm fuzzy feeling spread through my chest. I was so happy they'd finally started looking toward their future. Maybe he was right... maybe it *was* time look toward mine, too.

TRUE TO HER vague hand signals, it wasn't long before Heather popped in. With a squeal, she ran over to me in my little folding chair and gave me a hug.

"Mabel, this looks great! How are you doing? Have you had fun?" She was bouncing on her toes, and it may have been the most physically animated I'd ever seen her. It was infectious.

"Yes! This has been so much fun. Don't get me wrong, I'm exhausted. But I'm glad I got forced into doing it."

"Hey, sugar!" Dottie shouted loudly from the sidewalk as she waved and headed this way with all the subtlety of a freight train.

"Speak of the devil," I whispered to Heather, and we both dissolved into a fit of giggles.

"Hello, Dottie," Heather greeted her with a kiss on the cheek as she walked fully into the tent. I'm glad she regained her composure faster than I did.

"Hey, Dot. You enjoying the festival?" I kissed her cheek too, then offered her my chair with a gesture of my hand. She had stopped in first thing this morning to say hello and good luck, and I had a feeling she'd been going wide open ever since. She promptly swatted my hand away.

"Honey, you know it! I've been all up and down and in and out and sideways and back again. How've you been doing in here?" She looked around as if taking a visual inventory, comparing what was here now to what I'd started with this morning. For all I knew, she knew exactly what I'd sold better than I did. Woman was still as sharp as a tack.

"I've had a ball."

"Well, sugar, I knew you would."

"Yeah, yeah. I thought I'd hate it, I don't really like peopling-"

"Amen." Heather chimed in.

"- or the salesy aspect of creating things. But it's been... less painful... than I imagined it would be."

Dottie snorted loudly, making me laugh. "Well, I'm so glad you haven't been miserable. Now, your reward is time off for good behavior." She ginned at me with a twinkle in her eye.

"Wait, what?"

Heather laughed. "I'm going to go and run The Pet Parlor booth and Dottie is going to run your booth so that you and Elliott can walk around a little bit together." She smiled at me kindly while I gaped at the two of them.

"Go on, sugar, go get your beau and let me handle this for awhile. Might do me some good to sit for a spell anyway. I got my eye on a few things I need to go back for on round two." She winked at me and sat in the chair, and I knew it was more a tactic to get me to leave than from actual need to sit and rest.

I took my cell phone out and snapped a picture of her. "Thanks, Dottie. We won't be long."

Heather started pulling me by the arm out of the booth while Dottie yelled, "Take your time!" to our backs.

"Wait!" I dug my heels in a little at the front of the booth. "Will you take my picture? I've never done a craft festival before." I handed my cell phone to Heather and stood awkwardly at the front of the booth.

"Never? Like, not even when you got started painting?"

I shook my head. "My first experience selling my art was in an art gallery in Columbus."

"Whoa. Okay then, we most certainly have to document this momentous occasion! Smile!"

I could feel my smile probably looked more like a grimace, but I hated posed pictures. I always worried about if my eyes looked to squinty or if I was positioned just right.

"Uh, let's just take a few..." Heather winced behind my phone and I assumed the picture she'd taken wasn't one for the books.

"You don't need to take a few, she always looks perfect."

Elliott's voice was smooth and deep, and when I looked over Heather's shoulder to see him poke his head out of his booth, I barely registered Heather's drawn out, teasing "Awwwwwww."

The phone camera made its copy cat camera click noise a few times, and she said "I've got a good feeling there's one in there you can use. Your face lit up when you saw him. Check and see." She winked at me and held my phone out.

Shaking my head, I took my phone back from her to scroll through the new pictures. She was right, there was a noticeable difference in the photos before Elliott and the ones after he'd made a comment. I picked the best one and sent it off to my mom with a quick caption.

> *Impromptu craft fair! Had some help setting up last minute. Call you tomorrow and tell you all about it. Love you!*

I locked my phone screen and put it back in my pocket. Heather and I walked arm in arm the few steps to meet Elliott in the middle of the sidewalk in front of our booths.

"Thanks for doing this," he said to Heather.

"No problem! I'll hold down the fort for awhile." She smiled softly as she walked away and disappeared into his tent.

"You ready?" he asked me, linking our fingers.

"Absolutely. Food first, please!" I bounced on my toes.

Laughing, Elliott leaned down and kissed me before gesturing to the opposite side of the square where the food trucks were set up. "Lead on."

We wandered through the whole festival, going in and out of booths and snacking on, well really almost every single food we wanted to try. Festival food was the best. After an hour or so, my phone started pinging incessantly in my pocket.

"Well someone is popular today." Elliott poked me in the ribs as we walked hand in hand slowly back toward our booths.

"It's a good possibility it's my mother. I sent her a surprise 'look what I've done' photo right before we started walking around." I said with a frown.

"What, did you rob a bank and not tell me? Really, Mabel, I thought we were close enough now you'd at least ask me to drive the get away car."

"Ha ha. No bank robbing today. I've been too busy running a booth at a craft fair."

"I'm assuming the problem lies in that sentence, but I can't find it. More words please."

I sighed. I hadn't mentioned any of this to Elliott, and I wasn't sure that the end of our pleasant stroll around the square was the right time, but oh well.

"Most of my painting business has been built around

exclusivity..."

"Ah. We're too low brow around here. Got it."

"Mmm. Also, I implied that I had friends to help me set up said booth. Which implies I'm making connections here. Which implies that I may not be as eager to settle Gram's estate and head back to Ohio as she thinks I am, or as I've let her believe rather, or as she wants me to be? Some combination of all of that." I huffed out a breath just as Elliott tugged me to a stop.

"Mabel, are you considering staying in town a little longer?" I knew he was trying not to pry or put any pressure on me, but it was hard to miss, or ignore, the hopefulness in his voice.

"I... I don't know? I'm finding it harder and harder to imagine myself any place else. But I'm feeling guiltier and guiltier about having to say that to my mother. And I genuinely don't like the idea of being so far away from her, although next door is too close. I just... I'm still working it all out." I'd said all of that to the chipped brick over Elliott's shoulder. I don't know how the brick felt about it all, but my stomach was in knots.

After a beat or two, Elliott tilted his head to get back in to my line of sight. "I told you, I'll take what I can get. I'm just happy you let me know what you were feeling. It's just a slight bonus to know that you're feeling like you may want to stay. At least for a little bit." He tucked my hair behind my ear and then tugged me back down the side walk to our booths.

ELLIOTT AND I parted ways on the sidewalk, and as I entered my booth, I hoped that Heather was having an easier go of it than Dottie seemed to be. For a second I panicked thinking there was a big problem, but when I took just an extra second to look around, I realized that she was just surrounded by customers. *Not a bad problem to have*, I thought to myself as I headed to the back of the booth to help.

"Hey, Dottie, thanks for holding down the fort!" I kissed her cheek and hip checked her to the side, toward the chair. "Take a load off and let me get back to handling things here."

"Well, sugar, you weren't gone all that long. Did you two get to see everything?" She never even missed a beat, wrapping up with the customer she was helping and smiling at the next one in line.

"We sure did. But I'm happy to take back over now." I turned to the next person in line and said, "Hey, I'm Mabel. Anything I can help you with?"

She was cute, in a very dark vibes kind of way, with her ripped black jeans and dark purple tank top that perfectly matched the purple streak through her jet black hair. She held out a small painting face down, and as I turned it over I had to work to keep the shock off of my face. The cartoon styled painting of a pink fuzzy kitty cat with crown and sprinkled cupcake was maybe the last thing I would have picked for her in the whole booth.

"Just this please. Are you the artist?" she asked.

"Yes. This is actually my first craft fair. I usually take requests for specific paintings." I tapped her card on the reader and started packaging her painting.

"Oh, that's cool. But you couldn't have made a better picture for me than this one, even if I'd told you what to do."

Her eyes were incredibly kind under her thick black eyeliner, so I asked, "May I ask why? Seems like there may be a story there."

She laughed. "Not really, I guess. My sister just moved across the country and I don't get to see her or my niece as much as I did when we all lived in the same town. I miss that kid like crazy. That," she gestured to the painting I was sealing in a brown paper bag with my sticker, "is her personality all rolled into one package, or painting I guess."

"Aw, that's a great story. Thank you for sharing." I handed her the painting, and she waved a little as she made her way out of the booth.

Just as I turned to Dottie to chat about all the goodies Elliott and I had eaten, a new, loud voice called out behind me.

"Did I hear you say you're the one that painted all this?" The woman was a few inches shorter than my five foot five frame, but she held herself in a way that said she was used to everyone paying attention when she spoke.

"Yes ma'am, I am. Can I help you with something?" My fingers started tapping on my thigh as I fought not to outright fidget.

"Well, I don't know what kind of booth you think you have here, but I think it's outrageous." She bristled and hiked her purse strap up a little higher on her shoulder.

"I'm not quite sure I understand. I'm sorry if you didn't find something you like, but art is subjective I suppose." I was truly at a loss for what to say. I didn't paint anything offensive as a general rule, and my eyes darted around the booth trying to see what had gotten this lady so upset.

"Art is subjective, but money isn't. Do you really think these are worth the price you've got on them? It's ridiculous." She turned her nose up slightly in the air, as if being too close to the offending price tags was painful, and that extra inch and half gave her some relief.

I looked to Dottie, who was sitting in my chair pretty as you please and completely unbothered. *Okay... no help there.* "I do understand everyone has a different price point. But I know I have fair market value prices on my large paintings, and I have some smaller items to offer as well." I thought my voice was steady, but I wasn't really sure. I hadn't had to argue about prices on my paintings since the very beginning, and then my mother was there to champion for me. I guess that was a perk of the current way I did business that I had been taking for granted.

"Well, I bet I could go home and sling some paint onto a scrap piece of paper and come up with something better than this. I'll give you five dollars for it." She gestured to a larger painting still sitting in an easel.

I wasn't sure how she'd done it, but she had managed to simultaneously insult me and make it seem like she was pitying me with a sale all at the same time. I absolutely hated confrontation, and there was no way to stop the nervous wringing of my hands as I answered her.

"I'm sorry, ma'am. That painting is clearly labeled twenty-five dollars, which in my opinion is still a very reasonable price for an original painting and not a print copy. The price is firm." The painting was a large fountain surrounded by overflowing baskets of flowers. It was more of an abstract style than realistic, but the flowers were vibrant and the placement was well thought out. I really didn't see the resemblance to slung paint, but maybe I was too close to the situation.

She huffed, and with a roll of her eyes said, "I'll give you ten dollars, but no more. And really, I can't believe I'm offering that for something that isn't even real art anyway, and a poor example of the subject at that."

"I... well I'm not really sure what you mean by subject. I just sort of made this up. And it is more abstract, so maybe that's just not your preferred style of painting. I could show you some of my more realistic-"

"Hogwash. I've been to this place before, and it's exactly like this painting, right down to the crack in the top of the fountain and the symbols carved into the rock in the base there. It was a lousy trip, so I guess in that way this painting represents it perfectly. Ten dollars is my final offer."

I could see it then, the flash of pain across her face when she looked at the painting and relived whatever memory it brought up for her. I truly thought I had made this scene up, but I did believe it was close enough to whatever moment she recognized in it to evoke those same feelings. Just like Nora and the painting of the flowers. The symbols in the rock were quite the coincidence though. I don't know what had made me add them in at the last minute. At the time, I'd thought it was just for a little added visual interest. But now...

"Well..." I was ready to agree just to get this lady out of here. I didn't know why she wanted to have the painting so badly if it reminded her so strongly of something hurtful. Maybe she wanted to burn it, I don't know. Didn't they say that was cathartic or something? But before I could say another word, two things happened.

Just as Dottie was about to come out of her seat, Alex, Heather, and Sarah walked fully in to the booth. By the looks on their faces, they'd over heard most of the conversation, and suddenly Alex was reminding me of Betsy when she was all fired up.

"I believe Miss Mabel here said the price was firm. Kindly either pay the woman, or show yourself out." Alex stood off to the side, and as she spoke Heather and Sarah moved as one to stand behind her and give the woman plenty of room to leave.

With a huff, she turned on her heel and left, muttering to herself the whole way. As soon as she did, my new friends surrounded me, Dottie's hand reassuringly on my back.

"What nerve!" Sarah said.

"Some people can just be so rude, I don't understand it," Heather said.

"I know you weren't about to give in to her, Mabel," Alex said with a frown. Heather smacked her on the shoulder. "What? She needs the tough love if she was about to let that horrible woman talk her down on price like that." Her face was almost as red as her hair, and I couldn't help the giggle that escaped. She narrowed her eyes at me, which just made me outright laugh.

"What are you all doing here anyway?" I asked, looking at each of them in turn.

"We texted in the group chat, didn't you see? We all agreed to meet here and help you pack up. The official part of the festival is almost over," Heather answered.

"Oh you guys, that's really kind but I can get it. I don't want to put y'all out. I'm sure you have things you need to do to get ready for tonight anyway."

"Yep. And so do you. Where do these go?" Sarah had grabbed what was left of the bookmarks into a tidy little pile and was reaching for the note cards next.

"Uh, in this box?" I reached under the table I'd been using as a command center of sorts and handed her a box with smaller boxes in it that acted as dividers. I'd been doing enough online shopping lately I'd put all the shipping materials to good use. Then it was a flurry of activity as they packed up and I passed out boxes and instructions. Dottie held down the supervisory position, and my chair.

In absolutely no time at all, the entire booth was packed up and my little cart was ready to wheel off to my car. The perks of all of your merchandise being completely flat is that it didn't take up a lot of room.

"Thanks, ladies." I looked around at the now empty booth, and had a thought I wish I'd had about fifteen minutes ago. "Hey can we all get a picture together?" They startled a little, and I realized I'd kind of blurted my question out of nowhere. Loudly. "It's just that I probably never would have done this without everyone's encouragement-" Dottie coughed from her chair "-and manipulation, but I had a great time. And I really do appreciate all the help. I'd just like to remember today."

"I can help with that." Elliott came walking in the tent, the empty bag the tent was stored in slung over his shoulder. "I came to see if you needed help packing up, but I can offer my photography services, too."

We all huddled up in front of one wall of the empty tent, Dottie and I in the middle with her arm tight around my waist. When Elliott tried to hand my phone back, I tugged on his hand and said, "Selfie!" He somehow managed to get all six of us in the camera frame, big smiles all around. As everyone parted ways with promises to meet up later, Dottie grabbed my hand.

"I'll walk with you to the car, sugar. There was this lovely candle holder I wanted in a booth that direction anyway. I'll see if they're still there."

We walked slowly arm in arm toward my car, dragging my little cart behind us. It reminded me so much of walking through town with Gram. I squeezed her arm a little tighter.

"Thanks for all the help today, Dot."

"Sure thing, honey. How about the manipulation?"

"Well, we wouldn't be family without a little manipulation, would we?" She laughed lightly. "Thanks for that, too. I'm really glad I did this."

"Even there at the end?"

I sighed. I knew a simple walk to the car was code for let's hash it out. But it was nice to be able to discuss a situation without immediately being told what I'd done wrong or what I could improve on. It was nice to figure out how *I* felt about it before someone else told me how to feel.

"The end wasn't great." I gave her a look, silently asking why she hadn't intervened when loudly intervening would've been such a Dottie thing to do. She ignored me. "I hate confrontation. And yes, I was considering letting her have that painting for less just so she would leave. And yes, I know in hindsight that's what she was after all along." I paused, and Dottie remained quiet as we strolled arm in arm down the inside of the sidewalk, avoiding all the last minute festival shoppers and the other people closing out their booths early, too.

"I've developed such a mindset of 'the customer is always right'. Really when you boil it down, that's what my entire business and livelihood is built on. People pay me to paint *exactly* what they want in exactly the style that they want it in. I guess I didn't realize that it was creeping over into the entire rest of my life, thinking like that."

"Mmmhmm."

"Dottie that is the most non-answer I think I've ever heard from you in my whole life and to be honest you keeping your mouth shut is starting to freak me out a little." We'd almost made it to my car, parked off what I was starting to think of as my side street, and I turned to face her fully.

Her face softened and she reached up to pat my cheek. "Mabel, you've been at this so long, and you grew up in those high falutin' artistic show pony places, sometimes I forget you're only twenty-five. You certainly don't act twenty-five. Lord child you've got more manners and are more polished than I've ever been at any point in my life."

"Some of it is the circles I grew up in yeah, but some of it is just me, Dot."

"I know, sugar. And it's not always bad. It's served you well so far, thriving business and limitless talent to boot. But do you think you'd be doing what you're doing now if it hadn't been chosen for you?"

My steps stumbled a bit, as her words hit my gut almost as soon as they'd hit my ears. She kept walking and talking without missing a beat, as if she wasn't picking apart my whole life while on a brief walk to the car.

"Constance used to mention it sometimes, when you'd gone back home from a quick visit. And since you've been back in town I can see it for myself. Sometimes I just worry that you've forgotten how to loosen up... that you've forgotten how to determine and go after what *you* want without someone telling you what that is first."

All I could do was blink at her a couple of times. Somehow, she'd been able to wrap up what I'd been feeling in two sentences.

I'd made the, somewhat rash, decision on my own to come and stay in Painted Creek for a few weeks, yeah. But I'd been rudderless ever since. And before that, I was just going through the motions of my life, but it was predictable and stable and safe. I think the only things keeping me from rushing back to Ohio each time my mother mentioned it now were the new relationships I'd found, ones I'd never had before, that were becoming more and more important to me.

And I realized suddenly, no one in those new relationships was trying to tell me what to do. I knew how they felt, sure. I knew that Dottie would love to have me close by all the time. Elliott had made it clear our relationship had the potential for so much more. Even my new group of friends, the coffee shop ladies and Charlotte, had adopted me without question. But no one had ever made it a decree or an ultimatum about making a choice to stay. I was in charge of deciding my own life.

Dottie's phone pinged from her tiny little handbag. "Oh hell, sugar, I gotta run. I always keep Becca overnight after the festival so Sarah can sleep off her hangover a little longer the next morning. I best go start gettin' ready."

I gave her a huge hug. "Thanks again for the help, Dot. Couldn't have done it without you. I'm sorry you didn't get to check on your candlestick though." I frowned. I hadn't even thought about it as we'd passed the few tents that were still up on the way to the car.

"Don't worry about it. It was from the shop on Spruce Street anyway. I'll stop in Monday and see if they still have it. Have a good time tonight!" She winked and then hustled off, more energy and spunk left in her pinky toe than I had in my whole body.

I quickly loaded the car and climbed in. While the AC worked to cool off the stuffy air, I flipped through the pictures from the day smiling. I sent the group selfie to Dottie, Elliott and the group chat with my new friends, all with the caption 'Painted Creek fam'. I clicked my phone off, tossing it into the passenger seat and pulled out of my parking spot before I could rethink it.

THIRTY-THREE

AT ABOUT FIVE minutes till eight, I walked up to the front door of the coffee house. The sign was flipped to closed and most of the lights inside were off, making it dark enough that the lights in the square from the second off-the-books festival reflected in the windows like twinkling stars. I stood for a minute and watched as many of the locals talked and bartered with one another over all kinds of things. From this single spot, I could see a table of crocheted items, what looked like baked goods, and even one table that appeared to have frozen casseroles ready to take home.

The festival had been fun, but I liked this small town gathering better. Really, it was just friends and neighbors coming together to share their gifts with one another. I looked down at all my bags in my huge travel tote. I may have gone a little over board in snacks, and I packed some extra things the girls didn't know about. I guess in a way, I was honoring the spirit of the second festival and sharing some of my gifts with my friends, too. As I looked down at all I was carrying, I felt the first little ping of anxiety.

"Too late now," I whispered to myself as I opened the door.

I really had no idea what to expect tonight. There weren't many details past what food everyone was bringing, which was a lot. I'd decided on comfortable but cute clothes of leggings and a tunic length top and my favorite leather sandals. It had taken a lot of talking myself down to leave the house looking so casual... I'd had to chant 'play date not meeting' over and over to myself to keep from changing clothes.

"Well, look what the cat dragged in..." Sarah called from behind the counter. One of the machines was whirling away, and I was thankful there was going to be some kind of coffee to start the night. I didn't know a craft booth would be so tiring.

"What do you mean? I'm five minutes early! I'm so sorry if everyone has been waiting on me." I felt my face flush, and I gripped the handle of my huge tote as if holding it tighter could stop the embarrassment from spreading through the rest of my body.

"Mabel, it's fine. I was only kidding. Everyone else is here but only because they came from the square, not a ways across town." Her tone was somewhere between apologetic and exasperated at having to explain. I focused on the former.

"Is there anything I can help you with?" As I walked closer, I saw that she had a huge serving tray laid out with to-go cups, lids and two full coffee pots.

"Nah, just going to carry this up when we go. I have a coffee pot upstairs but I'm spoiled and it just tastes better from down here. That, and if y'all are as tired as I am, we're going to need more than four cups worth."

She moved out from behind the counter and I instantly felt better about my clothing choices. She had on leggings too that looked soft and worn in the best way, like comfort clothing, and an off the shoulder breezy top that made her look so much younger than she was.

She shuffled over to the door, locking it and pulling down all the blinds on the windows. When she turned back around I could see in her eyes that she was tired, but there was a smile on her face too that told me she was looking forward to the evening.

"I think I could clear four cups by myself. I had no idea how tiring that would be, especially when I didn't even have to set up my own tent."

"You sure lucked out there. Let's head up. Alex and Heather are already up there, and if we leave Alex unattended too long she'll bake something else and wreck my kitchen in the process."

She checked the lock on the back alley door as we walked by and began climbing the stairs to the apartment above the coffee shop. I paused on the first step, looking back around at the now empty shop.

"Do you need to set a security alarm or something?" I asked, still hesitating in case she turned to come back down.

"Nope." She popped the 'p' and kept climbing. "All the security I need is leaning against the wall right next to you, and I've only needed that once against a raccoon, not a human."

I looked down, and leaning under the hand rail in the corner was a metal baseball bat. I shook my head, trying to dislodge all the intrusive thoughts that were fighting for dominance in my brain. I called out a weak "Oh, okay," and hustled to follow her up the stairs.

I'd managed to catch up to one step behind her when she opened the door to her apartment. She called out a greeting to the other women, who were in fact in the kitchen, and I followed behind quietly.

"We're here! Alex get the hell out of my cabinets. We're not cooking, baking, or fixin' up anything else. Mabel's brought four different dishes herself from the looks of it. We've got plenty of food."

Alex straightened from where she had indeed been trifling through a bottom cabinet. A mixing bowl and large wooden spoon were laid out on the counter, but no food ingredients had been brought into the mix yet.

"I just wanted to do one more thing. And it's not really food. And it'll totally be worth it...in about three hours or so." She mumbled the last bit, probably hoping that no one would hear or care about how long whatever she was up to would take.

"What in the world is going to take you three hours? We don't have time for that." Sarah said as she flipped on a double coffee pot warmer and placed the full pots on top.

"She won't tell me, which is why I won't move. Hey, Mabel." Heather was leaning casually against the refrigerator, blocking it very nonchalantly with her body. "I'd like to say this is just post-festival behavior, but it's not."

"It would be perfectly normal behavior if you two would just trust me!"

"No," both Sarah and Heather said in unison.

I couldn't help but laugh. When Alex turned to me with a pout on her beautiful face, I started pulling dishes out of my tote. I hoped maybe distraction, and the presence of even more food, would pull her off of whatever she had her mind set on making.

"Here... I have cream cheese brownies, homemade pizza bites, cheese straws and sausage balls... well more like sausage boulders. I got tired of rolling tiny balls. Hope it's enough to add to your rather impressive stash here." All of a sudden, I was looking at the pile of food and then looking at the four of us. "Wait, are there more people coming?" There was no way we would even put a dent in this. And I hadn't emotionally prepared myself for peopling with strangers. That was a very different skill set.

"See? Mabel thinks there's so much food we've invited other people over to watch us act all grumpy and brain dead." Sarah poked Alex in the shoulder as she walked by, working efficiently at gathering all the standard coffee fixing items from a cabinet next to the sink.

"No other people are ever invited to the post-festival craziness." Heather was shaking her head solemnly.

"I thought you said this was normal behavior? I'm so confused." My head was ping ponging between Sarah and Alex, who had erupted into some sort of fake hand slapping fight and Heather, who looked amused but like she just wanted to sit down.

"The Alex being crazy and trying to cook every recipe she's ever come across for every single gathering is normal." She sighed. "This-" she gestured to the other two, who were now hip checking each other out of the way as Alex pulled out measuring cups and the like and Sarah just as quickly put them back away, "-this is post-festival mania. They both wake up ridiculously early to cater to the locals who are setting up for the festival, then they run their shops all day for locals and tourists alike, and THEN they insist that... whatever this is... is more relaxing than, you know, *sleep* in the evening." She shrugged. "I just close the store down for the day."

"Oh my God stop! You're scaring Mabel!" Sarah was starting to laugh in spite of herself as Alex used her height difference to lean over her and get to an upper cabinet with another mixing bowl in it.

"Don't bring me in to this..." I held my hands up and started to back away, but I was giggling now, too.

"Fine! You all win! I'll quit. I guess we didn't really need pineapple upside down cake jello shots anyway."

You could hear a pin drop in the kitchen for about two seconds. Then simultaneously, in a way that only comes from being close friends, Heather opened the refrigerator and got out the pineapple juice, Sarah started pulling out all the cooking equipment she'd been fighting to put back, and Alex winked at me with a self-satisfied grin on her face.

WE ALL PITCHED in to make the most complicated batch of jello shots I'd ever seen in my life. Alex barked out orders like she was on *Chopped*, and by the time the little tiny silicone molds were gelling in the fridge, we all collapsed onto the couch with our first plate of food and an extra large cup of coffee.

"Are jello shots always a staple at your get-togethers?" I asked, looking at each of them in turn. "I'll be honest, I don't really drink. Well that's not true, I never drink. Unless you count wine. I mean, I have wine, that doesn't count, but I don't have *real* alcohol. I mean, not so much that I don't have it but I've never had it. So yeah, I don't drink much."

"Oh lawd, the post-festival mania has gotten to her, too..." Alex stage whispered to Heather. "Add her nonsensical rambling quirk to the list..."

Sarah giggled as I covered my face and groaned. "Okay, that was bad even for me. I'll just see myself out now."

Heather chuckled but said very kindly, "No, jello shots are not normal for us, we usually just have a glass or two of wine to go with our whine. And you don't have to have any, Mabel. We're just glad you're here."

"And we're glad you brought these brownies." Alex said around a mouthful of said brownie. She was staring at what was left of hers as if she could break it down into its original ingredients by focusing hard enough. She probably could.

"I'll give you the recipe."

We chatted for a little bit, about everything and nothing, while we all finished our food and went back for seconds. When everyone was leaned back in their seats groaning, Sarah lolled her head to the side to look at me.

"I never offered you a tour. My bad. Mabel, this is my place." She waved her hand back and forth, more like she was trying to fan away an odor than she was presenting her apartment, but I got the idea. "Welcome." She let her hand plop back on to the sofa and when she slow blinked, I wasn't one hundred percent sure her eyes were going to open back up.

"Oh, it's okay. We kind of jumped right in to... whatever that was in the kitchen. You have a lovely home though. How long have you lived here?"

"Becca and I moved in when her dad split four years ago. Until then, it was just storage from his life before me and my life before him and random coffee shop extra supply stuff. But that ending up being a blessing, too. I was able to get out of our apartment lease quickly and sell a lot of furniture for cash. We just kept what we needed, and then I didn't have a double rent payment for this place and the apartment."

She'd said everything with her eyes closed, but I caught the looks of pain and anger on the other two's faces on her behalf.

"I think you've done more than just kept what you needed. It's cozy and warm and has good vibes. That's what really matters."

And it was. The whole place was tidy and well cared for. All the furniture was comfy and inviting, and the decor was warm and homey. Pictures and obvious souvenirs littered every flat surface like a little road map from a happy family of two.

She cracked one eye with a lazy smile and said, "Thanks, Mabel."

"Welcome." I smiled at her and the others, and then giggled at everyone's super relaxed state. "So... I brought something for us to do, but we totally don't have to. Everyone looks pretty content to become one with the furniture."

"What is it?" Heather asked.

"Goop beads." I couldn't help but smile broadly as I waited for everyone's reaction.

She sat up a little straighter on the couch and her eyes sparkled. "You made some flower clay beads? That's so awesome! I want to see!"

"Me, too! I had no idea what you guys were talking about that day. I want to see how they turned out." Alex was looking my way with interest, but she had yet to move any muscles other than her eyes.

I hauled myself out of the deep chair and back over to my bag on the floor by the stairs. Grabbing the supplies, I plopped down on the floor in front of the coffee table and started spreading everything out.

"I know we're not teenagers anymore, but I brought some beads and string to make bracelets. If y'all want to use the goop beads, you're welcome to... there's enough for all of us to have three. I thought it was fitting since I don't think I would have ever tried it if it weren't for the extra encouragement from my new friends."

I smiled at them briefly, but my mind also went to Charlotte. I hadn't bumped into her lately, but I'd also been so busy getting ready for the festival she could've stopped by every night and I never would have known. I made a mental note to make her a bracelet using the new batch of beads that was drying at home.

I pulled out the little container of chamomile goop beads and poured them onto the lid. They were all about the same size, and after I'd sanded them a tiny bit, they were reasonably smooth. According to everything I'd read, they would continue to smooth out and shine up a little with age and wear. They had more of a rustic feel now, but I still thought it was amazing that I'd made usable beads from what would have otherwise been thrown away after making my natural ink.

Heather clapped her hands together and perked up a little. "Mabel, this is awesome! I think these came out so well. Are you happy with the results?"

"I think so? I guess we'll see how they hold up to actual wear. It says that some times the scent of the flower can come back after you wear them awhile and they absorb your body heat, although that was talking about roses which smell stronger than chamomile, so," I shrugged. "We'll see I guess." But now that I was thinking about it, that did kind of open up some other possibilities for maybe some aromatherapy jewelry of some kind. I'd have to try some with lavender and see what happened.

"That's cool. But where in the world did you get all of this?" Sarah was eying the strands of beads I was still pulling out of a bag and laying on the table.

"You didn't notice all of my packing supplies for the festival were online shopping boxes?" I laughed. "I've been spoiled by getting exactly what I want and never having to leave the house!"

Looking at the coffee table now, I did wonder if I had gone overboard. I'd found a cute little shop on Etsy that carried gemstone beads and practically bought a strand of every one that caught my eye. We had a large enough variety everyone could make ten bracelets and I'd still have leftovers.

"Ooooh let's make more than one, then we can wear them as a stack!" Alex had wiggled herself down onto the floor too, and was looking over the selection of beads while drumming her fingers together like she didn't know where to start. Either her coffee had finally kicked in, or she was genuinely excited. Maybe both.

"We should all make one for Becca too, if that's okay Sarah," I added the last part in a hurry. I hadn't forgotten my warning talk about getting attached if I didn't plan to stay. "You can give them all to her when she gets home."

"She would love that." She smiled softly at me, but I didn't miss the look of hesitance in her eyes. That was fair, I guess. I'd never made any mention to anyone that I was even remotely considering staying in town.

We all dove into the beads, and after Sarah passed out some paper plates for us to lay things out on, we were bracelet making machines. We all ended up making one matching bracelet to go in our stacks that used the goop beads, and that meant more to me than they could ever possibly know. Slowly, I think I was building a tribe for myself here in Painted Creek. Or maybe they just adopted me, I don't know. But either way, it was nice.

"What was up with that lady in your booth, Mabel?" Alex broke one of those weird silences that they say fall over conversations every seven minutes or so. "And why in the world were you about to agree to a price cut?" She seemed to be intensely focused on stringing her next bracelet, but I knew at least half of her brain was listening and ready to lay into me for any reason I might have for giving into that customer that involved putting myself down.

I sighed, wondering how much of the truth I could give them without having to explain too much about my visions. I just wasn't ready yet.

"I think that painting reminded her of a place she'd once been. It didn't sound like the happiest of memories, but for some reason she wanted the painting anyway."

"Then she should've just paid for it instead of insulting you like that," Alex huffed.

"True. I think sometimes memories are hard. Like maybe she wanted to remember whatever good had happened on that trip but she hasn't been able to move past whatever pain she remembers to be able to enjoy the memories. I don't know if that makes sense. But honestly, I almost feel like that painting belonged with her. Maybe it'll find its way to her some other way."

Heather was slowly nodding her head, like she completely understood. Not for the first time I wondered if she had some sort of similar thing to my frisson when she picked out books for people. She'd certainly known exactly the book I needed, not once but twice.

"Well, you're nicer than I am." Alex grumbled.

"Not nicer, just more patient maybe," Sarah laughed as she took the string Alex was trying to tie in a knot from her, finishing it off before handing it back.

"Thanks." Alex stood and stretched. "My fingers need a break. Who wants a jello shot?"

Instantly three hands shot into the air, mine included. It was time I learned to enjoy my life and my new friends without constantly worrying about my image or other people's opinions, and a pineapple upside down cake jello shot seemed like exactly the way to start.

TWO HOURS AND an entire empty tray of jello shots later, we were all piled in a heap on the couch giggling. Pineapple was my new favorite flavor.

"What was your old one?" Heather said.

"What?"

"Your old favorite?"

"Favorite what?" I was confused, but she was obviously talking to me.

"Your old favorite flavor if pineapple is the new favorite flavor." Somehow, Alex was the one that chimed in to explain things rationally. Alcohol was weird.

"Did I say that out loud? Huh." I gigged again and Heather rolled her eyes.

"Well, since you obviously have lost the brain to mouth filter, tell us about Elliott!" Alex singsonged his name while bouncing up and down on the couch like a teenager.

"What about him? He's cute. Turtle is nice. Did you know she's a tortoise and not a turtle?" I felt like I needed to steer the conversation away from my new relationship, but I wasn't sure why, and alcohol was never a good steer-er anyway.

"Uh huh. Turtle is great. Ten out of ten for a reptile." Heather was bobbing her head up and down, more like she was listening to music than agreeing with me, but I pointed at her in solidarity anyway.

"Aw, she's even in love with Turtle already! Does that mean you're going to stay forever and you and Elliott will have tiny little turtle babies?" Alex batted her eyelashes at me and I guffawed out loud.

"I don't think that's how it works? And she's a tortoise. And I don't want to adopt a bunch of baby turtles... don't they have to like swim or something? I forget. But they'd run away if I put them in the creek. I'd be a bad turtle mom." I could feel myself frowning now while it was Alex's turn to laugh. But really, I couldn't fence in the creek for a bunch of baby turtles could I? I shook my head to clear the thought, but that just made the room spin.

"Okay fine, no baby turtles. But I do hope that getting close to Elliott means you're thinking of staying in town. Long distance relationships suck."

"But it's not impossible." Heather chimed in. She was smooshed all the way in the corner of the couch, but it was more like she'd made herself a cozy nest than run out of room, her legs thrown over Alex's lap. "Plus, we've grown accustomed to your face..." She sang the last part in her best Henry Higgins impression, which wasn't bad if slightly off key, while Alex leaned backward from propping against my shoulder to boop me on the nose.

Swatting at Alex's hands with zero percent accuracy, I said, "Y'all are crazy. It's too soon to think about uprooting my whole life for a boy. Isn't it?"

"Fine, then stay for me. I'm in love with your brownies." I snorted, but Alex had probably cleared most of the pan by herself.

"You're a baker, I think you'd be fine without me. I'm still working it all out. I can't stay. I have no idea what to do about my mother..." I trailed off, trying to pull a solid thought from the swirling fogginess in my brain. "He is cute though, isn't he?"

"I assumed your mom was a girl?" Alex asked.

I felt the couch move as Heather dug her toes into Alex's ribs. "I think she meant Elliott."

"Oh, that makes much more sense."

Quicker than any of us had a right to be moving, Sarah got off the couch and walked into the kitchen. I scooted over into her spot, causing Alex to fall backwards. We both giggled, but I stopped laughing when I saw the look of concern on Heather's face as she watched Sarah stomp around the kitchen.

"You two leave her alone. She can't uproot her whole life over a boy just because he's cute. She's got to make sure she wants to put up with everything in this crazy ass town too for longer than just a damned vacation."

I looked down at Alex's face, and she was frowning now, too. I mouthed 'sorry' to both her and Heather, feeling like I was the cause of Sarah's new bad mood. Alex just shook her head while Heather mouthed back 'not you'. I appreciated the reassurance even though I didn't believe it.

"You know what? I think I'm going to bed. I'm sorry, I think the red wine and the rum made me grumpy. All y'all are welcome to stay, but Becca'll be back around nine in the morning so I hope you like early hung over wake up calls." With that, she turned on her heel and walked into her bedroom, shutting the door more softly than I expected behind her.

"Ugh, I'm sorry. I shouldn't have talked about moving or leaving or whatever I said wrong. Wait... she doesn't like Elliott does she?!" My fuzzy head was making it harder to think than normal, but that was always a possibility wasn't it?

"It's not you, Mabel, and no she doesn't like Elliott. I don't think she likes anyone but us and Dottie. She probably just doesn't want to think about you leaving since she's gone and decided to like you." Alex reached a hand up to pat me on the cheek, but it landed as more of a slap. "Sorry," she laughed, "you were closer than I expected."

"Are you two staying?" Heather asked.

Alex nodded. "No one is driving home tonight. And no more jello shots. Who's idea was that anyway?"

Heather rolled her eyes as she pulled herself up off the couch. "I'll get the extra blankets."

"I'm just going to call Elliott..." I rolled off the couch and went to sit in the stairwell to the sound of a chorus of 'oooooos'. I was still giggling as I shut the door behind me and the call connected.

"Hey, Mabel." Elliott's voice was low in the phone, and I let my head fall back onto the wall as I closed my eyes to talk to him.

"Did I wake you?" I asked.

"No, but I am already in bed. It was a long day. Some of us had to set up tents you know."

I giggled again. I'd never considered myself a giggler, but I seemed to be doing it a lot lately. "Thank you kind sir. I a-ppre-she-ate you doing the setting up for me."

"Mabel, are you a little drunk?" I could hear the smile in his voice through the phone.

"Maybe. Probably. I don't really know, I've never been drunk. Not soshally expectable. But I'm tired of being expect-a-ble, I want to be me."

"Socially acceptable behavior is boring, remember? And I think you're perfectly acceptable the way you are."

"Really?"

"Yes. And I'm certainly not bored."

We talked for a few quiet moments and said good night. When I snuck back into Sarah's apartment without waking anyone, I crept around the room pretending to be a ninja and chuckling in a very non-ninja-like way. Heather had left a blanket for me on the over sized chair, and despite the awkward moment with Sarah, I was as content as I could remember being as I curled up and fell asleep.

THIRTY-FOUR

I WAS NO longer content. There was an ice pick trying to dig its way out of my forehead, and there were obnoxiously happy and cheerful noises coming from the kitchen over my shoulder.

"What even is happening?" I groaned, regretting sitting up instantly.

"You're hung over and I'm cooking breakfast for all of you before Becca gets home and sees our own rendition of the living dead. Now get up and come drink your juice."

It was Heather that had spoken. I heard her voice. Saw her lips move. But that wasn't Heather's attitude that was coming through loud and clear from the other room. I rubbed my eyes viciously trying to make the pounding stop so I could think clearly.

Alex groaned from the couch. "Why do I always forget how

you are in the mornings..." She rolled over just as a spatula came flying through the air, hitting her in the back and bouncing to the floor. "Ohmahgahstaaaahp! I'll get up!"

I was already making my way to the kitchen, where Heather had three glasses of orange juice laid out on the counter. I took the one closest to me, murmured a thank you, and then backed away slowly.

Heather grinned at me and gestured vaguely around the kitchen with what I assumed was a cooking spatula, not a throwing spatula. "These two are horrible in the morning after a ladies' night. I'm not normally a morning person, you know that, but for whatever reason, I never wake up hung over. Apparently even when jello shots were involved. And seriously, Alex, what were you thinking with that?"

"Wanted to impress Mabel. Stupid. Won't happen again."

I laughed and then groaned when it rattled my skull.

"Take these. It's ibuprofen for the headache you must have. Especially if you don't normally drink." She dropped the capsules into my hand and I chased them with the rest of my orange juice. While the cheerfulness was somewhat obnoxious, the care giving was a nice bonus. "Becca will be back by nine, so get moving ladies. No grogginess when the princess comes home. Sarah is already in the shower."

Alex was up folding the extra blankets, poorly, but she was up. I folded the ones on the chair and started gathering my things. "I'm going to head out before she gets home," I said while pulling two papers and paints out of my bag. "After last night, I think it would be better if I wasn't here, for both her and Sarah. Text me a picture when she gets her bracelets though!"

As quickly as I could, I sketched out two paintings. One was for Becca, and was another painting of Mocha the bunny wearing some new beaded bracelets. The other, an up close shot of a pair of hands clasped together, one larger and one child sized, both wearing matching bracelets, was for Sarah.

"I'm sure that's not necessary..." Heather said a little hesitantly.

"No no, it's fine. It's probably best. I'm going to need to call my mother anyway and get stuff sorted from yesterday." I finished gathering my things as quickly as I could and then gave Heather a hug. "I had a great time. Thank Sarah for letting me stay, and I'll text you all later." I finger waved at Alex, shuffled down the stairs, and snuck out the alley entrance to avoid the already bustling coffee shop with its loud noises and even louder customers.

I wish I had known that the loudest of sounds would sneak up on me in my car. My mother's ring tone pierced the silence I'd found at ten or so decibels above its normal volume. I swiped at the screen trying to make the noise stop, and accidentally answered the call.

"Hello," I barely avoided groaning out a greeting.

"Good morning, darling. Nice of you to answer a phone call since you avoided all my texts yesterday."

The groan slipped out. "Mother, I don't think I can have this conversation right now. Can I call you later?"

"Mabel, are you okay? You don't sound well. Are you sick?" She went from snarky to genuine concern in less than two seconds. A huge wave of guilt washed over me, and I sighed.

"I'm fine, Mom. Just a headache."

"It sounds like you're in the car. Where are you going this early if you don't feel well?"

"I'm actually on the way home. I stayed with some friends after the festival."

".....Are you hung over Mabel Rose?!" Her volume rose with her indignation, and felt somehow even louder after her slight pause as she worked out me staying out with friends and having a headache.

"Mom-"

"Don't you Mom me. Mabel, what will people think, you getting drunk out in town at night? Really, don't you have better sense than that?" She harumphed into the phone, and I felt what little patience I had, that was not under the effects of my first good and proper hangover, snap.

"Yes, Mother, I do have better sense than that. I was in at a friend's house all night, we never went out, and I spent the night as to not drive home. No one but you will think one single judgmental thing about the way I spent my Friday night after a hard day's work at my first ever arts and crafts festival. I also have better sense than to continue this conversation right now. I'll call you later. Bye."

I hung up the phone without waiting for a response, and continued the short drive back to the cottage in blissful, guilt-filled silence.

AFTER A QUICK shower and an extra strong French press coffee, I felt marginally human again. I had a text from Elliott, half checking on me and half teasing me for what he assumed was an epic hangover. We made plans to meet for dinner tomorrow, and my mood improved even more.

I spent a little time unpacking all the things from the festival the day before, and when I really took stock of what was left, I was pleased with how things had gone. It was nice to see what people would pick up on impulse instead of what they would order after a lot of thought and planning. I put everything back up in the dining room, and appreciated how well the space was organized in its chaos.

I spent a leisurely afternoon flipping through several of Gram's journals. The corner that I had propped up in inside Gram's closet had gained a few more pillows and a spare lamp, and was now quite cozy. I'd pull a journal at random and flip through a few entries before putting it back and choosing another.

Idly, I wondered if I should start journaling too, although it had never really been my thing. But the presence of Gram's journals and the much older ones upstairs kept weighing on my mind, urging me to try again. Maybe journaling was some sort of family legacy I knew nothing about. I made a mental note to go upstairs and find the oldest journal. Maybe journaling was just something special between Gram and her mom. My dad had never kept a journal, at least not that I was aware of.

Thinking about my dad made me choose the next journal a little more carefully. I searched through the totes until I came across the year 1990 which, if I wasn't mistaken, would've been the year my parents got married. When I sat back in my pillow fort, the journal fell open in my lap to an entry dated the week before my parents' wedding. It read:

Well, we're officially a week away from Anthony and Marissa's wedding. I can't believe it's finally here, and in a week my baby will be moving eight hours away from Painted Creek to be with his bride. I understand the move, it is truly best for them and the beginning of their new life together, but oh how I will miss him!

I knew the day he came home talking about the intern he'd met at the hospital that he was already gone fool over her. He loved her with a fast fierceness that usually fizzles out just as quickly, but as soon as I saw them together I knew he had found his one true love. What a rare and beautiful gift! Watching them these last few months, I can see how she pushes him to be better, and how he supports her to go after everything she's ever wanted (including him, ha!).

I'm so incredibly sad to see him go, but I can't wait to celebrate their love here in Painted Creek, and I can't wait to watch him carve out his own path in this world.

I sat thinking about the short entry for so long my feet went numb underneath me. I knew my mother had gone to medical school like my dad, but I didn't know that she'd gone far enough to be an intern. She'd always stayed home with me while dad worked crazy hours as a doctor, and I'd never once questioned what she wanted to do with her life since I'd become an adult. She just fit so seamlessly into my business, helping with the shipping and marketing and what not, that I never wondered if she wanted anything different.

On impulse, I took a picture of the journal page and texted it to my mother. I'm not quite sure why I did it; if it was to remind her how much Gram and my father had loved her or if it was to remind her that sometimes leaving home can be the right direction for your life. It was only a minute or so later when my phone pinged with her response.

You are the best parts of all of us, Mabel. I'm so thankful I still have you.

I wasn't sure how to respond, so I didn't. But I did call her before bed and tell her all about the festival, each of us acting as if nothing out of the ordinary had ever happened between us.

THIRTY-FIVE

SUNDAY PASSED AS those lazy Sundays can do, and it was perfect in its unhurriedness. I spent the day accepting, painting, and finishing a few commissions, and I even got to start on the painting for Heather and her book store. I was most excited to finish and deliver that one, and I couldn't wait to be able to focus on it and nothing else.

Spending the whole day in a serene painting state was just what I'd needed after the physical exertion of the festival and the emotional exertion of the next day. But the thing that makes lazy Sundays so special is that they're usually followed by Monday madness.

Mr. Findley met me bright and early at the building Monday morning, and this time, he brought a key.

"I'm sorry again, Mabel. It certainly would've been a lot more convenient for you to come and go on your own. Making a decision may be easier if you could let yourself in and out whenever you wanted to have a look. You're almost out of time now." He unlocked the door and ushered me inside.

I winced and said, "Don't remind me."

"You really still don't know what you want to do?" He looked concerned, like a caring uncle would when his favorite niece was floundering through her life.

"That's just it, I think I *do* know what I want to do. I know it more surely than I've ever known anything. I'm just not sure I can bring myself to actually do it."

He frowned at me and shifted his weight, putting one hand on his hip. He vaguely gestured with the other hand to the wide open space we were standing in.

"What would the dream for this be then? Fix it up and rent it? Passive income is never a bad thing."

I nodded slowly, but I let my eyes wander the empty space. I could almost imagine it as a little shop, with cute display tables and art on the walls.

"The dream would be a gift shop of sorts, with a kind of art gallery thrown in. I've always wanted a little gift shop. This is... more than that. So much more. I can't explain it, but, I think I could do it."

Probably... I could probably do it.

Maybe.

"I think that would be wonderful. You seemed to do well at the festival. Plus, you'd never have a fight with your landlord." He chuckled softly at his own joke while I suppressed an eye roll. "Speaking of landlords though, should I be drawing up a lease renewal for next door?"

"That's what I'm leaning toward, yes. But don't go to the trouble yet until I actually make a decision. I'd hate to waste your time if I decide to go in another direction. I still haven't had a conversation with my mother about my plans."

"Hmm. Yes, well, I suppose you're paying me for my time. So

that's a sound financial decision." He didn't comment further, but it was obvious he didn't think it was a good decision at all, the possibility of not renewing the lease, financial or otherwise. "Speaking of paying for my time, I still have yet to look into the building's history, but I will try and have that for you by Friday as well. Maybe it'll help you reach a decision."

"Maybe. But I'll let you know something before Friday. One way or another."

"Very well. You have the key now, so just come and go as you please. I'm going to head on out, if you don't need anything else."

We said our goodbyes, and Mr. Findley left me alone in the building I owned with thoughts that seemed to own me. Everyone always said things like 'do what's best for you' or 'you have to do what feels right' or 'it's your life, you get to decide how to live it'. And they always said it like it was the easiest thing in the world, to just make decisions based solely on what you wanted or needed without any regard to what anyone else felt.

I just wasn't built like that. Who knows if it was nature, nurture or a little of both, but I cared deeply about the people closest to me. Their feelings and opinions mattered to me. Was that really so bad? Wasn't there a way to do both?

I had slowly walked a huge circle around the main space of the building. I wanted this for myself so badly! A place to display the art I made just for fun, a place for people to discover new treasures and be reminded of old memories through paintings, and maybe even a place for community and other creators. It sounded like the perfect next step. And here I was, building a community and inheriting literally everything I needed to make it happen. Well, almost everything.

I couldn't inherit the emotional fortitude it would take to make my dream a reality. Because that would mean crushing my mother's heart in the process.

Rationally, I knew that I was an adult, and well past the age of leaving the nest at that. But we'd always been so close, and it had just been the two of us for so long that I wasn't quite sure either of us knew how to be without the other. We had our little bubble, and though it didn't include any other people to speak of, we were happy, I think. She had given up so much to raise me, to help me turn my love of painting into what it is now. It felt selfish, like I was abandoning her for something else. Even if it did feel like it was possibly something more.

Plus, I had so many regrets now about not spending more time with Gram. And for what? Some feud or hurt feelings that I genuinely did not understand or know anything about? How many times throughout my life had I wished that we lived closer to each other, to be able to spend more time together. Was I seriously considering moving away from Mom and putting myself in that situation again?

My thoughts were spinning around in my head like a hurricane; full force in a never ending circle and leaving destruction in their wake. I walked back to the front door and with one last look around, I began locking up to head next door to Artful Brew. I had almost a full week left to figure everything out. I did my best thinking at the last minute anyway.

"Lies I tell myself..." I whispered as I turned and walked away.

THE FAMILIAR BUSTLE of the coffee shop didn't do as much to calm my thoughts as I wanted it to. I was hoping the caffeine buzz would help, but realistically I knew in a few minutes I'd just have a lovely dose of physical jitters to go with my racing mind.

"Morning. You missed Monday coffee." Sarah got straight to the point, as usual. Honestly I was kind of surprised I'd even gotten a greeting before she jumped right in, especially after the awkwardness of the whole are-you-staying-in-town conversation Friday night.

"Good morning. I know, I'm sorry. I had to meet with Mr. Findley. Did Becca like her bracelets?"

A small smile crept across her face, as it often did when anyone talked about Becca. "She loved them. But I think she loved the new painting of Mocha even more, especially since he was wearing bracelets, too." She paused, and then met my eyes. "And I felt the same about my painting. Thank you."

I swallowed an unexpected lump in my throat. In her own way, I think she was apologizing for the outburst Friday, but I didn't deserve it. After all, I was still keeping something pretty big from her.

"My pleasure. And I'll be sure to come to the coffee meeting on Wednesday."

She nodded once, as if the whole thing was settled, and I guess it kind of was. Since no one else was in line, I'd come right during her mid-morning lull, I asked, "Hey have you ever had a neighbor in the store next door? It looks like it's been empty awhile. Do you wish there was something in there?"

Don't ask me what I was doing. I don't even know, other than making the whole lying to my new friend who already didn't trust people easily situation worse by playing stupid. So, so stupid.

"There hasn't been anyone in it since I've been here. I do okay on foot traffic from all over the square though, so I don't really mind. You should ask Elliott though, he might have a different opinion. Although, I guess if someone moved in there and wanted to cause trouble they could complain about Turtle being out back." She shrugged, but I felt as if she'd just dropped a bomb I hadn't even been aware I needed to worry about. Outright selling the store would never be an option, and if I rented it to anyone else there would be some sort of weird stipulation about loving your neighbor, even if they were a tortoise.

"Makes sense. A coffee shop probably gets more traffic than a pet store anyway. And speaking of coffee..."

"Want to pick your own today?" she asked.

"Nope. Just the normal amount of caffeine though please. I'm scattered enough as it is today, I don't need to add fuel to the fire." Approximately two minutes later, she passed me an extra large coffee cup, lid in place and steam snaking through the hole in the top. "What is this?! Doesn't this hold like four cups of coffee? What happened to less caffeine today?"

Sarah actually laughed at the genuine look of terror on my face. Normally, I'd be all over a coffee bigger than my head, but I really didn't think it was a great choice for today.

"It's only half full of coffee, the other half is vanilla cold foam. I put it in the extra large cup so you could have what's probably about two cups of coffee and then an equal amount of cold foam. The coffee is flavored with mocha and caramel syrup, and when the vanilla cold foam begins to melt and swirl in, you get a magical mixture of all three flavors in each sip. I call it a Milky Way Galaxy."

I took a small tentative sip and practically purred. "Okay, this is amazing. Seriously my favorite so far. I'd even say it's out of this world." I waggled my eyebrows at her over the top of my cup.

"Get out." She pointed toward the front door with a straight face, but I could see the twinkle in her eye as she turned to the new customer that walked up behind me to order.

With an equally straight face, I said to the man, "Sir, Sarah here just made me an incredible coffee. I'm really over the moon about it. You should ask her if she'll make you one, too. It's the shooting star of the menu."

"Seriously, get out."

"Fine. But my love for you and this coffee is still astronomical." I shot her some finger guns and began backing toward the door. "Imma just spacewalk on outta here."

I turned to leave, because let's face it, as much as I wanted to moon walk my way out of the shop there was no scenario in which I was coordinated enough to do so.

Just as I reached the door, I heard the man at the counter say "I'll have whatever she had," followed by Sarah's loud groan and the other barista's laughter.

I rode my space pun high all the way to Elliott's shop.

I WALKED RIGHT into The Pet Parlor without hesitating, hoping that it wouldn't result in some kind of daring fuzzball escape or bird fly by. All was quiet though, which honestly was actually more troubling than all the racket that I'd grow accustomed to in this shop.

"Well hey there, pretty lady. What brings you around these parts?" Elliott was behind the counter reading. He grinned when he saw that it was me, a double dimple grin.

"You." I shrugged with an answering grin of my own.

"Well, can't beat an answer like that..." He leaned over the counter to give me a kiss that lasted longer than would've been polite had anyone else been in the store.

"Quiet today?"

"Yeah. It gets like this sometimes, but it's okay. I don't mind the break."

I frowned, looking around the empty pet store. I could see the fish swimming around in their tanks peacefully and just barely hear the scurrying of some of the smaller animals in their habitats. I'd never wondered if the deserted store next door had any impact on Elliott's business until Sarah mentioned it. I was an awful almost-girlfriend.

"That's an awful long face you've got there to be coming around for a visit. Is everything okay?" He leaned on his folded elbows over the counter, settling in for whatever trouble I was about to unburden on him. But I wasn't sure I could tell him what was on my mind without revealing some of the secrets I'd been keeping since the first week I'd been back in town.

"There's nothing *wrong* wrong, like no big emergency or crushing bad news or anything. Just still working some things out in my head about Gram's estate, or I guess I should say my inheritance." I shuddered. "That sounds so final. If I still say Gram's estate, it's like she's still here and I'm just managing things for her."

"You've certainly had to make a lot of decisions since you've come into town." He nodded slowly, like he was trying to figure out where I was going with all of this while still being supportive. Cute.

"Has the empty store next door ever affected your business here?" I tilted my head to one side to study him and started drumming my fingers against my leg.

"Hang on..." he shook his head and scrunched his eyes up for a second. "Give my brain time to do a complete 180 to keep up with yours..."

I giggled and then took a deep breath. "The two topics are

related, but answer my question first."

"Well, I suppose I may get a little more unexpected foot traffic if there was something cool in there to draw people in. But then there's the potential of the new owners complaining about Turtle being back in the alley, even though she has every right to be there and I have all the necessary documentation..." He narrowed his eyes at me slightly, and after a pause said, "Why are you asking me about the empty store next door, Mabel?"

I'd moved on from tapping my fingers on my leg to touching each finger in turn to my thumb, over and over again. I know he noticed, but if he was going to ignore it then I was going to take the small fidgeting win and keep doing it.

"Um, you see funny thing is, I may have inherited that building from Gram." I took in a long breath through my nose and held it, waiting for his reaction.

"Ooookay. So you own an empty building now. That's-"

"And the Artful Brew building, too." I said as quickly as I could while letting out the entire breath I'd been holding. I leaned over the counter, unceremoniously smacking my head on top of my arms trying to hide my face.

"Oh, shit. Okay. Well. You really have had a lot on your mind then haven't you?"

I nodded my head quickly without raising it, probably causing tangles in the hair around my face but whatever. I deserved them.

"Want to talk through everything with me? Sometimes hearing it out loud with another person just hits different."

"Yesh preash." My words came out all smooshed sounding since I still refused to lift my head from my arms.

"Okay, so you own the cottage and the empty building next door and the building with the coffee shop in it."

I nodded again.

"And Sarah doesn't know you're her new landlord."

Not a question, but I nodded anyway. I felt his hand come to rest on the top of my head, and he started stroking my hair in a soothing gesture that somehow just made me feel worse.

"Mabel, why haven't you said anything to anyone?" His tone wasn't accusatory, more like he was just trying to understand my thought process, but I still felt the lead weight of guilt I'd been carrying around grow a little more.

"I don't know? A lot of reasons I think. At first, I didn't think I would be staying in town and so I thought it didn't matter anyway. Then when I got to know people, I was scared of everyone's expectations about what I would do with the stores and if I would stay in town or if I would sell out and would I really sell the cottage or, ugh just all the things…" I trailed off, trying to get the rest of my thoughts together. Elliott tapped me on the top of the head.

"Think maybe you could stand back up so I don't have to try and decipher a muffled conversation?"

I let out a huge groan into the counter, but I stood up. When I finally raised my gaze to his, he was looking at me with sympathy instead of judgment. Some of the tension eased, but not enough to erase the frown from my face.

"Hi." He smiled, and propped his chin on one hand on the counter.

"Hi." I waved at him, like the dork that I am.

Chuckling, he said, "Got yourself quite the pickle here, don't you?"

"Yes?"

"Question, not statement. Okay, what about this whole thing isn't pickled then?"

"Well, I guess no one really ever has to know. Gram was her landlord all this time and no one ever knew because she ran things through Mr. Findley and a property management company. I could just do the same thing if I choose to renew her lease."

His eyes narrowed again, but this time it was definitively more accusatory than merely trying to figure out what I was saying.

"Mabel, what do you mean *if* you renew her lease? When is the rent agreement up?"

I tried my best to pull my head in between my shoulders like Turtle, but I didn't quite make it. "Friday?"

He ran a hand down his face, and hearing myself say it out loud made it sound worse than it did when it was just rattling around in my head. I was out of time.

"Um, that is one hundred percent a pickle my friend. You better hope that Sarah never finds out that you're the landlord if you don't renew her lease and you don't give her any notice either. That's their home too, Mabel."

"I know, I know. And I could never do that! I know I could never do that. Of course I'm going to renew the lease and they can stay there forever for all I care. Hell, I hope they do, she makes a damn good cup of coffee. Speaking of, have you had the Milky Way Galaxy before?" I did a chef's kiss in the air.

"Focus, Mabel."

"Right. The coffee shop is safe. I'll just continue the lease through the management company like it has been and nothing will change. I don't even have to live in town to do that, I can handle it all remotely."

I caught the shadow that passed over his eyes, but he covered it quickly. My stomach knotted up when I saw, yet again, how unfair I was being to Elliott, sort of leading him on this way. But we'd agreed that whatever this was was only while I was in town. So I didn't actually need to feel this gaping wound of guilt and sadness in my chest each time I mentioned to him that I may not stay. Right?

"Well, it sounds like you have that worked out. And I've seen you at the cottage. I can't imagine you just putting that place up for sale. I assume you'll keep it."

He went right on trying to help me sort my pickled problems, but I didn't miss that his voice had cooled just a fraction when he spoke again. I couldn't blame him.

"You're right. I can't let the cottage go. And honestly, I don't even think I could rent it out... it creeps me out a little to think of other people living in Gram's house, even just as a B&B."

"So you keep it as a vacation home. Solid plan. That just leaves the empty building." He'd settled back on his stool behind the counter and crossed his arms while he talked to me now, a physical barrier between us. I felt my shoulders creep back up an inch or two as I fought the urge to wrap my arms around my waist.

"Right. The building. Well. I've always wanted to open a gift shop slash art gallery. And the upstairs space is absolutely perfect for a studio. The lighting is amazing with all the windows."

Elliott sat unmoving, just staring at me while I talked. I swallowed hard and kept going, running through my thought process out loud.

"But of course, that would mean staying in town permanently. It would just be too hard to do remotely, shipping in inventory and having someone else run it. Plus, and I really can't believe I'm saying this, I would miss out on the personal element of getting to talk to customers and chat about their purchases, hear their stories."

He raised one eyebrow slightly, nodded slowly twice. I did wrap one arm around myself now, but I wasn't sure if I was bracing against him or what I was about to say.

"But, if I stay, I'm leaving my mother behind. We've never been apart, and I'm all she has left now. I... I just don't know that I can be so selfish. That I can hurt her like that."

I felt my shoulders roll in with the weight of everything I was feeling. This really was my entire problem, boiled down to this one decision. Elliott was right, when I said everything out loud to another person, all the other choices were just no brainers. The biggest decision of all, and really the only one left, was whether I move to Painted Creek permanently or go back to Ohio with my mother. This is the one that was so hard, so painful.

Elliott was still just sitting, not really staring at me now but just watching me. I knew he had something to say, but I wasn't sure if I wanted to hear it.

"Do you have any thoughts on the matter?"

He snorted humorlessly. "Do I have any thoughts on the matter. Yes, Mabel, I have so many thoughts about whether or not you're going to stay in town permanently that it keeps me up at night. But right now, my thoughts are really irrelevant. You have to decide what is the right thing for you. I don't know if you've never been told that or if you've just never learned how, but that is really what this entire situation boils down to."

At first I was a little taken aback by what he'd said. Did everyone else just instinctively know how to do what was best for them?! And now that I really thought about it, I wasn't sure that I *did* know how. I'm sure if I examined it a little closer I'd find that I'd never been asked to choose what was best for me either. I was always so eager to please everyone else, no one ever needed to ask me what I wanted. Because what was best for me had always been what was best for or easiest for someone else.

"Selfishly, I want you to stay. And I'm only saying that out loud because I think you already know. But if being away from your mother would make everything that you stand to gain meaningless, then staying obviously isn't what's best for you." He sighed, and it was like his whole body deflated with the motion. "Mabel, doing the best thing for you doesn't always feel *good*. Sometimes, the decision comes down to what feels less *bad*."

I just blinked back at him. I really don't know how he just got into my head like that and seemed to know what I was thinking or worried about or needed to hear, but he always did. I guess I'd always just assumed that making a decision on something just for me would feel good in the end. But I guess life wasn't always so black and white.

"Well, that sucks."

He shrugged. "I will say though, keeping all these secrets is a dangerous game around here. And no offense, but have you heard yourself when you start rambling? Don't get me wrong, I personally think it's adorable, but you do tend to say things that you don't mean to say out loud. You should consider weighing whether keeping the secret is worth the potential damage to the new friendships you've made here in town."

Too much. It was too much to think about all of a sudden, and I was ready to be done with this conversation that I was so obviously unprepared to have. So, I reverted to humor.

"Thank you, Dr. Scott. What do I owe you for today's session?" I smiled at him, although I could feel how weak it was.

My smile completely melted away when he said, "You don't need any kind of psych degree to know that, Mabel. Listen, I've got to go feed Turtle, but I'll call you later, okay?" He slid out from behind the counter and headed to the back alley, with no invitation to me to follow.

I wasn't sure if the dismissal or the tough love hurt more. After standing motionless for at least a full minute, I slipped out of the pet store and went back to the cottage alone.

THIRTY-SIX

I ABSOLUTELY WASN'T in the mood to paint. I didn't want to work on commissions or paint for fun or try new techniques or really even look toward the dining room at all. It was like a bad grown up version of a children's book... I will not paint here or there I will not paint anywhere. My spat with Mom on the phone this weekend on top of the weight of the looming deadline and then this conversation with Elliott had left me grumpy. When dinner came and went and he still hadn't called, I headed out into the back yard for a stroll, hoping the fresh air and sound of running water would bring me some clarity.

Instead, I found Charlotte cussing a blue streak on her way into the herb garden.

"Char... are you okay?" I was still a good ways away from her on the porch, but there was no mistaking the words or the vehemence with which she said them.

"Hey, Bell. I'm fine. Just madder than a wet hen." She actually stomped her foot as she said it, and I stuffed the laugh that wanted to come out at the sight deep, deep down. I knew better than to laugh at a fighting mad woman.

"I'm sorry. What's wrong? Can I help?" I picked up my pace toward her a little, worried maybe she was hurt.

"No, no. It's nothing really I'm just being dramatic. My favorite gathering apron broke just as I was on the way back. Nothing I can't fix up later. Nothing like a minor inconvenience to finally put you over the edge, hmm?"

I'd made my way over to her, and sure enough it looked like the gather stitch on the main pocket of her apron had just given up on its job. The pocket fabric had fallen away from the main apron fabric, and everything she'd collected from the herb garden lay at her feet in a pile.

"Here, I can at least help you pick all this up." I crouched down and began gathering up all the cut stems, hoping she was familiar enough with them that she could sort them back at her house.

"Thanks. Fancy a chat?" In a move that was more graceful than I could ever hope to be, she folded one leg beneath her and sank to the ground without using her hands to brace herself on the way down.

"Damn ninja..." I whispered more to myself than her as I lowered myself to the ground with all the finesse of a panda falling out of a tree.

She untied her apron and laid it out on the ground next to us. She started unceremoniously tossing clippings on top, so I followed suit.

"Bad day then?" I asked.

"No, not particularly. I guess I've always been a bit short tempered. At least that's what my momma always said." One side of her mouth lifted in a wry grin, and I smiled back at her. "How about you?"

"Oh, I'm pretending I didn't have a day. Then I don't have to think about it."

"That sounds like an interesting plan. How's it working for you?"

"Not very well." All the herbs were laying on the apron, and I reached over and grabbed what I knew was a small sprig of rosemary and began twirling it between my fingers. The smell washed over me, and with it a small wave of peace. Not like everything was suddenly right in the world, but more like suddenly everything was figure-out-able. I'd take it.

"You know it's funny, I can smell this so strongly around the house, sometimes even inside. I keep meaning to look for the big rosemary hedge in the yard but I never remember when I'm outside walking around. I always just come straight out here."

"It is a strong scent, I suppose, but my favorite. Try this one." She handed me a large leaf she'd just pinched off of another sprig. "Lemon balm. Soothing and uplifting."

I bruised the leaf a little before bringing it to my nose, though I didn't really need to. The lemony scent mingled with the rosemary perfectly, and I realized I was glad I hadn't gotten caught up in painting tonight. I would've missed this moment, sitting in the grass with a friend, just being present. When was the last time I'd done that?

"Nice. Kind of like the Mabel Grey geranium, just less flowery and more minty."

"Your name sake I suppose?"

"I guess? I don't know why my parents chose it. And Gram always preferred roses, so I don't think it was her input. She liked the big shrub kind. Said they were more hardy and stubborn." Charlotte snorted, and I grinned, thinking of Gram and her gardening.

"So what's happened in this day we're pretending doesn't exist? Must be pretty big." She was absent mindedly shredding a blade of grass, and I was happy I wasn't the only one who fidgeted their way through conversations. I kept playing with my sprig of rosemary.

"I don't think I've told you too much about why I'm still here in

Painted Creek after my initial visit time frame passed by..."

"Not specifically, only that you had to work out estate stuff."
She stiffened slightly beside me. "You decide to sell the cottage?"

"No!" I surprised myself at the adamancy in my voice, but she
visibly relaxed. I guess maybe she relied on Gram's herb garden
more than I thought she did. I cleared my throat to try again. "No, I
could never sell this place. And I can't imagine anyone else living
here either, honestly. The cottage is mine."

She never looked up from her new blade of grass, but a small
smile played across her lips. "Okay, I can see how deciding to keep
a beautiful house and grounds all to yourself would make for a
miserable day. Dreadful really. How sad for you."

I plucked a handful of grass from the ground and threw it at
her. "Har har. So funny. It's not the cottage, it's me. I guess I'm at
sort of a crossroads of where I've always been and where I think I
might want to go. But either path I choose has the potential to hurt
someone. I'm just still trying to figure out what damage I can live
with."

Talking with Elliott today really had gotten me thinking, as
much as I was trying *not* to think about it. He was right, there was
no easy solution for me, I just had to go with what hurt less. And
for the first time in my life, I think someone else's sadness and
disappointment may hurt me less than my own.

"You, my new friend, are a people pleaser."

"Thank you captain obvious. Good talk."

"A snarky people pleaser. Rare breed, but no less dangerous to
themselves."

I cut my eyes over at her and waved for her to carry on with
what she really wanted to say.

"My momma wanted me to be a nurse. She saw my love for
taking care of people with all my homemade remedies and what
not and thought that was the obvious career choice for me. I used to
help her make medicinal tinctures and infusions... I think maybe
she wished she could've been a nurse, and projected that on to me
when I took an interest in herbs too. Mad as hell when I got married
and opened up a kind of apothecary instead."

My fingers began to tingle, and as I spun the rosemary sprig in my hands, it moved up my arms and hit my shoulder blades with enough force that I visibly shivered. The picture in my mind solidified in such a vivid way I knew I would be able to sketch it out when I got back in the house. I would probably even be able to use my hyper realism style if I wanted to, all the details were there with sharp clarity. When I looked up, Charlotte had a wry smile on her face, so I was fairly confident that everything had worked out for her in the end. "I guess she came around then?"

Her face got a far away look, and she glanced up toward the cottage, not meeting my gaze. "Eventually. Not that it was easy, mind you. Took awhile, some painful and awkward moments along the way. But Mabel, I think you'll come to see that in finding yourself and choosing your own path, you'll find your people along the way. And the people that've been there all along, the ones that truly love you, will come around in the end. Sometimes it takes seein' with your own eyes that someone knows what's best for themselves better than you do to loosen up the apron strings a little."

I wasn't quite in the mood to actually participate in this conversation, but I was hearing her loud and clear. My fingers itched to pluck off all the little tiny prickly leaves from the rosemary, but I couldn't bring myself to destroy it like that. I picked off one, and began to slice it into tiny bits with my fingernail.

"Careful, that'll stain your fingers. Anyway, in the end I guess we were both right in a way. My daughter has never wanted to be anything but a nurse."

"Shut up. I didn't know you had a daughter! Seriously Charlotte, I know ninjas are all secretive and stuff, but damn. I can't believe she's never come up before now."

"Oh, she's always around I assure you. Just usually off with a mind of her own. I think it runs in the family." Her eyes twinkled and it was so good to see her talk about someone she loved. More than one someone I guess, since it was obvious she cares for her mother. And that her mother thinks she's as stubborn as she thinks her daughter is.

"Bring her with you one evening. Unless this is your alone time, I wouldn't want to mess that up. But I'd love to meet her. I bet she's just as beautiful as her mother."

She pretended to fluff up her hair, "Oh, that runs in the family too, dear." I threw more grass at her as we both laughed.

"Oh! I bet she knows Becca! Well, I mean I'm just assuming I guess but you don't look a day over twenty-five at the most, and I guess she could be older than Becca by some, but you would've been so young...which is fine of course I don't mean-"

"Mabel, do shut up. I'm not offended. Things come to us in our own time, yes?"

"Yes.." I smiled, grateful she was letting me off the foot-in-mouth hook, but I realized she didn't actually answer my question. I wondered again how old she was when she'd had her daughter. "You'll both have to come to the coffee shop one morning. I meet some new friends there three times a week, and one of them takes Becca off to school. We could all go together."

"Maybe so. But for now, I best be going. Have to fix this blasted thing when I get home now anyway. Here," she handed me a couple more sprigs of rosemary, "you seem to like this one, too. I'm sure you'll find a good use for it."

We stood up, ready to go our separate ways, me with a sketch to draw and her with a bundle of herbs in a broken apron. As we each dusted off, I said, "I'm really glad I ran into you tonight. I've missed seeing you out in the yard. Last week was... a lot."

"It's okay, Mabel. It's your life. You don't even have to poke your nose out that back door for a single second if you don't want to. But if you do, I'm usually around in the evenings."

"Please feel free to come up and knock on the door some time. I can make us some tea, even if it's not as good as Gram's." I shrugged.

"No, I suppose it's not. But tea was always Constance's thing now, wasn't it? Have a good night, Bell."

I smiled at the nickname. I'd thought it was a joke the first time, but I think it was growing on me.

"Night, Char. Be safe walking home." She shook her head, but threw up one hand in a wave as she walked away.

Turning back toward the cottage, I hustled up the hill almost as fast as I'd come down earlier. I wanted to get this picture sketched out before I couldn't recall all the details anymore. It was so vivid in my mind, but I never knew when the image would start to fade and I would have to blunder around trying to fill in the details that had slipped away.

Finally reaching the house, I hustled into the dining room, more out of breath than I would like to admit just from walking through the yard. "I need to walk outside more Hedgie. That was almost brutal. Embarrassing really."

I grabbed a piece of paper and a pencil and set about sketching. I wasn't exactly sure what this building was called, some kind of old stone cellar of sorts. It was nestled into the forest, not in a nature reclaimed the building kind of way, but more in a the building has always just sort of belonged there kind of way. A small herb garden ran along the sides, just a few plants and honestly it almost looked more like landscaping than a garden, as if the person who came here just loved these particular herbs and wanted them around. Rosemary bushes stood out on either side of the door, with flowering lavender adding a cheerful pop of purple on either side.

As I finished up the sketch, I glanced at the rosemary sprigs that I had clutched in my hands in my hustle back up to the house. They were bruised, but not badly, and suddenly I knew without a doubt what I was going to do with them.

Floundering into the kitchen so quickly I ran into the corner of the island again, I set about putting a pot on the stove, preparing to make a natural ink from the rosemary. I was fairly certain it would come out a yellowish brownish and maybe a little greenish color, and I was hoping that a monochrome painting with this ink would make something that looked close to a sepia print.

I had no idea what this little tiny cellar meant to Charlotte, but I was trusting my frisson vision, and I knew I had to paint the sketch and give it to her as a gift. It was just a bonus that I could paint the whole thing with ink made from the cutting she'd given me from my own garden. I laughed out loud to myself, "Oh, the tangled webs we weave..."

I decided I'd keep the rosemary goop, and forget finding a better name for it, it would forever be goop now, and make some beads from it. I'd make one for Charlotte to go with her painting, and one for myself to go with my stack. I smiled as I thought that all my new friends were represented in my new jewelry obsession. All but Elliott, but I had something in mind to fix that.

As I flitted from the kitchen to the dining room and back late into the night, I didn't spend much time thinking over the decisions I needed to make or the back lash I would face no matter what I did. I just worked, and sang out loud, and talked to Hedgie, and felt a deep sense of *rightness* that I knew I would never find anywhere else in the world.

THIRTY-SEVEN

I MET TUESDAY morning with a renewed energy that didn't match the amount of sleep I had gotten by the time I'd finally fallen into bed Monday night. I finished Heather's painting, all the open commissions I had accepted, and made good progress on the painting for Charlotte. I decided not to take any other commissions for the next two weeks, until the end of the month. One of the perks of working for myself the way that I did was being able to take an impromptu vacation of sorts. I changed the auto-response on my website to reflect the break, and breathed a sigh of relief to have a little time to myself.

I'd texted my mother to let her know the changes too, and then declined all her calls to discuss it. I knew that I worked hard, had been working hard since I was sixteen, and I felt secure in my business and clientèle. Two weeks off wouldn't hurt, while I took the time to examine what I really wanted my future to look like.

And it was looking more and more like my future was here in Painted Creek. New friends that could become a found family, old friends who were already more like family, and a relationship that I could see deepening into the biggest adventure I'd ever had, if I let it. But I still wished that I didn't have to leave behind everything I'd had with my mom to chase after everything I never knew I wanted.

And I did feel like I'd be leaving it behind. Mom hadn't stepped foot in Painted Creek since I could get to town on my own. I knew she would never be interested in moving with me, and I wondered if she would even visit if I did move here. She made it blatantly clear when I first came here that I was to sort things out and come back home. I'd been too chicken to even imply that there was a possibility that I might want to stay in town, but I didn't really have to test the waters to know how she was going to react.

Even if we didn't see eye to eye, she'd always had my back. And now that we'd had some space from each other, I was beginning to see that she was using me as a crutch to not live her life. She'd been living for me and through me since Dad died. But you can't make people see what they don't want to see, even if it was clear as day to you, and it wasn't something I felt like I could point out to her either.

And if we were being honest, I had used her as a crutch, too. I was not a people person, and letting her make all the social choices for me was easier than trying to make them on my own. Did it mean that all my acquaintances were older and stuffy and I had no real friends my own age? Yes. But it also meant I never had to put myself out there as *myself*, so I never risked being rejected.

I think it was time we both started taking some risks. Independently.

When Wednesday morning came, two days till my deadline to sign paperwork with Mr. Findley, I was filled with a kind of restless energy that didn't translate well to sitting and relaxing like I had hoped when I decided to take some time off.

I tried to paint, but the few things I'd attempted came out

looking like a jittery mess. Idly, I wondered if it could be a series to sell at Artful Brew... we could tell people they were painted after drinking one of Sarah's café con leches. Honestly, it seemed plausible to me, that drink should come with a warning label.

By mid-afternoon, I had ten missed calls from my mother that I was still ignoring, and I'd given up on relaxing or being productive. I decided I'd make a trip into town to deliver Heather's painting. I was really pleased with the overall effect of the painting, even if it was the most confusing frisson painting I'd ever done.

In a few ways, it was actually like two paintings in one. The left side of the painting was dark, with an almost ominous feeling. The grass and trees were gnarled and sinister looking as they swept across the page. The right side was bright and hopeful, with thriving flowers growing along the edge of a cobbled stone path that led to an iron gate. The gate was cracked open, as if in secret invitation, with light pouring from the other side. I'd done the base layer of both sides with traditional paints, but most of the detail work was done with natural inks, giving the whole painting an earthy vibe that I hoped would fit into The Secret Book Garden perfectly.

A bridge connected the two scenes, drawing the eye from the darkened, dead forest into the light of the stone path and beyond. I didn't know what journey this represented, but I was hoping my new friend was in the light and not trapped in the dark.

BY THE TIME I'd gotten Heather's painting all packaged up and ready to go, it was late in the day and almost closing time for all the shops along the square. Since it was so close to dinner, I figured I would see if Heather wanted to go grab a bite to eat somewhere after she closed up. I still hadn't had the chance to try out or rediscover most of the restaurants in town.

The little bells tinkled as I pulled open the door to The Secret Book Garden, and the store was no less amazing the second time as it had been the first. Unconsciously, I said, "Wow," under my breath as I walked in, and I heard Heather giggle in response from behind the counter. I looked over to her and smiled a little bashfully, but then shook my head and said, "Seriously, Heather, do you ever get used to how amazing this place is?"

"Not really." The look on her face was full of pride and something else I couldn't quite put my finger on. "But I do make sure I'll never be bored in here. Have you noticed all the squirrels?"

"I'm sorry, what?" She didn't respond, only grinned bigger, and I turned my attention back to the store. Looking everything over and paying, what I thought was close attention to details, I still didn't know what she meant. "Nope, don't get it. Explain please."

She chuckled, and started pointing out little tiny squirrels that were hidden all over the shop. They were a variety of sizes and materials, and most blended in with their surroundings to become almost invisible.

"What?!" I started laughing. "Oh my gosh they really are everywhere! How many?"

"I don't even know anymore. If I see one I like when I'm out thrifting and it's small enough, I'll add it to the store. Sometimes when I'm cleaning or rearranging, I'll come across one I've forgotten about." She looked around the store as if searching out hidden squirrels, and I fell a little more in love with the shop.

"Hey! If you find them all, you could make like a squirrel scavenger hunt! Give them all little names and have a card your customers can fill out as they spot them. If they ever find them all they win a prize. I could even paint you a little squirrel reading a book or something and you could make prints!"

Heather was laughing, but she was also jumping up and down, clapping her hands. "I absolutely love that! How fun! But maybe instead of trying to find them all myself first, there can be a bonus if you find one not on the list. Maybe I can ask Sarah or Alex to have some sort of specialty item that you get if you find a sneaky squirrel."

We both dissolved in to a fit of laughter, but I thought she was on to something. "Seriously, Heather, I think it's a great idea. You should text the group chat and we'll all help make it happen. And I love the idea of getting a bunch of the stores on and around Main involved, connecting the community. You should totally do it."

"You know, I think I will. Thanks for the idea, Mabel!" She came around the counter and gave me a quick hug. "As grateful as I am for the impromptu marketing scheme, what brings you by? Need a book?"

"No, actually I have your painting. It's finished!" Reaching into my tote, I pulled out the package and handed it to her. "I hope you like it."

She squealed and immediately put it down on the counter, sliding her finger under the sticker to pop open the large cellophane bag. I waited with baited breath as she slid the painting out and flipped it over. She held it up in front of her, and it was pure torture that I couldn't see her face as she took in the painting for the first time.

I waited a second or two, but Heather hadn't moved at all or made any noise. I had no idea if she was just processing what she was seeing and feeling or if she was trying to figure out how to tell me she hated it. It was so much more nerve wracking for me, waiting for any kind of response on a frisson painting. I didn't really know what I was painting or why, and if it even meant anything to the person in the first place. Although, come to think of it, my frisson visions had never been wrong...

"Heather? Are you okay? You've been completely still for like a really long time..." my voice was soft as I stepped to the side to touch her shoulder, and I realized that she had been silently crying this whole time. "Oh no, what's wrong? I'm so sorry, I thought... well I don't know what I thought but I didn't mean to upset you. Heather, say something please." I was wringing my hands in front of me, not sure whether I should try and hug her, rip up the painting, keep my mouth shut or what.

"I... I can't." She spun on her heel and ran to the back of the store. Just before I heard the storeroom door slam I heard her heart wrenching sob echo through the empty shop of books. My eyes teared up, and my stomach swirled with regret over the pain I caused my friend. *And I don't even know WHY,* I thought to myself.

I glanced back toward the storeroom, but respected her obvious wish to be alone. On the way out the door, I flipped the open sign to closed hoping no one else would come in and bother her. With one more glance through the window, I walked away feeling worse about my painting "gift" than I ever had before.

THIRTY-EIGHT

EVEN THOUGH THINGS had been a little cooler between us the last couple of days, the only person I wanted to see right now was Elliott. By the time I walked to the pet store, I had silent tears running down my face and was finding it harder to breathe, walk, and cry at the same time. Pulling open the front door, I walked straight around the counter and into Elliott's concerned arms.

"Mabel, what in the world?! Are you okay? What's wrong?" He soothingly stroked my back up and down while holding me tight, but I just shook my head. That was too many questions in a row and I was too upset.

"Are you physically hurt?" he asked. One question, I could do that.

"No."

"Is someone else physically injured?"

"No." I felt him relax a little, and then felt an added layer of guilt that I had worried him. After all, everyone that I had come to care about in town he had known for years and he cared about them, too.

"Okay. We can figure out everything else when you're ready. It's okay." He just continued to hold me, rocking gently side to side, until my breathing evened out.

I could feel my phone vibrating in my bag, but chose to ignore it. I knew who it was anyway, and I just didn't have the strength to face what I knew would be an argument on top of feeling so badly for the way I'd left Heather a minute ago. I shuddered with an exhale when I pictured her face crumpled in tears all over again.

"What happened, Mabel?" Elliott's voice was soft. He gestured to his chair but I was too upset to sit down and be still while I rehashed what had happened for him.

"You remember I told you about my frisson vision paintings?" I asked him.

"Didn't know that's actually what you were calling them, but yes, you did."

Ignoring his attempt to lighten the mood, I said, "Well, the last time I got a book from Heather, she said she'd rather trade for a painting than for me to pay for the book. And when we were talking about it, I got the tingles, but this time it was kind of weird."

"What, like in your toes or something?" he broke in with a confused look.

"No, my fingers. The picture in my head was weird." I returned his confused look, because I rather thought that would be obvious, but whatever. "Anyway, I finished this painting and even though I didn't understand it I thought it was still beautiful and I was excited to give it to her so I took it over today and we had the most lovely chat and when I gave her the painting, she cried!"

I'd said all the words in a single breath and my voice cracked at the end. I'd hung my head in my hands and waited for his response. I could hear my phone vibrating again in the silent pause.

"Oookay… well… Mabel, sometimes tears are good tears you know…"

"She ran away from me, Elliott! Literally said 'I can't' and ran into the back storeroom. I could hear her crying from the front door."

"Oh. Well, that's different I suppose. But really, baby, it may not be as bad as you think. Sometimes people can have a really strong reaction to something but it doesn't necessarily mean they're as upset as you think they are."

More vibrating from my bag.

"You really think so?" I finally peeked through my fingers when his hands closed around my wrists, lifting my face closer to his.

"Of course I don't know for sure, but I do know Heather rather well. I'd say when she calms down there will be a fair bit of embarrassment and then an explanation. And even if she is as upset as you think she is, you have to trust her to tell you that."

And, more vibrating. I should have put it on silent.

"Are you going to answer that? What if it's Heather?" He asked, glancing at my purse as if it might explode.

"It's not. It's my mother." I leaned my head back and looked at the ceiling, closing my eyes in resignation. I had to answer her or she would just keep calling.

"Are you sure? Maybe you should check…" He picked my tote up off the floor where I had flung it down before crashing into him and handed it to me.

Reaching in my bag I said, "I say it's my mother, you say it's Heather. Loser buys dinner?"

"I'll take a bet that ends in dinner with you anytime."

I pulled my phone out and showed him the once again lit up screen with my mother's picture on it.

"I'd like another burger please." I said, but I didn't have the heart to grin or gloat.

He nodded toward the back alley. "Go talk outside with Turtle. She has a way of calming me down when I'm upset."

"I'll try anything." I called over my shoulder as I pushed open the alley door and answered the sixth incoming call to my cell phone since I'd left the book store.

"MABEL, FINALLY! WHY haven't you answered my calls?"

"Hello to you too, Mother. How can I help you?" I walked over and gave Turtle a few scratches, and she gave me a look that I interpreted to mean she was rooting for me on this phone call. I put the call on speaker so I could hold it out while I interacted with Turtle.

"Don't you give me your customer service voice young lady. Plus, you won't need it anymore if you keep taking time off. Why does your website say commissions are closed? You assured me that you would keep up with your business painting while you were on this silly little trip."

"It's not been a silly little trip, Mother. It's actually been the most at home and settled that I've felt, well, since maybe the last time I was here." She didn't respond immediately, so I took the opening and ran with it. "Mother, I'm considering moving to Painted Creek. Permanently."

More silence.

"It isn't just the cottage that I've had to sort out since I've been here. Gram owned some buildings here in town too, one empty and one with a long standing tenant. I can't just back out of a lease with no notice, and I think I could finally open the shop I've always wanted to open in the empty building. I-"

"That's enough. I'm not going to entertain this conversation any more, Mabel. You are not destroying everything that we've built for you over an old house and some rinky dink real estate in the middle of that God-foresaken town. Start packing up and come home."

"Respectfully, no." I could count on one hand the number of times I'd said no to my mother and meant it, but this one was going to stick. Once I'd said the words out loud, I knew there was no better option for me than staying here in Painted Creek. I just had to get through this hard bit first and come out on the other side in one piece.

"I'm sorry, did you say no? You've carried on there quite long enough young lady. Call the lawyer and sell just like we planned and get back home!" Her voice lifted in incredulity at the end, and I was afraid we were getting close to yelling at each other. Not that we'd ever actually done that. The silent treatment was much more our style, but there was a first time for everything.

"I did say no. I'm not selling anymore, Mother. And this is not a God-forsaken town, it's full of lovely people who have become friends and a community that goes out of its way to make you feel welcome. And it's not rinky dink real estate either, it's prime real estate on Main Street that holds the perfect location for an artsy gift shop and the best local coffee shop I've ever been in!"

I felt more than heard the sharp intake of breath from the other end of the alley, and I knew immediately who it was. I slowly turned around to face Sarah, lowering the phone to my side in the process.

"Sarah, I can explain." I held one hand up as if to hold her off, but she hadn't moved a single muscle since I'd turned around.

"Do you own this building, Mabel?" Her voice was deceptively quiet, and her hands had clenched at her sides.

"It's not quite what you think-"

"DO YOU OWN THIS BUILDING, MABEL?"

I lowered my hand, but looked her square in the eye as I simply said, "Yes."

"And you were never going to tell me? And from the sound of it, you weren't even sure you were going to KEEP it? Mabel, this isn't just my business, my livelihood, this is my *home*. Becca's home." Her voice cracked on the end, and I wished she would go back to yelling. At least I didn't have to wait long to get my wish.

"I know that now. I didn't know in the beginning, but then when I got to know you..."

"Then you were just too chicken to give me a heads up that I might need to be looking for a new location. A new place to live. A new job. And definitely new *new* friends. And to think, I was on the way over to check on you since you seemed upset. My mistake."

"Sarah..."

"No. I was right to be wary of you all along. You never planned on staying. You never cared about any of us past a fun little vacation and a break from a job you obviously hate. So do whatever you want with this building, Mabel, but notify me through Mr. Findley's office. I don't want to talk to you again." She ripped open her alley door and let it slam behind her.

I walked over to the edge of Turtle's enclosure and sank down to the ground. Leaning against the brick of the building, I pulled my knees up and draped my arms across them, hanging my head.

"Mabel, are you there? Can you hear me?"

Shit. I'd never hung up the phone with my mother. Wincing, I pulled the phone back to my ear, turning off the speaker.

"I don't suppose there's a chance you didn't hear any of that?"

"Oh darling, I heard every word. I'm so sorry, sweetheart."

I sniffled, surprised at the sincerity in her voice as she tried to comfort me.

"I really do feel like I belong here, Mom. I've been painting better than I have in years. I've made new friends, and I even met someone. I just... I just feel like I have to stay. I need to stay."

"I hate to hear you so upset, Mabel. You wouldn't be feeling like this if you'd left after a couple of weeks." Her voice softened, and I didn't know if it was in an effort to convince me or if she really did believe that what she was about to say was the best thing for me. "Come home, darling. It can be like it's always been, just you and me. I bet you just needed a change of scenery to revive your painting. We can travel more together, and then you won't have to worry about these so called new friends talking to you like that. You know we never argue."

I sighed. I felt all the fight drain out of me and I wanted nothing more than to say 'yes Mother' and give in. But I'd come this far now. I had to finish this conversation.

"We never argue, Mother, because I never challenge you on anything. You control my job, my social circle, or lack thereof, even what I wear most of the time. And I've always let you, because I didn't want to cause you any pain. Your happiness has always mattered more to me than my own. But I can't keep doing this. I have to live my own life. I still want you in it, more than you know, but I have to make my own choices, and I have to get out there and *live*. God Mom, aren't you lonely? Isn't there more that you've wanted for yourself?"

"No, Mabel, I'm not lonely." Her voice hardened considerably. "I have you, just like I've always had you, and that's enough. Now, that horrible town took your father from me, I'm not going to let it take you, too. Pack up and come home, and we can talk about all the rest of this nonsense then."

It hit me then for the first time, why my mother hated this town so much, why I was only allowed infrequent visits as a child and why she would get so upset and angry when I drove here as an adult. She blamed Gram and Dottie and maybe all of Painted Creek for Dad's death. They'd called and asked him to come help with some renovations one weekend and he'd never made it back home. She couldn't see past the pain to remember any of the good times we'd had here as a family. And she'd let it ruin her relationship with Gram, too.

"This town isn't taking me from you, Mother, but you're doing a good job of pushing me away on your own. It didn't take dad either, that was some dumb ass drunk driver on the interstate flipping his car into dad's lane when he was just trying to get back home. Stop blaming Painted Creek and Gram for something no one could control!" I was riled up again, and so done with the emotional roller coaster I'd been on the last hour or so.

I heard her gasp, but I couldn't stop now. It was like the dam that had always been holding back my opinions and thoughts and feelings had busted, and I wasn't sure that I wanted to try to repair it now anyway.

"I'm not coming back to Ohio. I know that hurts you, and I am genuinely sorry for that. I am thankful for everything you have done for me, the way you helped shape my business into what it is, allowing me to make a good living out of my passion. But I have to make more than just a living, Mother. I need to make a life. And right now it feels like that life is here."

"If that's how you feel. We'll discuss this later. Goodbye,

Mabel."

She hung up on me before I could respond.

I SAT FOR another minute or two with Turtle, just listening to the muffled sounds carrying over from Main Street and trying to collect myself enough to go finish my conversation with Elliott. With a few last shell scratches, I stood, dusted off, and made my way back into the shop.

He was just flipping the sign in the window to closed, and when he heard the back door shut softly he turned and gave me a tentative smile.

"Everything okay?" He winced. "Stupid question I know, but you know what I mean."

"Could be better."

"Could be worse...?" he said hopefully, but I just shook my head.

"I think that may be the first actual fight I've ever had with my mother. Although, I'm not sure if you can call it a fight if there wasn't any yelling?" I stopped the manic pacing I was doing in front of the door and cocked my head to the side, considering. I think I was caught up in the semantics so I didn't have to think about the actual conversation. "Nope, not a fight. There was no actual screaming. It was merely a disagreement, an argument of epic proportions, if you will. People scream at each other when they fight, right?" I continued my pacing.

"Er, sometimes I suppose, but not always..." He trailed off like he wasn't sure if that was a hypothetical question or not, and eyed me warily.

"We had a not so calm discussion about how I can't return to Ohio because I feel like my life is here now, or at least it could be." I heard his intake of breath, but I kept going without looking at him. One life altering conversation at a time.

"So here I am, shattering my mother's illusions of just the two of us living happily ever after as spinsters together when my stupid mouth gets ahead of my brain and I tell her all about the two buildings that I own in town and how they aren't rinky dink real estate but right on Main Street and one of them is the best coffee shop ever but of course I didn't know Sarah was in the alley so then I got to not-fight-argue with her too just as an added bonus to this really shitty day. Although come to think of it, she did yell at me, so maybe I did have a fight with Sarah."

"Oh Mabel, baby, just wait a minute-," Elliott tried to break in but I was on a roll.

"Just as a recap, I broke Heather to the point of sobbing uncontrollably-"

"-you didn't break Heather, I told you if you'd just-"

"-I broke my mother's heart, probably completely out of nowhere since I never gave her any indication that I was unhappy with my life and I was too chicken to tell her I was considering staying all this time, and now I'll probably never see her again since she freaking hates this town-"

"I'd imagine that's probably a little bit of an exaggeration..."

"-and I managed to completely blow up another new friendship because I couldn't keep my big mouth shut in a shared space while I was fighting-not-fighting with my mother. I don't even know why I dug my heels in on wanting to stay in town after my fight with Sarah anyway..."

"Now wait a minute..." Elliott had his hands up toward me much in the same way that I had mine toward Sarah a few minutes ago. It wasn't working any better for him than it had for me as I did my best to wear a path into the tile floor.

It was like I could see the train wreck about to happen, but I was powerless, or unwilling, to stop it.

"Don't you think you're getting a little bit ahead of yourself? I don't think that anything that's happened today can't be undone, if you worked to make it right." He seemed almost desperate to get me to see reason, as if he could sense what was about to happen and was desperate to stop it.

"Seriously?! Heather and Sarah have every reason to hate me now. All the friendships I've made are gone in one big poof because I know that Alex is going to take their side, and she should, shouldn't she? I mean who am I anyway to come in here and mess up the friendship they have after just a few weeks. I won't be able to go out in town without running into one of them or someone who knows them and OH MY GOD I bet the whole town will shun me now. Then, even if I did open up a store, no one would come anyway and I'd go out of business and then have to admit my mother was right. I might as well just go home now. No friends, no business, no nothing. I guess there's just not anything worth staying for!"

My mouth snapped shut forcefully. The pounding in my head that had begun when I realized Sarah was listening in the alley intensified to something akin to ice pick stabs to the brain. Of course it was too late though. I saw the hurt flash across his face briefly before it morphed into anger.

He calmly walked over and opened the door to the store. "Sounds like you've got it all figured out. You certainly don't need my help." He stood motionless, just staring me down. I guess this would've been the perfect time to take a deep breath, apologize, and try to talk like a rational human being who breathed between sentences and thought before they spoke.

Instead, I picked up my tote bag and left, only slightly wincing when the door slammed shut behind me, followed by the loud click of the lock.

THIRTY-NINE

I DIDN'T REMEMBER driving back to the cottage. It was a blur of hot angry tears and bitter regrets. By the time I pulled up in the driveway, it felt like it took a minor miracle to find the motivation to just get out of the car and go in the house.

The air in the driveway swirled around me as I trudged up the walk, and I took a second to stop and breathe in the fresh air. The ever present smell of rosemary was still there, but it seemed a little fainter than normal with the rose shrubs in full, fantastic bloom. Seeing the large yellow flowers made me miss Gram so much the ache in my chest grew to match the headache that had stayed with me since I left Elliott's shop. I dropped my head, feeling fully defeated, and went inside.

It was probably time for dinner, but I couldn't stomach even the thought of eating right now. I clicked on my favorite lamps in the house for after the sun went down, but I honestly wasn't in the mood to be surrounded by all the cheerfulness anyway. I stood in the middle of the cottage and looked around. Was this really where I was meant to stay? This morning I was so sure, but it all went to hell so fast I was truly wondering if it was the right decision now.

I wandered aimlessly outside, then made a beeline for the creek. Throwing my shoes off when I reached the water's edge, I started stomping through the water, kicking up water and sticks and leaves, anything that got in my way.

I was so angry! Angry at myself mostly, but that just made me angry *and* sad. I should've known better. I should've known not to get attached to anyone here in town when I was really just an outsider. I should've known not to get comfortable with those stupid frisson paintings again, too. I didn't have enough control over the outcome, not knowing what they really were or why I was painting them. It just wasn't a risk I should take anymore.

And I should have known better than getting so close to Elliott. I knew before that first date that it wasn't going to end well. I should have kept my distance. The thought almost took my breath away, and that only made my anger grow.

Most of all, I should have known better than to say the things I'd said to Elliott. He was just trying to help, and he certainly didn't deserve for me to take my pain out on him.

I kept stomping down the creek, kicking water up over the bank with every step, oblivious to the rocks underfoot. When I reached the slight curve in the creek's path, just before the herb garden, I looked up for the first time and saw Charlotte watching me. The look on her face was inscrutable which was fine... I didn't have the energy to try and figure it out anyway.

"Oh, don't stop on my account. Looks like you've got something to work out. I'll just get what I came for and go... unless you want to talk it out, that is."

"No." I'd stopped kicking, but I was still breathing hard and it came out short and rather rude.

She narrowed her eyes at me, and I had the strangest sense I was about two seconds away from being scolded like a child. For a second, I felt sorry for her daughter if she ever stepped out of line. Without another word, she hopped across the stones in the creek and had half her body through the vine curtain before I stopped her.

"Wait. I'm sorry. You didn't deserve that, and I appreciate the offer." She turned back toward me, and for a moment I was distracted by the way her hair blew around her face, almost shimmering as it had the first time I'd met her. She just stood there and waited for me to start talking, but I wasn't sure where to begin.

"This morning, I decided to stay in town." She raised one eyebrow, and I hated how it reminded me of Sarah.

"Oh?" There wasn't really any inflection, and I couldn't tell if she was happy with the news or didn't care either way.

"But then, I delivered a painting to a new friend and I think I hurt her feelings, she left crying. Then, I upset my mother by telling her that I wouldn't be returning to Ohio, and I'd never disappointed her before now, so that sucks."

She was at least nodding slowly now, so I kept talking.

"Next, Sarah overheard a secret I'd been keeping that kind of involved her and she got really upset. She says she doesn't want to speak to me anymore." I took a shaky breath and kicked at the water a couple of times. "And I basically told Elliott that without everything and everyone else, he wasn't worth staying in town for. So I think we broke up. If we were ever together enough to actually break up in the first place." One more kick splash for good measure.

"Well, Mabel, you've had quite the day, huh? No use in stewing over what happened now. Not going to change it any. So my question is, what are you going to do about it?" She'd moved her hands to her hips, and I got the impression that when things got tough this woman rolled up her sleeves and got tougher. I don't think I'd inherited that gene from anyone in my family, but I certainly wish I had.

"What do you mean what am I going to do about it? There's nothing I *can* do about it. Everyone is hurt and angry and upset and it's all because of me. I already did that. There's no way I can undo it now."

"That's one way to look at it. One really whiny, unproductive way, but still an option." She cocked her head to the side much in the same way I'd done earlier, but I doubted she was trying to determine if we were fighting or not. I got the feeling if you were in a fight with Charlotte, you'd know it. "What ever happened to intent versus impact?"

"What??" I could feel all of the frustration and anger from earlier bubbling back up, and I was trying not to lose my patience and yell at her, too.

"The impact may have been that you hurt them all, but was that your intent? Did you set out today thinking 'hmm I wonder how I can hurt everyone I've come to care about today'?"

"Of course not!"

"Then apologize!" she yelled, throwing her arms up in the air as if she was as impatient for me to understand her point as I was for her to get to it. I startled a little, causing my feet to slip on the big rock I was standing on in the creek. When I regained my balance, she'd walked over to the water's edge and was all but glaring at me from a couple feet away.

"Mabel, if you didn't intentionally cause anyone harm, there's always an opportunity for you to make it up to everyone and mend the relationships you were beginning to build here. It may not be easy, but I can bet you it'd be worth it. The way I see it, the only way that you'd truly be at fault here is if you took the coward's way out and just left things the way they are now and ran away." Her hands went back to her hips as she stared down at me. Literally and figuratively, I think.

Glancing down into the creek, I said, "What's the point? I'm sure it wouldn't work anyway. I should just leave everyone to their lives and go back to Ohio, where I know what the hell I'm doing."

When I looked back up at Charlotte, I wasn't prepared for the look of utter disappointment on her face. "I guess you're not who I thought you were then. Goodnight, Mabel." She turned and walked away, back to the woods toward her house instead of into the herb garden. I couldn't help feeling like 'goodnight' was actually goodbye, and the weight of disappointing another friend turned my feet into lead as I trudged back up the creek and into the cottage.

THE SMELL OF roses was almost overwhelming when I re-entered the house. I checked to see if the front windows had been left open. Finding one cracked, I slammed it shut and locked it for the night, missing the smells of rosemary and lemon drop that usually blended so well with the roses in the night air.

Stomping through the creek certainly hadn't done anything to improve my mood, and I felt so much tension built up in my muscles I thought I was going to explode.

I walked into Gram's room and went straight for the closet. I was hoping that something, anything, would call to me as a distraction. I flipped through a few journals, a few different entries, but nothing could hold my attention. With a huff, I slammed the last book shut. In my anger fueled carelessness, one of the pages turned in on itself and creased when I shut the book.

"Well that's just great. Now I'm destroying property, too. Good times." I straightened out the page, and with much more care put all the journals back the way I had found them and left my little reading nest in the closet.

For the first time, I eyed the chair that sat at Gram's desk on the opposite side of the room. I'd still not cleaned out the desk, and I was pretty sure it was the last thing in the house that needed going through. I knew how much Gram sat here, took care of all her paper work and card writing and things, so it had still felt too personal, too final. But as I pulled the chair out and sat down, I was hoping that a little of that connection was still left, and maybe I wouldn't feel so absolutely alone with the mess I'd made for myself today.

It didn't work. It just made the little ball in my gut with Gram's name on it roll around something fierce and grow in size, and it was the last straw in my shit-tastic day. I laid my head down on her desk and cried. I stayed that way until all the angry had drained out of me and my arms had gone numb, leaving the rest of me feeling hollow and cold, too. As I stood from the desk and turned to leave the room, the journal that had been out on the desktop since the day I came back fell to the floor, falling open to the beginning of an entry.

I really wasn't in the mood to try and read one of Gram's stories anymore, the allure of that distraction drying up with my tears. I fully intended to close the journal and save this last adventure for another day. But when I bent to pick up the book, the first words written caught my eye and pulled me in. I sank back into Gram's desk chair and started reading the entry from last year.

I miss my momma. Of course, I think about her often and in the most unexpected of times since the day I lost her, but lately I miss her with this deep bone ache that stays with me from the time I wake until the time I go to sleep. Last night, I dreamt of her for the first time in years, the two of us out in the herb garden as we used to be. I think it's coming close to time for me to be called home.

I've had an amazing life. I took what my family taught me and what their family taught them and molded and shaped it into what suited me, and I couldn't have asked for anything better. I'll forever be grateful to my Gramma Faye for teaching my momma all about the herbs and the ways they speak, and to both of them for teachin' me how to listen. And we all certainly had different ways of using what we heard!

I've loved my teas and the conversations they've embellished for practically my whole life. They haven't been working for me quite the same lately, no, but that's all for the best I guess. Maybe I'll go find Momma's recipe book and see if I can make some of Lottie's famous beauty oil one more time for these old wrinkles. Sure would be good to smell it again.

I think of how Gramma Faye would tell stories of all her concoctions and how they would 'save the family' back in the day when they couldn't get on to a doctor like we could. But I guess with a family that big, ten kids and all the animals too, you had to have a trick or two up your sleeve to keep them all patched together. Then my momma comes along and takes that knowledge and turns it into a thriving business for herself, practically unheard of in her day. Shew, I'm sure Gramma Faye was fit to be tied with such 'frivolous nonsense'. Now I know I wasn't around for that conversation, but I never knew anything but love and encouragement between those two, so it must've all worked out.

Healing and doing good comes around in a lot of different forms, I've found.

Then I came along and shook up EVERYBODY. Oh, I can just about see my momma's face clear as day every time I had some new fangled thing to show her, the patience she would find from deep down somewhere to keep encouraging me 'till it all clicked. And click it did, making dried tea blends finally fulfilled something in me I didn't know was missing. Doesn't mean it wasn't painful sometimes, but all that pain helped me grow stronger in my craft, too. My teas have served me and everyone else well for all these years. I'm so glad that connection to my roots was there when it felt like my branches were gonna snap off in the hurricane of life.

Which leads me to my Mable. Oh how I love that girl! I think I'm gonna start fixin' up this old place, just in case. Can never be too prepared. I wish I'd had more time to teach her everything I know. I wish I had more time to tell her about everything her family has accomplished and what they made out of their lives and talents and passions. Our family wouldn't be what it is without each one of us shining bright in our own power, quirks and all. I just hope that Marissa can finally wade through her own grief enough to allow Mabel the same freedom. Lord that girl can shake a mean paintbrush! I hope she uses that gift in every way she can. And maybe someday she'll find a way that connects her to the roots she doesn't even know she still has, too.

I hope I'm still here to see it. But even if I'm not, I know she'll find her way. It all always comes to us in our own time, doesn't it? Now, where did I leave Lottie's book? I think it's going to be a cookin' up day...

There was a lot here. So much to unpack, as Elliott would say. I was just sitting stock still; blinking, breathing I think but I'm not really sure, trying to pick a direction to go in my brain to make it all make sense.

Gram knew she was sick. Well, that's not quite right, but she definitely could sense that something was wrong. And wasn't it just like Gram to start making her contingency plans, just in case she was right? I looked through her open door into the main living area with a new sense of gratitude. She hadn't thought the place needed a face lift... she'd done it all for me.

What stood out next was how little I actually knew about my extended family. I'd missed all the stories of my dad's side growing up, and my mom never spoke about her family at all. Actually, until my dad died, I always assumed she thought of his family as hers more than her own blood family. I brushed my fingers over the open pages, thankful to have these journals and all the other sets, too. I had access to family history, and I could learn it all anytime I wanted to. These journals were a bigger gift than fixing up the cottage had been.

What took a little more pondering was all the references to Lottie and Gramma Faye. I'd never really heard Gram talk about her mom or grandmother much before, but I'm sure that's who she was referring to. I decided to tear the house apart all over again until I found the books she was talking about, and then maybe I'd find her tea recipes as well. Just like she'd wanted to try and recreate her mother's beauty oil, I'd love to try and recreate the tea she always made for me. Even if I knew in my soul it wouldn't be the same, just like she did.

Closing the journal gently, I laid it back on the desk top, stood, and pushed the chair under. I had so much to sort through in my mind, but I couldn't do it here in Gram's room where the pull to go through the other journals was now stronger than ever. Glancing into the back yard, I turned on all the string lights that crisscrossed over the creek, and stepped out into the otherwise dark yard. Maybe the creek hadn't calmed me before because I wasn't ready to calm myself. With a deep breath, I dug my toes into the cool grass, ready to try again.

FORTY

I WALKED SLOWLY down to the creek, mindful of each step not because I was worried about my footing but because I was trying to be present in the small journey. I was especially grateful for Gram's love of lights tonight. There was no way I would be out in this big yard surrounded by woods at nearly midnight otherwise.

When I reached the edge of the water, I stopped to really listen to the sound it made as it washed over the rocks and knocked against the earth on the bank. The crickets were singing softly, and I finally began to feel a tentative calm envelop me for the first time today. I took a step into the water, and slowly walked to the swing to settle in.

I loved this swing. I wasn't sure why I hadn't spent more time in it, but I suppose I hadn't spent much time just... being... since I came back to the cottage. I'd have to carve out some time when everything was said and done to just escape into this space and listen to nature, and my heart.

It was so peaceful, the sounds of the water continuing to ease the tension of the day and the full moon casting a soft light over the whole yard, brighter even than the string lights. Dad had always said two things about a full moon; they made the emergency rooms crazy, and they were for letting things go. I wasn't sure what I wanted to let go of, but it was becoming more and more clear what I wanted to keep.

I wanted to keep this cottage. No, I *had* to keep this cottage. It wasn't just the wonderful memories I had here. Now that I knew generations of my family had made lifetimes of memories here too, there was no better place for me than this to go through those journals and learn about it all. The cottage was mine.

And I was staying in it. Yes, I could come back and forth, keep it as a retreat of sorts or something, but that's not what I wanted. That was a distorted kind of compromise that put everyone else's feelings above my own, and I was done doing that to myself. This was my new, permanent, home.

So what about the people in town? The friends that I'd made and the feelings I'd hurt? I could become a hermit I suppose. Let's face it, I wasn't that far off now, especially when I was in the middle of a big painting project. But Charlotte was right, that was the coward's way out. I wanted to fight for my place in these people's lives. I wanted to share in their joys and adventures and heartaches. I wanted to spend every second I could giving everything that they'd given me back ten fold. I was going to earn my place here, not as Constance's granddaughter, but as Mabel Morrison, the girl who creates art and memories with spilled coffee and falls for escaped tortoises and preserves random, forgotten memories.

I looked up at the moon and thought of one more thing I *didn't* want to release into the universe, and that was my frisson vision paintings. They weren't always perfectly constructed like my commissions, and they were almost never easy, but they were my gift. I hadn't really seen it as a gift, more a burden, until tonight. But reading Gram's journal entry made me realize that denying a part of myself that came to me as naturally as breathing was no way to live.

Did these special paintings line up perfectly with the path I'd taken in my life and business? No. But every one that I'd created had helped people remember or hold on to a memory that was important to them or had changed their lives. And THAT was something worth holding on to and celebrating. For the first time, I truly believed that it was.

I paused to really think about all of the reactions and comments from my new friends when I'd given them their frisson paintings. They were always grateful for the painting, even if the memory had been a difficult one. They all connected to it deeply, and it was almost as if the painting served as an affirmation that they were on the right path now.

Maybe all the memories we make along the way, both good and bad, are as important to our lives and our healing as the decisions we're making right now. Recognizing how we handled a difficult situation, or how we cherished a pivotal moment, helps us grow into the journey we're on now. I could only hope that Heather's painting had shown her something similar, that the tears weren't grief but perhaps relief at realizing how that memory from the past had brought her to where she was.

I decided, either way, I'd be here to find out.

I was done pushing people away when things got hard. I realized, sitting there in the swing and listening to the crickets, that was exactly what I had been doing. I didn't know how to work through confrontations because I had always just given in. I didn't work to fix any arguments or hurt feelings because I'd decided that it was easier to let a misunderstanding destroy a relationship than it was to explain what happened and face the possibility that the other person would leave. I was so busy trying to protect myself from any more loss that I was losing myself in the process. I was officially done dimming my light to try and keep others comfortable, to make sure they would stay.

"That's what I want to let go of moon," I said softly into the quiet night sky. "The fear of loss."

I rocked slowly in the swing for another few minutes before making my way back into the cottage. I walked with more determination, my head held high. Tomorrow was going to be long, but I knew what I needed to do to try and set everything right, and there were a lot of preparations to make. I threw open the windows I had slammed shut earlier, inviting the night air into the house and appreciating the little boost of encouragement I felt every time the wind blew.

I spent another couple of hours before bed slowly making my way through my mental to-do list for what I was referring to as Operation Mabel Stays. When I finally started tucking the house in for bed, I glanced into Gram's room one last time. When I put the journal back on the desk earlier, I'd put it back exactly where it had been laying since I arrived a month ago. Looking at it now, there was no way I could've knocked that journal off without practically sweeping the desk clean. And come to think of it, I wasn't super familiar with physics, but it seemed unlikely that the hardback, leather bound journal would have fallen to the floor and remained perfectly open onto a single page like that.

Shaking my head slowly, I smiled. "Thank you for the little push," I said aloud into the empty house. "I hope I make you proud."

I turned toward my bedroom and collapsed onto the bed. I think my eyes were closed before I'd fully landed, still in all my clothes with dirty creek-stomping feet. But a soft smile still remained on my lips as I drifted quickly to sleep surrounded by the scents of lemon, roses, rosemary and home once again.

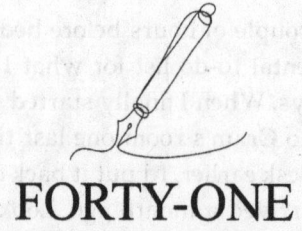

FORTY-ONE

THE ALARM ON my phone blared ear splittingly loud, but I wasn't even mad at it as I bounded out of bed the next morning to the shower. There was much to do for Operation Mabel Stays today, and I was anxious to get to it. There was no better motivator than finally making a decision and having something to work towards. Having a few wrongs to set right never hurt either.

After a quick shower, I checked my phone for the first time while towel drying my hair. I had several missed texts from Dottie asking if I was okay and if I wanted to talk about anything. I grinned as I sent her a quick response, telling her I would stop by this afternoon, but nothing more. I'm sure she probably had more information about everyone else's viewpoint than I did by now anyway. But she didn't know what I was thinking. I grinned only a little evilly as I finished getting dressed. Good to surprise her every now and then and keep her humble.

I had laid out everything that I would need to take with me the night before, so getting myself out of the cottage took no time at all. I had nothing but determined confidence in this little list of mine as I peeled out of the driveway. First stop, Mr. Findley's office for some paperwork. I had a feeling some of my other stops might require more proof of my plans than just my word.

I WAS KNOCKING on the door to Mr. Findley's office at exactly 8 AM, which was an hour before he actually opened, but I could see his car in the parking lot and was hoping he would make an exception on his office hours, and his tolerance threshold for crazy clients, just this once. Just as I was about to start calling him and pounding on the door at the same time, Carol poked her head around the corner. She waved through the glass with a concerned smile on her face.

She didn't step back as she opened the door to invite me in, and the forward momentum I thought I would need rippled down my legs as I began bouncing on my toes.

"Good morning, Mabel. Are you alright? Oh, you know we aren't technically open yet, right?"

"I know, Carol, I apologize, truly I do. But I just have some things I need to sort out as soon as possible and I don't think I'm going to be able to pull it all off without Mr. Findley's help. And then when I saw his car was here I just decided to make a nuisance of myself until he answered. I didn't mean to interrupt your morning, but it really is important."

I'm not sure what she saw in my face, the pleading or the determination or something else all together, but before I could register what was happening her face split into a wide grin and she pulled me into a hug.

"Oh, I'm so happy! You're staying aren't you? Here in town I mean? Oh, I just knew you would!" When she let me go, her eyes were a little misty and I knew I could add her to the list of friends I'd made since coming back to Painted Creek. Granted, she might be the only name on the list after today if I couldn't make things right, but one is better than none.

"Yes, I am. No one knows yet, and I'm a little worried it's going to take some convincing to believe me..."

"Oh, it will for sure. I hope you have some big grand gesture planned. And I mean for Sarah, not Elliott."

"Oh, good Lord," I murmured under my breath, and Carol laughed quietly. "What are the odds that the whole town doesn't know how badly I've messed up?"

"Zero. Oh, but that means they'll all know when you make it right again, too! Come on, you can be Phil's first official appointment." She ushered me down the hallway, and with a light rap on the office door, pushed me inside.

"Your first appointment is here. Now you make sure you help her out." With a wink, she turned on her heel and left, shutting the door behind her.

Mr. Findley sat behind his desk with an amused expression on his face, tilting his chair back and forth.

"What?" I finally asked when I couldn't take the speculative silence anymore.

"Oh, nothing really. Just trying to work out the puzzle before you give me all the answers."

With a sweeping gesture of my hand, I sat in the chair across from him. "By all means, tell me what you've got."

He chuckled. "Well, you're staying in town or Carol would've come in crying."

"Yes, and?"

"That means your obviously keeping the cottage, as you should. And if I were a betting man, I'd say you're keeping the rental agreement for Artful Brew as well."

"Point two."

"You and that group of women hit it off too good for you to come to any other conclusion. And to meet Becca is to love her, I knew you wouldn't jeopardize her in any way."

"So very true. But don't stop now you're on a roll."

"Ah, well that's where my confidence runs out. Just what did Mabel decide to do with her empty slate of a building with the perfect studio space for an artist, so I've been told?"

"Oh, come on now, double or nothing, just take a guess." I had on my best poker face. But I also didn't play poker, so I couldn't completely smother the grin that was fighting to break free.

"You're keeping it and turning it in to a shop of some sort."

"Ding ding ding we have a winner ladies and gentlemen!" I'd thrown my hands in the air to wave them around while I wiggled in my seat. He was giving me a warm, genuine smile, and as I settled in my seat once more, I felt again like I was talking to an uncle that was proud of me. I may only have one living relative left, but I was certainly overflowing with found family.

It was nice.

"Okay then young lady, what do you need from me?" He leaned forward over his desk, crossing his hands and waiting intently for what I was going to say.

"Well, there's nothing that needs to be done with the cottage, Gram saw to that. I'll need the lease renewal drawn up as soon as possible. I'll probably still want you to manage that through your company if you don't mind, since everything runs so smoothly. I'll sign an official copy for you before I leave, but I do want to take a copy of it with me today, please. What's this?"

While I had been rambling, Mr. Findley had been pulling papers out of a file in his desk drawer. He'd slid a pile over in front of me and was now pointing at a signature line.

"Sign and date here please. This renews the lease for another six months. If, after that time, you wish to change the term length you can do so. There are also options for lease to own, if you'd ever find yourself wanting out of the rental business..."

"You had this done already?" I was absolutely gawking at him, but I couldn't help it. "Why?"

"Wishful thinking? Blind faith? Gut feeling? I don't know. But I'm glad I did. Now you don't have to wait for me and you can get on with your day. I'd imagine you have some things to take care of." His tone of voice was completely professional but his eyes were twinkling.

I groaned. "Seriously, how bad is it? What have you heard?" I covered my eyes with one hand and made a let's have it motion with the other.

"Well, some people claim to have heard you in the alley on the phone with your mother all the way from Main Street."

"Fabulous. What else?"

"Lots of people allegedly heard Sarah giving you what for in the same alley. And rumor has it she was so mean the rest of the day that her staff made her quit early and go home when Becca got in from school."

"Good, good. Just the person that supplies the entire town's caffeine hit mad as a grizzly bear. Cool. Anything else?"

He was shaking his head slowly as he printed off a copy of the rental agreement. "Not one single bit of any of it matters, Mabel, except for what the people involved say to you and you say to them. The rest of the town is going to make up stuff and fill in the blanks on their own no matter what. Just make sure that you take care of your business in a way you're proud of and don't even think about the rest."

He leaned back in his chair, reaching to a smaller, locked cabinet, pulling out a single envelope before locking it back. "This is from Constance. I have no idea what it says, but I was instructed to only give it to you if you decided to stay in town and keep both buildings." He slid my papers across the desk with the envelope on top, and gestured with his head toward the door. "Now get out. You have things to do and I have clients to see who actually make appointments."

He stood to see me out, and I think I surprised us both when I walked around his desk to give him a hug. "Thank you for all the help. Thank you for believing in me."

I put the envelope in my bag for later, grabbed the copy of the rental agreement, and all but jogged through the building to leave.

I threw up a hand in a quick wave to Carol on the way out as she shouted, "Oh, go get 'em honey!"

And that's exactly what I planned to do.

FORTY-TWO

I WOULDN'T SAY I was closer to Dottie's house than I was Main Street, but that's where I found my car headed next. I had some questions for her that I really wanted to talk about before I pushed through the rest of Operation Mabel Stays. The answers wouldn't change my decision, not at all, but maybe they'd settle something in my heart that was more agitated than I realized.

As I shut the car off in her driveway, Dottie opened the front door and smiled at me through the screen. My eyes misted over, but this time it lacked the burn of pain and grief. Countless times had I pulled up to the cottage, only to be greeted by Gram and Dottie, sometimes Betsy and Nora too, just like Dottie was standing now. Like the few moments it would take for me to come over and knock on the door was just too long to wait to see me again. And you know what? Maybe it was. Maybe this is what life and love was all about, the small moments that you didn't fully appreciate until they were gone.

In that moment I was so incredibly grateful to still have someone to stand at the door and wait for me to get out of the car. Slamming the car door behind me, I rushed up the porch steps and wrapped Dottie in a big hug, little girl style with my head tucked into her shoulder. I felt her chuckle when I tried to make my taller frame shrink against hers, but I just held on tighter for a second or two more.

"Come on in, sugar, and tell me all about it." She patted me on the back and then led me in the house, one arm around my waist.

In no time at all, I had finished a rapid fire, chain of events recap of the last twenty-four hours or so. Dottie had remained uncharacteristically quiet the whole time, although it may have just been because I was talking too fast for her to interrupt anyway.

"Well, say something, Dot. You keepin' your mouth shut might be the strangest thing that's happened in all this mess." I smiled at her, but I really was anxious to hear her thoughts on everything.

"Sugar, you don't need me to say a gosh darn thing. Sounds like you've got it all back on track to me, or you will when you're done wrappin' up all you've got left to do on that list of yours."

"But... you... I... nope, you have to say something. Anything, really. I need some commentary or reassurance or something. Even an opinion, you're good at those." I reached across the couch and poked her in the shoulder as she swatted at me with a throw pillow.

"Child, you don't need any of those things. This is *your* life, a fact which you just decided to embrace if I'm not mistaken. You don't NEED anything from me, blessing, reassurance, opinion, nothing."

"But-"

"But if you WANT it, you're doin' good, sugar. You said some things and made some mistakes but instead of just leavin' it at that you're fighting to set it all right. I'm down right proud of you, honey. And I'm so glad you're staying in Painted Creek. I'm glad your roots and new found wings have brought you to the same place."

"Me, too," I said quietly, tracing the patterns on the throw pillow in my lap with a fingernail.

"I reckon I only have one question now."

I looked up at her to see her head turned sideways, studying me once more like she had when I first got back into town. "What's that?"

"What in the hell are you doin' here talking to me instead of out righting wrongs and tackling whatever else you had on your Mission Mabel list?"

"Operation Mabel Stays."

She didn't even acknowledge that with a response, so after a beat and with a huff I answered her.

"You knew Gram better than anyone on this planet did, probably better than Betsy and Nora put together." She started to protest, but I held up a hand and kept talking. "Now I'm not arguing that all y'all weren't thick as thieves and then some, but we both know it's true that you and Gram were closer than that even. My point is, you knew Gram better than anyone and there's something that has just been eating at me. I'm hoping you can explain it to me."

"I'll try."

"I always knew Gram's tea was special. I never could find anything that came even close to making me feel the way that her blends did, or tasting as good or even looking as pretty in the bag. But I always thought that it was just because she'd made it for me, and she was my grandmother and that's what made it special."

Dottie had relaxed into the couch and was smiling softly at me, as if she already knew what I was going to ask and was thrilled that I was going to ask it. She waved her hand to encourage me on when I'd paused talking, but she didn't say a thing.

"So imagine my surprise and confusion when I started getting these stories from people all over town about Gram and her tea and how they missed sitting and having a cup with her. Even Elliott looked like he saw a ghost when I offered to make him a tea! He looked shocked when he asked me if I could make tea like Gram did..." I trailed off and just looked at Dottie, waiting to see if she'd offer up anything, but of course this silent streak of hers today was still going strong.

"I never heard you ask a question, sugar. What is it you want to know?"

"What was it with Gram and her tea? At first I thought it was just people being neighborly and keeping an old woman company, but the stories are going back decades! She mentioned making tea in her journals countless times. Why do people act like she had all the secrets of the universe closed up in perfect little bags full of herbs? And why didn't she ever talk about it?!"

Dottie sat still for a moment, staring off into space, and for once I was able to sit still without fidgeting and wait for her to gather her thoughts. When she finally looked at me again, she looked settled in a way that she hadn't been since I came into town. I don't know what I'd said to make her relax on such a deep level, but I was glad to see so much tension leave her.

"You found the journals."

"Yes, ma'am."

"Well, I imagine if you start at the beginning and read them, you'll have all the answers you need. But I'll tell you what I know, or I guess what I've come to understand over the lifetime I had of loving Constance and being her friend."

I nodded once, thankful for any insight I could get.

"Constance had a way with tea, and not just making the perfect cup but using it to connect with people and help them through seasons and storms in their life. Now I don't know the hows or whys mind you, we never really talked about it in so many words. But through the years I watched her get this far away look on her face for just a split second, and she'd bustle off to make a tea. Sometimes she'd package up the dried herbs and set off to deliver them, and sometimes she'd bustle around the kitchen making up a gorgeous little tea service for someone who would show up out of nowhere five minutes later. Damnedest thing I ever saw."

"So she just... knew?"

"She just knew. Sometimes it was like she was looking at something only she could see, and I'd see her rubbing her palm with her thumb like it ached or tingled for just a second before she'd snap out of it and launch into a flurry of activity making her teas. Now, I may have imagined it, but I do believe I've seen some similar behavior out of you a time or two, sugar. Don't suppose that's a coincidence is it?"

"No... I don't suppose it is." I knew with a certainty deep down in my soul that Gram got the same kind of tingles I did, only she was seeing what kind of tea to make to soothe someone in the present. I seemed to be seeing paintings to help soothe someone's relationship with their past. I frowned. That would take some more examining later.

"Well, I sure would like to have that conversation another day, sugar, if you're willing. But for now, to answer your question, Constance had a way of knowing what tea blend would help people when they needed it, whether it was with a headache, a stomach flu, or a broken heart. And the conversation that came with the tea was most likely just as healing as the tea itself.

"She didn't talk about it, sugar, because she didn't have to. People would find her when they needed her or she'd go hunt them down in town if she thought they needed her. And she was never wrong. Took her a good few years to believe it, to trust it, but she was never wrong."

We both just sat with our thoughts for a minute. Suddenly, I wanted nothing more than to read every single journal cover to cover. I wanted to read all the stories of Gram and her teas and her love for her friends and neighbors. And for the first time, I wanted to write my stories down too. I had been afraid of the frisson paintings for so long, maybe it was time I learned to fully trust myself and my intuition and gifts, just like Gram did.

"Dottie, we'll have that conversation soon, I promise. But I have two more things to ask of you right now and then I've got to get going."

"I'll hold you to that. What else can I do for you, sugar?"

"Do you happen to know anyone in town that's a good contractor? I have some plans for a new store that I can't pull off on my own."

She reached over the arm of the couch to the side table and ripped the top piece of paper off of a note pad that had been laying there. She passed me the paper with a smile.

"Larry is expecting your call. He's the best in all the surrounding counties, and he's the one that helped Constance with some things at the cottage."

My mouth fell open. "You already had this written out! And you've already talked to him?! How did you know I would even need it?"

"Your family may have had the sight, sugar, but I'm not blind. I always knew you'd stay. You just took the rocky path to come to the conclusion yourself."

This woman. She'd always been there, cheering me on from Gram's side and then right out in front now that Gram was gone. Through a lump in my throat, I took her hand and said, "You know, I once had a grandmother that you remind me of... I miss her a lot, but you make a good substitute."

"Ah, sugar. You know, I once had a friend who was a lot like you... I miss her, but you make a good substitute."

"I'm glad you can see her in me. I'll try and live up to it."

"You keep on being your shining self, Mabel, and that's all you need to live up to. Now, I love you honey, but get out of my house."

"Dottie!" I swatted at her, but laughed as I leaned over to give her a hug. "Thank you." I whispered.

She stood and followed me to the front door. "You're welcome. Call me tonight and tell me all about it!"

"I will! Oh, hey Dot?" I skidded to a stop a few feet from my car and turned back toward her. "Can I go sit in your swing for a minute? I have a phone call to make."

With a knowing wink, she said, "Sure thing, sugar. Good luck."

With a small wave she went back in the house. I grabbed the

painting I had done for my mother out of the car and walked around to the gazebo in the back yard. I set the painting up on the swing, snapped a quick picture, and sent it to my mother.

Sliding the painting to the side of the swing, I sat and waited for her to call.

I DIDN'T HAVE to wait long. My mother's ring tone pierced the tranquility of Dottie's little backyard oasis, and I took a deep breath as I swiped to answer the call.

"Hi." My voice was soft, even to my own ears, but I really had no idea how this phone call was going to go. I knew what I hoped for, but there were too many variables at play here for me to make a good guess at how it would all go over with my mother.

Last night, almost feverishly, I'd sat down in the middle of my planning for Operation Mabel Stays and finished this entire painting in one sitting. I'd been thinking of the non-fight fight I'd had with Mother, and gotten a frisson vision that had almost taken my breath. I'd known the subject beyond a shadow of a doubt, but I didn't know the back story or why this moment in time would've been so important. But I stopped what I was doing and didn't come up for air until I sat looking at the finished painting with tears in my eyes.

"Mabel, darling," she took a second to collect herself, and I wished so badly that I could hug her through the phone. "It's absolutely beautiful."

I let out a sigh of relief. Glancing at the painting next to me I said, "I wasn't sure you would like it. The style is very different from what you're used to seeing from me. But I was hoping the scene depicted in the painting would make up for it."

Two people were sitting with their heads close together, and the point of view was from behind and slightly above, as if you'd walked up on a private moment. The style was very loose, almost eluding to shapes and figures more than actually painting them, the colors all washed out and faded. I'd used all of the natural inks that I had created since my return to Painted Creek, and the result was subtly striking; a marriage of tones that I don't think I could have created any other way. The most pigmented part of the painting was their clasped hands, resting in the space between them.

It was a painting of my parents, sitting in this very swing. I don't know why they would've been here, as far as I knew Mom never came over to Dottie's when we were in town and she had never been particularly close to her, but Dad had called her Aunt Dottie for my whole life.

"You're right, it is very different from the paintings I am used to seeing from you. I also think it is the best work you've done in years." I gasped, not expecting such high praise for something I wasn't sure she would like. "Oh, Mabel, I'm sorry if I ever made you feel like anything other than the style you became known for was less than spectacular. You are spectacular. You. Everything you make regardless of style is just a reflection of that."

"Thank you." I didn't really want to say more, not now. I knew we would have more discussions about my business and the directions I wanted to go in, but for now, I would take the small acknowledgment that the new things I was doing were good, too.

"I can't believe Dottie told you about this. Whatever in the world were you talking about to bring it up?"

"Dottie didn't tell me anything, Mother. I just saw the scene in my head and painted it. I'm assuming it's you and Dad in this very swing, but I don't know any more than that. I'd like to though, if you're willing to share."

"The frisson has come back then." Not a question, but she did say it with an inflection that could have been interpreted as relief.

"Yes."

"I see. Well. You hit this one right on the head, darling. I don't know how you do it."

She went quiet for a second, and I imagined she was staring at the picture on her phone much like I was staring at the painting next to me. Her voice had a far away lilt to it as she began telling me about a small moment in time, many years ago.

"It was the day that your father and I were to be married. Constance insisted that spending the night apart was tradition and my staying in a hotel room was out of the question, so I had stayed in the cottage that night, while your father stayed at Dottie's house. In the early morning hours, before I had to start getting ready and before anyone would miss me, I snuck out and went to Dottie's, hoping to get a glance of Anthony when he went on his morning run. I was just too excited to wait until that evening to see him. I was so in love with that man. I still am."

A sharp pain sliced through my chest, and with it a new realization. I felt the loss of my dad every single day, but the older I got the more it became just kind of the way things were than an actual something-is-missing loss. But my mother had lost the love of her life. That was a different kind of loss.

"Anyway, he came out and saw me lurking on the street, and the biggest grin split his face. He waved me over, and we sat on Dottie's swing, hand in hand without saying a word for I don't even know how long. Eventually, Dottie came out and shooed me back to the cottage with a twinkle in her eye. I snuck back in and as far as I know, Constance never knew I'd left at all."

"Oh, I'm sure she did. Gram knew everything."

Mom chuckled, which surprised me. "Yes, you're probably right."

"Thank you for sharing. It sounds like a lovely memory."

I heard her take in a fortifying breath, and I braced for whatever she was about to say. I was half expecting her to demand I come back home, that she couldn't stand to feel like she was losing me, too. I didn't expect any of what she said next.

"Mabel, I owe you an apology."

"Um... I'm sorry, what?"

"Actually, I owe you years' worth of apologies. But I'll start with this one and we'll go from there."

"Oh...kay..."

"I never dealt with your father's death, not really. At the time, I had a young, gifted daughter to think about, and I threw everything I had into raising you and trying to give you all the opportunities both your father and I wanted for you. But along the way, with every new milestone or accomplishment, I became more bitter that your father wasn't there to see them, too.

"At some point, that bitterness turned into resentment... toward Constance and Painted Creek and every little thing I could associate with the accident that took Anthony. I was so focused on what I had lost. I never stopped to be thankful for what I'd had, and what I still have."

I swallowed the lump in my throat and shook my head. "You don't owe me an apology for that, Mom. Everyone grieves in their own way."

"Maybe so, but I passed on some unhealthy coping mechanisms to you. I kept us so tightly together trying to avoid losing you too that I cut you off from other things and people that could have helped you flourish. I ran from anything uncomfortable or difficult because I'd forgotten that sometimes the best things are worth fighting for. I was so worried about facing another loss I forgot to be thankful for all of the small moments that added up to a love big enough to create such devastation in its absence.

"Your painting reminded me of that. Of all the small, quiet moments that I hadn't let myself remember because I was so angry that I wouldn't have any more of them. But that doesn't honor your father's memory. That all but causes it to fade, like the edges of the painting you did."

I was speechless. I had never heard my mother open up and talk about her feelings like this, and the catalyst had been a painting that I'd done my way; from the frisson to the natural inks to the painting style. For the first time, I was hopeful that I could pattern my life in a way that suited me without a permanent strain on my relationship with my mother.

"Mabel, I'm not saying that it won't take me time, or that I'm not upset and sad about the fact that you won't be living close by. But I have thought about what you said yesterday, and after seeing this painting I know you're right. It's time for you to do things your way and see where it can take you."

"Mom, please come visit." I don't know what made me say it, but as soon as it was out of my mouth I knew it was the right thing for both of us. "You don't have to stay long if you don't want to, but please, just come."

"I think I'd like that, darling, very much. I'm proud of you, Mabel. Always."

We talked for another minute or two, and much like Dottie, she made me promise to call her and let her know how things worked out for Operation Mabel Stays. I only lingered a moment when I hung up the phone. I was eager to keep moving... I had more bridges to mend, after all.

As I ran to my car and hopped behind the wheel, I threw a double thumbs up to Dottie, who had her nose stuck in the space she'd parted in her blinds. She stuck a thumbs up back into the window and I laughed as I drove away, feeling lighter than I had in a long, long time.

FORTY-THREE

I PARKED ON the side street next to the pet shop and took a deep breath. Honestly, I was most anxious about this stop. I didn't know how to argue with someone. I didn't know if our disagreement yesterday was the end or if it was something we could overcome, but I did know that I would never forgive myself if I didn't at least try.

So, I grabbed the small bag out of the back of the car, dug down deep for some confidence, and headed into the store.

It was still reasonably early in the morning, just after opening but still before an afternoon rush. I looked around the empty store, and the quiet was almost eerie. It was as if even the animals were holding their breath, waiting to see what would happen next.

I heard the back alley door shut softly, so I stood up at the counter and waited patiently for Elliott to come back to the front of the store. I knew he knew I was here, but I wasn't about to rush him if he wanted to make me sweat it out a few extra minutes.

"Can I help you with something?" When he finally made his way around the counter, his tone was calm and cool, but his eyes gave away the pain that I'd caused him with my careless words. I decided then and there that I'd do everything I could not to let it happen again.

"Yes, if you could just listen, that would be great." He nodded once, expression never changing, so I carried on, trying to stick to the speech I'd made up in my head on the way over from Dottie's.

"First of all, I owe you an apology. Not because I want something from you so I'm trying to make nice, not because I don't want you to be mad at me, but simply because I was an ass and treated you unfairly. I said some things I certainly didn't mean because I was upset and looking for any excuse to run away. But I don't want to run away anymore."

I pushed the small bag across the counter and nodded my head toward it, gesturing for him to open it. I waited as he pulled out two tea bags, a chamomile and a chai, and the necklace I had made for him. It was a simple leather cord with a single pendant.

"The pendant is made from flower petals from the beautiful bouquet you brought me the first night we went on a not-date. I knew you would be someone special to me, and I found a way to have a physical reminder of that feeling forever." I shook my wrist at him, the bracelet I had made with beads from the bouquet the only one I was wearing right now. The other beads that made up the rest of the bracelet were all different colors, just as the bouquet had been.

He was studying the pendant, a simple flat tear drop shape that I had free formed by hand. It didn't seem like he was going to respond, so I kept talking.

"I understand if you aren't interested in us any more. I never gave you any reason to believe that I was in this with you the way that you deserve. I've never shown you that I would fight for this, that I'm here to stay for good. I've only ever acted as if I might take off at the first sign of things getting hard, whether it was with my mother or here in town. I realized last night that I never wanted to get too close, because I didn't want to risk having something to lose... I would love the chance to show you that you're worth the risk."

He looked up at me through his lashes at first, not raising his head as he regarded me silently. When he finally straightened, he crossed his arms over his chest and took a step back away from me. My stomach sank, but I held my ground and simply waited for him to speak.

"Have you talked to Heather? Sarah?" he asked.

"Wha... no? I came to see you first."

"And what if they're mad at you forever? What if Heather says she hates your painting and you crushed her, and Sarah can never forgive you for lying? What if everyone in town thinks everything you've done here has been unforgivable and cruel?"

His face was hard, and in that moment I was sure that I would be walking out of here and straight to the grocery store for a log of cookie dough to eat later while I binged all the break up episodes of *The Gilmore Girls*. But, I looked him dead in the eye and gave him the most honest answer I could, and I hoped that the more times I could speak it out loud the easier it would be to believe it myself and make it come true.

"Then so be it. I am confident in all my abilities, artistic and otherwise, and will stand behind them even when it's difficult. Because my gifts *are* gifts, and they're worth it. I'm worth it."

"Good to know." He slowly raised the necklace to clasp it around his neck. "Thank you for the gift. And thank you for the apology."

"Elliott, truly, I'm so sorry for letting my mouth get away from me. I didn't mean what I said. I promise I'll try my best not to let it happen again. That is, if you still want to spend time with me..."

"I won't lie to make you feel better, Mabel, that was pretty low, trying to make me feel like you didn't care for me at all so I would get mad and then it would be easier for you to tell yourself there was nothing here for you..."

"Yes."

"But couples fight. Couples hurt each other, intentionally and unintentionally. It's what they do afterward that determines whether or not they can work through all the hurt feelings and disagreements and come out stronger together. If you can promise me you won't run away when things get difficult, I can promise that I'll always be here to talk through it with you. You're worth the risk, too."

A slow smile spread across my face, and I took a tentative step toward the counter at the same time that he leaned over on both elbows.

"Mabel, could I take you to dinner tonight? On a real date? As my girlfriend?"

I leaned over and kissed him softly before whispering against his lips, "No."

He jerked back and said, "Wait, what?"

I laughed and grabbed the front of his t-shirt, pulling him back toward me. "Make it a to-go dinner and meet me in the middle of my new gift shop for a floor picnic and you have yourself a deal." I turned my head slightly and grinned, waiting for his response.

"See you at seven," he said and I felt his answering grin against my own.

After only a kiss or two, or twelve, I pulled back with a pat on his chest. "I have another stop to make, and honestly, I kind of just want to get it over with. If you don't hear from me in time for our date you should check the dumpster out back for a dead body."

He just laughed. "You'll be fine. Be yourself, be honest, and it'll work out one way or another."

"Wow. Super inspiring pep talk. I feel so much better."

He shrugged. "It is what it is. Good luck."

With that ringing endorsement, I set out for two doors down, hoping that my difficult conversation luck would hold for just a little while longer. I lingered outside of the pet store and dialed the number that Dottie had given me for Larry the contractor. Luckily, he answered quickly and was already familiar with the buildings and the potential project from speaking with Dottie. It was always nice when the small town gossip train worked out in your favor.

Just before we hung up, I got the best, craziest idea for the big gesture that Carol had mentioned earlier. I got the reassurance I needed from him, and looked toward Artful Brew with a devilish smile on my face.

I PICTURED A scene from an old western in my mind as I pulled open the door to the coffee shop. All that was missing was the swinging doors flapping behind me as I walked inside, and a tumbleweed blowing down the deserted street outside. It was quiet, the morning rush long gone and the crowd trying to fend off their afternoon slump hadn't quite come in yet. I made a bee line for the order counter and braced myself for the wrath that I knew would greet me.

Sarah didn't say a word, just raised her eyebrow, and I almost cracked a smile at the familiarity that the gesture already had for me, but that probably would've been a death sentence. She simply continued to stare, so I decided to just jump right in. Again.

"I don't think I'd trust you to pick a coffee order for me today, no offense. So I'll just take a plain black regular, my go to."

She frowned at me, and it almost looked like she wanted to argue until she remembered she didn't care that much any more. When she turned on her heel to go pour a coffee, I smothered a grin and decided that maybe poking the bear was the best way to play this after all.

"Sarah, I know you said that you didn't want to talk to me at all about this building, and I'll respect that. All correspondence about your lease here can go through the property management company and Mr. Findley as you requested." I was slowly walking down the length of the counter, moving to the 'pick up here' section and talking loudly to her over the whirl of all the machines. She was studiously ignoring me.

"But you never said anything about discussing the building next door, which you now know that I own as well."

I saw her shoulders tense, but she kept her back to me and kept moving.

"So I was just wondering, now that you know, if you had an opinion on what I should do with the space. You know, since you'd be neighbors and all, I thought it was the right thing to ask you, get a feel for what might mesh well, that kind of thing..."

She turned and set my coffee cup down on the counter with enough force to slosh some coffee out of the small hole in the lid. I kept my face as neutral as possible, but I was starting to feel giddy with anticipation.

"Do what you want with it. It's your decision obviously. You don't need my input."

"Oh, but I do. I could rent it out I suppose, but maybe I should fix it up first. Hang some lights, put up some wall paper that kind of thing? You know, I could even hang a disco ball right from the center of the store and have speakers installed along the walls. I suppose it might rattle the shared wall though, that could be a problem. What do you think?

"Mabel, I don't give a single damn what you do with that store or anything else in your life. You could knock a hole in the wall for all I care. Please take your coffee and go."

I knew the grin that overtook my face was practically feral as I said, "Oh, I'm so happy to hear you say that..." I practically skipped to the back staircase, where I knew Sarah's aluminum ball bat would be waiting.

"What are you doing? I asked you to leave!" Sarah called as she rounded the counter to chase me down. Her eyes went round when she saw me standing with her bat thrown over my shoulder. Was this what Harley Quinn felt like all the time? I cackled a little at the thought, but I did love the feeling.

"So where do you think? About here?" I pointed the bat at the wall where the brick turned into plaster, taking aim.

"Mabel, what the hell?! You are not going to knock a hole in the wall! What are you thinking?"

"I was thinking that I'd really like to be able to walk next door and see my neighbor without going outside. You see, she makes the absolute best coffee ever, and she knows exactly what drink I need for the day when I don't even know myself, at least when she's not being a grudge-holding, sarcastic ass."

She actually stomped her foot in response, and I could see Becca clear as day in the way she stood facing me. I threw my head back and laughed before I continued on with my little speech.

"I figure running a gift shop and art gallery is going to be hard work and will surely call for extra caffeine. Just seemed like a good idea to me." I shrugged, like it was no big deal, and just stood holding the bat down at my side waiting for all I'd said to slowly sink in.

"Your neighbor."

"Yep." I popped the 'p' and shrugged again.

"Gift shop and art gallery."

"Seems to be a pretty reasonable next step for an artist, don't you think?"

"You're staying?" Her voice had gone quiet, but the distrust was still in her eyes as she narrowed them at me, regarding me cautiously.

"Yep again. I have copies of your new rental agreement in my bag if you want to see them, although you truly will have to go to Mr. Findley to sign the official copies tomorrow. I'm keeping all of the management for this building through him, as per your request, but the building next door seems like the perfect blank canvas for me, albeit a different kind." I gave the bat a twirl at my side and eyed the wall once more. I sighed, and turned to face Sarah, hoping that she could see how much I meant my next words.

"Sarah, I apologize for keeping the ownership of this building a secret from you. Originally, I was trying to keep everything as Gram had done it, but obviously I just can't keep secrets like she could. Did you have any idea she was your landlord all this time?"

She shook her head no but didn't speak.

"I foolishly thought that I could keep it all separate from the relationships I was forming with the people in town, but that's just not who I am. I know it may be hard to believe, but I never would have canceled your lease here... this is meant to be your store. Look around at all you've done with it. I know Gram could see it and so can I."

She shifted on her feet a little, like she wasn't used to getting compliments. When she met my gaze again, her eyes had thawed a little. She raised an eyebrow, waiting for me to continue, but the hostility was gone.

"I am staying in Painted Creek. Can I tell you with certainty for how long? No. Maybe forever or maybe I'll leave for some other grand adventure a couple of years from now, who knows. But for now, I am committed to moving to Painted Creek, opening a shop next door, dating Elliott, making friends and putting down deeper roots. And I'm going to do that whether you're still mad at me or not. So my question to you is," I gestured to the wall with my free hand, "how close of a neighbor do you want to be?"

It didn't take as long as I expected it to before she smirked at me and tilted her head. "You know, it would be kind of cool to walk from one store to the next. But the landlord here is kind of an ass, so I don't think I'll take the first swing. Don't want damages to be added to my rent."

With a loud laugh, I took the end of the bat and rammed it like a sledge hammer into the wall. A satisfying spiderweb of cracks appeared in the plaster as chunks fell to the floor. I flipped the bat around to Sarah and offered her the handle.

"I'll deal with the landlord, so by all means, please, take a swing."

She grinned at me, took the bat and swung at the wall. The cracked plaster didn't stand a chance, and when the dust settled we stood looking at the back of the plaster wall of the building next door.

"Well, you get points for theatricality, I'll give you that. But now there's a hole in my wall…"

"I'll paint you something to hang over it for a few months." She shoved me on the shoulder and we both laughed.

"A gift shop, huh?" Sarah was walking back toward the counter, so I followed, standing on the other side on the worn spots in the floor.

"I think so. I'll have some spaces for art, but I think I'd like the majority of it to be natural based products, like soap and essential oils and candles and teas and stuff."

"Hippie. I like it."

"Not hippie, per say. More like healer." I reached for the coffee that had been left on the counter earlier, but Sarah swiped it away.

"Don't drink that. I'll make you something else." I didn't want to ask if it was because it was a boring, plain black coffee or if it was because she'd done something to it.

A moment later, she slid another cup to me and said, "Dirty Dalmatian. It's a dalmatian hot chocolate with an espresso shot."

"Dalmatian hot chocolate?"

"Half dark chocolate half white. Kind of a sweet celebration drink."

I took a sip and sighed. "It's perfect, as always. I should get going though. Suddenly, I have a lot of work to do."

"I'll see you at coffee tomorrow then." I glanced up at her, touched that she was so quick to include me again. "I may have let my temper lead yesterday. I probably owe you an apology, too. That's what friends do."

I smiled at her over the lid of my coffee cup. "Thanks. But I may skip coffee mornings for awhile. I don't think it's fair to Heather. I want to give her some space." I didn't even ask if she knew what I was talking about. I figured if a contractor I'd never spoken to already had the schematics to a building I owned, then Sarah knew what had happened with Heather yesterday.

"Heather is fine, but that's her story to tell not mine. You should text her."

"Maybe. Thanks for the coffee, neighbor!" I held up my cup in a mock salute and left the coffee shop, stepping out into the sticky afternoon air.

Turning left, I stopped outside what was truly *my* shop now and looked in through the front door. With a smile on my face and a renewed sense of purpose, I turned the key and went inside.

FORTY-FOUR

I TOOK IN the quiet of the store for a second, just appreciating the space in a way that I hadn't allowed myself to do yet. I always knew it was an incredible space, but picturing much more than that would've been extra heartbreaking if I'd ended up leaving town.

I walked around the edges of the room slowly. The plaster was cracking and falling, layers of paint giving a small glimpse into the building's past. I walked along the wall between my store and Elliott's, running my hands over the plaster and daydreaming about the potential in this big room.

With one last slow spin through the large, empty room, I headed up the back staircase. I was still trailing my fingers along the walls as I went, and the railings and the doorknobs, really anything and everything as I got acquainted with the building. Just as I was about to reach for the knob in the old glass door to enter the little apartment, my fingers fell into a dip in the brick door casing. Flipping on the flashlight on my phone, I aimed the light at the door frame to find two initials carved into the brick.

"C and L. How sweet." I took a quick picture with my cell phone and made a mental note to ask Mr. Findley about the people who owned the pharmacy. Maybe they'd want a picture or a transfer drawing of the initials to remember their time here. Pressing my hand over the rough letters one last time, I turned the knob and stepped into the upstairs apartment.

I didn't really remember much about the upstairs from my quick look around with Mr. Findley, only the magnificent windows. Now, looking at the whole space from just inside the doorway, I got a shimmer of excitement up my spine when I thought about what the space could be.

There was so much room for a studio! I could put in a small kitchenette, so there would be running water for washing equipment and painting, and of course for snacks. The windows allowed in so much natural light that I wanted to highlight, and I was excited about the potential. I could set up six easels or more if I wanted to.

Suddenly, a strong frisson hit and I got tingles over my entire body. It was almost as if I'd been electrocuted, every hair standing on end and my skin covered in goosebumps. I blinked rapidly as, before me, the space shimmered and seemed to transform before my eyes. No, that wasn't quite right. I closed my eyes, and a vision of the new studio space was as clear as a photograph in my mind. When I opened my eyes again, instead of seeing the space only as it was now, it was like there was a transparent film of what it could be, would be, overlaid everywhere I looked.

It was the first time ever that I could almost actually see the visions that I got with the frisson phenomenon in real life, not just as a picture appearing in my mind. And it wasn't going away. Every time I turned or moved or looked somewhere else, it was like I was seeing the present and the future at the same time, one superimposed over the other.

And it was more than I could have imagined.

The studio space was gorgeous. The windows gleamed with sunlight pouring in directly onto six easels. Small side tables sat next to each easel, ready to hold all of the supplies needed to help create whatever masterpiece was at the station.

In the middle of the room, four small tables big enough for six people or so each sat waiting to be filled, and I immediately imagined small classes and maybe parties, too. It had never been on my radar before, but I knew without a doubt it was something I wanted to do, to share my love of painting and art with other people. I was adding it to the next chapter here in Painted Creek. It was perfect.

I turned and took the stairs two at a time on the way down, hoping whatever magic transformed the upstairs would last long enough to show me the main shop as well. I rounded the bottom of the stairs and hustled down the back hallway, heart pounding in my ears, and skidded to a stop at the back of the cavernous room with a gasp.

It was magnificent. Tin tiles covered the ceiling, paint chipping off in that way that gave the space a shabby chic charm without looking too run down or too perfect either. Standing from the back of the room, the wall to the right connected to the coffee shop with a gorgeous brick encased arched doorway. The whole wall, floor to tall ceiling, was an art gallery, tens of paintings and other types of art displayed on the white washed brick with little tags underneath for descriptions. Shorter tables in a light warm wood held sculptures and paintings alike just waiting for people to walk through and admire them.

As I turned to look at the other side of the room, I quickly blinked away the tears that sprung to my eyes, worried they would wash away whatever magic had taken over. But there, almost directly across from the door to the coffee shop, was an identical arched door that led to the pet store. I smiled, still blinking rapidly, and tried to take in the rest of the main store space.

Little display stations were set up charmingly throughout the open floor, all blending together even though they each had their own unique personality. The vision around each shimmered, obscuring what was displayed, but I didn't care. I would forever be grateful for this gift, this glimpse into what could be. I knew without a shadow of a doubt that somehow I would make it happen. This is where I belonged.

A KNOCK ON the door startled me, and as I jumped the film I was looking through shivered and disappeared. I blinked a few times, looking around at the dusty, run down space once more.

"Wow," I whispered.

A light tap sounded again, and when I turned toward the front door, Heather was standing on the other side, hand held up in a silent wave and arms full of books. I motioned her in as I headed toward the door to help.

"Hey. Thanks," she said as I took some of the books from her arms and shut the door behind her.

"Sure. Um, hi." Now that she was in the building and out of danger of toppling over from the weight of the books she was carrying, I really didn't know what to say. I dug a little design in the dust on the floor with the toe of my shoe.

"I hope it's okay that I stopped by," she started quietly. "Maybe I should have texted you first. But Sarah said you were still here when I went in for coffee. So. I took a chance."

"Of course it's okay with me. I just didn't think you'd want to see me."

"Mabel, I owe you an explanation. I'm really sorry that you blamed yourself for my reaction to your beautiful painting. You fit so seamlessly into our little misfit group that sometimes I forget that you haven't always been here. That you don't know everyone's dirty little secrets and old heartbreaks and new beginnings."

"Thank you?"

She chuckled somewhat humorlessly at my confused response, but kept talking. "I forgot that you'd never heard the full story of how I came to own the bookstore, and you'd have no idea why I would be so upset. I actually didn't even think about it until my phone started blowing up last night. Then I decided I would just hunt you down somewhere today and explain in person."

"Well, I'd offer you a chair, but..." I gestured to the old space around us and shrugged.

"That's alright... we'll go for the Reader's Digest version this time anyway. I don't want to take up your whole afternoon."

"Okay..."

Her eyes clouded over, but she took a deep breath and dove into her story. "My aunt left the bookstore to me in her will. Her son was irate, to say the least, since he was her only child and I guess he just assumed that she would've left everything to him. He contested the will, we spent months in court, but the will was ironclad and the store belonged to me."

The longer she talked, the sadder I watched her become, and I hated seeing that something in the past could continue to cause my friend so much pain.

"My family all thought that I should turn the store over to him, that it really belonged to him and I had no right to keep it even though my aunt had left it to me. I had loved that bookstore my entire life, and she knew that I would take care of it, do it justice. At least I like to think that she did."

"And you have, Heather. I hope you know how amazing that store is."

"Thanks." She smiled briefly, but it didn't reach her eyes. She shifted the books she was still holding from her hip to wrap her arms around them in front of her chest, like a shield. "Anyway, most of my family thought I should give him the store, and they weren't quiet about it. They said some awful things, taking his side while he played the victim. I just knew in my gut that he couldn't get the store, but I never knew why or had any proof of what made me so anxious about it, so they all just said I was greedy.

"When I started fixing the store up and making it my own, most of my family shunned me. It was a really difficult time. Turns out, my cousin owed tens of thousands of dollars to loan sharks from gambling debts and some other really shady extra curricular activities. He was planning on burning the building down for insurance money... not even selling the shop but just destroying it all. They found evidence of his plans while searching his apartment on a warrant for drug charges. He's still in jail now. My family tried apologizing afterward, but it was kind of too little too late to mend some of those bridges. Things have never really been the same since."

"Oh Heather, I hate that you went through that. But I'm glad you stuck to your gut feeling and fought for the shop. I don't know that I would've been strong enough to."

"That's just it, even though I love the store and have poured so much of myself into it, sometimes I still wonder if I did the right thing. I've never been able to fully accept compliments about The Secret Book Garden without feeling some sort of guilt about keeping it in the first place. But something about your painting, Mabel, I don't know... when I saw it, it was just like a confirmation that I was in the right place. That everything I had gone through had been for a reason and that the beautiful business I had re-imagined for myself was well earned, not 'stolen' from someone else. You gave me such an incredible gift and you didn't even know it. That painting unlocked an acceptance that I was still denying myself, acceptance of myself and my choices and the whole situation."

There was a lightness around Heather now that she had finished her story. I studied her looking for any sign that she was just trying to make me feel better, but I found none.

"Thank you for sharing that with me. I'm still sorry I made you cry, but I feel a tiny bit less bad now that I know the reason."

"You shouldn't feel bad at all. You should feel amazing. I don't know how you did it, how you came up with exactly the right scene to unlock all those feelings, but you did and I'm really incredibly grateful for it."

Shifting the books I was holding for her to one arm, I gave her a one sided hug and said, "I'm just glad you're okay, and we're okay. We are okay, right? Still friends?"

"Definitely!" She beamed back at me and then smacked a hand on the pile of books in her arms. The sound echoed around the empty space, and she looked around, letting out a low whistle. "You've got some work to do in here I'm afraid."

I laughed, and looked around too with a more critical eye than before. "Oh yeah. But it'll be worth it. Now, what is all this, other than heavy?"

"Um, I may have gone a little over board. But Sarah mentioned that you were leaning toward natural and handmade items in the shop, so I brought books on interior design, soap making, marketing, and some other stuff. You can flip through them and just bring back whatever you don't want. But it might give you some ideas to start."

"Thanks! I've been kind of just standing here letting the space speak to me, and I think I have a general direction to start with. This will all be excellent research material. And you've not steered me wrong yet!"

Just then, Elliott opened the front door, picnic basket in hand. "Hello ladies, am I interrupting?"

"No, no," Heather said. "I'm just leaving. See you tomorrow morning for coffee?" she asked me.

"Wouldn't miss it."

Elliott placed the basket on the floor and took the remaining books from Heather. With a wave, she was out the door and on her way.

"There's a blanket on top." He gestured to the large basket. "I thought we might need something to sit on. There should still be room for us after we put all the books down, I think..."

We got the blanket spread out, and Elliott set a sub sandwich and small bag of chips in front of each of us. "To our first meal in your new shop. How's it feel?"

"Scary. Good." I looked him in the eye. "Right."

"Good. Now eat." I was rewarded with a double dimple grin and I savored every second of the seemingly small moment.

Later, with dinner finished and some of the books flipped through, he said, "You know, most of these buildings used to connect..."

"Oh really?" I tried to smother my grin as I batted my eyes at him innocently.

"Yep. I mean, I bet if you tried hard enough, you could even bust through with a baseball bat or something."

"A baseball bat? How uncivilized!"

"You're right I suppose. That's just too scandalous. What would people think?"

"Indeed." I looked at our joined hands on the blanket, and then glanced around the empty store. It was rapidly growing dark, and the space felt like a cave, mysterious and full of possibilities.

"I should go soon. I want to get back to the cottage before dark and try and catch my neighbor out in the yard."

"Okay. I can help you pack up in a minute." He looked down at me and ran a finger over my cheek. "Hey, Mabel?"

"Hmmm?"

"I'm so incredibly glad that you decided to stay."

My thumb moved back and forth across his, and I'd never felt more at home than I did when I was in his arms, like I belonged.

"Hey, Elliott?"

"Hmmm?"

"Wanna reattach our stores?"

"I thought you'd never ask."

I leaned against his shoulder and felt content, sitting in the silence with the possibilities of our future swirling around us. Later, I would paint this scene, a twin to go with the painting of my mother and father in Dottie's swing.

AFTER A LINGERING goodnight kiss and a promise to call before bed, I made it home just as dusk was painting the sky in various shades of purple. I hurried through the house, flipping on lights as I went so it wouldn't be pitch black when I came back in.

I didn't really have a plan other than to sit out in the yard and hope that Charlotte would stop by tonight. I wouldn't blame her if she didn't, my behavior wasn't exactly friendly last night, but she'd left without whatever she had come to collect from the herb garden. I was hoping that that was enough to bring her back.

I waited in the swing over the creek, watching the tree line as the sky got darker and darker. Just as I was about to give up and go inside, I heard the snapping of tiny twigs under foot and looked up in time to see Charlotte emerge from the trees.

I hopped off the swing and all but jogged down to meet her by the hanging vines. Her face was a mask of calm indifference, but she wasn't openly yelling at me. I'd take it.

"I wanted to apologize for my behavior last night. You were only trying to help, and I was hell bent on pushing everyone away. I hope we can still be friends?"

"You been sittin' out here all night?"

"Yes. You left without cutting any herbs last night... figured you'd show up sooner or later."

"What about everyone else you were determined to push away? You hunt them down today, too?"

"Yes. You were right. I was being a coward and running back to what I've always known because I was too scared to fight for what I actually wanted. I'm staying here in Painted Creek, opening a new business, and I even got myself a boyfriend." I waggled my eyebrows at her and was relieved when I saw her lips twitch as she fought back a smile.

"Well, it's about time. I'm right proud of you, Mabel. I knew you had it in you."

"Thanks. What made you so smart anyway?"

She did smile now, a melancholy sort of smile that for some reason made my heart hurt a little. "Oh, trial and error I suppose. Want to come help me?" She gestured to the herb garden and pulled an extra pair of scissors from her newly mended apron. "If you're stayin' for good you might as well get to learning how to take care of everything in here."

"Why? That's what I have you for." I bumped her with my shoulder. "Actually, I have something for you. I'd hate for you to have to carry it home in the dark though. Why don't you meet me at the coffee shop in the morning and I'll give it to you then! You can sit with me and Alex and Heather and harass Sarah while she works."

"What time do you go?"

"Around seven-thirty! Yay!! I'm so glad that you'll come! It'll be nice to have all my new friends in one big group."

"That's early. Best be getting what I came for and getting back home then." She was halfway through the vines before she turned back and grabbed me by the shoulders. "It's good that you're staying. This is right where you belong, girl. I wasn't sure there for a minute, but now I know you're going to be just fine."

"Thank you, Charlotte. I don't think I've told you enough, but I'm thankful for your friendship. I think you're actually the first official friend I made on my own here in Painted Creek. I'm glad I have you."

"Well, I'll always be around." She gave me a little finger wave and slipped into the herb garden. I made my way back up to the cottage and went through my nightly routine. I was excited for tomorrow. I couldn't wait to give Charlotte her painting and introduce her to everyone else. I got the feeling that she could use some other people in her life too, and I might be biased, but I thought the tribe that I had stumbled into and claimed as my own was the best you could ask for.

It occurred to me, in that vague way that things come across your mind when you're almost asleep, that Charlotte never actually agreed to meet me at the coffee shop. I just assumed she'd meant that she would.

If she didn't show, I'd just finally have to go track her down myself.

FORTY-FIVE

SHE DIDN'T SHOW. After a lovely morning coffee date with the rest of my friends, a brief stop in to say good morning to Elliott, and a mad dash to the bakery for cronuts, I went back to the cottage and put together a little package for Charlotte. I wrapped the painting as I always did, and added an extra bag around the outside, just in case. I would be walking through the woods after all, and it would be just like me to trip into a mud puddle or fall in an abandoned well or something similarly stupid while on my trek to Charlotte's house. I threw in the bracelet that I had made with the rosemary goop beads, wrapped two cronuts, and placed them in the gift bag, too. Grabbing my keys and phone, I was off on a mini-adventure.

I strolled through the yard, taking in the sounds and smells of the beautiful spring morning while giving a little thank you to the universe that it wasn't raining. As I reached the tree line, a well worn path became visible, and I whispered another little thanks that I wouldn't be making up the directions as I went. This path had obviously been walked countless times and was easy to follow.

The woods were calm, the brush not too thick, and I realized it was almost like an extension of the yard that was allowed to grow up rather than the dense forest wilderness I had been imagining. After walking for about five minutes, the path gave way to a small clearing, but there was no other house in sight. On the other side of the clearing, the path disappeared and the forest did seem thicker there, creeping in to restake its claim on the land as wilderness.

I looked around, confused. She always came and went this direction, there had to be a house here somewhere. Paying closer attention to the edges of the clearing, thinking I had missed another path, I noticed several wooden box structures sitting in a row. They were about waist high, and almost looked as if they had tiny little roofs on top, slanting back down toward the ground. They looked old, decades old easily, and I walked over to get a closer look.

"Beehives?" I asked the open air as I examined the boxes. I was pretty sure that's what these used to be, the boxes seemed to have layers stacked on top of each other like a little bee high rise. "What in the world is going on?"

The breeze shifted then, blowing from the direction I had come, and the overwhelming scent of rosemary surrounded me, invigorating and familiar. I turned back to face the path and search for the plant, and that's when I saw it. There, just to the left of the path as it comes into the clearing, was the exact stone structure from my vision, its painted replica tucked safely in the bag slung over my shoulder.

I walked over to the stone cellar and unceremoniously plopped down onto the ground in front of the small door. The plants all around the outside were overgrown, but the rosemary was easy to see, and it was still thriving, the bushes almost as tall as the cellar now.

I pulled my cell phone out of my jeans pocket and dialed Mr. Findley. Another perk of small town living was that he had given me his cell phone number in case I'd needed anything when I first got to town. I appreciated not having to go through Carol or his voice mail to reach him now.

"Good morning, Mabel. What can I do for you?"

"Good morning, Mr. Findley. Sorry to abuse the power of knowing your cell phone number this morning, but I find myself with a bit of a mystery and I needed your help, well, right now."

"Alright…"

"Do you remember that first night I came into town, and you were telling me about the cottage and how you'd left groceries and what not, and you mentioned that there were neighbors but that they all kept to themselves and we all had big yards and I'd probably never see anyone?"

"Uh, yes I seem to remember something like that."

"The neighbors off to the left, where would their house be?"

"Mabel, you don't have neighbors on each side, only the house you pass by on the way to the cottage, which would be on the right in the way that you're describing."

"No, I've met Charlotte. She would come to visit Gram and help with the herb garden. She's always walked over from her house, saying it was just through the trees a ways."

"I'm sorry, Mabel. I don't know what to tell you. Everything to the left of the cottage is still your property. It has been for generations. I think I remember Constance telling me about some beehives and maybe an old root cellar or storage building or something out there. But there's no other neighbors."

"Oh, right. Okay. I must've been mistaken." I knew I wasn't mistaken at all, but I also didn't have a reasonable explanation right now, and arguing with Mr. Findley wasn't going to get me anywhere.

"Hey, while I have you on the phone, I was able to get some more information on your building together for you. I forgot to give you the printed material when you were here yesterday, but I'll save it for you. Would you like a brief description now?"

"Yes, I very much would, thank you." I sat up a little straighter as tingles ran down my neck and across my shoulders, a sure sign to pay attention.

"Well, it turns out that building was owned by none other than your family in the early 1900's. Your great grandmother Lottie sold it after World War II when her husband was killed in action overseas. The point of sale contract had a stipulation stating if the new owners ever wanted to sell the building that your family be given first right of refusal to buy it back. That must've been how Constance knew that it was up for sale before anyone else. Did her letter to you say anything about that?"

"Oh! Oh my gosh I can't believe I forgot about that letter. In all the craziness yesterday I put it in my bag at your office and never thought about it again." I could not believe that I forgot about Gram's letter! A month ago when I rolled into town, I would've stopped everything and ripped it open just to have one more memory from her, and now here I'd left her last letter to me in the bottom of my tote bag. I shook my head at myself, and slowly got to my feet off of the damp ground.

As I finished my call with Mr. Findley, I walked closer to the cellar. My very real fear of snakes kept me from trying the door to see if it would open, but I could make out all the details of the little structure that I hadn't seen in my vision. It was larger than I thought, and I decided that as soon as we could I would bring Elliott back with me to explore it a little further.

I walked back to the cottage slowly, thinking of a plan on how to find Charlotte. I realized that somehow I had never really mentioned her to the other ladies, as if the two sections of my life were separate. I could always start there, especially with Sarah who may have seen her around the elementary school while she was there with Becca. I wondered again why she would lie to me about where she lived, and I only hoped that she was safe and not in some sort of dangerous situation that caused her to keep her home life a secret.

As the cottage came into view, thoughts of Charlotte drifted away as my mind returned to Gram's letter. My steps quickened along with my heart, and by the time I reached the porch steps my breathing was coming out in embarrassing puffs as I fought to catch my breath. I ran inside and dug through my tote to retrieve the letter, and returned to the big egg rocker on the porch to read it.

Sliding my finger under the seal, I lifted the letter from the envelope. It was several pages thick and held together with three paper clips across the top, and I resisted the urge to peek at the other pages as I settled in to read Gram's letter first.

Sweet Mabel,

I'm so glad you decided to build a life here in Painted Creek. This town has meant so much to me, and I know it will be good to you, too. I hope that the decision to stay connected to this town was yours and yours alone, and you make this life you have everything that YOU want it to be.

I didn't want to burden you with the history of the empty building until you'd made a decision for yourself on what its future was to be. Guilt and a sense of loyalty can make us do funny things, and I didn't want that for you, my dear girl. But if you have this note now, there's no harm in passing on a little history to go with the rest of your inheritance.

My momma owned that now empty store when I was a wee little thing, and my daddy, Connor, had a suit shop next door. I spent my days there playing upstairs and in the store room while Momma tended to all the customers out on the floor.

She made the most amazing soaps and women's beauty items, all from scratch mind you, with the most amazing smells from all the flowers and herbs that we grew ourselves out back at the cottage. Her momma, Faye, even made some of the decoctions and tinctures she'd used on all her children through the years and sold them in the shop, too. They had a little shop of remedies, and I think that's why they could thrive during such hard times, by offering something folks still needed, all while making it from things they grew themselves.

Oh, my momma would even encourage me when I would come up with the most ridiculous schemes to make spending money of my own by selling things in her shop. I didn't start out making teas you know... that took some trial and error! But you aren't the only one who loves ice cream shops, so I suppose I figured it out in the end.

When my daddy died overseas, my momma decided to sell the shops. She lost both great loves of her life that year, her husband and that store. But we kept on making things that the folks in town had come to rely on us for, and eventually I added in my teas and for awhile I even had honey bees! We did good for ourselves, even using the old root cellar off the edge of the property to store extra tinctures and such. It was a good life.

When I got the chance to get the stores back, I couldn't let them go. Not because I wanted to run a store, mind you, that was never my dream. But honey, so many times in my life I saw the people in our family choose the path that was right for them, only to have it always somehow circle back to this town, and healing people and helping the community. In case your path ever brought you back here too, I wanted you to have this piece of family legacy to help you along your way, if that was what was in the cards for you.

I've attached some old photographs to this letter. Maybe if you ever do fix up the old store, you can hang them to remind yourself of how far we've all come, and to remind yourself that you're never alone.

I love you Mabel,

Gram

P.S. - I hope by now you have found my journals, and perhaps my mother's journals, too. While a lot of the entries will just be the ramblings of two crazy women, there is a lot of information in them too, some about our herbal practices and even more about our family. Maybe one day you can sift through it all and pull out the important bits. Maybe one day you'll have your own important bits to add, too.

I only hesitated for a second before sitting up and laying the stack of papers in my lap so I could carefully remove the paper clips at the top. When I moved Gram's letter to the back of the stack, the face looking up at me from the first photograph was all at once familiar and a stranger, the context making it difficult for me to believe what I was seeing.

Her raven hair seemed to sparkle and shine even in the aged photo, and there was no mistaking the set of her posture, feet firmly planted on the ground, shoulders back and head held high as if challenging fate itself. It was unmistakably Charlotte, her hand resting on top of what I assumed was her daughter's head, affectionately ruffling her hair. Another, older woman stood to her other side, stern and solemn looking, keeping a watchful eye on the both of them. They stood in front of what I assumed was my shop, though it looked much different in the photograph, shiny and well cared for and loved.

I flipped the photo over, searching for a written description that would confirm what I already knew in my heart. There at the bottom in Gram's handwriting was a note that read '*Faye, Lottie, and Connie in front of C & L's Sundry, 1944*'.

The second photograph was of the interior of the store. It was pristine, and even in the black and white photo the personality of the space came through. It was laid out much like what I had imagined or seen yesterday while I was at the shop alone, and I was determined then to keep the similarities that I noticed as a tribute to the women who came before me, who made it all possible. The store in this photograph was full of life and love, and I vowed it would be again.

I leaned my head back on the chair and just rocked with my eyes closed. The weather was still blissfully mild for the season, and I took a moment to ground myself with the sound of the birds chirping, the warm sun on my face, and the sweetly scented air.

"Thank you. For pushing me. For believing in me." I wasn't sure who I was talking to, Gram, Charlotte or maybe the house itself, but I was overwhelmed with gratitude for the women of my family, my mother included, for paving the way to allow me to follow my passion and purpose. I wouldn't let them down.

Slowly rising from the rocking chair, I turned to face the house and I knew that it was time to start acting like it was MY house, that I wasn't just a visitor or caregiver here. I walked inside and threw open the windows to let the sweet spring air fill the house, then walked straight into Gram's room and made a beeline for the desk.

I opened the long top drawer to place the photos in for safe keeping, and there, as if it had been waiting for me the whole time, was another leather journal. This one was engraved with beautiful flowering vines over the entire cover, and a darling little metal clasp held the book closed. The paper had rough cut edges, and I instantly loved it. Instinctively I knew that this book was the one I had been searching for, that it was different from the rest of the journals.

When I opened the journal with trembling hands, there were all Gram's recipes for every tea she had ever made. I was so thankful they weren't lost! I already knew that they wouldn't be the same if I tried to make them myself, what made them special was Gram, no doubt about it. But herbs were medicinal no matter who mixed them up, and they would still do their jobs to some extent no matter who brewed the tea.

A thought crossed my mind all at once, and I wondered what would happen if I made a natural ink using all the herbs in one of Gram's blends. Most would probably be some shade of brown, but that would make a lovely sepia toned painting. I'd have to try it sometime.

Flipping a little farther back in the book, I realized that Gram had rewritten some of her mother's recipes for soaps and body oils and things as well. I was sure that I would find them written in Lottie's own hand in her journals upstairs, but for now it was nice to have them all in one place.

I lovingly placed the journal back in the drawer and set the photographs on top of it. I had a lot of things to get in order to make my dream of owning a store front come true, and to honor the women of my family that got me here.

I clapped my hands and rubbed them together. It was time to get to it.

Epilogue

OPENING DAY WENT off without a single hiccup or snag. The last six months were grueling, but the store was finally finished and the love and support from everyone in town had been simply staggering. While the day was a huge success, I was thrilled to be home, swinging over the creek with my toes in the cold water as the moon overtook the sun in the sky. The sound of the flowing water helped ease the adrenaline out of my system, and I relaxed for the first time as I reflected on the day.

We had reconnected the three buildings, and I loved nothing more than being able to walk into the coffee shop for a mid morning, and afternoon, and evening, pick me up or to walk over and see Elliott any time I wanted, too. The arched doorways were some of my favorite features of the renovation, and the brick door frames on my side had been painted a lush navy blue to stand out against the rest of the white washed brick walls.

An unexpected bonus had been that Becca could now pop over any time she wanted, and she was fast becoming my 'bestest and cutest employee', as she would tell anyone shopping that would listen during the soft start weeks that led up to today's grand opening.

In the center of the large art gallery wall, I proudly displayed a grouping of natural ink paintings. I had learned to care for the herb garden at the cottage myself, and was now able to make the inks using my very own herbs from what I had started calling the generational herb garden. They were always some of my best paintings, and they seemed to hum with their own energy as they hung on the wall.

Several times today, someone had walked by a painting on display and stopped dead in their tracks to stare. The paintings had spoken to them in some way, reviving a memory or strengthening one, and they had taken them home with a look of wonder on their faces. I didn't think I would ever get tired of that feeling, of watching strangers reconnect with themselves, rediscover a lost love, or heal a long festering wound by seeing it in a new light. At its core, that's what the shop was about to me. That's what painting and art were made for... feeling.

I had selected several vendors to be a part of the gift shop portion of the store, and I was thrilled with what they had to offer. Carol was the first person that I had asked to claim a display space, and she had cried when I told her that I didn't want to open without her being a part of it. We'd redesigned a logo for her business, and she now had displays in the sundry, Mr. Findley's office, and a special pet safe display in The Pet Palace.

Another local woman that made soaps and lotions approached me about vendor space, and I was thrilled to welcome her to the shop. While she made some of her own things too, she had happily agreed to recreate some of Lottie's recipes for me, selling them to me wholesale. I had painted labels for all of those, along with some of the teas, and called them all LC's Specialties, for Lottie and Connie.

It was hard for me to think of the woman with the raven hair as Charlotte now... I'd been through many of the journals, both her's and Gram's, and it was getting harder and harder to remember the friend I had made in the herb garden versus the great grandmother I had never known. Somehow, I missed them both.

The photographs that had been attached to Gram's last letter now hung proudly behind the counter in my sundry, just as Elliott's 'origin story' paintings were hanging in his store. It was humbling, and a joy, to be able to see their faces every day and remember where this shop had begun.

A partnership of sorts with several of the local businesses had bloomed and blossomed, and I was thrilled when they continued the trend amongst each other, connecting all the shops up and down Main Street and the square in ways they hadn't been before. I offered a discount on custom pet portraits if you ordered them through The Pet Parlor, and Heather had a display of painted book marks for sale that came with a coupon to the sundry shop. Once a month, Sarah offered certain hot teas that were available in tea bags in the sundry shop, too. The feeling of community support and involvement was an added bonus I never expected.

My mother came for the opening, and she shocked me when she said she was moving to Asheville. There was a community college there, and she had decided she wanted to go back to school for a business and marketing degree. She often talked about the joy she got from guiding my new career, and I thought it was perfect for her. After all, I never would have had the success in my business that I did if it weren't for her support and guidance.

Sitting on the swing over the creek and reflecting on the success of the day, I couldn't help but look around at the new changes to the cottage with a smile. Elliott had begun staying with me soon after I decided to move to Painted Creek for good. He helped me change Gram's suite into my suite, and then our suite, and we turned my old bedroom into a gorgeous library. All of the journals now had a beautiful home, and I'd begun the tedious process of scanning them all for posterity's sake, too.

Larry the contractor had been kind enough to add a tortoise habitat to the top of his project list. With his hard work, Elliott's expertise, and my fantastic landscaping and yard crew, Turtle had the most spectacular habitat a girl could ask for just through the trees on the other side of the creek. We had actually decided to put Turtle between the cottage and the clearing I had found the day that

I was searching for Charlotte's house. We continued cleaning up the path past her habitat and brought the clearing back to life too, the landscaping around the cellar looking as it did in my painting once again. It was the perfect place for picnics and stargazing and quiet and peace.

Movement down close to the hanging vines of the herb garden caught my eye. Standing there smiling, arm in arm, stood Charlotte and a young, vivacious version of Gram that I had only ever seen in pictures. Tears instantly sprang to my eyes, and I placed a hand over my heart. Instinctively I knew that this wasn't a visit in the way that I had interacted with Charlotte, but a brief reminder that they were always there, watching over me and supporting me and guiding me to be the best version of myself that I could be.

They whispered something to each other and laughed, and I found myself smiling through my tears as they each raised a hand to wave at me one last time. I waved back, and blew them each a kiss. It was a poor representation of how thankful I was to them both, of how much I loved them, but it was all I had.

The air around them shimmered, and as they turned to walk back toward the woods as I had seen Charlotte do so many times before, they simply faded into nothing. I expected to feel some sort of loss, but that was silly. After all, they weren't really gone.

A strong October breeze whipped through the woods, aiming all its force up the hill toward the cottage. I took a deep breath and laughed, surrounded by the strong scent of rosemary, roses and lemon drop.

Acknowledgments

SO MANY PEOPLE deserve to be acknowledged here, and I know inevitably I'd forget someone if I tried to name you all individually. So, if you find yourself reading the following paragraphs and think *Oh, I helped do that!* then please do consider this your thank you, too.

To my husband and children, thank you for giving me so much grace during this very new process of writing, editing, cover creating, and marketing a book. When I began this journey, I wanted to try and keep it as minimally invasive to our lives as possible... present me is laughing at past me, but it was a nice thought. Thank you for always celebrating the small milestones, for taking the dog out twenty times a day so I could keep working, for talking through problems and offering suggestions, and for always being an inspiration to every part of my life.

To all of my parents and sister, whether it be legal or blood, thank you for always supporting me and cheering me on. Whether it be sharing stories, editing advice, asking with interest about my progress, or a million little other things that add up to complete unwavering support and encouragement, this book would not exist without each one of you and I'm so thankful to have you all in my life.

I was fortunate enough to have friends that were so enthusiastic about this project that they became beta readers, street team, cheerleaders, and so much more. This book would not exist in this version without your support and hard work. Your excitement and unconditional faith in me has meant so much to me and never went unnoticed or unappreciated.

To all the established authors, aspiring authors, and social media aficionados, whether I've met you in real life or we connected online, thank you for all the support and encouragement along the way. A nudge from fate can come from anywhere, encouraging that first scary step, and what wonderful things can happen when you listen!

Last and certainly not least, a big thank you to all the readers. Thank you for seeing this book, falling in love with it, and championing it to the world. Words could never adequately describe what it means to me to know that you fell into Painted Creek and will take parts of it with you always.

Thank you all for going on this journey with me. Love to all of you!

P.S. - NOW, WHO wants to take this ride with me again? After all, you did such a fantastic job the first time, and there are more stories to be told...

About the Author

ROBYN KILGORE LIVES in East Tennessee with her husband, kids, dog and business manager (the cat). When she's not working on a writing project or reading, you can find her chauffeuring her kids to activities... usually by way of a coffee shop drive through.

Her love of vintage treasures, whimsical findings, and seeking magic in every day life led her easily to write magical realism novels. Robyn also has a small handmade jewelry and craft business, her first (and forever) passion turned business venture. She gives a nod to the experience of making jewelry in her first novel, *The Magic of Painted Creek*.